A Fool's Paradise

Nancy Flowers Wilson

Flowers In Bloom Publishing

Copyright © 2000 January 2000 by Nancy Flowers Wilson
Cover art by Bernard Stanley Hoyes
Cover design by NHEA
Author photo by Ken Johnson

FIB Publishing and the logo Reg. U.S. Pat. & TM Off.

First Flowers In Bloom Paperback Fiction edition 2001

For more information, or to contact the author, address correspondence to:

Nancy Flowers Wilson
Flowers In Bloom Publishing
P.O. Box 473106
Brooklyn, NY 11247

Or visit: www.nancyflowerswilson.com

Wilson, Nancy Flowers—1971-
  A Fool's Paradise

Library of Congress Catalogue Card Number: 2001086642
ISBN: 0-9708191-0-2

5 4 3 2 1

Printed in the U.S.A.

Acknowledgements

I thank God for giving me the talent of creativity and story-telling among other gifts and my mom for believing that I could do anything that I put my mind and heart into.

I'd like to pay tribute to two literary pioneers who paved the way for African-American authors of yesterday, today, and tomorrow, Phillis Wheatley and William Wells Brown. If not for their strong will and perseverance as literary scholars I would dare not think where I'd be today.

Much praise to all the authors who inspired me from my childhood to the present: Toni Morrison, Chinua Achebe, Alice Walker, Marita Golden, Claude Brown, Assata Shakur, Connie Briscoe, E. Lynn Harris, Bebe Moore Campbell, Tina McElroy Ansa, April Sinclair, the late James Baldwin, Richard Wright, and Zora Neale Hurston. I thank each and every one of you for giving me alternative reading options and allowing me to see the light. A special thanks to Terry McMillan for making African-American contemporary fiction both popular and very commercial.

To my brother, Prince Wint, you are definitely my knight in shining armor. I appreciate your help and insight more than you'll ever know.

To my husband, Sheldon, thank you for giving me the time to work on this project even when it interfered with "our time." I know those two years weren't easy, so again thank you for your patience. I can't begin to repay you for all the time that you spent helping me edit, or can I?

Claudette Wilson, my mother-in-law pressed me to finish the manuscript, so that I would stop giving it to her piecemeal. Thanks for the love & advice about how true patois is written and spoken.

My best friends, Majida Abdul-Karim for her words of inspiration and Leone Williams (who typed many chapters for me and contributed the poem, My Star), hugs and kisses to both of you.

Dawn Green, girl it's finally done! I appreciate your spreading the word about the book when it was merely a tadpole. Now set up those interviews, girl!

Big shout-out to Tracy Green Boutin (a.k.a T-Lover there is no other), and Aleshia Harmon for being such fabulous friends. My boy Raymond O. Griffith, Esquire, for your friendship and legal expertise. Raymond, you are the man!

To my sands, Akwete Hines, those weekends you let me chill at your place inspired many chapters. The good company was helpful, along with your constant words of encouragement.

Marvette Richardson and Carla Tucker, I want to thank you both for loving the very first draft.

Breggie, thanks for the e-mails and words of advice. Patrice Gaines and Evelyn Palfrey, thank you for extending yourselves to me. It means a great deal to those of us just starting out. Patrice you were a savior for helping me locate Carol Taylor one of the finest editor's today. Carol, thank you for being so exact with my work (smile). I only hope that the book lives up to your expectations. Chandra Sparks Taylor, thanks for seeing my vision. You are truly a wonderful editor, and I look forward to working with you time and time again.

Thank you, Bernard Stanley Hoyes for the use of your beautiful art piece "Prelude to a Kiss" and Nhea Duncan of Author Promotions Unlimited for her creative services.

All my love to the Spring 1993 line of the Alpha Gamma Chapter of Delta Sigma Theta Sorority Incorporated. Let me not forget about all my Morgan State University Alumni peeps.

Finally, if I've left your name out it wasn't done intentionally. If you know the number, holler at me. If you don't have it handy, e-mail me at *nancyfwilson@aol.com*. I look forward to hearing your comments.

Much Love,

Nancy Flowers Wilson

Jamaica, West Indies

1984

Prologue

My father, Trevor, called me Star, so I grew up believing that I had the ability to attain anything the world had to offer. As a result I grew up with very high aspirations and determined to reach for the sky—or die trying.

I have three passions: My boyfriend, Donovan, is the first one. We've been friends from infancy. The second is school. I love learning new things. The last thing is my desire to travel to America. Jamaica, my birthplace, and the country where I reside, is in an economic decline and the opportunities are becoming few and far between. Whenever I watch American programs on television I see how differently the people live, and I want to one day experience that lifestyle. I've dreamed about this ever since I can remember. Seeing black people like Benson assisting the governor at his mansion and like the Jeffersons who were moving on up, I, too, wanted a piece of the pie. I could just imagine being in America where the streets would glitter like gold with unlimited opportunities. The only catch was that I wouldn't be able to have all three of my passions. I would have to give up one or two, but which would it be?

The sexual attraction that Donovan and I have for each other was sinful. I can't recall a time when I was able to visit him in closed quarters and we were able to accomplish anything other than good, hot sex. When Donovan caressed my breasts and kissed the nape of my neck I could feel the wetness oozing out of me. Just imagine popping the top from a bottle of champagne and the flow of liquid that rushes from the bottle. That's exactly what Donovan did to me.

Then there's school. Presently, I'm an honor student studying premed at the University of the West Indies. The challenge of working hard and learning something new gives me a rush. In the end my reward is a well deserved A. Generally, good grades especially A's lead to acknowledgement from my parents and professors for my exemplary efforts. There is nothing more gratifying or fulfilling.

I would love the chance to travel and go away for a while, but such a situation has never presented itself to me. If it had I know I, Anne-Marie Saunders, would jump at the chance.

As it turned out, one of my passions would eventually be my downfall. The other would do me the most harm, and the third would be my salvation.

Chapter One

Donovan Miller is the father of my unborn child. We have known each other since we were toddlers. My mother has boxes full of the silliest pictures of us as kids kissing each other at birthday parties. It seems like it was only yesterday that we were children ourselves playing in our favorite spot. It was a desolate, but not too far off place from our homes located right behind the old Wallace Sugar Refinery, which had been abandoned for years.

When Donovan was about seven or eight he started playing with more boys his age. They generally played rough, male-dominating games. Nevertheless, he always made special time for me. Donovan was not only my best friend, but he also served as my consoler, confidant, and inspiration. As we got older he also became my lover, which all stemmed from a simple kiss.

There was a beautiful mango tree in my backyard. Its branches always full of heavy ripe fruit, which scented the air throughout the house. It was under that same tree that Donovan and I experienced our first kiss. It was because of that simple kiss that he became my lover. It was a typical hot and humid Jamaican afternoon, so we sought out the shade of the mango tree. The tree provided us with the right amount of obscurity, as well as a refreshing fruit while we relaxed from a long day of playing. We sat there eating our mangos, both too drowsy from the sun to say much. Suddenly out of nowhere Donovan turned and kissed me. The kiss sweetened by the mango juice could not have lasted for more than a couple of seconds. I was startled, and it must have shown, because Donovan's face flushed with embarrassment. Looking back, I'm sure it was something that he had been contemplating for a while.

I always perceived Donovan as strikingly good-looking. Evidently, the other girls in school thought so, too, because they would act silly and fawn all over him. I was simply naïve at the time, because I wasn't aware that he thought of me, Anne-Marie Saunders, as girlfriend material. To me he was more like a big brother. It surprised me that he thought of me as anything other than a friend.

When we were in primary school the kids always teased me, especially the girls. They called me names like tomboy and teacher's pet, but Donovan always came to my rescue. I never questioned his actions. We were just kids, and I had no reason to feel that he had an ulterior motive. Our relationship was based on openness and honesty. When I got older, I realized that the girls were simply jealous that Donovan was interested in me, and the boys envied me because I was smarter than they were.

Today Donovan is six feet two inches, and is 190 pounds of taut muscle. He is beautifully bronzed with his Chinese mother's almond-shaped eyes. Aside from his eyes Donovan is the spitting image of his father. He has his father's high cheekbones; smooth bittersweet-chocolate complexion highlighted by reddish undertones; and thick, coarse head of curly hair. But Donovan's secret weapon is his beautiful smile. To me Donovan is perfect. He's smart, sincere, thoughtful, loving, caring, with a great personality to match. However, on occasion Donovan can be rather quick-tempered and irrational, but he never directed his anger toward me. Apart from that I thought he was almost too good to be true.

My period hadn't come for three months. I knew that I was pregnant, but I was trying to push the idea to the back of my mind.

I purposely failed to see Dr. Keene during my last trip home last month for fear of hearing the truth, but I knew I had to visit him soon. I had papers and finals to worry about, and the last thing I needed was another distraction. There was also the chance of Dr. Keene telling my parents. There was little discretion in our small town of Cambridge, St. James, Jamaica. The news and gossip have legs of their own and travel faster than the speed of light.

During my last visit from school Donovan and I talked hypothetically about what ifs. The pregnancy subject came up, because he paid me a surprise visit at school one weekend, and my prescription for the pill had run out. It didn't stop us at the time, and we figured the risk was minimal. But hindsight is always twenty-twenty. Donovan expressed some concern, but reassured me that he loved me and would support my final decision if the unexpected did occur. My sentiments were that if Donovan and I consented to unprotected sex then we had to deal with the consequences. It was as simple as that. I'm not exactly a kid anymore, and neither is he. I'm nineteen soon to be twenty in a couple of weeks heading into my senior year at the University of the West Indies. I'm also in the top five percentile and the youngest of my graduating class, so this pregnancy may have been unplanned, but I will never look at it as a mistake.

Talking with Donovan relaxed me a bit, but now I had to muster up the courage to tell my parents. Even though I hadn't told Donovan yet I already knew he supported me. However, my parents would be more than a little disappointed to say the least. My father, Trevor, would definitely be more upset than my mother, Faye, because I was his Star, and he had high aspirations for me. I knew he wanted me to attain all the things he hadn't.

My father was usually pretty lenient with me. Mama on the other hand was an entirely different story. She was obstinate and argumentative and hated to admit she was wrong. Expecting an apology was definitely out of the question. She would stubbornly walk away like a child. It was unheard of to talk back to your parents, but I did have the right to explain or express myself. At least I thought so, but Mama saw it as me acting feisty and fresh. As much as I would have loved to raise my voice, I had to control myself and remain calm. She would talk over me loudly. Her voice increasing a decibel with each word and eventually drowning me out altogether. My father usually served as the buffer between us. When we quarreled and my father knew she was wrong, he would come to my defense while she would grasp at straws.

"Faye," he would say in his deep and robust voice, "go rest yourself, and have a sit down. Leave the child alone." Most of the time she would just suck her teeth and mutter something under her breath. Cooking, gossiping, and macramé were hobbies in which my mother found great solace. If she didn't have someone to gossip with mainly my younger sister, Nadine, she would start cooking or do her macramé. That was the scenario if she were wrong. Forget about it if she were right. Mama would get so riled she became almost unbearable.

"Who do you think you're chatting to? This blasted child needs to be disciplined. She is too rude, and out of order so don't come and *frig* with me unless you want some too." My father didn't tolerate profanity and since *frig* was basically *fuck* in Jamaican patois he'd get riled too. At this point I was usually in the clear, because my mother knew better than to take that tone with my father. They would get into a loud and brawling squabble, which I'd feel awful for causing, but before long it was over, Daddy being the triumphant victor.

My mother sometimes acted like she despised me. I tried to stay out of her way by hiding out under the mango tree with my textbooks or out on the veranda studying. My older brother, Patrick, and my younger sister were her favorites. In fact, Nadine could do no wrong. She was Mama's fair-skinned princess. She didn't treat Patrick badly, because he was a boy. Although Patrick was the type of person that wouldn't have cared one way or the other. Patrick didn't brook with any foolishness, and he would tell you exactly how he felt.

When I do decide to break the news about my pregnancy the shit will surely hit the fan, and it's gonna stink. I wish that I didn't have to be present when breaking the news. Quite honestly even if it was Nadine, I wouldn't want to be present. Then again I would, because I'd love to see the look on Mama's face. Daddy probably wouldn't be that surprised, but the news would break our dear mother's heart.

The thought of being home for summer break and spending time with Donovan put an instant smile on my face and being able to sleep in my own bed always afforded me a good night's rest. I also missed Mama's delicious cooking. If I wasn't careful I'd be going back to the university with an extra ten pounds on my five-foot-eight, 135-pound frame. Everyone in town knew that Mama could cook up a storm, and her food was simply irresistible.

I could smell Mama's handiwork wafting throughout the house from the kitchen. On any other day the smell of the food would have me jumping out of bed to stuff my face. Especially to eat the fried plantains, which were one of my favorites. But today the smell was making me queasy. I manage to pull myself out of the bed and shrug into my robe. I made my way out of the bedroom to see who else was home and to get something to munch on, hoping the nausea would go away.

The house was rather quiet, and the only sound that could be heard was the radio in my parents' bedroom. Mama was listening to the Jamaican pirated version of Madonna's latest song, Like a

Virgin, and Nadine was nowhere in sight, probably out flirting or being a nuisance.

On the kitchen stove was a plate with fried plantains, a small pot with chocolate tea, and a larger pot with boiled yams, pumpkin, and green bananas. The large covered skillet contained steamed liver sautéed with onions and tomatoes. It had been almost two months since I last had the pleasure of eating such good cooking. I poured myself some chocolate tea and cut two slices of hard-dough bread to accompany the liver and plantains. While eating I prayed to be able to keep it down, because it was actually the smell of the liver that was repulsing me. When I finished eating I decided to sew myself something pretty to wear since I was in such a good mood.

After several hours of sewing, my new summer dress was finally finished. I decided to take a shower and prepare myself to go see Donovan at his father's shop. Donovan didn't know that I was back home from school so he would be pleasantly surprised. As I dressed all I could think about was how to tell Donovan about the pregnancy. Rehearsing opening lines in my head I slipped on my dress, and with the help of a girdle it fit beautifully. It wasn't apparent that I was pregnant yet, but my stomach appeared a little plumper than usual.

I applied some lipstick and put a small amount of powder on my face to help prevent perspiration. My dresser had a complete array of perfumes, and during my last visit Donovan gave me a new fragrance called Jean Naté. I sprayed a generous amount on my wrists, neck, and behind my ears. I brushed my hair back into a bun and clenched the bobby pins between my teeth as I tried to make a perfect swirl with the length of my hair. It was the first day in July and too hot to have my hair hanging down my back, or in my face. Next I chose small pearl earrings to compliment the ensemble. I walked over to my full-length mirror and was pleased with the image that appeared before me. The dress did wonders for my ample breasts, long legs, and mocha complexion.

With a tinge of excitement I grabbed some money from my bureau and yelled out that I was leaving.

"Mama, I'm going down to Miller's to buy a *Gleaner*." It wasn't often that I had free time to read the newspaper so I decided to buy a copy while I was out.

"Do you want anything?" I asked.

"Yes, please tell Mr. Miller to trust you some brown sugar, nutmeg, currants, and mixed fruit."

"How much?"

"About ten pounds of sugar, and five pounds of the mixed fruit. I already have the rest of the ingredients. Your father will come down to pick them up."

"Are you making black cake?"

"Yes, I'am," Mama replied, in a sing-song voice.

"For the house or a customer?"

"You know Maisey's wedding is this Saturday?" she responded, asking more than she was telling me.

"This Saturday? I thought it was at least another couple of weeks or in early August. Time sure does fly."

I walked out the door, and started down the veranda steps when I heard the screen door close a second time. It was Mama. She came out to ask for another favor.

"Anne-Marie, ask Mr. Miller what my balance is, please."

"Sure."

As I was making my way down the knoll I could see my father approaching. He was exhausted, barely dragging himself up the hill. When we were finally facing each other I kissed him on his cheek and gave him a warm embrace, which he returned, unlike Mama who shunned affection of any kind.

"Hi, Daddy."

"Hey, Star, glad to see you back! What time did you get in last night?"

"Pretty late. I think everyone was asleep when I got home. You look beat."

"*Yeah, mon.* I need some serious rest and relaxation. I left Clifton in charge of the bar, and I came to get your mother to run the restaurant for the rest of the day."

"How are Clifton and Dottie doing anyway? The last thing I heard was that Dottie had thrown him out."

Clifton was my father's best friend since grade school. Dottie, Clifton's girlfriend, had attended grade school with them. She now teaches third and fourth grade. Daddy and Clifton used to own the bar together, but Clifton had a drinking problem. When he began to drink heavily he went broke, and my father stepped in to buy his portion of the bar. My father still felt obligated to keep him employed, but Clifton was trifling. He came home all hours of the night drunk, and acting crazy, not to mention his frequent infidelities. Clifton wasn't very prudent about his activities. Dottie had found him with other women humping away in their home on more than one occasion. She finally told him to shape up or ship out. Quite frankly I thought Dottie needed to give him up altogether. Even if Clifton managed to stop drinking, chances are he would still be unfaithful. It would be almost impossible for him to give up both bad habits. There was always room for change, but the ultimate question was would he? He served as a discredit to Dottie, a very smart woman, and one of the best teachers I ever had, but her choices in men were terribly inept.

"Well you know Dottie means business this time. She still hasn't allowed him to come back home. Clifton's *koching* over at Uncle Sammy's."

"Uncle Sammy will soon kick him out, too, and you know Aunt

Beverly don't like people in her yard too long," I said.

"That's the truth. That sister-in-law of mine don't play," he said chuckling to himself, feeling a sense of pride and admiration for Aunt Beverly's strong character. She was a no-nonsense kind of woman.

"Well, Daddy, he's going to have to make a change. A positive one, and soon. Something's got to give. Nobody wants a drunk, and he's starting to look pretty bad. Clifton used to be such a sharp dresser, but now it's almost as if he doesn't care about his appearance anymore."

"That's what happens when you treat your body like a garbage bin. It starts to act like one."

"Daddy, then why don't you fire him? It's too hard for him to resist the liquor, especially if he's always surrounded by it. He's obviously an ardent alcoholic."

"A what?"

"An ardent alcoholic. He loves to drink. It's like a strong passion that makes it really hard for him to give up."

"Star, don't bother me with your big words. My head is swelling enough from a hard day's work. Furthermore, you can't expect me *fi just fire de mon*. I know Clifton since we were this high." He raised his hand to his waistline.

"If you don't, he'll never stop drinking, Daddy."

"I feel so damn bad for him. You know we started the business together, and he wasn't always an *ardor alcoholic*."

I started to laugh, because I knew what he was trying to say.

"Ardent," I said, and slowly repeated it with the correct pronunciation—"*ardent* alcoholic." He sucked his teeth in frustration, because I was making fun of him.

"Whatever you call it." Daddy didn't like to be mocked. "I hope and pray that he will soon realize how he's mashing up his life. Anyway, you smell good. Where are you on your way to? He already knew and was just being facetious. Smiling and showing all of his pearly whites he answered his own question.

"Miller's?"

"Yes." I felt myself blushing like an idiot.

"And look here, that looks like a new frock." Daddy pulled at the hem of my dress to feel the fabric, and I playfully snatched it away from him.

"It's new. I just finished sewing it today. Donovan gave me the material. It's from China." Donovan's father had a lot of goods exported many foreign countries.

"You like it?" I asked, turning around slowly, putting on a little fashion show for him minus the runway.

The dress was a floral print on a white background made out of a cotton and linen blend. The bodice was made into a halter with spaghetti straps, and the bottom flared. It fell gently below my knees and showed off my long legs. The top clung slightly to the curves of my breasts, but left enough to the imagination. I'd made a shawl with the remaining material for the cool Jamaican evenings in the fall, and I was pleased with my work.

"It's beautiful, anything you make always looks good. When you see Mr. Miller, tell him I need some material for a suit. Star, I beg you to make me a pantsuit."

"When?" I asked, sounding surprised and curious at the same time.

"This week. I know it's short notice, but I have been so busy lately. You know I'm providing the beverages for Maisey's wedding reception?"

I gave him a stern look, and frowned as if I was really upset.

"Please," he continued to plead, attempting to get pity from me. Daddy knew I wouldn't deny his request, but this was a grand opportunity for me to get something out of the deal too.

"And what do I get?" I asked.

"Anything you want, Star."

"Well, since you're being so generous, when I was down at Cambridge Square I saw a beautiful leather book bag. It's exactly what I need to carry those heavy textbooks around."

"Star, if that's what your heart desires, it's yours!"

"When I get back, I need to take your measurements."

"Why? You already know my measurements."

"Because you're starting to develop a gut," I said as I patted his stomach. "Plus I can't remember the last time I made anything for you."

"Your mouth is going to get you in a lot of trouble, young lady. It's too fresh," he said, but with a smile.

"I'll pick the fabric, and I'll tell Mr. Miller that you will be down to pick it up no later than tomorrow morning. I'm going to need to start work on it by tomorrow afternoon. It's already Monday."

"Thanks, Star." He bent down and kissed me on the cheek and headed home.

"You're welcome, Daddy. Now go get some rest."

On my way to the store I greeted a couple of the town people. It felt like I never left home as I strolled passed the familiar colorful shanty houses and soda shops with zinc roofs. Men pushing carts with large umbrellas sold shaved ice with flavored syrup, as the old timers sat on their makeshift porches, and kids played at the water pump in an attempt to stay cool. Others simply sat under large banana trees on the side of the road enjoying the shade.

Donovan's father's name is Benjamin Miller, but we all called him Mr. Miller. He had the best general and novelty store in the area, called Miller's. Although there were two other stores in town, Miller's was the favorite, because it had largest quantity and the best items. Mr. Miller ran a very prosperous business, and since Donovan was an only child he would one day inherit it. Mr. Miller was a widower. His wife, Sue, had died from glioblastoma cancer, an inoperable brain tumor that spread at a rapid rate. Donovan was a kid when she passed away. Glioblastoma's effects were usually paralyzing, the results terminal. Mrs. Miller deteriorated quickly and died the same year she was diagnosed. Devastated, Mr. Miller never remarried. Instead he remained devoted to her memory and committed to his son and business. The cause of the cancer, and how and why it strikes victims so randomly is still unknown. After seeing the pain it caused Donovan and Mr. Miller I decided to become a doctor to research the nature of cancer and hopefully one day find a cure for the disease.

When I entered the store the bells above the door rang. Startled, Mr. Miller who was behind the counter having what appeared to be an intense conversation with Ms. Margaret, stopped talking to turn around and see who had walked in. They greeted me then picked up where they left off without skipping a beat.

I wandered aimlessly throughout the store fingering the richly colored fabrics and smelling the fragrant soaps and incense. After five minutes wasting time while they finished talking I picked up a bag of plantain chips. Mr. Miller, who always treated me like a daughter, allowed me to take items like candy, soda and chips for free.

About ten minutes later, I'd finished the chips and was getting tired of looking at the same items. Mr. Miller would occasionally look in my direction to assure me that he wouldn't be much longer. The entire time they talked in hushed tones, which was odd. No one really liked Ms. Margaret, because she was a bitch, to put it mildly. When we were little kids she always kept a watchful eye over her daughter, Colleen, who was my best girlfriend. Ms. Margaret would always bust up our games with her loud screaming. She always needed to know where we were and what we were doing. Most times we were interrupted before the sun even went down. We use to think the reason Ms. Margaret was overprotective was because Colleen was born prematurely. Though, she was always much smaller than the other children, Colleen was healthy.

Colleen, still petite, now stands about five feet two inches. When we got older Colleen and I realized that Ms. Margaret was just a miserable nag with nothing better to do than chastise poor Colleen. Eventually she became mentally and physically abusive to Colleen, who finally decided to pack her bags and move out. The relationship that I had with my mother wasn't the greatest, but she didn't physically abuse me and we got along from time to time. Colleen wasn't able to experience a fraction of what Mama and I shared when we were on good terms.

Mr. Miller finally started wrapping Ms. Margaret's purchases, so I went back behind the shelves to make myself scarce. After looking to see if I was nearby Mr. Miller came from behind the counter and stood in front of Ms. Margaret, gently placing his hand on top of hers. It lingered there a little longer than necessary. She smiled up at him then picked up her groceries. On her way out she made a slight detour to come over and talk with me.

"Anne-Marie, how has life been treating you these days?"

"Fine, and you?" I said a little startled. Ms. Margaret has said barely a dozen words to me since I've known her. Colleen even told me that her mother thought I was a bad influence and I was doing things in which young unmarried ladies shouldn't engage. It was the pot calling the kettle black. Ms. Margaret was only six-teen when she'd gotten pregnant with Colleen, and even though she got married, it wasn't until after Colleen was born. I'd love to hear what she has to say about me once she finds out that I'm pregnant.

"Not so bad. Things could be better, you know how it is," she responded.

"Mmh hmm. Yeah," I heard myself say aloud, even as I thought, *no, I don't know how it is*. I knew her dream had come true when Colleen left. Ms. Margaret had her house all to her lonesome self. I would have thought things couldn't be better.

"When was the last time you saw my Colleen?"

"It's been a while. Probably not since my last visit home."

I knew that Ms. Margaret was just trying to be inquisitive. Surely she didn't think that *I* would volunteer any information to her. If she wanted to know something, she had better go directly to her daughter.

"Well when you see her tell her I said hi, and that I asked after her, okay."

"Of course I will. Take care, Ms. Margaret."

She was so full of shit, and I don't know why she was trying to play the concerned mother now. Ms. Margaret knew where and how to contact Colleen. Speaking to her put a bitter taste in my mouth. When she exited, the bells above the door rang once again

Mr. Miller finished putting the money in the till and closed the drawer. He then walked over and gave me a big hug. We talked a bit, and then I wrote down the items that my mother wanted so he could gather them while I went to look at some fabric for my father. Finally, I decided on a lightweight rayon resembling linen. It would be cool and very easy to work with. I pointed it out to Mr. Miller, and I told him the fabric was for my father. He knew exactly how much to cut without any direction from me. When he was done cutting and wrapping the material I asked him if he knew where Donovan was.

"He's in the back of the shop with Bigga, Winston, Joshua, and Hop."

They were Donovan's childhood friends. Bigga's real name is

Errol, but it was common to call men that were on the hefty side Bigga. Hop's proper name was Clive, but he acquired the name Hop in grade school. When he was younger he broke his ankle, and he never got the proper medical attention. As a result he walked with a slight limp. Winston and Joshua were brothers and Donovan's closest friends out of the group. Although Winston and Joshua were two years apart, they looked like identical twins. Both had received certificates in business management and now held management positions at different hotels in Montego Bay.

When I walked into the back room they were sitting at the table playing a lively game of dominoes and talking loudly over one another. The room was half the size of the front room, and the wood-paneled walls made it dim and drab in comparison. It was mainly used for storage, and several large boxes were stacked to the ceiling. There was a poster from the movie *The Harder They Come* auto-graphed by Jimmy Cliff and another of Peter Tosh.

"*Bam*. See here, boss! You can't touch that," Bigga exclaimed.

Donovan saw me, got up from the table, and came over to greet me. The game was over, and Bigga was obviously the winner. He was talking a whole lot of nonsense to the rest of the group.

"I'm the master, you must bow down to me," Bigga yelled triumphantly. He began thumping his chest and carrying on. He looked over at Donovan.

"*Yu gwaan* . . . walk away. I know you don't want *nuh more ah dis*. You lucky that your girl came to rescue you, because you were about to get another ass beating." Bigga took himself much too seriously and liked to blow things out of proportion. I detested Bigga's very being. He was arrogant and a slob. But mostly I didn't like him because he used to hit on me. I definitely didn't want him. I'd rather be alone than be with Bigga. He was barely six feet, weighed at least 250 pounds and had an ass that was larger than any woman I knew. He had a muddy-brown complexion, bad skin, and an overbite.

The first time I mentioned his behavior to Donovan, he said that Bigga was just being playful and didn't mean anything by it. I failed to see Bigga's advances as playful. He was blatantly disrespecting my relationship with Donovan. It didn't seem to matter to Bigga that Donovan and I were a couple. It took a little more coaxing and actually telling Donovan exactly what Bigga said before he finally saw things my way. I don't think Donovan wanted to believe that his friend would betray him that way. He finally confronted Bigga, who of course, denied coming on to me. He claimed that he was just being friendly. I wasn't sure what Bigga's definition of friendly was, but asking me when we would get together wasn't my idea of friendly. He even had the audacity to ask me one time when I was going to leave Donovan to get some of the Bigga stuff.

Donovan was real smooth in telling him to back off and watch his step. Donovan is mindful of him now. He isn't worried about me leaving him for that creep, but he is aware of how uncomfortable Bigga makes me feel.

Bigga was still mouthing off and Donovan was apparently annoyed with his incessant bull.

"*Shut yu blood-clot mout' already nuh.*" Then he turned around to give me his undivided attention.

Bigga didn't say a word after that, and the room fell silent. A few seconds later the rest of the guys turned to acknowledge my presence.

"*Wha'pin gyal?*" Donovan asked slipping an arm around my waist.

"Nothing much. I came down to pick up a few things from the shop and see my man."

Donovan smiled and bent over to gently kiss my lips. The feel of his lips made me giddy as his manly smell lingered under my nose. I had an immediate hankering for him. He held me at arm's length to admire my dress. "Looking good, girl." He smiled to give me his seal of approval.

"Thanks. I take it that you approve," I said, beaming from ear to ear.

"Baby, even a blind man would approve."

Again, I blushed. I was feeling extremely splendid today, and not Bigga or Ms. Margaret could ruin it. I got on my tiptoes to give Donovan another kiss, and he leaned forward to meet my mouth. His was warm and sweet as I moved my tongue slowly. I was close enough to feel him begin to rise. I was tempted to reach down and touch him, but resisted the urge. Instead I pressed my body closer to Donovan's, and he wrapped his arms around me. I heard Hop say, "*It de start fi get hot in here. A due time we leave.*"

We ignored his comment as other thoughts danced in our heads.

"You wanna go up to my house?" Donovan whispered, looking down at me with a sexy, mischievous grin. It was hard to resist the temptation, and why should I? The damage had already been done.

"You know I do, but first I need to know where the food is. I've been smelling it ever since I came back here."

"Over there in the brown bag."

"Good. I'm starving. I neglected to eat lunch because I was busy making this dress. It was well worth me completing it today, too, since you can't seem to take your eyes off it."

"It's not the dress I can't take my eyes off. It's what's inside of the dress."

"You're so fresh."

The guys all came over to hug me and ask about school. Then one by one they started to leave. Hop came back to ask Donovan if he was going to play cricket with them later. I thought to myself, *Not if I have anything to do with it.* Donovan went over to him to chat a bit longer, and I left them to talk in private. I hurried over to get the brown bag with the food and started to devour it like a scavenger. It wasn't hot, but I couldn't wait to get to Donovan's house to heat it up. I went to the small icebox to take one of Donovan's carrot-juice concoctions.

Donovan made the best drinks. He made stuff like Root Tonic, Sorrel, Ginger Beer, Irish Moss, and Egg Punch and many others that Mr. Miller sold in the shop. They went fast, too, especially the Tan Pon It Long, which is believed to give men stamina and help increase the longevity of their sexual performance. I didn't know if I believed it or not, but Donovan loved drinking it, and he certainly had stamina.

As I polished off the remainder of my juice I felt Donovan hovering over me. He reached down and gently cupped my breasts in his large hands. He was commencing, and we hadn't even left the store yet. I could feel my whole body beginning to tingle. I got up to face him and looked down only to see him protruding through his slacks. It had been a while since we'd last been alone, and I knew that if we kept gyrating like we were that he would probably explode right on the spot.

"You ready?" I asked mischievously, pushing the chair back, and leaning against him.

"Anne-Marie, I was born ready for you, woman."

"Then let's get out of here." He grabbed my hand, and we walked out to the front of the store. We were about to step out when Mr. Miller looked up at us and gave a knowing smile. "And where are you two going?"

"Nowhere special, probably down by the river to catch a breeze." Mr. Miller knew that I was lying, but I know he didn't expect me to reply *"to your house to fuck your son."* That would be a little too forward. "Mr. Miller, can you please put the parcels under the counter. My father will be down for them later on this evening. Thanks for your help."

Donovan had already stepped outside to wait for me. I looked at him through the glass door and for the first time noticed that he was letting his goatee grow. It made him look ruggedly handsome. Donovan was naturally sexy, and I knew that if we had a son he would look just like him.

"Okay," I heard Mr. Miller reply in the background, but I was caught up in other thoughts.

"Bye. I'll see you later, Mr. Miller."

"All right, dear."

Hastily I walked out of the store and grabbed Donovan's hand so we could hurry over to his house. I knew we didn't have to rush, because I heard Mr. Miller tell Ms. Margaret that he gave Arlene, the woman who worked at the shop part-time the day off. Therefore, I knew he would be closing up later.

Donovan slowly disrobed me as I lay flat on the crisp white sheets and began to kiss the nape of my neck. His mouth was warm, and his breath faintly smelled like the manacu stick that he chewed on our way to his house. He kissed me deeply while I gently fondled him. He was already standing at attention, and the feel of him excited me. As I massaged him, I planted sweet kisses on his chest, and the look on his face was one of satisfaction. His hand moved downward to feel the inferno that was building between my thighs.

Sucking on my left breast he moved his tongue in slow circles around my nipple. His free hand was softly kneading my other nipple so that it stood erect. I wanted him so badly it hurt. I dug my hands into the small of his back, and he knew I was ready. Guiding him inside me, we rocked back and forth. I felt myself gasping for air and began to moan softly. I was elated, because to me this was one of the best feelings in the world.

My head was spinning from the overwhelming sensation. Wrapping my arms around him I pulled his head toward me to kiss his lips. His eyes were closed tightly as if he were in another world. We both made groaning sounds of pleasure.

My body began to shiver, and I could feel myself getting weak. When I climaxed, all I could do was cry out. I laid there stiff without motion. Donovan's groans got louder, and his body grew frail as he shuddered.

We both collapsed onto each other, and lay there silently. It was a blissful moment that I wished didn't have to end. I was gonna have to tell Donovan the news later because I was too tired to have a serious conversation today. We continued to lie on his queen-size bed cuddling. Then he pressed his fingers to his lips, and put them on mine. I smiled and put my head on his chest, wrapping my arms around him before I fell into a light slumber.

Chapter Two

I t was still pretty early when the light filtered into my bed room. My room, which used to be my older brother, Patrick's, was in the rear of the house. A few years ago when Nadine and I had a falling out, I decided to let her keep the larger room that we shared. Although this room was smaller, it had the best view, and no one else appreciated it the way I did. I've always had a fascination for enchanting sights. In the morning I could gaze out of the window at the lush green land and beautiful foliage on the countryside. I could capture the sunrise as it set the dusky gray sky to cobalt and indigo before settling for sky blue with hidden rays of sunshine. Nightfall was even more entrancing as the sun set the sky ablaze from shades of amethyst into a copper-red. It could only be described as breathtaking.

I could tell the day was going to be a scorcher. The temperatures were already soaring in the high seventies. I felt like I could sleep all day, but I had errands to run. The thought of Donovan and last night instantly came to mind and made me smile.

I smelled food, which meant that my mother must have finished cooking at the restaurant and returned home early to prepare breakfast. My wonderful sister, Nadine, couldn't cook if her life depended on it. The closest she ever came to making food was buying it from the store. I was hungry, but felt queasy when I lifted my head off the pillow. I decided to lie down for a couple more minutes with the hopes that this feeling would quickly subside. Prior to this week I had managed to avoid all ailments that normally accompanied pregnancy. Now all of a sudden I was under attack, and I had to run into the bathroom and hold my head over the toilet.

When I returned to my room, I reached for my robe, slipped my feet into my favorite old slippers, and headed to the kitchen. I had a full day ahead of me and realized the morning would pass me by if I didn't get a move on.

As I walked through the long corridor I peeked into Nadine's room, but she wasn't there. The day I moved out of that room it became a sty. I don't think Nadine ever lifted a finger to clean. The twin beds were still there, but she insisted on using the empty one to store her dirty laundry. Empty perfume bottles were on the dresser, and the small garbage pail was overflowing. Along the way to the kitchen, I began straightening out the many family photographs that hung on the walls. It was one of my many anal habits. I always felt the urge to fix, sweep, dust, and straighten things. I hated to see things out of place, and the sight of dust disgusted me. We also need another paint job, because the peach-colored walls were beginning to fade and peel. The living and dining room formed a large L shape. If not for the kitchen being partitioned it would have been a perfect square. In the living room we had a settee, a love seat, and a lounge chair that my father had, front and center, facing a floor-model television. The wine-red sofas were covered in plastic, so when you sat down they made a sighing sound of relief. I avoided sitting on the couches because the mixture of heat, plastic, and skin did not make for a pleasant combination. Even the chairs to the formal dining room set were covered with plastic, and the solid, mahogany oval-shaped table donned a lace tablecloth with plastic beneath it too. It was a shame because it took away from the fact that the dining set was an eighteenth-century design. If not for the beautifully crafted curio cabinet and credenza, it would have been a waste.

I could hear the bantering of my mother and Nadine in the kitchen. They were gossiping as usual. When I stepped into the kitchen, their conversation ceased, but not before I heard my mother say something about catching Ms. Margaret. If I hadn't heard Ms. Margaret's name I would have sworn that they were talking about me.

"Good morning," I said with a sweet smile. Neither of them bothered to look up at me.

"Good morning." they both mumbled.

Both were seated at the table, my mother with her hands clasped. She and Nadine gave each other an annoyed look, which I ignored. When I walked in my mother got up from her chair and started fussing with the food.

Mama was dressed in red, which was her favorite color. Her shoulder-length hair was in an upsweep and gave focus to her beautifully chiseled cheekbones and fair complexion. The narrow nose, soft textured hair, and red undertones were all features inherited from her Arawak lineage. We were about the same height and size, and... I resembled her the most out of my siblings. The only thing I didn't have was her complexion. Nadine got that. Mama definitely didn't look like she bore three children, didn't look a day older than thirty, knew it, flaunted it, and loved the attention she drew.

Nadine reached for the *Gleaner* and started flipping through the pages. I must have really disturbed an important gossip session for Nadine to pretend to be interested in the newspaper. I was in the mood to be a pest, so I sat across from her. Nadine shot me a look over the paper, and Mama noisily tapped a big silver spoon against the large black cast-iron pot on the stove. I decided to break the monotony. My presence alone was not enough to annoy them.

"I saw Clifton last night on my way home," I spouted.

Nadine sighed heavily and got up from the table and went over to the stove to help herself to a plate of the ackee sautéed in tomatoes, and onions and codfish. Then she continued to make a huge racket with the utensils and ran the water at the sink for a long time. Nadine slowly dragged her feet as she walked over to the refrigerator. When she was done pouring the drink she slammed the fridge door shut.

"Yeah, and?" Mama replied with her back to me.

"Did you know that he was staying at Uncle Sammy's?"

"That's what I heard."

"Well it's true, but he was heading over to Dottie's when I saw him."

"If Dottie takes him back, she's a fool. That man is a damn idiot. I don't see how she could take up with him in the first place."

"Love can make you do strange things."

"Love? What kind of damn love is that? After all the grief that man put her through. He's a drunken asshole, and he sleeps with any woman that he can get his nasty hands on."

My mother was so fired up it seemed like Clifton was screwing around on her.

"If that were me I would have left him a long time ago. You would think since he doesn't own half the bar anymore that he would save the little bit of money that he makes. Instead he drinks it away and now he don't have a pot to piss in much less a pillow to lay his head on." Mama was on a roll now.

"Well for once he didn't look drunk. I think he was sober. We spoke for a while, and he sounded sincere when he said that he wanted to change and get his life back together. His clothes were nicely pressed and... " I was unable to complete my sentence before Mama interrupted me.

"Change what?" Mama retorted. "The type of alcohol that he consumes or the type of woman that he sleeps with next? That's exactly the same type of crap he used to pull on my sister."

"Ma, Dottie is not Auntie, and that was a long time ago. Maybe he really does want to change."

I was growing weary of hearing her talk about Clifton and the past. I was also getting fed up with Nadine. I now regretted staying in the kitchen with them. Hearing Mama talk about my aunt and how Clifton destroyed her was ruining my morning.

I can sympathize with my mother's strong dislike for Clifton— what he did was wrong—but if my aunt was able to get on with her life and start a new family then why couldn't Mama forgive and forget? She had a bad habit of harvesting negative feelings.

I tuned her out as she continued to relive her detailed recurrence of the whole ordeal. It was bad enough that she treated Clifton badly every time he stopped by the house, which was now rare. But her bad-mouthing him was putting a strain on my parents' relationship, which was once very lively, but now resembled that of business partners who occasionally had sex.

My mother became very bitter and distrusting of all men, including her husband, after the way Clifton had treated her sister. Things only got worse when Clifton and my father opened up the bar together. To this day Mama doesn't understand how Daddy continues to be Clifton's friend. She never fully forgave Daddy for what she saw as putting Clifton before her.

I was hungry but didn't want to stay in the kitchen with them. I got up from the table to get a mug and pour myself some mint tea to take back into my room.

The moment I left the room they started gossiping again. Nadine began laughing uncontrollably. It amazed me how my younger sister and I had almost nothing in common. When I moved into Patrick's room, our relationship became even more distant.

Daddy was concerned that we barely spoke to each other and asked all the time why we didn't do things together. I'd make up excuses to appease him, but he knew that I was lying. Mama wasn't the least bit concerned, as long as she had her "princess" to gossip with, nothing else mattered. Nadine and Mama made quite a team when it came to gossiping and spreading rumors. They were the chatterboxes of Cambridge and had more than enough *labrish* to spread.

I was standing in front of the picture window staring at the weathered plastic chairs on the porch and looking at the zinc roof of Miller's shop when the doorbell rang. Happy for the distraction I ran to the door. I couldn't believe my eyes.

"Colleen, is that you, girl?"

"Girl, you expecting somebody else this time of morning?"

"I'm so glad to see you," I said, giving her a big hug. "I totally forgot that you were coming here today."

"Getting a little absentminded in our old age, huh?" Colleen joked.

Even though Colleen had moved to Montego Bay a few months back to live with her Aunt Lorna, she still came to visit whenever she knew I was home from school. In her last letter to me she said that she had started working at the Montego Bay airport as a ticket agent. Between going to school, studying, and spending time with Donovan, I didn't see Colleen as often as I wanted.

Colleen looked wonderful. She had a glow about her that I'd never seen before. Even her clothes were different. Normally she dressed in long skirts, or long loose-fitting dresses in dark colors. But today she was in a vibrant electric-blue halter-top and matching gauchos. The color made her bronze complexion look radiant. Her clothes flattered her petite and very shapely figure. She no longer wore her hair in girlish bangs. Instead it was pulled back from her prominent forehead, making her look bold and confident. This new look was great, and it seemed like the move was really doing her some good. I grinned as she stepped into the foyer and took a few steps back so she could see me checking her out.

"Well, well, well, don't we look—" I didn't get the chance to complete my sentence before Colleen jumped in.

"Look what? Say something smart, and see what I do to you!"

"I was only going to say that you look nice. Aren't we touchy?"

"Girl, I'm so sorry. I'm a little annoyed."

"Why? What happened?"

"I saw my mother, and she couldn't wait to criticize the way I look. Everything that came out of her mouth was so hurtful. She's so awful."

"Let me guess, she said something about your lipstick."

"Yes, but not just that. I don't understand why she's so friggin' miserable. If I had stayed at her house a little longer, one of us would have ended up dead. I can't stand her. She was on her way to church, but that didn't seem to matter much. She still found time to be insulting."

"Don't let her bother you. You don't live there anymore."

"Anne-Marie, I know that. But if you can't say anything good then don't say anything at all."

"That's the truth."

"She said that I was dressed like a whore. Does this outfit look whorish to you?" Colleen asked, looking to me for reassurance.

"Colleen, look at me. You know your mother is a wicked woman. She's being spiteful. Don't let her ruin your day. Besides you look fantastic."

"Thanks, girl. I'm trying not to let her bother me, but I still don't understand why she's so evil."

"I can't help you find an answer to that, but try your best to avoid her."

"I won't have to try very hard. The next time I see her will probably be months from now anyway."

"True. I always wondered how you survived for so long. At least I have my father to help me keep my sanity around here," I said, nodding in the direction of the kitchen.

Colleen smiled. "I used to tune her out or try not to be in the same space with her for long. But enough about her, talking about my mother depresses me. Anyway guess what?" But she didn't wait for me to answer. "Do you remember Lloyd?"

"Lloydie? Of course."

"Well," she hesitated and looked to see if anyone was around. We were still standing outside on the veranda. "Let's go in your room. Where is Mama Faye?"

"She's in the kitchen gossiping with Nadine."

"As usual. Let me go in there and say hello. Then we can go in your room and talk." She then stopped suddenly and dug into her bag. "This is for you. It's a top like mine. I knew you would like it."

"Well, thank you very much, Miss Rich." I playfully grabbed the bag from her, reached inside to pull out the top and held it up for inspection.

"Pink—my favorite color. So where's the bottom?" I looked into the bag again like it would magically appear. Colleen hit me playfully on the arm.

"Don't even try it, miss. You're so ungrateful." We both burst out laughing because our parents always called us ungrateful wretches if we didn't do cartwheels or flips when they gave us something. As we passed by the kitchen door Colleen said good morning to both my mother and Nadine. They barely stopped long enough to acknowledge her, they were so immersed in their conversation.

"Shut the door behind you," I said when we entered my room. "Now what about Lloyd?"

"I'm seeing him."

"Lloyd Hall?" I questioned.

"Yes!" Colleen answered enthusiastically.

"You're a damn liar."

"Anne-Marie, for real. I'm dating Lloyd."

"Colleen, you're kidding me."

"After all these years, you of all people should know I don't have a sense of humor. I'm serious."

"How long has it been?"

"The last month or so."

"I can't believe what I'm hearing. You didn't write about it in your last letter to me." I sat down on the bed and tried to regain my composure. This was a shocking piece of information. Colleen never really dated before because Ms. Margaret was so strict. There was nothing wrong with Lloyd. He was a rather nice guy, but he was also eight years our senior. He didn't really seem like her type either. I pointed to the chair in front of my vanity for Colleen to sit down.

"Have a seat. So, are you two serious?"

"Somewhat."

"Details, girl, details."

"Well," Colleen started, "one day when I was at the airport waiting for the bus to take me home, he drove up in his minivan. He offered to give me a ride home and said he wasn't taking anymore fares for the day, so I accepted."

"Mmh-hmm." That was all I could manage to say as I hung on to her every word.

"He drove me to Aunt Lorna's and was surprised when he found out that I had moved to Mo' Bay. He lives in Mo' Bay, too, over by Gully. He also owns a record shop there with a friend."

"Mmh-hmm," I said, again prompting her to go on.

"Well, he started picking me up every morning to take me to work, and in the evenings he would drop me home. He said it was on his way in the morning since he picked up tourists at the airport to take them to their hotels anyway. Lloyd makes a lot of money too!" she said excitedly. "He said the tourists tip *big,* and in American dollars. You know some of them don't change the currency until they get to the hotel, girl. Anyway, I said it was okay for him to pick me up as long as it wasn't an inconvenience. About two weeks later he asked me if I would go to the movies with him. I said yes, and we've been dating ever since then."

"What movie did you guys go see?"

"Have you ever seen that American movie *Purple Rain?*" Girl, it was good. I heard that it was Prince's true life story."

"I've heard of it, but I'm so busy with school I don't even have time for myself these days. So tell me, do you really like him?" I don't even know why I asked, I could tell simply by the smile on Colleen's face.

"Do I ever. You know he's really sweet, and good-looking, which doesn't hurt."

"Girl, don't let them good looks fool you. Some of these good-looking guys are only after one thing."

"I'm not saying I'm with him for his looks. I'm merely speculating the fact that he is handsome. He is my man, you know."

"Is that right? I said laughing. "The last time I saw Lloyd he was growing dreads. Is he still growing them?

"Yeh, mon. Him a Rasta, me dear, but dem locks look good pon him."

"Does this mean you will be growing dreads soon too?"

"Do I look like Rita Marley to you?" she replied sarcastically.

"I can kinda see a resemblance."

Colleen laughed. "Anne-Marie, you're so funny. You should be a comedienne."

"So, anything happened so far?" Colleen was probably the only virgin left that I knew, unless that recently changed too.

"Nothing like what you're trying to imply, nosy. We haven't screwed yet to answer your question."

"Yet," I repeated twice. "Yet, that is the operative word. You have been giving this some thought." That wasn't the answer I was expecting, and suddenly I felt like the protective mother, and though

I was in no position to give advice, it sailed out of my mouth anyway. "Don't make any rash decisions."

"Anne-Marie, is the word *fool* written across my forehead? It's not candy, and I'm not just giving it away. Give me some credit. I know you care about me, and I appreciate your concern, but please trust my judgment. I mean Lloyd is nice, but he's not that nice."

"I'm sorry, sweetie," I said, and meant it. If Lloyd put that glow on her face, he must be doing something right.

"It's okay, but don't let it happen again."

Trying to digest this news about Lloyd was going to take a while. Lloyd was so different from the other guys Colleen used to sneak around to date.

"I'm very happy for you." And I smiled. I could tell that she was really pleased with Lloyd. She talked about him nonstop for another hour or so. "How long are you planning to stay? The day or are you spending the night here with me?"

"Lloyd is coming to pick me up later this evening. I have to go to work tomorrow. I dropped by to spend time with you, tell you the news, and give you your gift. I still have things at the house that I want to pick up. Lloyd is going to help me move them back."

"Ms. Margaret will have a fit if she sees Lloyd in her house."

"Well she went to morning prayer, and probably won't be back for a while anyway. And if she sees us, fuck her!"

"Now you're talking a lot of shit. If she sees you moving the rest of your belongings you know that she will go insane and try to wring your neck. She may even try to attack Lloyd."

"She's not that mad."

"Listen, when you first threatened to leave she caused a big commotion. She even told the pastor so that he would talk to you. Then she stopped worrying about it because she thought that you were crying wolf. Ms. Margaret didn't think that you had a place to go, but when she found out that you were going to live with your father's sister she tried to kill you. Your mother thinks that your aunt Lorna is Jezebel resurrected. Remember you had to stay here with me, and it wasn't until she went to morning prayer that you were able to go back and pack up your stuff to leave. So please don't sit here with your newfound attitude and tell me you're not worried. I'm not convinced any more than I believe you are."

Her face told me that I had just crossed a very thin line, but she knew that I was telling the truth. I still wished that I could retract the last statement. I was probably being too harsh on Colleen. The tenacious exterior that she appeared to be wearing today was a front. She was still sweet, timid little Colleen. She glanced at her watch like she was pressed for time.

"Anne-Marie, I really don't want Lloyd to leave me, and he'll be coming soon. I gotta get going."

Without any argument I shook my head. After specifically telling her earlier not to let her mother ruin her day, I managed to do just that. I wanted her to stay here with me a little longer, but understood and respected her feelings.

"When do you think you'll be coming back this way?"

"Whenever," Colleen said curtly.

"Do you know your next day off?"

"No, not yet."

"Okay," I said, trying to be appeasing, but the damage had already been done, and trying to placate her now wasn't going to be easy. She was disgusted with me and understandably so. "Maybe I'll come and see you next time in Mo' Bay. I still haven't been by to see your new place."

"Sure. You can drop by one of these days."

"All right," I said to Colleen's departing figure. Moments later I heard the screen door slam.

I went back to the picture window in the living room, still upset about Colleen. Mama and Nadine were sitting on the veranda, unaware that I was in the window. I couldn't imagine what they could possibly be talking about after all this time.

I felt like I needed to clear my head. My day had started off badly and was getting worse. Was being pregnant making me moody and snappish? Colleen and I never bickered like that before. We had the type of relationship I wish I could have with Nadine. I'd wanted so badly to share my news with Colleen, but I'd blown it. I grabbed a Popsicle out of the freezer and headed back to my bedroom. I wanted to sit down and think of a way to make up with Colleen. After a couple of minutes of staring unseeing out the window, I decided to take a nice cold shower.

The pellets of water were beating down on my back. It was refreshing, and the water was nice and cool. I wanted to stand there for as long as possible. The sound of the water hitting cement was soothing and tranquil. It was one of the few places that I could think freely and collect my thoughts without being disturbed. Since my father added the extra room to the house and made the bathroom with indoor plumbing, hardly anyone used this outdoor shower anymore. The indoor bathroom was a big deal in our area. We were one of the few families with the luxuries like indoor plumbing, an icebox, and a color TV. We were considered a prosperous and well-to-do family. The majority of the people in our community came to us for storing meats and for ice. There were probably only about ten to fifteen families in the entire vicinity with such comforts. The only other person to use the outdoor shower besides me was Patrick. He didn't visit home as much as he use to though. Patrick lived in Kingston and spent most of his time performing and traveling with his band, Roots & Culture, which was starting to draw a lot of local attention. It also didn't hurt that my very handsome and strapping big brother was the lead vocalist.

I approached Donovan's house. My stomach was churning, with light beads of sweat making my shirt clingy and uncomfortable. This is a man that I've known all my life. I knew that I had nothing to fear, but my emotions were riding me like a roller coaster today.

Donovan lived in a fairly large brick house. It was painted off-white and had three huge bedrooms that his parents had hoped to one day fill with children. There was also a very large living room, dining room, kitchen, storage room, indoor bathroom, and a screened sunporch in the rear of the house. A white wrought-iron gate marked the beginning of their four-acre property.

The wooden steps to the porch made an awful creaking sound. They were old and weather stricken. I made every effort to be as quiet as possible as I climbed each step. The screen door was closed, but the door to the house was ajar. I opened the screen door and entered the foyer. It was painted a light green, and there was an oak desk and chair next to the door. Pictures of Donovan's family adorned most of the walls. One had two beautiful paintings of Mr. Miller holding Donovan when he was a toddler. The largest wall had one large picture of Mr. and Mrs. Miller on their wedding day, and it was a beautiful sight to see. Donovan's mother had been a very talented artist. She painted most of the pictures that hung in their house. Beneath the large picture with Mr. and Mrs. Miller was an exquisite handcrafted wooden bench. It was an heirloom from China and a gift from Mrs. Miller's family. The bench had an embroidered blue-and-white bolster cushion of wool yarn, which were compliments of my mother's craftsmanship.

Donovan's home was always immaculately kept. The wooden floor was shellacked and well maintained. Ever since Donovan's mother died, his aunt came by regularly to straighten up, iron, and sometimes cook.

The smell of incense lingered in the air. It made the house smell warm and comfortable. The sound of Bob Marley filtered through from the adjoining room. I walked in the direction of the living room following the melodic sounds of the music. Donovan was lying on the settee in his briefs with a damp washcloth on his face. Between the loud whirring sound of the fan, which was aimed directly at him and the LP playing he didn't hear me when I came into the house or entered the room.

I walked over to his stereo and lifted the needle on the record player to stop the music right in the middle of Bob wailing, "I shot the sheriff." Startled, Donovan jumped up. He removed the washcloth from his face to see what was wrong.

"Girl, you nearly gave me a heart attack."

"Sorry," I lied, and started laughing. I walked over to him on the sofa and sat down. He looked and smelled delicious. I leaned in close and buried my face in his neck. He smelled of talcum powder and Ivory soap.

"You shouldn't turn the music up so loud. You can't even hear when someone comes in. I even slammed the screen door loud enough for you to hear me come in," I said, telling him more lies.

"So what brings you here so early in the day? I thought you would be studying or starting on your father's suit. You came by for a replay of yesterday evening, didn't you, sexy woman?" He then pulled me farther into him and nuzzled my cheek.

I laughed softly. "Actually, I had to get out of the house. My mother and Nadine are home carrying news, and I really couldn't stand to be around them much longer. Anyway, guess who came by this morning?"

"Who?"

"Colleen. She looked really good too. She definitely needed to get away from that witch Ms. Margaret."

"True. So what is she doing in Mo' Bay? She working or going to Teachers College? At one time she said she wanted to teach."

"She got a job at the airport. And guess who's making her so happy?"

Donovan laughed. "Anne-Marie, I'm not even gonna try. Tell me who it is."

"Lloyd! Remember Lloyd Thompson."

"Thompson? The name sounds familiar. You mean the Thompsons who live on the other side of the church?"

"Yes. Lloyd drives the van, and sometimes he would pick up barrels for your father down by the airport."

"Yes, yes. He's older right, about twenty-seven or twenty-eight? He moved about three years ago after his father died. Mrs. Thompson still lives there though. I saw her the other day. She stopped by the shop for some groceries. Nice lady."

"Well that's him, and Lloyd is Colleen's new man."

"She doesn't think he's a little too old for her? I can barely even remember Colleen dating when she was here. I hope she knows what she's getting herself into. She's like my little sister, and I don't wanna have to rough up nobody."

"Stop worrying. I had the same concern, but then Colleen helped me realize that she's not a *pikny,* anymore. We had a brief argument about that, and then I got on her nerves about Ms. Margaret. In two hours she was out the door. Colleen is really mad with me right now. She claimed that Lloyd was picking her up, and she didn't want to be late.

"Anne-Marie, *wah mek yu so flighty*? Sometimes your tongue is too sharp, and you know how sensitive and moody Colleen can be. She's miserable like her mother, and she doesn't even realize it. You have to stop trying to be everybody's mother. Now you never did answer my question. Did you come by to replay scenes from yesterday?" He put his lips over mine and started rubbing my thigh with his hands. My heart started to race. This is not what I came here for today, and I needed to stay focused.

"Donovan–Donovan," I said, trying to get his attention. I removed his hand as it began to wander beneath my skirt. I had to put a halt to his actions and what was obviously about to happen. As much as he made my adrenaline rush, and my head spin I wanted him to stop. This man had obviously cast some kind of spell over me. I could barely contain myself. Why couldn't I be within close proximity to him behind closed doors without us always ending up in bed? I was tired of beating around the bush. I had to mentally prepare myself, and I took deep breaths to help calm me down so I could regain my composure. He continued making advances, and I used all my will to pull away from him.

"Donovan, I came by because we need to talk, and it's very important." I stressed the word *important*. I intended to nip this in the bud today—and fast.

Chapter Three

C olleen walked to the kitchen to get the stepladder. She was still fuming from the earlier run-ins with Ms. Margaret and her best friend, Anne-Marie. She didn't expect much from her mother, but Anne-Marie had disappointed her. She'd been insensitive, harsh, and judgmental. She was supposed to be a friend. Instead Anne-Marie made her feel like crawling under a rock to hide.

Earlier Colleen was full of anxiety because she couldn't wait to tell Anne-Marie her news about Lloyd. If she had known that things were going to turn out the way they had she wouldn't have taken the day off. She really could have used the extra money. Especially since she was trying to get her own apartment.

The original agenda for the day was to pick up her paycheck, which she did. Then Lloyd took her to town to get the gift for Anne-Marie and from there they headed to Cambridge. Unfortunately her timing was a little off, and she ran into Ms. Margaret right after Lloyd dropped her off. That should have been Colleen's first sign that her day was going straight down the tubes, but she was still riding high even after her mother's petty insults. Her mother was always miserable and chased away everyone who ever crossed her path. She even managed to lose Colleen's father, and he was the type of man that was very easy to please and even harder to upset. After their divorce, Ms. Margaret used Colleen as her moving target, because misery loved company.

Ms. Margaret claimed to be a devout Christian, however, her behavior and actions were quite the contrary. She was capable of disguising her awful demeanor around strangers, but once a person got to know her, the truth was obvious. Ms. Margaret was sick and twisted as far as Colleen was concerned. She wasn't sure if she even wanted her mother to be a part of her life again. Colleen thought she had put the past to rest. That was until Anne-Marie had brought up the horrible memories of how her mother mistreated her and how susceptible she was to the abuse. It really got under Colleen's skin because she knew there was some truth to it. Colleen felt so strong earlier when she'd stood up to her mother. She didn't cry, lose control, or run away. Neither did she do an about-face or cross the road when she spotted Ms. Margaret walking in her direction. They went at it head-to-head and toe-to-toe. For the first time Colleen wasn't going to allow her mother to bully her—although at first sight her heart was momentarily suspended.

Colleen couldn't stop replaying the incident in her mind. She'd wanted to prove to herself that she could be the bigger person and attempted to take a different approach by being friendly.

"Good morning, Mommy," Colleen said when she was face-to-face with Ms. Margaret. For a moment she wasn't sure if she should address her mother as Mommy or Margaret, but she used her better judgment. She realized the repercussions that would come if she called her mother by first her name.

"Mmh humph. Good morning," Ms. Margaret responded like someone was forcing her to speak. "So what are you doing here? I hope you don't think you can come back home to stay with me." Already she was picking a fight.

"Actually, I came to visit Anne-Marie. I have no intentions of staying with you." Colleen knew that her mother was on her way to morning prayer because she had her Bible in her hand—and she needed it.

"Well good, because I'm in the process of turning the bedroom into my new sewing room. She gave Colleen a once over and continued. *"Ku Ya! Hoh yu fayva buguyaga to ras with that bright red lipstick! Yu reek of sin."*

Colleen could feel her heart racing, and her jaws locked as she grinded her teeth in anger.

"You need to come and get your good clothes that you left at the house, because that scanty outfit you're wearing now is shameful! I don't want people thinking that I raised my daughter any kind of way."

Colleen couldn't hold back anymore and decided to let loose. She'd given the bigger-person thing a try, and it had failed.

"I'm sorry it's not to your liking, but I didn't buy or wear it to please you."

"What you saying—those clothes are yours? I thought they were Lorna's. I guess her slackness has rubbed off on you. Well I pray to God that you are not picking up her ways. That woman is too skettel and nasty. I really hope the two of you are visiting God's heavenly temple. Do you hear me? I hope that you been going to church."

"Margaret," Colleen said without hesitation this time, "you're the one who needs to go to church. You need help, because a true Christian would never act this way."

"Who you calling Margaret? It looks like you think that you're talking to one of your little friends. *Yu think say yu too big fi mi to give you a lick cross yu face, because I have half a mind to box you right pon that big forehead of yours. You need fi continue wear yu bangs and cover up that high forehead.* In the bible it says *honor thy father and thy mother.* Exodus chapter twenty, verse twelve."

"I can recite verses from the bible the same way too. It's funny how you've never stumbled across Ephesians chapter six, verse four. It says something about not provoking your children to wrath. I know the bible just as well as you, only I know more than Exodus and the twenty-third Psalm, which is all you seem to know how to read. And the difference between you and me is that I understand and adhere to the word."

"What's that suppose to mean? Do me a favor, and make sure that you take your belongings out of my house this afternoon. I don't want anything to do with you. You hear me ever. After today I don't have a daughter named Colleen. The child I raised would never speak to me like that. *Gyal,* move from my sight with your rude and out-of-order self."

"I've always bitten my tongue to please you, but not today! And you know what, Margaret, in my entire life you've never given me an encouraging word. You have never said or done a nice thing for me. The only thing you have done is to criticize me. You made me self-conscious about everything. I always felt that something was wrong with me, but today I realize that you're the one with all of the shortcomings. I plan to be a better person than you could ever hope or expect to be. I will be a better person, no thanks to you. I deserve the same amount of respect that you have come to expect. Though I doubt that will ever happen. And since I no longer live under your reign, I don't have to deal with that anymore. *Yu see me, I would ratha sleep ai door than live with yu.* If you choose not to see me again that's your business. Today is a new day, and I promise myself that I will not fall victim to your abuse ever again, so believe me if I never see you again, that's fine with me too."

At that very moment Colleen could feel the heavy weight lifted off her shoulders. All she could do was look at her mother with the scorn and pity that she felt for her. She never wanted to have another confrontation like that again in her life. Colleen walked away and left Margaret with a stupefied look on her face.

Colleen quickly snapped out of her meditative state. With the stepladder in hand she went into her former bedroom to sort out the belongings that she wanted to take. Most of the clothes that hung before her were part of her past and the way she once was, timid and vulnerable. She wanted to burn them, but didn't believe in being wasteful. She could put them to good use by giving them to someone who needed them. The clothes Ms. Margaret use to sew for her made her feel ashamed of her body. Colleen had a closet full of long skirts, dresses, and oversized blouses. She was never allowed to dress like the other children her age. The clothes weren't ugly. Most of them were actually nice, but were better suited for an older person—perhaps, someone who no longer wished to reveal certain parts of her body. Colleen decided she would give them to Mrs. Val who was a struggling widow.

Colleen took the clothes off the hangers and folded them. The pictures of her and her father still remained on the bureau. Her perfume bottles were still there too. Bending down and looking under the bed she stretched her hand as far as she could to reach for her shoes, which were neatly hidden from plain view. She managed to pull out three pairs and put them to the side to pack later. She was definitely taking her hair dryer and curlers. She could also take the sewing machine if she wanted to be spiteful. After all it did belong to her, and what good was a sewing room without a sewing machine? Colleen's father bought it three years ago for her on her sixteenth birthday, and when Ms. Margaret's machine broke she never bothered to repair it. Instead she resorted to using Colleen's. Colleen didn't really mind, because she rarely used it. Besides, there wasn't enough room at Aunt Lorna's house for her to store it there.

Colleen climbed up the ladder to get her traveling bags. She expeditiously began to fold and pack her personal items. When she was done she went in the back room and returned with a large shopping bag. She stuffed as many of the unwanted clothes into it as she could. She left her room with the traveling bags in one hand and the shopping bag in the other. Dropping them both she realized that she was leaving her jewelry box and its contents, photo albums, and framed pictures of family and friends. Colleen didn't want to leave anything of sentimental value behind. She wanted to make sure she would never have to step foot into her mother's house again, so she had to find a way to carry everything out.

When she finally walked out the door she looked back at the pale blue walls and the antique furniture that filled the room. It suddenly dawned on her that she would probably never come back to this house again, and tears began to stream down her face. Colleen knew that this time it was really good-bye to the house that she was born and raised in, the house that she had experienced the most pain, and where she also shared a lot of laughter with friends and even her mother before the divorce. It was everything she knew, but it was time to close that door in her life and branch out to explore new avenues.

Deep down Colleen was heartbroken to know that her mother resented her so much. Sadly, at that moment, the feeling was almost mutual. Maybe one day she could forgive her mother, but it would take some time. For now she was only human, and being the bigger person was easier said than done.

Almost three hours had passed since she came to the house to pack and there was still no sign of her mother. Maybe Ms. Margaret didn't want another run-in with Colleen either and was giving her enough time to get everything together and leave. Colleen went down the road for Lloyd to pick her up. It was almost five in the evening now but she still had more than an hour to kill. Colleen decided that she would go to Mrs. Val's and drop off the bag of clothes and grab a bite to eat if time permitted. With all the commotion, she had forgotten to eat lunch, and it was almost dinnertime now.

Mrs. Val wouldn't stop thanking Colleen for the clothes. She said that Colleen shouldn't have bothered, but she was happy to have something nice to wear to Maisey's wedding that weekend. Colleen had forgotten all about her aunt's wedding.

Mrs. Val enjoyed Colleen's company and wanted to talk. She went on and on about her high blood pressure, grandchildren, deceased husband, and how she was looked forward to attending the wedding. Colleen wanted to oblige and stay around to chat, but she really had to get going. Lloyd would be arriving soon, and she didn't want him to have to wait around long.

Colleen was walking toward Miller's when she saw Ms. Margaret headed in her direction. She didn't know if Ms. Margaret spotted her, and she would never know because Ms. Margaret ducked into Mr. Miller's store where Colleen was also going to get a soft drink. As Colleen passed by the store she peeked in and saw Mr. Miller flipping the store open sign to store closed. It was only ten minutes after six, and Mr. Miller was already closing up the shop? That was rather peculiar since he usually closed at nine-thirty. Colleen sped up because that probably meant that Ms. Margaret would hurry to make her purchases and more than likely head home.

Colleen was relieved when she saw Lloyd's van. He got out to open the passenger door for her and took the luggage to put it in the back. When she got into the van, there were two D&G Cream sodas in a paper bag and a beef patty with coco bread waiting for her. She was so happy that she and Lloyd were together. He was a real man. If he only knew how much he perked up her day simply by being thoughtful. She would ignore Anne-Marie's earlier comments regarding Lloyd's intentions. What did Anne-Marie know anyway? Anne-Marie wasn't much more experienced with relationships than she was, and as much as Anne-Marie loved Donovan he was still only a boy himself.

The more Colleen thought about the upcoming wedding, the more she couldn't wait to go to show off her man.

Chapter Four

"Donovan, seriously, look at me and stop being fresh," I said, removing his hand from my breast. "Remember when you came to school to visit me back in April?"

"Of course I remember. That was the weekend your roommate left us alone, and we had sex all night long. I'd like to experience that day again if you'd let me."

Donovan pulled me into his arms, kissing me deeply, leaving the taste of his honey in my mouth. I was left feeling breathless and giddy. Taking advantage of my vulnerable state, he proceeded to caress my neckline with sweet, sensuous kisses. And without missing a beat his hands delved beneath my top to trace the curves of my breasts. He was working his magic again and was causing me to lose my train of thought. I willed myself the strength to push a few inches away from Donovan with the hopes that he would stop his advances.

"Well, Donovan, I'm glad that you remember it so clearly, because I'm pregnant!"

Donovan's bittersweet-chocolate skin became devoid of its usual richness, and his head fell back into the cushion on the couch while he stared at the ceiling in awe. He finally came to and asked, "Are you sure?"

"Well, I haven't had my period since."

Donovan reached over to cradle me in his arms. He kissed the top of my head, and I settled into the warmth of his chest. I could feel his heart beating fast, but the longer I lay there, the slower it became.

"Donovan, you know that's what got us into this situation in the first place," I said with a mischievous grin on my face. Our earlier talk about the pregnancy went seemingly well. It felt good to know that I wouldn't have to face this journey alone. Donovan's support meant the world to me. Without it I would have been lost.

"I'm not worried about it. Everything will take care of itself, and I will take care of you and the baby," Donovan said while taking a slow drag on the spliff and trying to pass it over to me.

"*No mon*, I'm not smoking anymore. I'm pregnant, remember?" Donovan's body glistened with perspiration from our little workout. It never seemed to fail. As long as we were together and alone, surely the outcome would be that we would make love.

I lay there silent with my eyes closed and let my thoughts wander. Just the thought of how well everything had gone gave me a real high. I was feeling almost as high as Donovan was without the joint.

"My father made some oxtails with rice and peas last night. You want me to heat some up for you?" Donovan asked.

"Please, baby. You know I'm eating for two now, so don't be stingy with the food."

"I'll put the entire pot on the stove, and when it done heat up then you can come and share out the amount of food you want. I don't want you complaining that I gave you too much and *me ah try fi get yu* fat or if *me nuh give yu enuf yu lie and say me ah starve yu.*"

"Stop the talking and go warm up the food." He took one last pull from the spliff and got up from the bed naked. I made myself comfortable since I knew Mr. Miller was manning the shop alone and wouldn't be home any time soon.

Already missing Donovan, I got up and started dressing. When I went to the kitchen I found him wearing a pair of shorts, and the table was set. The smell of good food was overwhelming. I took a seat at the solid oakwood table.

Donovan looked over his shoulder at me. "So, you know that you have to go to the doctor, right?"

"I know, but I don't want Dr. Keene running to my mother and father yet. At least not until we talk to them first."

"Don't worry about it. I'll go with you tomorrow morning and have a little talk with him. Trust me, he won't say a word to your parents," Donovan assured me.

"What makes you so sure?"

"I said don't worry about it."

"I thought you had to open up the shop in the morning."

"Look, Anne-Marie, relax. For once, let someone else handle things."

"You're right. I'm just scared. Is that okay with you, Donovan?" I asked rhetorically.

"Anne-Marie, I understand," he answered, coming to sit next to me and taking my hands in his. "I just want to make sure that everything is all right with our baby. You of all people should understand my concern. Believe me, I understand what you must be feeling, but you need to take care of yourself and stop worrying about what people are going to say. As far as opening up the shop, I'll ask my father or Arlene to open up. I'll tell my father the situation, and he'll understand.

"You're going to tell him about me and the baby tonight?"

"Of course. Why not? My father isn't like your mother or your family. What do you think he's going to do? Tonight when he comes home we'll have a sit-down, and don't worry I will make sure and tell him not to mention it to anyone. My father is very private anyway. He's the last person we would need to worry about."

"Thanks, sweetheart. I know you think that I'm being paranoid but…"

"You just need to relax and let me take care of you."

As Donovan began to serve the food, I slipped into my own thoughts. Everything was happening so quickly. Was I really ready to have a baby, to be someone's mother? It was hard to believe that something was living, breathing, and growing inside of me. This miracle of life was truly happening to me. I wasn't sure whether to laugh, cry, scream, or simply curl up into a ball in the safety of my bed. My entire lifestyle was going to change. A whole new set of responsibilities was being thrown at me, and I hadn't a clue if I could handle it all.

Abortion was definitely out of the question. The thought of taking an innocent life bothered me. When I first realized that my period was late I attributed it to stress from school. I also failed to refill my prescription to the pill, which helped regulate my already sporadic cycle. But, I'd never missed it two months in a row. That's when I started to fret and cry myself to sleep. Then one evening I had the door to my room open and my favorite song was playing. Bob Marley was crooning *No Woman, No Cry* over the airwaves. It was almost as if he was singing the song directly to me. When he uttered, "Little darling, don't shed no tears," mine immediately ceased. At that moment I knew that crying wasn't going to solve my problems. Now whenever I'm feeling depressed, I listen to Bob's song, and it helps me remember that everything is going to be all right.

Donovan had a lot on his mind. Things were starting to happen to him at an unbelievable pace. Anne-Marie's pregnancy was the most exciting and unbelievable news yet, but on the same note it was also terrifying. But funny enough, he wasn't surprised. Donovan knew that the pregnancy test results would confirm what they both already knew to be true. The only question that remained was how far along she was.

Although Donovan would never show his true feelings in front of Anne-Marie, he was scared. When she told him that she was pregnant, his stomach had done flip-flops, but for her sake he maintained his composure.

This wasn't the first time that a girl had told him she was pregnant by him. When they were fifteen, and Anne-Marie wasn't ready to give up her virginity, they separated. Another girl, Annette, had been chasing him down for what seemed like ages, so he let her catch him. On several occasions she expressed her willingness to do what Anne-Marie flagrantly denied him. Annette was willing and able, but it was just sex. Donovan didn't care for Annette the way that he cared for Anne-Marie.

Afterward Annette bragged to everyone at school that she was his girlfriend. When word got to Anne-Marie she wouldn't speak to him. He knew he'd hurt her and tried to get her back, but to no avail. So he did the most sensible thing a fifteen-year-old boy with raging hormones could do: He continued seeing Annette. A few months went by before Annette came with the disturbing news that she was about four months pregnant. At the time he didn't know if he should've kicked himself for messing around with her in the first place or knocked that shrewd smile off her face. Donovan thought Annette was crazy, because she was happy to be pregnant at fifteen. It wasn't uncommon for girls to get pregnant and marry young, but at least they finished secondary school. He wasn't going to propose to her since he didn't love her and had never told her so.

Donovan told his father the situation. Mr. Miller was more than a little disappointed in his son, but was glad that Donovan felt comfortable enough to come to him with the truth. Mr. Miller had a talk with Annette's parents who apparently had no idea she was pregnant. When Annette came to school the following day she looked tired and distraught. It was also obvious that her parents had taken a belt to her. She received the whipping of a lifetime. About two days later Donovan was told that she had miscarried. The news was sad, but Donovan couldn't help but feel some sense of relief. He vowed never to be that careless again.

After Annette he dated several other girls and some older women. A year went by before he and Anne-Marie became a couple again. The time seemed to go by in slow motion to Donovan, and he was grateful to have Anne-Marie back. That was the longest and most unbearable year that he could remember. Nothing he did seemed or felt right. To make matters worse, none of the women that he screwed were able to fill his void. Although the sex felt good, it still wasn't worth losing Anne-Marie.

Anne-Marie was well on her way to begin her undergraduate studies at the University of Kingston. She was the youngest of the five students to pass the exams to get into the premedical program, and she had the highest score. Anne-Marie was well aware of his flings and would not be easily won over. She had other things going on that were more important than having a boyfriend and was pursuing her dreams of becoming a doctor.

The fear that he felt when Anne-Marie said that she was pregnant wasn't linked to his new forthcoming responsibilities. The fear was due in part to the pain that Anne-Marie was going to have to face from her family. She was going to be ostracized, and he didn't want her to regret being pregnant.

The record player that Donovan had on earlier was still spinning and was at the end of the record, making a skipping sound. He sat there staring at the blank wall almost as if he were under hypnosis, oblivious to the annoying sound. His legs were spread apart, and his head rested on his clasped hands under his chin. Donovan had been pondering the situation and didn't realize how late it had gotten. The sound of his father walking in the house startled him. Donovan wanted to find the right words to tell his father about Anne-Marie and the pregnancy. He knew after tonight things would never be the same. He was going to be a father. First and foremost, he knew that having a baby wasn't a chore that he could put to the side. It was a huge responsibility, and he wanted to be like his father as far as parenting was concerned. Most of his friends were in one of the several categories: they knew their fathers, but didn't live with them; didn't know them at all; or their fathers didn't care about their existence. Since Mr. Miller was always there for him, Donovan was going to make sure that he and Anne-Marie did the same for their child.

When he was younger and didn't understand the meaning of death, Donovan resented his mother. He resented her for leaving him at such a young age, but as he got older, he knew that it wasn't by choice. It was a painful experience for him to grow up without his mother, because as a small child he remembered her being there, and then one day she was gone. So for that reason alone, he didn't plan on taking his new responsibility of being a parent lightly.

When his father and mother got married they weren't much older than he and Anne-Marie were now. As a matter of fact, his mother was his age, twenty and his father was twenty-three. They were still children working on becoming adults together.

Donovan had always been upfront and straightforward with his father and wasn't about to start keeping secrets from him now. Their relationship was more the way an older brother would be with his younger sibling. They shared intimate stories from time to time, not really ever going into detail, but sharing enough information to know what was going on. The two of them had a bond that others often envied. His father never pressured him to do anything that he didn't want to do and gave him the freedom to have his own opinions. If there was ever a problem, Donovan always knew Mr. Miller understood how much he cared for Anne-Marie, and Mr. Miller adored her very much. He described Anne-Marie as a bright and amiable person. Always genuinely concerned about the welfare of others. He also joked that she could be bossy, constantly doling out advice when she was never asked, but he loved her all the same.

Donovan heard his father exclaim, "What a long and tiring day." Then he took a deep breath and sighed loudly. "Donovan, you here?" he called out still in the foyer area.

"Yeah, I'm here in the room." He heard the keys to the shop jingle as they dropped and hit the sofa table. He instantly knew that if he were to walk out and meet his father, he would be unlacing his boots as he stood in the doorway. Mr. Miller never walked in the house with his shoes on. It was a habit he picked up from his late wife. He'd neatly line them up with the rest of the shoes that were already sitting by the doorway.

"How long have you been home?" Mr. Miller inquired.

"A couple of hours now—why?"

"No particular reason. I was just asking. I didn't know if you came straight home after you left the shop earlier today."

"Were you expecting someone to stop by or something, because I didn't come directly home? I stopped by Bigga's, and then Anne-Marie came over for a while."

"No, no—never mind. I wasn't expecting anyone." Donovan noticed that lately his father's behavior was a little peculiar. He was often preoccupied, rambling about absolutely nothing or daydreaming while they were in the middle of a conversation. Donovan was sure something was going on, but he decided to wait until his father told him the problem voluntarily. It didn't seem serious enough for him to worry about it, so he let his father be. Tonight though Donovan wanted and needed his father's full attention.

Donovan felt the presence of his father standing in the doorway now, and any other time he would have welcomed him to have a seat. However, tonight his lips seemed to be locked shut from nervousness.

"Donovan, are you ignoring me purposely, or didn't you realize that I've been standing here?"

"I was just sitting here thinking. I saw your shadow, but I figured you would just come in."

"You must have been thinking really hard. What's on your mind today?"

"A whole lot of things, but mostly my mother. I was just thinking about how I miss not having her around. So many questions are going through my head."

"Well, you know that you can always talk to me. Whatever questions you have, you can ask me, and I will try my best to answer them. I'm telling you... I wish she were still here. I miss her so much. There's not a day that goes by that I don't think about her, but you know I carry her around with me in my heart."

"I know. How did you feel about her? Like how did you know that she was the one for you?"

"Asking me that question now sounds silly, because of who your mother was. But I think I understand what you mean. There was no question in my mind when it came to your mother. I loved her the moment I saw her. She was the sheer essence of what a woman should be. When I say that, I mean she was strong, smart, witty, and very focused. She had caring ways, and yet she had a demureness about her. Through her eyes you could see that she had seen the world, was well-versed about her environment, and comfortable with her surroundings. She was patient, and loved to talk, but not about nonsense. There were so many different qualities about her to enjoy. I'm so sorry that you didn't get to know her the way I did, but in many ways, you remind me of her so much. I watch the things that you do or say and sometimes it's just like your mother is here."

Donovan listened intensely immersed in his father's words. He was intrigued with the way his father talked about his mother with such fierce passion. It made him wish that his mother and father were still living happily together.

"What are the qualities that I have that remind you of her?"

"Well, several things, but the one that comes to mind is your natural ability to play instruments like the guitar without any formal training. Like your mother you're very talented, and more than anything when I see you sitting there at your mother's easel and you start to paint, it always ceases to amaze me. Your mother shared the same passion for the arts as you do. She worked wonders with instruments and a paintbrush."

"I remember you mentioning that you had problems with her parents before or something."

"*Yeh, mon.* You should thank god that Anne-Marie's parents like you. Getting with your mother wasn't the easiest thing. For years, I knew that I wanted to be with her. We were friends, and her parents were fine with that. But when they found out that I had other interests beyond being friends, things quickly changed. Suddenly they were against me and forbade her to see me. I wasn't good enough for their daughter. At least that's what I thought. It really did *hot* me that these people could find themselves clear in Jamaica surrounded by black people, but have a problem when their daughter wanted to date one of them. As it turned out, they had some kind of prearranged marriage business back home. It was a part of their custom. If they failed to honor this tradition, it would reflect poorly on them. Her parents were raised in China, and they retained traditional ideas of honoring elders, ancestors, and pure lineage. It took a lot—and I mean a lot—of convincing and battling back and forth before they would even consider the notion that I wanted to marry their Sue."

"What finally made them change their minds?" Donovan asked.

Prior to today, he never knew the entire story.

"It was your mother's doing. I told you she was a strong woman. Sue wasn't keen on the idea of getting married to an absolute stranger. She was going to have to move to a foreign country. Remember she was born there, but she was raised here in Jamaica. China was very foreign to Sue, and she was happy with the life she had here. If she moved, she was going to have to learn an entirely new way of living and adapt to a culture where the women were submissive to their men. That would be a real adjustment for anybody, and it was more than Sue was willing to sacrifice. Suppose you find out that you don't like the person you're chosen to be with? In their culture, it doesn't matter one bit, because you're stuck. You don't have a choice, and I couldn't see your mother being submissive to anyone or moving and adapting to such an adverse environment. You can't raise a person one way and then expect them to change their entire lifestyle overnight. Your mother was too accustomed to her freedom and refused to give it up."

"You know, I can't believe we never discussed this before. Now did she love you then or did she learn to love you? I mean… did you ever think she may have settled because she was afraid to go back to China into that fixed marriage business?" Donovan was finding the conversation much more enlightening than he imagined. It helped to put his mind at ease.

"*No, no, mon.* Trust me, your mother wasn't the kind of woman to settle, no matter what the circumstances. We loved each other. If Sue didn't love me I wouldn't have wasted my time. The decision to stay together was ours. Now your mother was promised to a family before she was even born. The thing is that her betrothed wouldn't accept her if she were no longer a virgin. Sue had to have remained pure. Since her parents couldn't be convinced otherwise, we decided to get pregnant. To tell you the truth, I wasn't really the one to decide that it, she did, but I didn't have a problem with it either. Your mother was virtuous in every respect. I would never have taken advantage of her like that. Now I, on the other hand, was no saint. I had been at a couple of rest stops. You know what I mean," he said with a crooked smile on his face, nudging Donovan in his side. "But being with your mother for that first time is probably one of the most memorable experiences ever. The only thing better than that was when we had you and the look on Sue's face when she held you. Sometimes I sit back, and I still see her smiling face. She's been gone... what fourteen years now. You were a kid and probably don't remember much about her."

"Yeah, I remember some things." Donovan remembered more about his mother than his father could ever imagine. He remembered her smell and the perfume that she used to wear. Sometimes she would paint on her canvas or sketch pictures of him while he sat in the big rocking chair in the back room, which was now the guest room. At night she'd recite the letters to him in Chinese, making a song out of the alphabet.

"I really remember that she loved the globe," Donovan finally responded. "She used to sit me in her lap and tell me to point to any place on the globe. Then she'd tell me stories about the people that lived in that region and about their culture. You know, for years I felt like she abandoned me. Of course now I know better."

"It takes a while to come to terms with death. Everything happened so suddenly at the time. I'm still not fully over her, you know, but I have to move on with my life. I can't leave it at a standstill, and your mother wouldn't want me to do that either."

"Is that why you never considered marriage again?" Donovan asked.

"Marriage is not something you jump into, but I haven't totally dismissed the idea. If I meet the right person I would definitely marry again," Mr. Miller replied.

"It seems now like it was so long ago."

"I used to ask God why? Why your mother—my wife? She was such a good person, and there she was inflicted with this cancer that couldn't be cured. We even flew her to England, because their hospitals and medicines are supposed to better than ours. But the doctors said that it was no longer in the incipient stage. She was long pass that, and all they could do was monitor it."

"That's the glioblastoma cancer. Anne-Marie did some research for one of her classes about it. She was telling me some of the warnings and symptoms."

"*Yeh, mon.* One day she was fine smiling, laughing, and walking around. Not one complaint and suddenly without any warning she got a dizzy spell and could barely stand on her own. She was debilitated and couldn't even talk. All the creative energy that she had was gone."

"I don't remember how long she was sick. I just remember her being in the bed for a while."

"Sue didn't suffer long. It all happened in a matter of months. When she realized that she wasn't going to be up and about and she was bedridden, it killed her spirit and her will to live. She was such a great person, and she brought out the finer qualities in me. Kind of like you and Anne-Marie."

"Anne-Marie?" Donovan said, surprised.

"Yes. Anne-Marie kind of reminds me of Sue. I mean her intellect and strong will. Now, Anne-Marie is a lot more aggressive and bold whereas Sue was assertive but reserved. Nevertheless Sue got her point across just the same. Anne-Marie means well, but she can be very brash at times. You know what I mean!"

"Well to tell you the truth, I do. Today we were talking about how she runs her mouth and needs to watch how she talks to people. But it really makes me feel good that you think so highly of Anne-Marie."

"Of course I do. Why wouldn't I feel that way? Anne-Marie is a wonderful person. You know I think of her as a daughter. That really shouldn't surprise you. She's very charming and bright. I can't say the same for many of these women around here. These young girls come in the shop, and when I say young, I mean some of them went to school with you and even younger. You should hear the things that come out of their mouths. It can make even a grown man blush. Offering me things, and Donovan all I can do is shake my head in disbelief. They're fully aware of the fact that I know their parents, but most of them could care less. Now you tell me what road you think they're headed down. I feel so much shame for them, but Anne-Marie I'd proudly accept into my family. She has a good head on her shoulders."

"Out of curiosity, which girls have been hitting on you?" Donovan asked.

"You never mind. That's none of your business, but I'll tell you one thing, they need to put their heads to their books and think about a future instead of sleeping with all these men," he responded, unable to keep a straight face.

"So, you're holding out on your son? Since when have we started keeping secrets from each other?"

"It's not a secret, but it's not up for discussion. One thing I can assure you of is that I know you've been with a few of them."

"Why do you say that?"

"The things that they say. For instance, one girl said to me the other day 'If the son is hot, I can only imagine the father must be on fire' or 'The apple don't fall far from the tree.' Boy, I tell you, the mouths on these young girls are something else. The others are too vulgar to even repeat. I hate to even think that you were laid up with some of these girls." Mr. Miller replied.

"Those days are long over. I'm not surprised to hear that they hit on you. But if you were in your prime?"

"Then, yes it would be tempting. Those same girls were around back when I was growing up, son. Not much has changed, because they're like their mothers, and I'm telling you I been there, done that back then."

"*Pops, yu nah romp,*" Donovan said, almost falling off the edge of the bed and holding his stomach with laughter.

"The sad thing is they make themselves available for almost anyone. You see me, I wouldn't take advantage of them, but you have these men jumping at the opportunity. Then they give them a little pocket change. You think I don't know."

"I know you heard about Clifton and Dottie recently. That girl went to school with me and Anne-Marie."

"Yeah, I heard," Mr. Miller replied with a disgusted look. "I only hope you're not still out there messing with these slack girls."

"Pops, you crazy or something? I told you I'm past that. I ain't been with no other woman now for at least... " He paused to think about the length of time. "A good two years. It's all about me and Anne-Marie."

"That's good! That's what I want to hear. So, let me ask you how much longer she has in school before she graduates from the university? This is what her third or fourth year?"

"Mmh hmm, yeah about that." It never even occurred to Donovan what Anne-Marie was going to do about school. Although they didn't discuss it yet, he knew she wasn't thinking of going back to school way in Kingston next semester.

"Donovan, what do you mean something like that? The other day I thought I overheard her saying something about one more year to complete."

"Yes, she did have one more year."

"She did. So what happened now? It's shorter or longer? Don't tell me she changed her mind after she's come this far?"

"No, no nothing like that. It may just take more time than we thought."

"Tell me what's going on, son."

"Well, I've been wanting to talk to you, and I've been sitting here half the evening thinking of what to say and how to say it. Then I thought about you and Mom. I wanted to know how you felt about her and how you knew she was the one for you."

"Okay."

"Well, I know Anne-Marie is the one for me, because when we're together I feel good. She makes me feel special."

"Sound like your hormones chatting to you," Mr. Miller said, trying to make light of the situation. He could tell that something heavy was on his son's mind.

"Pops, seriously. I grew up with her, and it's funny to say this, but I've watched her blossom from girl to woman. She's headed in a direction that I definitely want to go. There is something that I want to tell you, and I don't want you to be upset."

"You're a grown man. Why would I be upset? Come on now, you know me better than that," Mr. Miller replied.

"Disappointed is more what I meant to say."

"You're starting to frustrate me. Is that more suitable to you? Now what is it you have to tell me?"

"The reason Anne-Marie may not finish school in the next year is because she's pregnant."

"Pregnant." Mr. Miller looked at him in disbelief. He got up from the bed and began pacing the room without uttering a word. Donovan didn't know if it was wise to interject the silence to break the tension in the room. But it killing him not to, so he finally spoke. "She's pregnant. We haven't been to the doctor, but we're going to see Dr. Keene to confirm it. We are almost ninety-nine percent positive that she is pregnant though."

Mr. Miller stopped pacing and took a seat beside Donovan. He put his arm around Donovan's shoulder and drew him closer.

"Son, you don't have to worry about me being upset or disappointed. I'm much more concerned about the two of you. Are you holding up all right? How is Anne-Marie feeling?"

"I'm fine, Pops. I was nervous about telling you, that's about it. The thought of becoming a father is really starting to sink in, and I still can't believe that this is happening to me."

"Has she told Trevor and Faye yet?"

"No, she told me not too long ago, and we decided to tell them this Sunday. I'm going over there for dinner, so we'll tell them together. I don't want her to be alone."

"Over the dinner table?" Mr. Miller questioned.

"Not necessarily over the table."

"Should I be there?"

Donovan thought about his father accompanying him to Anne-Marie's house as if he were a little kid, and scoffed at the idea.

"You have jokes now. Seriously, though, you know we wanted to tell them after Maisey's wedding. If we tell them tonight or tomorrow it would be the talk of the town. We don't need a lot of commotion and gossip, and you know that's exactly what would happen."

"Donovan, people are going to talk regardless. We live in a small town, and you can't worry about what people will and will not say."

"True, but the focus and attention would steer to us instead of Maisey and her celebration—people asking us questions, staring, pointing fingers, being rude—and I really don't want to be bothered."

"You have to learn to ignore people. Besides, the nosiest person that you have to worry about is Faye. And since Anne-Marie is her child she won't be so quick to spread the news. Trust me, she'll keep quiet, because the fingers will point in her direction for a change," Mr. Miller replied.

"Pops, any words of wisdom or encouragement for going to battle on Sunday with Anne-Marie's family?" Donovan asked.

"Good luck!" Mr. Miller said and patted Donovan on the back.

"That's it? Good luck?"

"What more do you want me to say? You already know what you're up against. Faye can be ignorant, so don't expect much from her. The rest of the family I think you can handle. A baby is something coming into the world not going, so they'll have to deal with it. Don't be surprised if you don't get the reaction you are looking for. I know you to be a responsible man, because I raised you to be that way. I'm not going to worry about the baby. I know you would do anything for Anne-Marie. I've witnessed you act a fool on more than one occasion, and I know you love her. Yes, I was shocked and a little taken aback when you said she was pregnant. The first thing that ran through my head was how you could be so careless. Then I realized there would be an addition to the family, and I'm going to be a grandfather. All I can really say is I know you'll do right by Anne-Marie. Donovan, you're my son, and I love you."

"Pops, thanks, and I love you too!"

Chapter Five

C olleen couldn't help being a little nervous about the prospect of seeing her mother at Maisey's wedding and being accompanied by Lloyd. She was an adult now and shouldn't have to dwell on such things, but she didn't have the average mother. Colleen explained the situation to Lloyd, and he told her not to worry. He was excited to visit home after an absence of a couple of years.

Lloyd occasionally dropped by to see his mom, but at the wedding he would see people he had lost contact with over the years. Lloyd also felt that no mother could possibly resist him, and Colleen's mother was no exception to the rule. Lloyd was confident that he was irresistible to women, and he knew how to spread the charm. Colleen still felt that she had to prep him in case they did have an unpleasant encounter with her mother. After all Colleen knew Ms. Margaret better than anyone else. Her mother wouldn't hesitate for a moment to embarrass her in front of a crowd. She lived for that sort of attention, be it good or bad. Colleen had also hoped deep down that someday she and her mother could become friends, but it seemed as though the relationship was becoming even more volatile. Colleen thought that if she moved out and put some distance between them, something positive would develop. Things had only gotten worse, and it was eating her up on the inside. She loved her mother despite her bitterness and their differences. Colleen was now at her wit's end trying to find a way to make amends between them.

Lately Colleen had been spending more time at Lloyd's house than she did at her aunt Lorna's. Aunt Lorna claimed she didn't mind Colleen staying with her, but she would always ask for her work schedule in case she was expecting company. Aunt Lorna was a single woman in her mid-thirties. She was about the same age as Colleen's mother, but you would never know it by looking at them. Her mother was young, but acted like Old Mother Hubbard, while Aunt Lorna basked in her youth. Ms. Margaret and Aunt Lorna had known each other since childhood, but they were never really good friends. For that matter they weren't friends at all. Even though Ms. Margaret had married her brother, Aunt Lorna always felt that her older brother was destined for better things and that didn't include Margaret. She felt that Ms. Margaret would bring him down and make his life miserable. Unfortunately Aunt Lorna's prediction came true. The misery lasted for a while, but Colleen's father finally came to his senses and divorced Ms. Margaret. At the time he felt obligated to marry her since she was pregnant with his baby. He later realized that he could still be a good father without having to remain with Ms. Margaret. He later remarried and was now happy beyond his wildest dreams. Anything would be a cakewalk when compared to dealing with Ms. Margaret. Aunt Lorna didn't know what her brother saw in Ms. Margaret. Even when they were in school Ms. Margaret had few friends and she was a tracer and a known troublemaker. The only good thing that came out of her brother's troubled marriage was Colleen. Aunt Lorna loved Colleen and wanted to do what she could to help her, but Aunt Lorna's clock was ticking, and time was running out. She needed her space for her men and hopefully one of them would eventually ask her to be his wife.

One day Colleen came home from work mid-afternoon because the airport closed early. The threat of the approaching hurricane seemed to be a reality, and all the flights were canceled. Colleen hopped in a cab and headed home, and since her aunt didn't have a phone she was unable to contact her. When Colleen finally made it home she was tired and exhausted. She immediately plopped down on the sofa that she slept on and was about to fall asleep. Colleen hadn't noticed any signs of Aunt Lorna, but she was notorious for keeping her bedroom door closed whether she was there or not, so Colleen didn't bother to check.

After a few moments of trying to drift off, she heard sounds coming from the bedroom. At first, Colleen dismissed them for the heavy winds introducing the arrival of Hurricane Maxwell. As the sounds grew louder and became more agitated, Colleen figured that Aunt Lorna must be home and cramping badly. She remembered her mother going through the same thing. Convinced that her aunt was suffering agonizing pain, Colleen decided to check to see if she could bring her anything for the discomfort.

Colleen knocked at the bedroom door a couple of times, but Lorna didn't answer. After getting no response, Colleen decided to just open the door. She was about to ask if everything was all right, and whether her aunt wanted her to make some tea or bring some aspirin, when her eyes opened wide with shock. Aunt Lorna was fully nude on the top of some man that Colleen had never seen before. She was carrying on like a wild woman hopping up and down on his penis. Colleen had never seen a man's penis up close before. After all she and Lloyd were still in the petting stage.

Aunt Lorna's room was situated so when you opened the door, the first thing that you saw was the bed. Lorna would have been totally unaware of Colleen's presence had it not been for the light that illuminated from the doorway. Colleen stood there in shock with her mouth wide open. She couldn't believe what she was seeing. It wasn't until Lorna yelled out, "Gyal, come outta me room, and shut me door," that Colleen realized she had been staring for quite some time and had better leave—and quickly.

She wanted to leave the apartment and would have if the weather weren't so bad. Colleen knew her aunt Lorna would be upset with her, and she didn't want her aunt and her aunt's lover to come out of the room and see her sitting there on the couch with nothing better to do. She sat there listening intensely so that when they emerged from the bedroom she could sprint into the kitchen and make herself scarce. Aunt Lorna and the man carried on for another half hour or so.

Shortly thereafter, Colleen heard the sound of keys jingling and loose change clanking, which probably meant that the man was getting dressed. Then she heard Aunt Lorna asking when she would see him again. They lingered a while longer and when the doorknob started to turn Colleen jumped up and shot into the kitchen. Aunt Lorna came out dressed in a robe, and from the kitchen light, Colleen could see that the man was extremely good-looking and fully dressed. On his way out, he leaned down and gave her aunt a peck on the cheek and said "Later." Aunt Lorna headed to the bathroom to take a shower. As she showered, Colleen sat on the couch awaiting her punishment or scolding for barging into her aunt's room.

When Aunt Lorna finished dressing she merely said hello to Colleen as if nothing happened and asked what she wanted for dinner. She didn't even mention that Colleen had invaded her privacy. It wasn't until they sat down for dinner that Aunt Lorna brought up the subject. Even then her only comment was "If my bedroom door is not ajar or you knock and I don't respond, I beg you please do not enter."

Colleen was happy that her aunt didn't make a big deal out of it. Although she couldn't help to think that had it been her mother, Ms. Margaret would've been extremely upset and handled it a lot less tactfully. Then again, her mother wouldn't allow herself to be caught in such a position.

After that incident at Aunt Lorna's, Colleen felt uncomfortable staying there and now understood her aunt's reason for always keeping the door closed.

When Colleen told Lloyd about catching her aunt, he found it extremely amusing. Lloyd laughed uncontrollably for several minutes. He thought Colleen's detailed description of her aunt bobbing up and down and panting like a woman from the wild was the funniest story he had ever heard. Colleen found it to be one of the most horrifying not to mention embarrassing moments in her life. Lloyd's only comment was "accidents happen."

Sex wasn't an everyday occurrence for Colleen. She barely discussed it openly, and had yet to experience it. Prior to the embarrassing incident with her aunt, the closest she had come to sex was talking to Anne-Marie. For years her mother made sex seem taboo. Talking about sex in her mother's house was unheard of. The only discussion that Colleen and Ms. Margaret ever had regarding sex was when Colleen first got her period. Ms. Margaret came to Colleen and showed her how to put on a pad and just as she was about to leave the room she turned to Colleen and said, "You know what this means now right?" Ms. Margaret wasn't really looking for an answer and continued. "It means that you can get pregnant now, so don't try anything stupid. No

S-E-X. You have been warned." Colleen remembered thinking then, at the tender age of eleven, whatever sex was she wanted no parts of it.

Colleen knew that Anne-Marie and Donovan were having sex, and they only spoke about it when Anne-Marie lost her virginity.

After that, there was really no need to discuss it further. Lloyd told Colleen that she was welcome to stay at his place anytime since she was uncomfortable at her aunt's house. So she began staying there late but she never spent the night. Colleen wasn't willing to make that kind of commitment with Lloyd yet.

Lately, she had been considering sex a lot more, but she wasn't able to let herself go all the way yet. She and Lloyd had been together now for almost four months although she had lied to Anne-Marie when she told her it was merely a couple of weeks. If she had told her the truth about the time, Anne-Marie would have been upset that she had not told her sooner.

Lloyd was a complete gentleman, and didn't pressure Colleen about having sex, but she knew that he was a man, and he had needs. She didn't want to take the risk of losing him or him fulfilling his needs elsewhere. He gave her a key and even suggested that she move in with him. There were several reasons that she didn't jump at the opportunity, the main reason being the fear of disappointing her mother.

Colleen lay on Lloyd's bed waiting for him to come home and enjoy the rest of the day with her. Thoughts of their relationship began clouding her head. She had dinner on the stove waiting for his arrival. When he walked through the door, she heard him say, "It smells like my baby's been cooking." Lloyd came into the bedroom and unbuttoned his sweaty shirt and planted a sweet kiss on Colleen's forehead. Then he headed to the bathroom. That was his daily routine: He showered every evening after a long day of hard work, then he would sit down to dinner. Since Colleen was there so often now, he rarely had to cook for himself anymore. He loved having Colleen around and really wished that she would take him up on his offer and move in. She seemed to have so many burdens that she need not carry alone, including her constant desire to seek approval from everyone and worrying about other people's opinion of her. All he wanted to do was take care of her.

When he came out of the shower Colleen had already left the bedroom to go into the kitchen and serve his food for him. Colleen rarely stayed in the room while he got dressed and when she did, she covered her eyes. Lloyd went out to the dining area where Colleen was sitting at the table waiting for him. He sat down and thanked her for preparing the food. Then they held hands and said a prayer before eating. Again Lloyd noticed that ever since they visited Cambridge the other day that Colleen was tense. He decided to find out what was bothering her.

"Colleen, sweetie, tell me what's on your mind. I know that something is bothering you since earlier this week."

"I already told you, but you didn't take me seriously." The conversation that she and Anne-Marie had on her last visit continued to haunt her. Tomorrow she would be attending her aunt Maisey's wedding and Lloyd would accompany her. Her father already knew Lloyd, and it helped that he was accepting of their relationship. However, Anne-Marie's comment that Ms. Margaret would "have a fit!" still rang clear as a bell in her head. It was starting to sound like a broken record, and suddenly she didn't feel quite as strong.

Lloyd interrupted her agonizing thoughts again.

"Tell me again, I didn't realize that it was that important."

"I told you about my mother and how she may react when she sees us together."

"Okay. I'm listening." Then Lloyd put his fork down, giving Colleen his complete attention.

"She may cause a scene. I don't want her to scare you off. She can be very irrational." Colleen knew the word she really wanted to use was crazy.

"She won't scare me off, okay, sweetie. And don't worry, I would never let you go that easily. If she behaves the way you say she will, I'll leave you two to resolve your differences. But don't wait for her to publicly humiliate you; walk away if she makes a scene. I won't allow her or anything else to spoil our evening. I promise," Lloyd said, turning his attention back to his meal.

"I'll try not worry about it, but you don't know my mother," Colleen responded. They ate the rest of their meal in silence. When they were done Lloyd told Colleen to relax while he cleared the table and washed the dishes. Shortly after he completed his chores, Lloyd took Colleen by the hand, helping her out of her seat.

"Come into the bedroom and let me give you a massage to relieve some of that tension." Colleen followed him into the room.

After ten minutes of rubbing her back he turned her over and began to kiss her arms and upward toward her neck. Colleen didn't immediately respond, but Lloyd was use to her being timid. He embraced her and kissed her softly on the mouth. Colleen wrapped her arms around Lloyd and passionately kissed him back. Lloyd was a little surprised, but continued. He knew she could kiss, but today seemed different. Lloyd felt himself starting to get aroused. He went back to kissing her neck and removed her blouse to expose her perfectly round breasts. He lightly kissed each nipple and slowly took one into his mouth to suckle. Colleen felt his manhood beginning to grow on her thigh, and she didn't stop him. Instead she enjoyed the moment. She could feel a hot, sticky wetness from herself, and her heart began to race. This wasn't the first time that they had done this, but things had never gotten this intense before. Usually she stopped him after he began sucking her breasts, even though she enjoyed it. Sounds of pleasure began to escape from her mouth as Lloyd guided her hand to his throbbing penis. Before she knew it, her blouse and skirt were both on the floor. Lloyd was now kissing her navel and slipping his hand inside of her panties. He separated her legs and slowly began to kiss her inner thigh. Her panties were slowly being slipped off. Just as they touched her feet, she realized what was about to occur, and she stopped him.

CHapter Six

They say good things happen in threes, and although I am not usually superstitious, I'm inclined to believe it's true today. Today was the busiest day that I've had all week. Donovan took me to Dr. Keene's office early this morning. If there was ever any doubt before there need not be anymore, because I'm definitely pregnant. I've long come to accept the idea, and the more I say it the more I like hearing it. Now I'm actually excited and looking forward to becoming a mother.

Prior to my visit to Dr. Keene's this morning I was awakened by what I thought was gas, so I made myself some mint tea to help relieve the pain. Any other time the mint tea would have helped. Then I felt another jolt, and I realized that it wasn't gas. The pain persisted and increased. I knew it had to be the baby making its debut to let me know that it was alive and well. I was experiencing the first stage of pregnancy. This would probably be the most memorable impression on a mother-to-be. The feeling was indescribable and the moment, amazing. I actually felt like a woman. I've always called myself a woman, but I was truly only a child trapped in a woman's body. This was the most phenomenal transition and there was still more to come.

Donovan came by my house to pick me up some minutes to nine. When we left, Nadine was still asleep, and my parents had already left to open up the bar. I mentioned to them late last night that I had several errands to run, including going back to Kingston to get my grades for the semester. So they didn't expect me back until later this evening.

Dr. Keene was the closest OB/GYN office within a five-mile radius of our small town, depending on where you lived in Cambridge. If you needed to see any other doctor you would have to travel a lot farther. We were lucky, because Donovan and I only lived about two miles away from Dr. Keene's office. Dr. Keene's office was a cheery bright canary yellow. All the walls were covered with pictures. There was one piece that amazed me the first time I saw it. It's a painting of a black Jesus kneeling down with hands clasped as he looks up into the heavens. This stood out the most, because Dr. Keene was the only person I knew with a picture of a black Jesus. The Full Gospel Assembly church that I go to didn't even have a black Jesus on display. The only things black in the church were the people, the bible covers and the pulpit the pastor stood at during his service.

When I first saw the picture I mentioned it to Dr. Keene. He asked me why it surprised me to see a black Jesus. I never thought of color when Jesus came to mind, but subconsciously I must have thought He was white to even ask. Dr. Keene asked me if I ever questioned pictures of white Jesus when I saw them. Of course I didn't, because I was raised to believe that He was white and accepted it.

He also mentioned that if I had any doubt or felt otherwise that it was clearly stated in the bible in the book of Revelation. I practically ran home after I left his office that day to read the bible, and I didn't have to read far. A full description was on the first page of Revelation. Since that incident Dr. Keene always made it a point to tell me facts about our heritage.

There is another picture hanging in his waiting room of a black doctor surrounded by his students. I just figured that Dr. Keene was one of the students in the picture and that the doctor was his mentor. As it turned out it was a picture of Dr. Charles Drew, the acclaimed physician who was the pioneer in blood plasma research and development. I really liked Dr. Keene because not only was he a genuinely concerned physician, he was like a wealth of knowledge.

The office was set up in a small four-and-half-room house. The waiting room was the largest of all the rooms. There was an examination room, Dr. Keene's office, a small kitchen, which was used to store patient files, and the lavatory. There were about twelve chairs in the waiting room, and they didn't face the door, so the people that were already sitting down in the waiting area couldn't see who was entering unless they physically turned around to be nosy.

When Donovan and I arrived, three other people were seated in the waiting room. I knew one of the women and greeted her. I didn't recognize the other woman, but we still exchanged pleasantries. I couldn't see the face of the man because he was slumped down, and his hands covered his entire face. He seemed to be either in deep thought or simply exhausted.

Dr. Keene's staff consisted of a nurse and a receptionist. I went to the front and told the receptionist the nature of my visit, and she told there was a forty-five- minute wait. Dr. Keene had two other people ahead of me.

Donovan took a seat in the back and was flipping through one of the many magazines that were spread out on a table. When he got through flipping the last magazine he placed it back on the table and began fidgeting. He was so nervous that you would have thought that he was the one coming in for the examination.

About fifteen minutes had gone by when Dr. Keene and Nurse Kelly emerged from the examination room. Dr. Keene walked back to his office while Nurse Kelly put the patient file on the receptionist's desk. The assistant asked if the patient needed another appointment, and Nurse Kelly told her yes. Then she walked into the storage room and came back out with medical supplies and headed back into the examination room. I put my head down momentarily and when I looked up the receptionist was talking to the patient that Dr. Keene had just seen. The woman had her back toward us. When she finally turned around I realized it was Ms. Margaret. She was wearing a long white skirt and a Hawaiian shirt covered with imprints of tropical birds. I almost didn't recognize her because she also wore a straw hat and large sunglasses.

As I was about to nudge Donovan to get his attention he stood up and said he had to go the bathroom. Before he stepped away, I pointed toward the front desk, and he briefly glanced in Ms. Margaret's direction and shook his head to say he had seen her and then walked out.

I really didn't want to speak to Ms. Margaret, so I started to put my head into my lap so that she wouldn't spot me. I didn't want her asking me why I was here or talking to me about Colleen as if she cared about either.

When I saw that Ms. Margaret was done talking to the receptionist I kept my head down low. I thought she was about to leave when I noticed that she stopped to tap the man with his head down in the front row. I her heard mention something about waiting for the results. The man responded but I didn't hear him. He got up to stretch and when he turned around I couldn't believe my eyes. It was Mr. Miller. I wondered what in the hell was taking Donovan so long. He must have gone to take a smoke. He had to see this. On the way out of the office Mr. Miller put his arm around Ms. Margaret's shoulders.

For a moment I thought that my eyes had deceived me. When I saw them at the store talking intimately the other day I figured something must be going on, but I wasn't sure. It was probably no coincidence when I heard my mother and Nadine talking about Ms.

Margaret on the veranda either. Even though I wasn't able to hear much of their conversation I should have been able to piece it together by the way they were being so secretive.

This was too much to process at once. It just seemed strange to see them together. Mr. Miller was so nice, and Ms. Margaret was such a bitch. What could he possibly see in her? I wondered if Donovan knew what was going on. Now that I think about it, I'm almost positive that he's clueless. Things could be happening right in front of his face, and Donovan would still be oblivious. Plus, if he did know he would have mentioned it to me when I came home.

Donovan despised Ms. Margaret almost as much as I did. I really wonder if Mr. Miller and Ms. Margaret really are involved. I don't want my imagination to start running wild when nothing is really going on. The biggest question was why were they at the doctor's office together? Was Ms. Margaret pregnant? Did Mr. Miller get Ms. Margaret pregnant? A barrage of questions and thoughts were rushing through my head. The most agonizing question was what the hell was taking Donovan so long to get back.

My mind must have taken me to a far-off place because I was in a daze and didn't even realize that Mr. Miller and Ms. Margaret had descended toward me. I looked up to find them standing over me. I immediately noticed that Mr. Miller had removed his arm from around Ms. Margaret's shoulder. They tried to appear nonchalant, as though it was normal for them to be together. But they looked as guilty as sin. They needn't worry, their secret was safe with me. Nonetheless, it wouldn't remain a secret for long since my mother and Nadine probably already knew about them being an item.

Mr. Miller spoke first, and Ms. Margaret stood there as if she were waiting for an invitation to speak.

"Hi, Anne-Marie, sweetheart. How are you doing today?"

"Good morning, Mr. Miller, Ms. Margaret. I'm doing well,

and how are you two doing?" I really wanted to ask what they were doing together.

"I'm fine, Anne-Marie, dear," Ms. Margaret said, finally deciding to speak. "So what brings you here today to see Dr. Keene? Is everything all right? You're not sick or anything like that are you?" She was doing a good job of pretending to be concerned, piling me up with questions that were none of her business. The only way she could ever know anything about me would be through hearsay, but never from my mouth.

"I'm doing just fine. You know I'm up at school most of the year so I'm just getting my yearly checkup."

"I really wish Colleen would follow your lead and go to school. I don't know why she wants to work at some airport. She's such a bright girl, but she never listens to me. Colleen is wasting her time at that job. Maybe you can talk to her."

"School isn't for everyone, and she has to learn to make her own decisions." I couldn't believe my ears. Ms. Margaret actually sounded concerned about her daughter's future. There's a first time for everything. She also claimed that she didn't know why Colleen moved away from home to work at the airport. How could she not know? Ms. Margaret made life at home miserable for Colleen. Working at the airport was probably the next best thing to heaven right now for Colleen. Anything was better than living with her mother.

"Yes we all must make decisions, but they should be wise ones. Nobody was stopping her from doing anything here, you know"

I thought to myself, what was there to do in Cambridge? The town offered no opportunities. Almost everyone in Cambridge worked in Montego Bay unless they had their own small business. I saw that it was no use in trying to teach an old dog new tricks, so I let it go and steered the conversation to her.

"So what brings you here today? Is everything okay?" The ball was in her court, and I wasn't going to let her off the hook that easy since she took the liberty of prying into my business. Her face turned red, but she shot me a "how dare you" look. I guess Ms. Margaret didn't think I would have put her on the spot like that. Then to my surprise Mr. Miller answered on her behalf.

"Margaret came for a checkup, too, and I gave her a lift since I didn't have to open up the shop this morning." I detected a hint of asperity in Mr. Miller's voice. It took a moment for me to realize that Mr. Miller wasn't being quite as pleasant as he normally would have been to me.

I wondered if Mr. Miller knew the true nature of my visit. The other night Donovan said he was going to tell his father. I didn't even bother to ask him if he did. Mr. Miller had always been like a surrogate father to me. I loved and respected him as such, and I felt no contempt for him. I certainly didn't want to come across as being disrespectful. All of a sudden I felt like a child searching for approval. I don't know what it was about the Miller men that had me practically kowtowing to their every beck and call.

Mr. Miller's tall frame hovered over me. His height held such power in comparison to my small existence. Mr. Miller's stature made me feel like he was a guillotine about to behead me. He was at least an inch or two taller than Donovan who was six-two. Mr. Miller turned his attention from me to Ms. Margaret. He gave her the car keys and told her to go wait in the car while he had a word with me. She obliged all too happy to be dismissed from my scrutiny.

Ms. Margaret was a cruel woman, and I resented her for all the abuse and sadness Colleen endured through the years. And even though I wasn't the one going through all the agony I could relate all too well. Unlike myself Colleen couldn't run to her father when her mother was being a bitch since her father lived far away.

I was the one that Colleen confided in. We cried together, and I was there to share the pain and help her through her darkest hours. I was aware of things Ms. Margaret probably wouldn't dream Colleen would tell me, but I knew. So when I talk to Ms. Margaret in a tone I wouldn't dare address others it was because I knew the truth.

After Ms. Margaret left the office Mr. Miller pointed to a chair for me to sit down. He instantly took a seat beside me and the disapproving look he gave me only moments ago changed to a burgeoning smile, which relieved me. I hoped he wouldn't reprimand me for my earlier behavior. He put his hand over mine the same way I saw him do to Ms. Margaret in the shop. Maybe there was nothing going on between them after all and that was just his way of showing affection to friends. His voice softened significantly as he began to speak.

"Anne-Marie, sweetheart, Donovan and I had a talk the other night, and he told me that I will be a grandfather soon. Is that right?" he said, smiling.

"It's true, sir. I'm just here today to see Dr. Keene to estimate how far I am and such."

"Good, good. Donovan did tell me that the two of you were coming to the doctor. So did you tell Faye and Trevor the news yet?"

"No. Donovan and I decided we would tell them together over Sunday dinner, and the time is flying by now. Only Saturday stands between us now."

"True, sweetheart. Well I wish you luck with your parents on Sunday."

"Thanks. I'm sure I'll need all the luck that I can get. My father I'm not too worried about. He will be a little disappointed, but when I assure him that I still intend on finishing school, he will be fine. It's my mother that I'm really worried about. You know how she can fly off the handle sometimes."

"Don't worry about her. She may surprise you. Just think positive. So I'll see you at Maisey's wedding tomorrow, won't I? I'm sure you've been sewing all week. I can't wait to see what you're wearing, little miss fashion plate."

"I'm not wearing anything special, just something out of my wardrobe. I have a few things that I made a while ago that I never wore. This week though I was busy sewing the suit for my father. He hasn't tried it on yet, and I may need to make some last-minute adjustments. It won't take me much time to finish that up tonight. It's been a busy week since I got back from school."

"Anne-Marie, speaking of school, how will you manage between school and your new responsibilities? Your education is important you know, and you've come so far. Will you have to put it off for a while?"

"Well, after this visit today I'm going to the school to get my grades for the semester. I will have a talk with the dean and my professors. I only have two more semesters and then I begin the med program."

"I thought that you were already in the medical program."

"Right now I'm premed. That is the preliminary before I can begin the actual boards and intern programs."

"Goodness gracious. You have to do a lot to become a doctor. *Lawd haf mercy pon dis chile*," he said, laughing and getting up from his chair. "Listen, I have to get going. I don't want Ms. Margaret waiting too long, and the car must be boiling," Mr. Miller explained.

"No problem. Donovan should be back soon anyway."

"Donovan is here?" Mr. Miller asked, looking around the room.

"He said he had to go to the bathroom, and I haven't seen him since."

"Well, Anne-Marie, take care of yourself and my grandbaby, and tell Donovan I'll see him at the shop later," Mr. Miller said, as he hugged me and proceeded to leave.

Just when I thought that everything was dismissed he stopped and came back toward me.

"Anne-Marie, I don't know what you have against Ms. Margaret, but remember, regardless of whatever it may be, she is the elder. If you have a grievance toward her, try and talk it out, but don't resort to being rude. It's not very becoming, and I know you to be a very respectful young lady."

"Yes, Mr. Miller." He embraced me again, then left. I watched him walk to the office door and head toward the car.

It looked like that witch Ms. Margaret had won after all. She could've burned up in the car for all I cared. For her sake I really hoped she wasn't pregnant. She didn't need to raise anymore children. Having a great father and a screwed-up mother wasn't the answer either, and I should know. I'm sure she thought that Mr. Miller was chastising me the entire time about my behavior. If she only knew that he let me off easy, she would be upset. Mr. Miller really could have been much harder on me, but he loves me and is thrilled that I will be having his grandchild. I hope that he didn't mention my pregnancy to Ms. Margaret. If he did she would go straight to the bar or up the hill to see my mother and let her know before I even made it back home. It really wouldn't matter since my mother will be finding out in a couple of days anyway, but it would be better if it came from me.

Five minutes later Donovan returned.

"You just missed your father and Ms. Margaret," I told him.

"No kidding," he answered, brushing it off as nothing unusual.

"They were here together. Don't you think that's strange?" I asked.

"Come on, Anne-Marie, you know my father. He doesn't turn anyone away when it comes to doing a favor." If he didn't see any reason to worry then why should I?

Nurse Kelly and Dr. Keene both emerged from the examination room and went into his office. Two minutes later Nurse Kelly came back out to the front. She read the sign-in sheet to see who was next and then looked up when she saw my name. Nurse Kelly has known me for years and knew my dreams of becoming a doctor. She would often ask me about my progress and my grades, always giving me encouraging words and advice. Once, she confided that when she was younger she, too, had dreams. Unfortunately, there were a few obstacles that didn't allow her to fulfill them. Instead, she became a nurse and to most native islanders becoming a nurse was the next best thing to being a doctor. Although the natives didn't think she failed, she felt she did, and Nurse Kelly always regretted that. That's why she took such an interest in me and was proud of my determination to accomplish what she had not.

"Hello, Ms. Saunders and Mr. Miller. How are the two of you today?" Nurse Kelly asked with spirited enthusiasm filling her voice.

"Good," Donovan and I responded in unison.

"So how is school coming along, huh? How much longer before I can start to call you Dr. Saunders?"

"Give me a couple more years. I have one more year to complete as an undergraduate and then I matriculate into the medical program," I said, smiling. It felt so good to have come so far.

Nurse Kelly went to get my chart, and I told Donovan that I was next. I asked him again if he was nervous, and he exclaimed "Nervous? Me? About what?" We got up and went into Dr. Keene's office for my consultation.

When we entered Dr. Keene's office he didn't look up immediately, as he was still completing paperwork on a patient. Nurse Kelly motioned for us to have a seat until he was done. I started looking around the office to see if he had made any changes or new purchases since my last visit. There was a new plaque on his wall, and he had replaced his oak desk with a new cherrywood one and matching file cabinets.

I thought about one day having an office of my own to decorate, but I wasn't planning on having a private practice. I was going to one day work abroad in a large research facility studying the cause and origins of diseases, helping to develop and find cures for them.

Dr. Keene closed the manila folder and handed it to Nurse Kelly before turning to Donovan and me. He was in his early forties, tall, fair skinned and slightly balding. He had a very jovial and peaceful-looking face. He always looked happy and cheerful. Dr. Keene was a well-educated and admired man. He read my folder, then he slowly glanced up.

"Donovan, your father was just here. Did you see him?"

"No. I didn't catch him. I took a little walk down the road and when I returned I heard that I missed him."

"Oh, too bad. So what brings you here today, Ms. Saunders?" Dr. Keene asked.

"Well I'm here today because I haven't had my period for quite some time now."

"What exactly is quite some time now? You are going to have to be a little more specific." Dr. Keene pointed to his desk calendar. I proceeded to show him the last time I had gotten my period. He then estimated the term I would be in if my approximation was accurate. I told him about my experience earlier this morning. Dr. Keene said judging from the calendar and my episode that I was in my third month. He said I could be anywhere between ten and twelve weeks pregnant.

Listening to Dr. Keene talk made me get even more excited than I already was. It gave me a rush. Donovan just listened intensely with an amazed look on his face. Dr. Keene told me what to expect from month to month and proceeded to show me into the examination room. He had a lot of new equipment, including a machine for sonograms. It could have been there all along, but I never took notice of it before since I had no use for it prior to this visit.

Donovan could no longer conceal his emotions. He took delight in everything that Dr. Keene said and did during the procedure. His face lit up as Dr. Keene took him through everything step by step. Donovan asked questions and seemed even more excited than me. After the exam Dr. Keene gave me a blue pamphlet entitled "So you're Pregnant." He also gave me a list of do's and don'ts, a prescription for iron pills, and a practical guide for a well-balanced diet. Dr. Keene said that it was important for me to thoroughly read through the nutrition guide and to follow it. When we were done I went to the assistant's desk to make an appointment to return at the end of my fourth month.

The entire way to the bus stop Donovan couldn't stop talking about our next visit so he could hear the baby's heart beat with the stethoscope. I'll never forget this morning. It was the first good thing to happen today and the most memorable part about being pregnant thus far.

After Dr. Keene's office, I took the bus to the university in Kingston. Kingston is probably one of the most vibrant spots on the island, and the pulse of Jamaica. The hustle and bustle of downtown, the ships in the harbor, the street vendors, the tall buildings, and parks set Kingston apart from any other parish in Jamaica. There was never a dull moment in Kingston, especially since it was the center of commerce and home of the central government. Whenever I had the spare time, I'd stroll downtown to the Coins & Notes museum or the Hope Botanical Gardens. You had to visit Kingston more than once to appreciate its many splendors.

My first stop was to see my professor, Dr. Ikembe who also

served as the dean of the department. An African, Dr. Ikembe recently moved from America to Jamaica with his family. He had a very thick Nigerian accent, and I'm sure he could say the same thing about my Jamaican accent. He was a stocky man and stood about five feet nine inches. It seemed like we were about the same height, give or take an inch. He always wore colorful African dashikis, thick-rimmed glasses and was as sweet as molasses. Every chance Dr. Ikembe got, he complimented me on my successes, and continuously involved me in every extra-curricular activity available. As soon as he saw me he smiled.

"Anne-Marie Saunders, so good to see you today. I was just thinking about you and wondering when you were going to return to get your grades. How is my top student?"

"I'm doing well, and yourself?"

"Life has been good to me, Anne-Marie. Have you gone to the board to see your grades yet?" Dr. Ikembe smiled, revealing his beautiful white teeth.

"No, not yet. I thought that I should stop by to see you first."

"Well, go see your professors and get your grades. When you are done, return to me. I have great news for you."

"Great news! What kind of great news?" He immediately got my curiosity.

"No. I will not tell you now. Go see your grades and professors and hurry back. I shall tell you when you return." Now he had my adrenaline rushing, and he was withholding this piece of great news from me. Why tell me you have great news if you're not going to immediately share it?

"I'll be right back then," I said, leaving him sitting behind his desk.

"Don't be long," Dr. Ikembe said as he got up to walk me to the office door.

What possible great news could he have for me? I already figured that my grades were going to be pretty good with the exception of the one *B* that I was expecting. I wasn't really happy about that, because it would certainly ruin my almost perfect GPA.

I walked over to the main office where the grades were posted by last name. I used my index finger to search for my name on the roster. When I finally came across Saunders I almost fainted. I couldn't believe my eyes. How could I have been so wrong? My eyes were deceiving me, so again I made sure that the posting read, Anne-Marie Saunders. But it was there, just like the first time I saw it plain as day, in black- and-white. I had managed to pull off all *A*'s. I had gotten one *A*-, but that was from the class that I was originally expecting to get a *B* from. This must have been the good news that Dr. Ikembe had for me.

The *A*- came from what started out to be one of my most difficult professors of the semester, Dr. Thorton. Originally from London, England, Dr. Thorton held a degree from Oxford University. She was always praising Oxford for one reason or another. It made me wonder why she was even at the University of West Indies since Oxford was *so* great. The class that she taught was comprised of twenty students, and eight of us were female.

At first I figured Dr. Thorton disliked the female students, but then I noticed she regularly called on them. However, she chose to disregard my existence by deliberately ignoring me. When I raised my hand to participate, she'd call upon someone else. She either chose me as a last resort or randomly selected someone that didn't even have his hand raised. Finally, I decided to stop volunteering and answered only when she decided to pick me. I couldn't figure her out. I never did or said anything mean to her, so I eliminated that thought. Then I figured Dr. Thorton probably disliked the fact that I was doing well despite her rancid treatment toward me. It almost seemed like she was trying to dissuade me of my current career choice. Though Dr. Thorton never singled me out, she'd often stare in my direction while making speeches and comments like "Some of you are not cut out to become doctors, so you may want to reevaluate your career goals before it's too late." This was a strange way to motivate a class.

Dr. Thorton didn't faze me one bit. I was only in her class because it was a prerequisite, and I needed it to graduate. I figured it was only for one semester, and it would fly by quickly. At the beginning of the semester I must admit that she plucked my last nerve. It didn't really seem to matter that the class was very easy. Dr. Thorton was pulling every trick to make it a living nightmare for me. Initially, it took an enormous amount of restraint for me to keep my temper in check. Then I realized that my purpose in her class was to learn and any animosity that I felt toward this woman would have to lay dormant.

One day Dr. Thorton beckoned me to stay after class. This particular day she acted different toward me. She refrained from making sarcastic remarks and even called on me when I emphatically raised my hand for a question that I really wanted to answer. To my surprise she didn't hesitate to choose me. Maybe this was a fluke, but I decided to raise my hand a second time. Again she chose me. After everyone left she sat down at her desk and in her clipped British accent, which was now also a cross with the Jamaican patois said, "Anne-Marie, may I call you Anne-Marie?" For most of the semester Dr. Thorton either called me by my last name, which was customary, or nothing at all, simply pointing in my direction, giving me permission to answer a question.

"Sure," I responded a little shocked that she cared to call me at all. "You can call me Anne-Marie, Dr. Thorton."

"Kathryn. Please call me Kathryn." Dr. Thorton was truly what you called strange. She was getting stranger by the moment, but I was interested in hearing what she wanted with me.

"Anne-Marie, I wanted you to know that this will be my last

semester teaching here at the university, and that it was a pleasure having you as a student." I couldn't believe my ears. She could have fooled me. Why did she feel it necessary to inform me about her sudden departure? Dr. Thorton had become even more mysterious. Just when you think the puzzle is complete, you realize a couple of pieces are still missing. Maybe today I would finally be able to piece it together. I didn't know how to respond. I'm sure telling her that I didn't care that she was leaving wasn't appropriate. Trying to sound as ebullient as possible without looking phony, I finally spoke.

"Dr. Thorton, I'm so sorry to see you go. I enjoyed your class and…"

"Anne-Marie, stop it," she said interrupting me. "You don't have to fib to me. True, you may have enjoyed the content and the theory but you hated my class. I made coming to it an absolute nightmare. Please don't be ashamed to admit it. Really, it's okay."

"Dr. Thorton, if I may speak candidly. Sometimes it did take all the willpower that I could muster to come to your class. Nevertheless, the material and content along with your lectures, which you stated were stimulating, kept me quite interested." It felt like I had taken a load off my back.

"I'm so glad to hear you say that. I've succeeded in all I've set out to accomplish. I know you must be a bit baffled. I want you to know that you are one of the brightest students that I've ever had the pleasure of working with. You, Anne-Marie, are my most prized pupil. You are inquisitive, bright, witty, never faltering under pressure, and I admire those qualities about you."

"Dr. Thorton, I appreciate your kind words." Her praise came out of nowhere and was a complete surprise to me. All of a sudden I felt like I was obligated to also make a confession or repay her with kind words. Words that would be almost impossible to gather much less say aloud. Dr. Thorton had no idea how right she was when she said that I was probably a bit baffled.

Dr. Thorton continued. "Listen, you have tremendous potential, and I want you to be able to experience all the world has to offer, but you have to be prepared. In this life, we are often faced with obstacles and barriers—some more difficult than—others and I want you to be prepared, armed, and fully equipped. The world can be a harsh and cruel place for women, and I know that you have been sheltered for most of your life. Things come pretty easy for you, but it may not always be that way. Not everything will be handed to you on a silver platter, so you must learn not to take things for granted, like your brain. Always use it to your advantage. It is especially difficult for women to survive in the medical field. Men feel that we should be nurses and even though you hold a medical degree, you still have to prove that you earned it. So if I've made this semester a living hell, I sincerely apologize. In reality, not everyone will be as nice as pie. I want you to stay focused, as you know how important this opportunity is to you."

"Dr. Thorton, I'm flattered that you've taken such interest in my personal welfare. I will take heed and follow all of the advice that you have so kindly given me today." I was pleasingly overwhelmed. There I was, all semester wanting to strangle her as she stood in front of the class with her pasty white complexion, round glasses, stringy reddish-brown hair, and tiny pursed lips. Though I still didn't agree with her strange tactics, I felt like I owed her a debt of gratitude. At least now I could understand what she was trying to do. We continued talking for a while, and she told me about some of the experiences that she encountered, and how she began her teaching career.

Dr. Thorton explained how hard it was for her and how she had to struggle every day to prove her self-worth among her male colleagues. By the end of our discussion, I saw her in an entirely new light. She made me see and put things in a different perspective. Dr. Thorton was correct when she said things probably always went my way. I have yet to encounter a situation that I couldn't handle. That went for school and my home life. I always had my father or Donovan to protect and defend me. Being open and honest with Dr. Thorton helped me to clear my conscience and remove all past hostilities I felt for her.

I had about three more weeks in her class after that meeting, and I knew I was going to miss her. Dr. Thorton would be leaving shortly after the grades were posted. She was going to the United States to teach and continue her studies. She gave me her new address, and it was located somewhere in New York. I promised to stay in touch.

Over the last couple of weeks, Dr. Thorton and I became fast friends, forming a unique bond. I wiped the slate clean, and it was as if we had always been friends. It was strange at first, but not everything in life made a great deal of sense. I stayed after class to make idle conversation and exchange theories. Dr. Thorton didn't ignore my waving hand in class anymore, and before she left she invited me, the only student, along with her friends and colleagues to her home for a good-bye celebration.

I was still amazed that she had given me an *A* for the class. Although I knew I deserved it, Dr. Thorton was known for playing hardball, and it was very rare that she gave anyone a high grade, much less an *A*. Even though we had become fast friends, I still prayed along with the other students for a decent grade. I'm not complaining, and I'm quite grateful to receive the *A*. My college career was almost impeccable with the exception of one lousy *B* that I received from another elective. I promised myself that if I had enough time and energy to spare I would repeat the course to remove the grade from my transcript. As it looked right now, I wouldn't be able to take it this summer. I needed to prepare for the upcoming semester, which was going to be brutal. Besides, it wouldn't kill me to keep the *B*. I only hope the admission boards would overlook it for acceptance to medical school.

I was still standing there in the hall marveling at my grades, when I felt a hand on my shoulder. I turned around only to see Dr. Thorton standing there smiling at me. She held her arms out to embrace me, and I reciprocated.

"Anne-Marie, you've had a splendid semester. I'm so proud of you."

"Thank you, Dr. Thorton. I'm pleased with the final outcome myself." I knew she was referring to the grade that she so graciously bestowed upon me.

"I've been standing here for a couple of minutes staring."

"Well you deserved those grades. You worked extremely hard, and it shows. Do you have a moment, I'd like to talk to you?" Dr. Thorton asked.

"Sure I do, but Dr. Ikembe wants to see me before I leave."

"This won't take long. Come, let's go into my office." We walked down the long corridor, which today was void of the usual student body. Along the way to her office, I decided that I would tell Dr. Thorton about my pregnancy and my visit to the doctor's office this morning.

"I was hoping that I would see you here today. I didn't know if you remembered the invitation that I extended to you a couple of weeks ago for my going-away party this evening."

"I didn't forget, Dr. Thorton. As a matter of fact I have something for you." I reached into my handbag and handed her a small box along with a card. After I got off the bus, I stopped at a gift shop and got Dr. Thorton a pair of silver handmade earrings, shaped like Jamaica. It was all I could afford on such short notice. The card was rather simple. It read, *There are those that say that they are going to do it* and the inside flap said *and those that actually do it. Good luck!* I signed, *Wishing you all the best, your friend, Anne-Marie.* She opened the card and read it intensely. I was hoping she wouldn't find it too impersonal. When Dr. Thorton was done reading she thanked me and opened the box. When she saw the earrings her face lit up. Her reaction was much better than I had imagined.

"Anne-Marie, these are beautiful," she replied holding them up to admire the craftsmanship. "Absolutely beautiful." Dr. Thorton removed the gold hoops that adorned her ears to replace them with the new earrings. She went into her desk drawer to fetch her compact. She held her hair up above her shoulders to admire the earrings as they dangled from her ears. I never noticed how much prettier she looked with her hair pinned up, so I suggested that she wear her hair off her shoulders in a bun. Dr. Thorton then confided that whenever she attempted to pin it up, it always fell back down. I offered to do it for her. I plaited her hair into one long braid, and with the length of her hair twirled it into a bun adding a couple of pins that were in my bag to keep her hair in place. She was pleased and kept thanking me for the earrings and the hairdo. I was happy that she was pleased. Finally, I asked her why she wanted to see me. She exclaimed that she, too, had a gift for me. Dr. Thorton reached under her desk and pulled out a beautifully wrapped box. Once again, she had managed to amaze me. I read the card, which was touching. It read, *If you're ever looking for a reason to smile, and to keep holding on always know that I'll only be an ocean away. To a wonderful person and a great future doctor. Wishing you great success. Kathryn.* I wasn't the sentimental type, but I was flattered. I went over to hug her, and she hugged me back tightly. It was very emotional since we both knew that after today we might never see each other again.

I could tell that she was a little misty eyed after we separated and didn't want me to see as she spoke urgently to me.

"Anne-Marie, open up the box already." I carefully unwrapped the paper trying not to ruin it. This was the kind of paper that my mother would have me save. Dr. Thorton was getting impatient and started to lend me a hand by tearing the rest of the wrapping off. She had gotten me my very own stethoscope. My initials were engraved on the round silver piece. I can remember being a child and playing with my plastic toy stethoscope. Even then, I had dreams of becoming a doctor. This was the best gift that I've ever received, and it was expensive too. I wanted to accept it, but it was too costly.

"Dr. Thorton, I love it, but I can't accept this."

"Why not? I got it especially for you, and your initials are engraved on it. You must accept it. Please."

I could see that if I rejected the gift, I would hurt her feelings.

"Thank you, thank you so much. I promise to put it to good use one day real soon," I promised, clasping her hands in mine.

"It's well deserved. Anne-Marie, go speak to Dr. Ikembe. I believe that he was planning on leaving soon. When you're done, come back around here, so we can leave together for the party tonight."

"I'll leave my gift here with you until I return, if that's all right with you."

"Of course it is." Dr. Thorton replied.

"Dr. Ikembe sounded like he had something good to tell me, so I'm anxious to find out what it is." I thanked Dr. Thornton again and hurried down the hall to see Dr. Ikembe.

Dr. Ikembe was still in his office, packing his briefcase and preparing to leave.

"Dr. Ikembe, I almost missed you. I apologize for taking so long."

"Oh good, Anne-Marie, I was wondering if you had forgotten to come back to see me."

"Dr. Thorton and I started talking, and the time just flew by. I apologize if I held you up."

"Don't worry about it. Well now that you have seen your grades

I want to congratulate you on your fantastic feat this semester. You have once again managed to outdo yourself. Even Dr. Thorton gave you an *A*. Now that says a lot and is very, very impressive. Dr. Thorton speaks very highly of you.

"The reason that I wanted to see you is because I have very good news to tell you. I'm sure you've heard of the foreign-exchange program that allows students to go overseas to continue their studies."

"Yes, I'm familiar with the program. I've also considered applying to some of the colleges abroad."

"Well, each year our faculty members recommend a couple of top students that should be eligible for the program. It's usually about ten to fifteen of our pupils in either their junior to senior year. After reviewing their credentials and transcripts we vote. In order to stay in the running they would need at least two thirds of the vote. This allows us to narrow the number of applicants that are selected initially. Ultimately our goal is to get the number down to about five to seven candidates. We then complete the paperwork and submit it. You, Ms. Saunders, were the first person to ever get one hundred percent of the vote, and your paperwork was submitted to several different schools."

"Dr. Ikembe, I don't know what to say. I'm speechless."

"Well that's not all. We sent your paperwork to Oxford, which is Dr. Thorton's alma mater; Columbia University, located in the United States, and where Dr. Thorton will be teaching in the fall. In addition to that list is Howard University, a predominantly black college where I served as dean when I lived in the United States. The list also includes Johns Hopkins, which specializes in cancer research, Harvard, and Meharry Medical College. All of the colleges have extended incredible packages for you to continue your studies. The only thing left for you to do is to decide which one of the schools you would like to attend."

I couldn't believe my ears. This was a dream come true, and I could hardly take the Cheshire grin off my face.

"Do you have material for me to review on each of the universities?"

"I have something even better. You will have the opportunity to visit the schools for a week, all-expenses paid."

"I can't believe all of this has been arranged for me. I'm feeling a little light-headed. Do you mind if I have a seat?"

"No, no, please sit down. Are you okay? I know that this all may come as a surprise to you. And I must tell you that you were our most qualified candidate."

"It does, and Dr. Ikembe, you don't know how grateful I am. I really want to thank you and the rest of the staff for considering me, and nominating me for this wonderful opportunity. You have been so good to me over the past year. Always having your door open to me, providing me with information and helping with my studies. I really want to say thank you." I walked over to him to give him a big hug. I couldn't believe how well my day was going. From my first experience this morning, who would have thought that it would only continue to get better. I couldn't wait to get home to tell Donovan. He would be so happy for me... but I was forgetting about the baby. How could I possibly take advantage of such an offer with a baby on the way? "Dr. Ikembe, I'm not sure that I will be able to accept this opportunity."

"Anne-Marie, I can't let you pass this up. In most cases students that are nominated only get accepted to three maybe four schools at best. You have surpassed that. You have Columbia, Howard, Meharry, and three other schools knocking down your door." Dr. Ikembe knocked on the wooden desk to emphasize his point.

"It's not that I don't want to go to one of the schools that you've mentioned. I'm sure they are all excellent. There's something that prevents me and probably won't allow me to take part in going overseas right now."

"If it's your parents, I'd be glad to arrange a meeting to come and see them."

"No, it's not my parents. Actually my mother and father would be delighted."

"If you don't mind me asking, please explain to me the obstacle that stands in your way!"

"Dr. Ikembe, I paid a visit to my doctor this morning, and he confirmed that I am almost four months pregnant."

He sat contemplatively, which made me nervous. "I see." Dr. Ikembe stroked his beard while his eyes wandered around the room. I could tell from the look on his face that he was in deep thought. "Perhaps we can work around this. What are your plans for the following semester? Will you be returning?"

"I plan on completing the upcoming semester. I'm due in early February, and it may take me a little longer than I originally hoped. I will more than likely have to sit the last semester out, but I do plan on returning so that I may complete it."

"Well, listen, maybe we can work out a solution. I have something in mind if you don't object."

"Dr. Ikembe, I'm open to any suggestions that you may have. It is still my intention to finish school."

"Good. I will meet with your professors for the following semester and explain the situation. You may need to rearrange your courses to take the most difficult classes in the first half of the year if you have not already done so. Instead of sitting out and waiting to finish, you can probably have home school during your second semester. I would really like for you to finish on time, as well as take advantage of being able to attend one of these prestigious institutions."

"That sounds great. Dr. Ikembe, I hope you're not disappointed.

I do intend on completing my studies."

"Anne-Marie, you have in no way given me reason to be disappointed in you. Things happen, and I believe that a strong will can conquer all. You have not been defeated, but you will be forced to work harder. Now I can't make any promises, but we will try to work something out for our prize student. I'm going to give you pamphlets and the information that has been forwarded to us from the universities. I know that this is your summer break and you may want to relax, but I would suggest that you use this time to study."

"I planned on doing just that, but I don't have the materials for next semester yet."

"Don't you worry, I will give you the necessary materials. Did you tell Dr. Thorton about your present, ahem..." He cleared his throat. "Current condition?" Dr. Ikembe said hesitantly.

"No, but I intended on mentioning it to her today. She invited me to her going-away party this evening."

"Yes, that's right. That takes place tonight. Unfortunately, I have a prior engagement that I couldn't cancel, so I won't be able to attend. My son is on the cricket team, and he is playing against a team from England today. They've made it to the finals. I'll see Dr. Thorton before she leaves this Sunday. I better get going. I don't want to miss any of the festivities before the game. I hope you all have fun."

"Well, Dr. Ikembe, I want to thank you again, and I will use my time wisely this summer. I won't let you down, and any arrangements or accommodations that you are able to make for me will really be appreciated."

"You are more than welcome," he said extending his hand for me to shake and patting me on the back. He packed up the rest of his belongings, and we walked out together. On the way out we saw Dr. Thorton locking her office door. Dr. Ikembe began talking to Dr. Thorton about a colleague he wanted her to look up at Columbia University when she arrived in New York. When we got outside to their cars, Dr. Ikembe assured me once again that everything would work out, and that he would be in touch. Dr. Thorton and I walked to her car, and we drove to her home together.

Dr. Thorton lived about ten minutes away from the university in a four-bedroom villa that she shared with two roommates. When we arrived at her home, one roommate, Leslie, was in the kitchen preparing hors d'oeuvres for the party. She, like Dr. Thorton, was also from London, and she worked as a chef. She was the head chef at the Royal Beach Hotel and Resort in Kingston.

Dr. Thorton invited me upstairs, and we started talking about her move to the United States.

"Anne-Marie, I'm so excited. I've visited the States numerous times, but living there will be an entirely different experience. Anyway, enough about me, were you surprised to learn about the exchange program?"

"I could have screamed when Dr. Ikembe told me. The number of acceptances that I received from the colleges is amazing." I shared my excitement with her and thanked her profusely for her recommendation.

"If you choose Columbia, then we will be near each other again. Or you cold attend my alma mater in London. That would be an experience as well. Though London doesn't offer nearly as much beautiful weather as we have here in Jamaica. You would miss that. It's always raining there, that's why I never plan to move back." She was peering into her closet trying to select an outfit for the evening as she spoke. "Any of the schools would be an excellent choice. Do you know anything about any of them?"

"I'm familiar with Oxford, because of what you've told me. I know all about Johns Hopkins, and I know a little about Howard University. That's really it."

"Don't you worry your pretty little head over it. We will give you so much information that you will be well versed and familiar with each one of the schools. Can you believe your dreams of leaving this little island behind have finally come true? How about that," she exclaimed.

"I smiled a little and didn't respond. Dr. Thorton instantly picked up on my change of attitude and left the closet to sit beside me.

"Anne-Marie, what's bothering you? I thought that this was what you wanted."

"Dr. Thorton, it is. It's just that some dreams are simply that. Not everyone is meant to take advantage of his or her dreams. This is one that I may have to reconsider, or at least think it through before making a hasty decision."

"Anne-Marie, that's malarkey. What is really going on? A couple of weeks ago you were singing a different song, and not too long ago you were screaming your head off. What is this sudden change really about?" I could tell that she was deeply concerned.

"This morning I went to the doctor. I found out that I'm pregnant. I already told Dr. Ikembe." Dr. Thorton believed that the baby would help strengthen my character and my will to succeed. She said she knew I had some concerns, but I had a good head on my shoulders, and I shouldn't let this stop me from living my dreams.

Dr. Thorton had more faith in my future than my own family. For a moment I wished that she were the person I could confide in instead of my mother. If only my mother had Dr. Thorton's attitude and outlook on life instead of always concerning herself with gossip and frivolous things.

Dr. Thorton went to the bathroom to get dressed. When she was finished we went downstairs to greet the first of her guests.

When the party started jumping, Dr. Thorton went crazy. She was much different from the teacher that stood in front of the classroom earlier this year, or even the person that I started confiding in over the last month. I could tell that she could get loose, but once she started drinking, forget it. Dr. Thorton was like a party animal. After about three hours, it was time for me to call it an evening. I still had a long bus trip back to Cambridge.

It was a good day overall, and it seemed like it would never end. Dr. Thorton's friends were nice, but I was exhausted. Before leaving, I found Dr. Thorton to let her know that I had to go. We promised to keep in touch with each other. She said that when I had the baby she would make arrangements to come back and visit. She drove me to the bus stop, and as I was about to get out of the car I wished her good luck and a safe journey.

"Dr. Thorton, I really want to thank you for being my personal mentor, for helping me out, being a friend over these last couple of weeks I wish you well."

"Anne-Marie, you were a breath of fresh air and a pleasure to be around. Anything that I can help you with, simply let me know. Before I leave, I want you to grant me one wish. Call me Kathryn, please. All of my friends call me Kathryn."

"Okay, Kathryn." I said, causing her face to illuminate. Then we hugged and bade each other good-bye.

Chapter Seven

It was a perfect day for a wedding. The early-morning breeze was crisp and refreshing. The birds were chirping happily in the nest perched above the waterspout on top of the house. The flowers were blooming and exuded a sweet, musty warmth and fragrance that filled the house.

Maisey's wedding was taking place this afternoon, and I still haven't decided what I am going to wear. I walked over to my closet with an idea of what I wanted to put on, and I'm sure the dress I have in mind won't fit. I put on a couple of pounds since I last tried it on.

Earlier this year I made a blue lace dress with sheer material beneath it. I'm positive that I didn't take it to school with me. It was too dressy for any occasion there. I searched my room from top to bottom, and the dress was nowhere to be found. Since I needed to go to my aunt Eileen's beauty parlor to get my natural hair straightened, there was little time left to waste looking for it. Not to mention that I had no idea how I wanted my hair styled. Now that I think about it, I would probably go for some drop curls. It really doesn't matter what I wear. It's not like it's my wedding day. My only concern is that I don't look like a ragamuffin.

Daddy wasn't home, and Mama was down at the restaurant with a couple of her friends, still preparing food for the wedding. She really loved cooking for a lot of people, and opportunities like this were few and far between.

Daddy woke me up early this morning before he left, so I could watch him try on his suit. Luckily for him, it fit, because I was not going to spend the rest of my afternoon sewing a new pair of pants. He would have had to run to town to purchase a ready-made suit.

Nadine was in her room sound asleep. For once she was a step ahead of me. She went to the hairdresser yesterday, and she had those large, hard-to-lay-your-head- down-in pink plastic rollers. The only curlers that I could use in my hair were the sponge ones. I don't know how Nadine did it, or anyone else for that matter, but she looked peaceful lying there. Instead of getting ready to get out of the house I was busy standing in her doorway watching her sleep. The last thing I needed was for her to wake up and see me standing there staring at her. I'd been home all week, and we still hadn't exchanged more than two words to each other. As bad as things were between us, I didn't see any reason for us not to speak. We weren't even pleasant to each other. To tell the truth, I never understood why we didn't speak like most sisters did anyway. We were only two years apart and should have had tons of things to talk about and share. We were both born in July—my birthday is the twenty-eighth, Nadine's is the thirty-first—yet we've never had a joint celebration. We did have a different set of goals in life, but that's a given in any family. You don't have to have the same affinity or passion to have a relationship. Instead, she preferred our mother's company, and Mama loved the attention.

About three years ago, Mama had asked if I could help Nadine with her schoolwork and help her prepare for the common entrance exam, which would enable Nadine to attend a specialized High School. I had attended Mountelvernia High School, which is one of the best secondary schools in Jamaica.

I told Nadine from the beginning that she had to remain focused and committed. I didn't have time for her to play games or become lazy. Nadine was notorious for procrastinating when it came to her studies. I compiled all of the work that I could salvage from my previous years to help her review. I tried to be as detailed as possible, so that I could see where her weaknesses lay. Everyone seemed to be counting on me, in order for her to pass. What everyone failed to understand was that I would not be the one taking the exam. Nadine had to want to pass for herself as well. Those days of common entrance exams were history for me, and I was successful on my first try. Everyone was given three opportunities to take the test.

Nadine wasn't taking her work seriously. If I wasn't around, she didn't study, and I couldn't be at her disposal all day. The first time she failed the exam I sympathized with her and even devoted more time to help her study. Nadine buckled down for three solid weeks, and there seemed to be some improvement. As her sister and tutor, I really wanted her to pass. By the fourth week I could barely catch her in the house. Before I knew it, she and some of her friends had caught a bus to Jarrett Park in Montego Bay to attend Reggae Sunsplash. Nadine would get in so late that she was too exhausted to get up in the morning to study, much less focus. At night she was gone again. Nadine didn't miss a concert. She went two weeks in a row, and by the time she was ready to study only a week remained before the second exam. Then she expected me to give up my time to help her.

Time sure flies when you're having fun, and I knew that everything we had reviewed that summer was probably long forgotten. Nadine became moody and impatient with me. It was difficult, almost impossible, to work with her. If she got an example incorrect, she would get upset, claiming I didn't explain it well enough. She was miserable and snappish, because she had messed up and knew no one was to blame but herself.

Nadine took the test the second time and was once again unsuccessful. For the third exam she decided that it would be a waste to study and didn't even attempt to lift a book. She left it in the hands of fate. If you didn't study then it was a waste of time to even bother taking the test a third time.

When Nadine failed the test the third time, I refused to comment. I kept my distance because she didn't deserve to be consoled. Maybe I was being selfish, but it was how I felt.

That evening when Mama came home she asked if Nadine passed the common entrance exam. When I couldn't offer her the answer that she sought, she ran past me into the bedroom that Nadine and I shared at the time. She did what any mother would have done and consoled her. When Daddy came home he also asked me if Nadine had passed. I gave him the news that she had failed. In confidence Daddy told me that he was very disappointed at how irresponsible and neglectful Nadine was toward her studies. He was well aware of the fact that had gone to Sunsplash instead of staying home to study. The final outcome saddened him because he really wanted the best education for his children

The following evening during dinner, our brother, Patrick who lived home then, inquired about the exam. She announced that she failed and attempted to explain how difficult the test was. Patrick cut her off in mid sentence disrupting her sorry excuses.

"You should have kept your butt home instead of shaking it at Sunsplash every night."

Patrick was blunt, always speaking his mind without contempt, and this evening would be no different than any other. Patrick added that while he was onstage one night as a deejay he spotted Nadine up under some guy who was far older than her thirteen years.

Daddy went ballistic. You could almost see the puffs of steam coming from the top of his head. He gave her such a tongue-lashing that even I could feel the sting. He didn't hold anything back. All diplomacy went flying right out the window. Daddy rarely got this upset about anything. Sure Mama annoyed him, but over the years he learned to accept and deal with her idiosyncrasies. The thought of his daughter out there flaunting her thirteen-year-old behind with some man was appalling. So he did what any loving father would have done: He ripped her a new asshole. This was the straw that broke the camel's back. Nadine sat there looking even more pitiful as the tears streamed down her face and bubbles of mucous filled her nostrils. She dared not speak a word.

Mama didn't say a word and Patrick kept eating his food as if he weren't the one to cause this stir in the first place. I sat there silently picking at the food on my plate, but I had lost my appetite. Even though I knew Nadine deserved all that she was getting, I felt sorry for her. Daddy never got that angry before, and it looked like he wanted to hit her. Nadine and I had never gotten beatings from our father, only from Mama. Daddy used to deal with Patrick, and he was too old for beatings now.

Patrick finished his entire meal and excused himself from the table. Daddy stopped raising his voice and began mumbling under his breath. Finally Mama felt that Daddy had gone too far.

"Trevor," my mother said to my father, "don't you think that you've said enough? I mean, damn, the child has locked herself in the house for two days now in mourning. Besides it wasn't all her fault. Maybe if Anne-Marie had dedicated more of her time to help her sister instead of chasing down Donovan, the child would have passed."

Now it was my fault that Nadine was dunce and failed. What the hell is going on here, I thought to myself. *I must be in a twilight zone or something. This was a bad joke.* I sat there mute, like a one-year-old, unable to say anything in my defense. The words that kept forming in my mind were, *This woman is crazy.* Mama had the audacity to say that I could have put forth more of an effort to help Nadine? The sad thing was she actually believed that it was somehow my fault Nadine failed. She must have dug deep to come up with that one. Was my mother listening to anything that Patrick had said at the table? That it was Nadine that he saw at Sunsplash. Not Anne-Marie, but Nadine. Mama never once bothered to acknowledge the assistance I gave to Nadine. It was me, Anne-Marie who got up early in the morning to help Nadine study. Almost daily, I had to put up with her whining. Perhaps, if I had devoted twenty-four hours a day to accommodate Nadine's hectic schedule, Mama would have been happier. If it wasn't important enough for her, then it sure as hell wasn't important enough for me. In case she had forgotten I pulled my weight on this end of the ship. It was Nadine who caused it to sink.

There's an old Jamaican proverb *Lazy people fenneh pon dem heel* or you can lead a horse to water, but you can't make it to drink. At the time, I had already completed secondary school and was into my first year at the university. I had done everything in my power except stop short and take the test for Nadine myself. Perhaps, that would have sufficed.

The expression on Daddy's face after Mama finished indicated that he wanted to knock her back to reality. Daddy was clearly disgusted and couldn't bite his tongue anymore.

"*Woman, wa di warra warra yu ah chat?* It seems that once again you've gone mad. Are you an idiot or something? When I wake up to go down to the bar seven—eight in the morning, it's Anne-Marie I see in the kitchen waiting for Nadine to wake up. *When I come home from work, one all two inna di morning, Nadine still nuh reach home yet. Now you tell me, something as important as the common entrance exam dey come up and you gone ah Sunsplash. Don't blame Anne-Marie you hear me. Blame that blasted pikny deh suh!*" he exclaimed while pointing at Nadine. "*So woman gwaan go sit down and stop chat foolishness.*" Daddy then got up from the table and left the house.

After he left, both Mama and Nadine looked at me like I had done something wrong. Mama was the one that decided to use me as a scapegoat, and it backfired on her. I felt uncomfortable sitting there with the two of them staring at me, and at that moment I was upset with my father for leaving me behind.

I politely excused myself and took my plate along with my fathers to wash and keep out of harm's way. While in the kitchen I heard Mama and Nadine talking about me. I left well enough alone, and when I was done in the kitchen I went to Colleen's house for solace.

Nadine's failing the entrance exam wasn't the end of the world. She attended Cambridge's Secondary school, which she completed this past June. After that night though it seemed as if Nadine and I only drifted farther and farther apart. And since I was away at school, it was even more difficult to fix whatever was wrong between us. As for my mother, we've always had our differences. Some parents claim they don't have a favorite child. They love all of their children the same. This did not hold true for the Saunders household. I was always my father's favorite, because I was bright and had a lot of his personality while Nadine was my mother's favorite, because she was light skinned. It didn't seem to matter that I was the spitting image of my mother, but had my father's complexion, which made me wonder, how she ended up with my father, who was by no means fair skinned. However, both loved Patrick, who had bushy eyebrows and was tall like my father, and a pointy nose and thin lips like our mother.

There was a lot of commotion going on down the hill. The people in our town were working like busy beavers. My father was helping his brother, Uncle Sammy, put the final touches on the deck that would be used as the dance floor for Maisey's reception. People were helping out in any way that they could. The children were carrying folding chairs to the deck, and the ladies were arranging flowers. There was so much hustle and bustle going on that I could barely walk a couple of feet without bumping into someone and stopping to have a quick conversation. It was nice to see everyone pitching in and being so genial to one another; it was times like this that I enjoyed being home.

Before I could even set foot into the beauty parlor I could smell the burning of hair. The smell of black Dax pressing oil and hair burning were very distinct. When I walked in the door the first person I spotted was Ms. Margaret. She was sitting under the hair dryer near the entrance, dozing off with a Jet magazine wedged between her handbag and her lap. I quietly stepped past her.

The tiny salon was packed. The familiar sounds of water running, clanking curling irons, and chatter were prevalent. Several of the bridesmaids were getting their hair done as well as Maisey, the bride. There weren't any seats left, and people were leaning or standing wherever they could find a spot. The salon wasn't large enough to accommodate all the women that were waiting. To make matters worse, the heat from outside combined with the heat of the hair pressing made it feel like an inferno. It didn't much matter that the fans were on, because they only blew around gusts of more hot air.

I walked through the crowd in the direction of my aunt Eileen to check out the length of the wait. I could pretty much judge for myself, but I was hoping she would let her favorite niece slip in. I really couldn't expect any favors. Especially since this was probably her busiest day, next to the Saturday before Easter Sunday.

Before I could get over to her, I felt someone grab my hand. I looked to see who it was and then I saw my uncle Sammy's wife, Beverly, and Dottie, Clifton's ex-girlfriend. I bent down to give my aunt Beverly a kiss on the cheek and hug Dottie. Aunt Beverly was fanning herself with a cardboard fan she carried everywhere. She looked as though she couldn't get enough cool air. Aunt Beverly was a tall, plump woman. My uncle Sammy obviously liked larger women. He was so small in comparison to Aunt Beverly. Uncle Sammy wasn't quite as tall as my father, but he did have a very muscular build that was partially due to all the hard labor he did.

Dottie and aunt Beverly were waiting for an available beautician to remove the rollers from their hair.

"Girl, chile, wah mek you wait so late to come down and fix up your hair?" Aunt Beverly asked as I hugged Dottie.

"I didn't think that it would get this crowded so quickly," I responded. "It's only nine-thirty. I thought that I could still beat the rush."

"Well Eileen opened at seven this morning, and I'm still here waiting. She had a long line of people waiting when she opened the door," Aunt Beverly answered and sucked her teeth.

"You'll be here until two maybe three o'clock. You see that long line in here. Some people even left, but they'll be back soon. I got here a little bit after Beverly arrived this morning. What you plan on doing to your hair?" Dottie asked while massaging her fingers through my hair.

"I wanted to get a press and curl, but I may have to go home and do it myself."

"All that good hair on your head. Child, you don't need to press it. Let it out and wear it wavy," Dottie replied, and Aunt Beverly nodded in agreement. "Why don't you ask your sister to press it for you. Don't you have a straightening comb at home?"

"Of course we do. Is there a house in Cambridge without a straightening comb?" I said, laughing. "But I think Nadine may be busy helping my mother cook at the restaurant," I lied knowing Nadine would never press my hair, not that I trusted her with a hot comb anyway.

A chair became available at the beautician station and even

though my aunt was the next person she told Dottie to go ahead of her. She wanted to spend a couple more minutes with me. Dottie jumped at the chance and left us sitting there.

"So, Anne-Marie, darling, how is my lovely niece doing and when did you get back from school? Yesterday?"

"No, Aunt Beverly. I've been back since earlier this week."

"And you mean to tell me that you couldn't even come visit? Me? Your aunt Beverly? What I do you? You don't love me? I can remember when you use to come home and the first place you would visit is my house. Now you're too grown."

"Don't say that, Aunt Beverly. You know I still love both you and Uncle Sammy. But since I've been back I've barely had a chance to rest and catch my breath. I've been so busy."

"Anne-Marie, not even five minutes?" she said, sounding resentful.

"You're right. I'm sorry I should have stopped by."

"I forgive you. So how is the school business coming along?"

"Pretty good. I can't complain. I went back to Kingston yesterday to get my grades, and I got all A's."

"What?" Aunt Beverly exclaimed excitedly. "You father is right to call you Star. I'm very proud of you. I expect to be one of your very first patients. Don't forget me, you hear?"

"I promise that I won't. How could I ever forget about my favorite aunt?"

"Make sure, cause I'm holding you to your word," she said as she got up out of her seat. "I'm going to let the beautician finish up my hair. *She soon finish with that girl there in her chair.*"

I looked over to the beautician, and she was spraying Afro-Sheen hair spray on the woman's hair.

"I'll see you later at the wedding, Aunt Beverly."

"All right dear." She walked away.

I got up to go talk with my aunt Eileen. She was about the

same height as me and favored my father the most out of all of his other siblings. She talked so fast that I could hardly interpret anything she said. However, I did manage to understand that she had at least six or seven more people to tend to, and the other beauticians were preoccupied as well.

I decided to hang around and catch up with everyone. I listened in on all the gossip and rumors that were circulating in the little salon. If you wanted to know the most up-to-date gossip, the beauty parlor or my kitchen were the places to be. I had already heard most of the information that was circulating, thanks to my mother and Nadine.

Everyone was laughing and cackling so loudly that you would have thought a party was going on inside of the shop. We would all be partied out before the reception even began. One of the women sitting down on the opposite side of the parlor made a crude remark about Clifton and his latest fling without realizing that Dottie was also in the shop.

"The man is nothing but a louse. *Mi surprise sey him dick nuh drop off yet."*

Everybody fell silent. I thought Dottie would jump out of her chair and beat the hell out of her, but she did the smart thing and ignored her.

Aunt Beverly quickly jumped in. "The man is an idiot. How can you have somebody like this"—she paused and pointed to Dottie—"and behave those sort of ways. *Pure foolishness I tell you. All I know is that him better find another place to cotch, because I soon kick him back side out pon de road."*

Everyone started laughing again including Dottie. I know Dottie must have felt like a fool for putting up with him as long as she did. Still, she covered up the hurt with a smile.

More people started crowding into the shop and space was beginning to be a little too tight for me. I was feeling a little claustro-

Since I got in at a quarter to two this morning I didn't get the opportunity to share my good news about school with anyone, besides Aunt Beverly. I decided to go to Donovan's house for a little celebration. He was in the kitchen, busy ironing his clothes along with his father's for the wedding. He was as happy to see me, as I was to see him. He held me for what seemed like an eternity, and it felt like he didn't want to let go. I was used to the affection, but today was definitely different. He rubbed my belly and asked how his baby was doing. Then it dawned on me that he was acting all sentimental because of the baby. I thought it was real cute that he was fawning all over me like that, and it felt good to know that he excited about the baby. I just reveled in all the attention that he was lavishing on me. When he went back to ironing I headed into the kitchen to make myself a cup of tea. There were several containers and water coolers in the kitchen almost blocking my passage to the stove. Donovan must have been up all night making these concoctions. It looked like there was a little bit of everything in there, and they were all neatly labeled.

Shortly after he finished ironing he came into the kitchen and joined me at the table.

"Did you get in late last night?" Donovan asked.

"Yeah, actually pretty early this morning. It was almost two o'clock."

"So how did it go? Were your grades as bad as you imagined?"

"I got all *A*'s," I replied with a smile.

"Say that again. And you were so worried all semester about getting a *B*," Donovan said and kissed me on the forehead.

"I know, but remember I told you that Dr. Thorton and I resolved our differences. As a matter of fact, I even went to her go-ing-away party last night. That's why I got home so late. She even recommended me for a fellowship."

"I always tell you that you worry too much over nothing. She knew that you were working hard," Donovan said, rubbing my thigh.

"Yeah. I know that now, but you couldn't tell me that a couple of months ago."

"So you said she recommended you for a fellowship. Tell me about it."

"First you tell me about the talk you had with your father about me being pregnant."

"There's nothing much to tell. I already told you that I was going to talk to him the other night. I told him, and it was cool."

"I was curious. Yesterday when I saw him at the doctor's of-fice he mentioned it, and I was surprised. He seemed really happy about it though."

"Like I was asking you before. Tell me about the fellowship."

I took a deep breath and started talking.

"Yearly, the department nominates several of their top students for eligibility in the foreign-exchange program. The department fac-ulty then votes to narrow down the selection. Each candidate must receive at least two thirds of the vote. After selecting the students the committee submits the necessary papers to the schools that of-fer the fellowships. My information was sent to several schools abroad and six of them have extended invitations for me to attend."

"So where are the schools?" Donovan asked.

"One of them is in London, and the rest are in America. I haven't had time to look at the materials that I received yesterday. I'll look at it later."

"But you're not really thinking about going abroad, are you? I mean you know with the baby and things."

"I haven't made any decisions yet, but if necessary I'm sure we can arrange something."

"What are you going to do about the baby?"

"Donovan, I said I haven't made any final decisions. You knew that I was interested in going abroad to school."

"That was before the baby. You know how important it is to me that we *both* be present for the baby. You know how hard it was for me not having a mother around." There was genuine concern in his voice. He almost appeared frightened.

"Donovan, you know how important my education is to me. I'm not implying that I'm putting my education or career ahead of our baby, but I have to fulfill my dreams as well. I told my dean that I was pregnant and he was supportive and said that I could probably make some kind of arrangements."

"Anne-Marie, I'm glad that your dean was so supportive, but he's not your baby's father. I don't know what kind of plans you intend on making, but you're not taking my baby anywhere," he finished.

I couldn't believe what I was hearing.

"This is our baby. Not yours alone," I retorted.

"Like I said, you are not taking my baby anywhere."

Donovan was being irrational and selfish. I didn't know where this was coming from Donovan and I never got into verbal disagreements like this. If he were upset about something, he would say his piece and let it be. If he were wrong he'd readily admit it. His erratic behavior was startling and uncalled for. He acted as if I was never coming back. My mother always says silent river runs deep. Today, for the first time, I understood that statement to be true. My calm and sweet boyfriend was showing me a side of him that I've never seen before. Going abroad was only going to be a temporary thing, and I would be traveling back and forth. Jamaica is my home, and Donovan is my heart, and the baby has my body right now. Did he expect me to put my dreams on hold? He was behaving like a child and acting like I've never discussed continuing my studies abroad. Everyone knew that. I felt like I was being pulled, and the strands were slowly unraveling on both ends. This decision was actually going to be tougher than I anticipated.

I pushed back my chair and got up from the table. I went to the sink, washed my mug, put it on the dish rack, and ignored him. I couldn't stand to occupy the same space with him anymore.

"Donovan, I'm leaving now." I said and started to walk out of the kitchen.

"Where are you going? We're not done talking," he said, reaching to grab my hand, but I pulled it away.

"I'm done talking, and I'm tired. The baby and I have to get some rest. We wouldn't want to upset the baby," I said sarcastically. "I'll see you later at the wedding. Good-bye." Then I heard him saying something about picking me up later. I kept walking, purposely slamming the screen door as hard as I could behind me.

I was exhausted, physically and mentally, and I still had to decide on an outfit and what to do with my hair.

I finally gave up searching for the blue dress and ended up settling for a satin burgundy one with matching gloves. I'd washed and greased my hair then plaited it into sections and took a nap while it dried. Afterward I took the braids out and wore it naturally wavy and pushed it back with a hair band the same color as my dress.

Donovan was a half an hour late, and because of him we ended up having to sit in the back of the church. Lucky for us the ceremony hadn't started on time.

It was sweltering in the church, but the smell of the flowers overwhelmed all of my senses. There was an abundance of beautiful white lilies and exotic peach-colored stargazers lacing the church benches. Everyone was fanning with anything they could get their hands on—cardboard fans, paper fans, and the wedding program.

After looking around for a couple of minutes I finally saw my parents sitting about five or six rows in front of us, but Nadine wasn't next to them. I couldn't find her anywhere. We sat on the same side as Maisey's family since we were guests of the bride. I was trying to locate Colleen, as I knew she was Maisey's niece and would surely be there.

The organ started to play the wedding march, and everyone immediately began turning to see the wedding party walk in. The cute little flower girl made her way down the aisle dropping peach rose petals. The processional seemed endless: There was the maid of honor and eight bridesmaids accompanied by groomsmen. They slowly strolled down the aisle and the cameras began to flash everywhere.

The wedding dresses were peach and the bodices were fitted with short puffy sleeves and the bottom reminded me of ballroom gowns, and they all wore matching hats. The wedding was laid out and a sight to see. The groom's family was wealthy, and most of them resided in Kingston, and the others flew back and forth to the United States. Rumor was that his family wasn't pleased that he picked some country girl from "back a bush." It's sad that people can be so simple. Love is all that should matter and should take precedence over everything else.

"Here Comes the Bride" began to play. The audience rose as the organ blared over the occasional "shhh" from parents telling their children to quiet down.

Maisey looked radiant as her brother Everton, Colleen's father, accompanied her down the aisle. She wore one of those fairytale dresses, like the one we all sat around the television to watch Princess Diana wear three years ago in 1981. The dress was off-white with chantilly lace trim but the train wasn't quite as long as Princess Di's. Maisey carried an elegant bouquet of white and peach calla lilies. Everything was so exquisite.

The silence was broken by one of the children saying "Mommy, her dress is so pretty." It seemed almost as though that was everyone else's cue to begin talking too. All you heard were comments about how beautiful the dress was or the hefty price tag that must have accompanied it. Even I was awestruck to see something so beautiful up close and personal. The people around me looked as if they could barely control themselves from reaching out and touching the fabric. When Maisey made it down the aisle, the pastor signaled to the organist to wind it down and asked that we all be seated. He said a brief prayer, and we all said amen. When he asked who gives this bride away today Colleen's father stood up and said, "I do." He was sitting in the very first row. When he sat down I was strained to see if Colleen was sitting next to him. On one side of him I could see his wife. There was another woman sitting on the other side.

Colleen had that new hairstyle everyone seemed to be getting lately. I think they called it a Jheri curl, and there was a guy with dreads sitting beside her. If I weren't mistaken it had to be Lloyd, Colleen's new man. I couldn't believe that she actually brought him to the wedding for Ms. Margaret to see. Colleen was definitely changing and getting very bodacious lately.

I began to search around again to see if I could find Ms. Margaret. I spotted Mr. Miller and knew that she wouldn't be that far away, and I was right. They were both sitting in the same row, but people were sitting in between them. It was all a ruse, because I knew what was really going on. They were trying to keep their relationship undercover. Even Donovan didn't have a clue. It wasn't my concern as to whom Mr. Miller chose to date. The only thing was that he is a good man and a great catch. I failed to see what he could possibly find so intriguing about Ms. Margaret. Of all the available, attractive, and kind women in Cambridge, why her? I find it hard to believe that anyone could be interested in that terror of a woman. Ms. Margaret was stunningly beautiful on the outside, but her personality detracted from her beauty. Personally I'd rather be with someone that was unattractive and had a beautiful personality than the reverse. Fortunately I didn't have to settle, because I already had a man with looks, charm, and intellect. I reached over to squeeze Donovan's hand and to ask him what he thought about Maisey's dress since he was silent the entire time. All he managed to say was, "It's nice." He was still in a mood.

I couldn't wait for the ceremony to end. Not only because of the heat, but there were too many crying and screaming children. The woman that sat beside me had the cutest little girl. She kept asking for her father. "Mommy is daddy here? Is Daddy here?" She was sounding like a broken record. The woman responded, "I think so sweetie, but Mommy's not sure." I wanted to say "get up and look, so she can stop whining already." Instead, I looked over and smiled. I began to wonder if I would be as patient and as soft-spoken with my child. There was no doubt in my mind, because I knew I would.

The ceremony seemed as though it would never end. I could hear my stomach growling and everyone else's. I couldn't wait to down some of my mother's good cooking. She slaved over that hot stove all last night and this morning. Cooking was the one thing Mama never tired from aside gossiping. She loved to cook, and everyone else loved to eat her food. People would always ask why I didn't cook like my mother, but then I'd point out that at least I could cook. Nadine could barely summon up enough strength to boil water. Our brother, Patrick, was a close second to our mother. If he ever decided to give up his music career he could easily go into business with our mother and cook full time.

The wedding party began the recessional, rows from the front started leaving first. Since we were in the back row we were going to be the last to leave. At least I got to see who was with whom, and what they were wearing.

Cameras started flashing from every direction. For a moment all I saw were spots from the blinding flashes. My parents darted out of the church along with Clifton who would be either behind the bar serving or assisting with the food. My mother wouldn't be serving, instead she would be giving orders and getting on someone else's nerves.

Mr. Miller waved to us on his way out the door, and Ms. Margaret trailed behind. Just as I was about to look at Donovan to prove my point about his father and Ms. Margaret, I caught sight of my sister, Nadine. She was wearing my blue dress— the same blue dress that I had been looking for most of the day. I didn't recall lending it to her. Nevertheless, there she was cheesing with one of the groomsmen in my dress. If we weren't in church I'd be compelled to snatch it right off her. Now I was pissed. I was fuming mad and felt like beating the crap out of her. Here I was stuck wearing this burgundy dress because she borrowed my dress without asking. Not that the burgundy dress didn't look nice. It's just that when you have your heart set on a particular thing only to have to give it up, it can be unsettling.

When we got to the deck that Uncle Sammy built for the reception I searched for Nadine like an animal hunting its prey, but she was nowhere to be found. I would have to deal with that later since this wasn't the ideal place to address the situation.

Colleen was on the other side of the deck talking with her father and Lloyd. It was definitely Colleen sitting beside her father at the church with the Jheri curl. She must have gotten it done right after she visited me. She was smiling and looking very happy. I guess Lloyd was pretty good for her.

I walked over to them and snuck up on Colleen, covering up her eyes with my hands. Laughing she was asking, "Who is it?" Her father, his wife, and Lloyd looked at me, smiled, and said they didn't know. After a few wrong guesses I removed my hands and asked her if she thought she was funny. Colleen was purposefully guessing incorrectly, knowing that it was me all along. I felt a sense of relief that she wasn't still upset about the other day. As soon as we were alone I wanted to make it a point to apologize and update her about my pregnancy and my news about school.

Colleen reintroduced me to her stepmother and Lloyd, and we all looked at her as if she were insane. I exchanged pleasantries with all of them.

"Don't you think we know each other? I've known Anne-Marie for years now. *Nuh true, Anne-Marie?*" Lloyd said. He said it more like an answer than a question. I laughed and nodded. I hugged Colleen's father who I hadn't seen in years. He told me that I've never even stopped by his yard to say howdy, and he heard that I attended school in Kingston. After about ten minutes of conversation I excused myself to mingle with some of the other guests. Colleen asked me to wait for her. She wanted to walk around with me. When Colleen was done talking to her father, she kissed Lloyd, and we left the three of them standing and talking together. Colleen looked happy and content. At least she had her father on her side.

"How does your father feel about you dating Lloyd?" I asked.

"You know how easygoing my father is. He said he never thought he would see the day when his little girl would grow up and start dating. Other than that, he's fine with it. This isn't the first time that they've met though. On the weekends we drive up to Kingston to see my father. I introduced them to each other a couple of months— I mean weeks— ago now," Colleen said, slipping up. I already had a strong suspicion that she wasn't being truthful with me earlier in the week anyway.

"Colleen, I'm sorry about the other day. I shouldn't have been so quick to pass judgment."

"Anne-Marie, don't worry about that. You were being you. If

you didn't question me then I'd have reason to be concerned. It's your mothering nature."

"I thought you were vexed with me. Speaking of mothering nature, I have something to tell you."

"I was vexed, but then I went home and thought about it, and I know you wouldn't try to hurt me intentionally. So what do you have to tell me?" Colleen asked.

"Not here. I'll tell you later."

"Just tell me. You can't keep me in suspense. Let's walk over there so we can have a little bit of privacy." She then led me to an unoccupied corner of the deck.

"Are you going back home tonight," I asked.

"Of course, why?"

"Because I wanted you to spend the night. I'm making dinner tomorrow evening at the house, and I wanted you to be there. Do you have the day off tomorrow?"

"Yes, but I had plans."

"Colleen, *stay nuh*. Don't make me beg," I pleaded.

"What kind of dinner is this, because after tonight's feast I'll have all the dinner I need for a week. Especially since your mother cooked."

"Dinner to tell my parents the same news I'm about to tell you."

"Damn it, girl. Tell me already and stop keeping me in suspense. If you want me to stay that badly, I will, but hurry up with the news."

"I think your mother is seeing Mr. Miller," I said.

"You're having dinner with your family tomorrow evening to tell them that my mother is seeing Mr. Miller? You're crazy. But what makes you think that?"

"No that's not why I'm having the dinner, silly. I just saw them arrive together over there." Colleen turned around to look. "I've been seeing the two of them together a lot recently."

"You're kidding. My mother and Mr. Miller? Are you sure? No, sir." Colleen shook her head to disagree.

"Serious. Yesterday I went to see Dr. Keene, and I saw them there together." Colleen's mouth was hanging wide open in disbelief. "What would Mr. Miller want with my mother?"

"She's a woman, girl. Open your eyes. Ms. Margaret may not be the sweetest person on earth, but she's a very attractive woman. You should know that, you favor her. Who knows, maybe your mother has some innate quality we're overlooking and only a man can see."

"Thanks for reminding me that I favor her. Thank goodness I'm nothing like her though," Colleen said, shaking her head in pity for whatever Mr. Miller was in for. "I hope he's not being naive and letting her charm and beauty blind him. My father's a good and caring man, and she managed to chase him away," Colleen said.

"Well, now that she's older, she may have changed, as far as relationships with men are concerned," I volunteered.

"I still can't believe it though."

"Believe it, because it's reality."

"So what did Donovan say when you told him that he and I were going to be brother and sister soon?" Colleen said, laughing herself into a fit.

"He doesn't believe me."

"Maybe he's in denial. Why else wouldn't he believe you? Maybe he's not ready to see his father with another woman."

"That's true. But he claims that his father tells him everything."

"I really doubt that. Donovan doesn't tell his father everything. I'm sure he leaves things out."

"Whatever. He's bound to find out sooner or later, and he can't say that I didn't tell him so."

"I'm still shocked. Anyway, what is it that you have to tell me?"

"Hold on a minute. I just saw Nadine, and she is wearing my damn dress. Come over here with me."

"So what if she's wearing your dress. She's your sister," Colleen said, laughing.

"Colleen, first of all I've been looking for that dress half of the day to wear it to the wedding. Second, she didn't ask, and third, sister my ass. She doesn't act like it, and you know that. Given the opportunity she'd stab me in the back first chance she got. You're forgetting that I'm talking about Nadine, aren't you."

"True. Let's go. By the way, that's a nice dress, girl. I've never seen you wear that before," she said facetiously referring to my blue dress that Nadine wore.

"That's because it's new. I made it a couple of months ago, and I didn't have an occasion to wear it. I finally decided to wear it today, but I couldn't find the damn dress anywhere."

We walked over to Nadine, and she was talking to the same guy I had seen her leave the church with earlier. She was in the middle of a conversation, and I didn't want to appear rude and interrupt. I politely waited and stood to the side to try and capture her attention. The guy Nadine was talking to saw us waiting and offered to get her something to drink. When he left I asked Nadine if I could have a moment with her. Nadine looked me up and down, as if to say, "What in the hell do you want?" I thought to myself, *Enough with the being polite shit.*

"Listen, Nadine, you're wearing my dress and didn't even bother to ask me."

"So," Nadine said her hands akimbo." For the first time I noticed that Nadine was nearly my height. She was about an inch shorter than me, but was probably still growing. She wasn't quite as full in the hips, but would eventually fill out. The women on my mother's side of the family were quite shapely.

"So? What the hell do you mean, so? You didn't know if I

wanted to wear it or for that matter you didn't ask me if you could borrow it."

"I didn't think you were coming to the wedding," Nadine replied as it that made a difference.

"Why wouldn't I come to the wedding? And that's beside the point. It's my dress. You didn't even bother to ask! I've been home all week, you could have good and well asked me then."

"I'm not going to stand here and let you embarrass me in public." She began to walk away. Nadine didn't see anything wrong with the entire situation and felt that she did absolutely nothing wrong or out of the ordinary. I looked at Colleen in amazement. Colleen shook her head looking as baffled as I felt. I followed Nadine as she started her trek back over to the guy she was with. I tapped her on her shoulder before she got to him, because it wasn't over.

"You know what? You better go home right now and take off my dress."

"Later. After the reception you can have your dress back."

Nadine was having a hard time understanding. Only God's good will was restraining me from grabbing her by the neck and strangling her. Donovan saw me talking to her and walked over to see what was going on. He knew it was rare for us to talk in public or anywhere else for that matter. So he automatically knew that a storm was brewing.

"*Wha'pin*, Colleen," Donovan said hugging her. "Hi, Nadine." Then he glanced at me.

Nadine didn't give him the time of day and ignored Donovan's pleasantries. She was still trying to find a way to go and mingle with her man friend. Donovan paid her the same respect and turned his attention to Colleen and myself.

"What's happening over here, ladies?"

"Nothing, sweetie. I'm just talking to Nadine. Nadine, I'm not going to tell you again. Go home and change now," I continued, trying to remain calm.

"What difference does it make now, Anne-Marie? Everyone has already seen me in the dress." Nadine was chucking it up now with a sinister smile on her face.

"You think that I'm fucking playing games with you? I'm not kidding. You better go."

Colleen was briefing Donovan on what was going on, and I heard him say "Oh, that's the blue dress. I knew that she said she was looking for it earlier."

"I said you'd get it later on tonight," Nadine said and walked off.

"Nadine, don't make me embarrass you right now. I will hurt you where you stand. Do you understand me? Take my dress off before you ruin it."

"Go ahead and tek it off of me nuh gyal. Gwaan," she taunted.

"Nadine, you better do what your sister asked you to do. There's no reason for all of this," Donovan interjected.

"Donovan, why don't you mind your damn business? This has nothing to do with you," Nadine snapped.

"Fine. I will. I was trying to save your ass from embarrassment, but Anne-Marie carry on."

Nadine's friend returned with the drink in his hand, and she knew that I would grab her up right then and there. Call me ignorant, but I would have taken her away from the reception and given her the beating of her life. I had more couth than to create such a disturbance at the party. Before I could say another word she started walking toward the exit. The guy she had been with was right on her heels like an obedient puppy. Nadine would probably fill his head with a bunch of lies. If she wasn't such a bitch and acted like a normal sister, none of this would have happened. If that were Colleen and she showed up in my dress I probably wouldn't even be upset. We would laugh it off, and I would get over it and move on. However, Nadine actually chose to challenge me. My original intention was simply to let her know that I was upset that she didn't bother to ask me to borrow the dress and leave it at that. But her entire demeanor aggravated me.

Colleen glanced at me to make sure that I was all right.

"She's got a lot of nerve. You won't be able to wear that dress anytime soon. I'm sure that she got a heap of compliments on it," Colleen commented.

"She is very fresh and out of order," Donovan said. "Don't worry about the dress. I'll get you a better one or more material if you need it."

"I'm not crushed over the dress. You know. It's the principle of the whole thing. When I get home I may *just dash* out the doggoned dress, but she better not ever find herself in my closet again."

"Did you tell Colleen the news yet?" Donovan inquired.

"No, just as I was about to, I saw Nadine waltzing by in my dress."

"I'll leave you two alone," Donovan said, smiling as he walked off into the crowd.

"Alright already. Stop procrastinating and tell me now. Did Donovan ask you to marry him?" Colleen exclaimed.

"Not exactly."

"Exactly what then. Stop playing and spit it out."

I leaned over and whispered in her ear. "I'm pregnant."

Colleen screamed so loud that she almost deafened me. It was a good thing that everyone was talking loudly and she didn't distract the people around us. Only a few people who heard the piercing scream gazed over. Colleen was jumping around and acting silly.

"I'm going to be an auntie."

"Calm down, girl. You're making a scene," I told her.

"You're pregnant. I can't believe it. This night is full of surprises. First Mom and Mr. Miller, then you and Nadine almost start to rumble right here on the floor, and now I find out that you're pregnant. What's next? I don't think that I can handle much more."

"The Nadine incident was a bonus," I said, laughing, and Colleen joined in. "Girl, let's go grab a seat. They are about to serve the food, and the baby and I have to eat. Are you sitting at the table that they reserved for the families?" I asked.

"I don't have to. Lloyd and I can sit with you and Donovan if you want."

"Good, let's find the men and grab a table."

Donovan was huddled in a corner with his boys—Hop, Bigga, Joshua, Winston, and a few others. I knew that they must have been talking about me, because as we approached them they stopped their discussion. Bigga and his big mouth was the first one to say something.

"What's up, Mommy?"

I shot Donovan a look of disdain. I couldn't believe that he would tell his big-mouth friends about the baby. Especially, Bigga, of all people. I, at least, wanted to tell my parents first. It would be horrifying if they heard it from strangers before I had a chance to tell them. Donovan gave me an apologetic look that melted my attitude.

"Baby, I'm sorry. I'm just so happy that I had to share the news with my boys. They won't mention it to anyone else. I told them that we hadn't laid the news on your parents yet."

"Well it doesn't make a difference," I said. "They'll know by tomorrow anyway."

Donovan moved toward me and gave me a hug and pecked me on the forehead. He seemed to be back to his normal self, but we still had unresolved issues to discuss.

"I came over here to get you so that we could grab a good table before they are all taken."

"That sounds good. You and Colleen go on ahead, and I'll join you in a bit. I want to rap with my boys a little while longer." Then he turned his attention back to them.

"We'll be somewhere over there." I pointed across the room.

Colleen reached over and tapped my shoulder to show me Nadine walking back toward the deck with her friend. I don't know if Nadine knew him prior to today's event or not, but I can't believe she took him home with her while she changed. She didn't see us at the table, and I wasn't about to draw her attention in our direction.

The deck was packed. Everywhere you looked or turned there was a person beside you. The evening was nice and cool, which was refreshing. It was better than having the reception inside a hall where there would be little to no circulation even with an air conditioner blowing. The sky was in full view, and it enabled you to see how beautiful all the stars were scintillating from afar.

My brother, Patrick, was setting up the music equipment on stage. I excused myself from the table to go over and see him. The last time I saw him was a couple of months ago when his band Roots & Culture had a gig at a club near my school. Patrick is the lead singer and guitarist. He goes by the name Roots, and the band is Culture. The group played other instruments like the drums, trumpet, and keyboard. A few of my friends came along with me that night to support him. My friend Keisha came with me and ended up leaving with my brother, so I didn't really get to hang out with him much afterward.

Keisha was American and was sent to school in Jamaica because her father is Jamaican. Keisha's father felt that she could get a much better education in Jamaica. He thought Americans to be lazy and lack discipline when it came to education. Keisha had been attending school in Jamaica since secondary school. She spent her summers in America, but she remained here throughout the year. Keisha used to come to my room for tutoring from time to time, and I had pictures of my family displayed on my dresser. She would always insinuate that if she ever met my brother what she would do to him, because he was *soooo fine*! When she found out that he was in a band and was the lead singer she really got excited. I really never paid her much attention, but after that night I never doubted anything else she said. Keisha and I became very good friends, but her relationship with Patrick never went further than the bedroom. Patrick was taught early on that anyone who gave it up that quickly wasn't girlfriend material. But he was a man, and wasn't about to pass up sex. It didn't hurt that Keisha wasn't bad to look at either. She was just overly aggressive. I think he, like most Jamaican's, was really fascinated by her American accent.

I stepped up on the platform as Patrick was bending down with his back toward me. He was fiddling with the wiring. I waited until he was done and when he turned around I startled him. He jumped back so far that if it weren't for the length of the platform he would have fallen off. Patrick finally regained his composure and gave me a big bear hug. He squeezed me so tight that I could barely breathe. He did that in return for my scaring him half to death.

I loved Patrick. I wouldn't trade him for the world. He reminded me so much of our father. He was down to earth, smart, charming, very business savvy, and laid-back. I never looked at my brother as being fine or sexy, but he was strikingly handsome. One day, he was definitely going to make some woman very happy. That's when, and if, he ever decided to settle down. Right now he was going through the "I'm a sexy motherfucker" phase.

"Damn, sis, you make a habit out of scaring the shit out of people, and you think that it's funny, don't you?" he said with a big grin. He couldn't stay upset at me no matter how hard he tried. "You see me working hard here putting the equipment together for the band so you can hear some good music and you come frightening me."

"I thought Maisey was hiring a professional band."

"Yu bettah creep afoe you walk, gyal," Patrick countered.

"Patrick, tek it easy nuh mon, and learn fi tek a joke."

"I can take a joke, but don't joke about my music. It's my life. So tell me, what was going on with you and Nadine earlier? I saw the two of you quarreling," Patrick said with a concerned look on his face.

"Nadine borrowed my frock without permission."

"That's nothing new. Is that why she changed? Because you embarrassed her?"

"I didn't embarrass her. And if I did she deserved it. I went over there to tell her that I didn't appreciate her wearing my things without my consent."

"No mon. You can't behave like that. Regardless of what goes on in the house, you can't carry your business out on the street like that. And before you jump to conclusions, I'm not taking her side. Trust me, I know how she is. Remember I used to live under the same roof as you."

"I know, but Patrick I simply went over there to talk to her. She was the one with the attitude, staring at me as if I were a piece of shit."

"I don't doubt a word that you're saying, but you could have let it pass until you got home later. If I saw the two of you arguing, you can bet these nosy neighbors we have were eavesdropping. Don't give people the opportunity to talk badly about you or our family."

"You're right," I said. That was one of the things that I always admired about Patrick. He never minced words no matter who you were and always helped to put things into perspective. I looked at him with an apologetic grin.

"How is your friend, what's her name again? Oh, Keisha," he said after pausing for a couple of moments.

"Patrick, don't act like you forgot her name. I bet you didn't have trouble remembering it that night that she left the club with you," I said while playfully elbowing him in the ribs as he pretended to be hurt.

"It slipped my mind for a second. So how is Keisha? I haven't spoken to her in a while. I've been so busy lately."

"I'm sure you have been. Busy finding more women to prey on. Keisha is fine. I didn't see her much at the end of the semester, and she goes home for the summer."

"I haven't had time for any women these last couple of weeks. You know me and the band got our first recording contract," Patrick said nonchalantly.

"Get out of here! I'm happy for you." I jumped up and gave him a peck on the cheek, and I held his hand tightly. I knew how much this opportunity meant for my brother. His band was really good, and they got a lot of local exposure, but the prospect of getting national exposure was sensational.

"Calm down, girl. We are still going over the paperwork. They were trying to cheat us with the money, but I have some friends in the business, and they told me what we should expect to get paid, and about distribution. Right now we are still in negotiations."

"Well some money is better than no money, right?" I asked curiously.

"Yeah, but when you see how much they make off you compared to what they pay you, it's a shame. And they think that we're dunces. We have to split this money between the four of us."

"In any case I knew you could do it, and I'm so proud of you. So which record label are you signing with?"

"An American label called Upside Down records, but enough about me. What's going on with you? How's school?" He bent down to complete the wiring while we talked.

"I'm pregnant," I blurted out, "and I got all *A*'s last semester."

"All *A*'s. Congratulations. What did you say before that? Something about a present because you got all *A*'s." Patrick was purposefully playing deaf.

"You know that's not what I said."

"Then what did you say?" he asked.

"I said that I am pregnant." Patrick immediately ceased tinkering with the wires and looked at me like I was a ghost. He was never any good at hiding his emotions either. For once he was at a loss for words.

He looked me over from head to toe. "How did this happen?" he asked.

"Patrick, you know exactly how this happened."

"No, I mean how could you let this happen? What about school, Anne-Marie? What about all of your dreams?"

"Patrick, things will work out. Donovan is there for me, and I'll work school out. I'm not about to give up school. I've come too far."

"I still have to ask, are you certain this is what you want to do?"

"There's no question in my mind. I made my bed, so I have to lie in it. Literally."

"My baby sister. I can't believe my ears."

"Not so little anymore." I felt bashful for the first time in front of my brother. I always looked up to him, and I felt funny telling him for fear of what he might say or how he would react, but I was slowly learning that this is something that I have to live with and no one else.

"So, who's the father?" Patrick said, clowning around.

"Patrick!"

"Kidding. I'm kidding with you. I can't get over the fact that my little sister is pregnant. Who else did you tell so far?" Before I could answer Raymond, one of the guys in the band, interrupted us.

"Patrick, Patrick. We need you over here for a minute." He waved Patrick to come over immediately. Patrick held up his hand to gesture that he would be there in a moment.

"Anne-Marie, I want to talk to you. Save me a dance later, okay?"

"I will, but if we don't get a chance to see each other later, come over for dinner tomorrow. I'm cooking, and I'll be telling Mama and Daddy the news. It would help if you were there."

"Anything for you." He quickly bent over to hug me and walked to the other side of the stage."

"Five-thirty," I yelled out to him, and he nodded. I watched him as he instructed the guys on what to do. I stepped down off the platform and looked out at the sea of people. I searched desperately through the crowd for Colleen and Donovan or any familiar face. I saw Clifton leaning on the railing with a drink in his hand and prayed that it was something nonalcoholic. For the first time I noticed how vulnerable he looked. He seemed lonely and displaced, and I felt sorry for him.

Quickly, I scanned the scene again, but it was too crowded. Then I was distracted by two very familiar-sounding voices bickering. The voices were faint but they seemed to be rising steadily. Again I scanned the room. This time I looked in the direction of the voices. I immediately saw Colleen and Ms. Margaret in what seemed to be a heated confrontation. Hastily, I bolted through the crowd to see what was going on.

Lloyd was standing next to Colleen looking very disconcerted and bewildered. Ms. Margaret stood across from them wagging her index finger in Colleen's face. This scene was all too familiar to me, only this time there were more people present to actually witness Ms. Margaret's ignorance. Ms. Margaret was trying to use her size to intimidate Colleen, but Colleen was standing her ground and wasn't backing down. I was so proud of her. I was sick and tired of her mother.

Donovan was standing a few feet away, so I walked over to ask him what the argument was about.

"Donovan, what happened with Colleen and her mother?"

"Last I knew Colleen, Lloyd, and I were sitting at the table. Colleen saw her mother and said she wanted to take Lloyd over to meet him. And I guess this is the result."

"They must still be going through the introductions," I said, trying to make light of the situation.

"Must be. I tell you I don't like that woman," Donovan said, disgusted.

"I don't understand why she has to act this way, and I don't know what your father sees in her."

"My father isn't seeing anything in her, because there's nothing to see."

"Okay, if you say so." Colleen was right. Donovan was in denial.

"I'm going to see if I can help break this up, because a crowd is starting to form."

I now stood beside Colleen and tried to gently pull her back, but she resisted my grasp and continued to talk in a calm manner, unlike Ms. Margaret whose arms were flailing in every direction.

"I'm not a child, and you can't rule my life anymore. I came over here as your daughter to introduce you to my friend."

"Friend! What kind of friend? *This knotty dread boy?* Let me tell you something. I don't know what kind of friend you are talking about, but I'm sure the almighty wouldn't approve."

Colleen had a look of horror on her face. She was clearly thrown by her mother's last remark. I felt the urge to intervene, but Colleen already indicated that she did not need my assistance. My strong desire to come to her rescue was overwhelming. Ms. Margaret needed to be put in her place. Not only was her last statement inappropriate, it was also unnecessary.

I could tell Colleen was carefully selecting her words. She smoothed down her dress with her left hand, and her right hand was firmly placed on her hip. The scowling look that she gave her mother was scornful and deadly. Her chest heaved up and down, her jaw was clamped tightly, together and her temples twitched impulsively. Colleen was exasperated, and I'd never seen her like this. Her voice was calm when she spoke.

"You hypocrite. You're not a Christian. If you were you wouldn't have said that to me."

"No bada fas' wid me!" Ms. Margaret exclaimed.

"You will listen to me," Colleen said, commanding her mother's full attention. "All my life I've done as you've said and lived according to your rules. I've tried to make amends with you because I know we left things in bad shape between us. All I did was try and introduce you to my friend. You didn't hear me say my lover, but you're so judgmental and ready to assume the worse. I'm done trying to appease you. You're not worth the effort, and I'll have to accept that we will never have a normal relationship. You've never given me the chance to open up to you, but I'm through trying."

Ms. Margaret was shocked that her daughter would take such a tone with her. You could see a little bit of hurt and a lot of embarrassment in her expression. She knew what Colleen said was true, and it hit home. Colleen made it clear that she was no longer seeking her approval. Ms. Margaret wasn't a nice person, and Colleen just said it to a small audience. Ms. Margaret would naturally try to respond in defense instead of walking away with what little pride she had left.

Colleen took Lloyd by the hand and started to walk away. Ms. Margaret grabbed her by the arm, forcing Colleen to turn back around. Before anything could transpire, Mr. Miller came barreling through the crowd. He took Ms. Margaret's hand off Colleen and gained control of the situation. He apologized for the disturbance and nicely helped disperse the small crowd. Mr. Miller then signaled to my brother onstage to play some tunes until the band was ready and hauled Ms. Margaret off the premises. They were talking outside on the deck, and you could see Ms. Margaret was trying to explain and somehow defend her actions. Mr. Miller didn't look too convinced. They stood outside for a few more minutes and then headed back toward home though I had no idea whose home they would be going to, since both were in the same direction.

Shortly after the commotion, everything settled down and the bridal party was introduced. Everyone with a camera was busy snapping pictures. It was a good thing Colleen's father was with the bridal party taking pictures when Ms. Margaret was carrying on. Colleen was his baby girl, and if he were present he would have lit Ms. Margaret up.

My song "You Send Me" by Sam Cooke was playing, and Donovan asked me to dance. We danced for what felt like forever, as we got lost in each other's arms. My brother was playing every feel-good song that existed. When "Always and Forever" came on by Heatwave, it made me happy to know that Donovan was my man. Donovan slowly kissed me, and it felt like the first time all over again. The emotions that swept over me made me tingle from head to toe, and Donovan's warm embrace told me he felt the same way. He whispered apologies in my ear and said that he loved me. I gently rested my head on his shoulder to show him my forgiveness. Colleen and Lloyd were dancing not too far from us, and they, too, were in their own little world.

Patrick got on the microphone and asked that everyone be seated so that they could begin to serve the food. In the distance I could see my mother doling out instructions to the help. She was pointing to the order in which the tables should be served. Colleen and Lloyd were wandering around looking lost. They forgot where we were sitting. I stood up and waved to them so they could come and sit with us.

The tables had peach tablecloths to match the bridesmaid dresses and a bouquet of flowers were in a vase in the center. Each round table sat no more six people with the exception of the wedding party's table. They had a long rectangular one and the bride and groom sat in the center of the group.

Colleen and I sat next to each other while Donovan and Lloyd sat on either side or us. There were two vacant seats still remaining at our table, and I prayed that it would remain that way, but Bigga and Hop came over and joined us. Even though I couldn't stand being around Bigga, it was better than having absolute strangers sit with us, forcing us to monitor our conversation.

It seemed like the toasts went on forever. At least thirty people stood up to say something. Everyone in the wedding party spoke, and there were sixteen of them, and both the bride and groom's parents spoke. It grew tiring. The food was finally served, and everyone ate until their heart's content. They weren't stingy with the servings either. Once again, my mother outdid herself. Everyone was complimenting the meal and praising the chef.

The guys got acquainted with one another and began talking nonstop. I wanted to make sure that Colleen was all right, because her performance could have been a front. Even if it were an act she still deserved a standing ovation. I now saw her in an entirely new light. She was transforming into a strong and beautiful woman. Not the same shy and timid girl that moved away from home a couple of months ago. We had a small exchange of words, and she assured me that she was fine, and that I needn't worry. She had prepared herself for the worse and pretty much figured her mother would react that way. Although she said she was really hoping that it wouldn't turn out the way it did. Trying to get through to Ms. Margaret would be an arduous task, but I tried to convince Colleen not to give up. Maybe in due time Ms. Margaret would come around. Ms. Margaret's feeble attempt to humiliate Colleen backfired, and she ended up looking like the fool.

Donovan turned his attention to me for a moment to ask if I had seen his father. I informed him that he left with Ms. Margaret a while ago. Colleen sucked her teeth at hearing her mother's name, and Lloyd held her hand.

Lloyd seemed to really care for Colleen. From what I could see, he seemed to have a genuine interest and sincere feelings for her. Lloyd was treating Colleen like his queen. He waited on her hand and foot, constantly checking to see if she was okay and trying to comfort her. Their love for each other was so new, it was enchanting. Perhaps this romance would blossom and bring Colleen the happiness she deserved.

We were all eating and talking when we were momentarily distracted. The cute little girl that was sitting next to me in the church whining for her daddy came over to the table and stood there. We all commented on how adorable she looked in her pretty red dress. Her hair was in a ponytail with a ribbon to match. Shiny patent leather shoes and white lace-trimmed bobby socks completed the outfit.

We continued with our meals and figured the little girl would eventually be on her way. She continued to stand there staring with her big bright eyes shining up at us and twiddling her hands behind her back. She looked like she wanted to say something, so I tried to help her along.

"Hi, pretty. What's your name?"

"Camille Icilyn Thompson," she said in a high-pitched voice. Her hands remained behind her back while she idly circled her left foot in front of her.

"Camille, that's a pretty name. It's almost as pretty as you."

"Thank you," Camille mumbled. I could barely hear her over

the background noise and the music that was playing.

"What did she say her name was?" Colleen said, turning her attention from the conversation at the table to Camille and me.

"Camille Thompson," I said unsure if the last name was right, so I nodded my head to Camille for confirmation, and she shook her head to reassure me.

"Why?" I asked Colleen. "Why did you ask her name?"

"Oh, because Lloyd's mother's name is Camille too. She turned to tap Lloyd to get his attention. He was still explaining his theory on the evolution of man and the Rastafarian way of life.

"Everyone, is a Rastaman deep down inside. You feel me," Lloyd lectured, "it is up to the individual to recognize his true identity.

Lloyd, Donovan, Bigga, and Hop had been talking about religion for so long that I could sense Donovan's relief when Colleen wanted Lloyd's attention.

"Lloyd, guess what?" Colleen said not really waiting for his response. "Her name is Camille Thompson like your mother's."

"Seriously," he said. "Come here, Camille." Camille hesitated, but stared Lloyd right in the eyes without blinking, like she was searching his face for something.

"I won't bite you." She took a few steps toward Lloyd, but kept her distance and continued to study him. She began to fidget, swaying from side to side and biting down on her bottom lip.

"What's wrong? Are you afraid of me?" Lloyd asked.

"No," Camille replied.

"It's really a small world. Isn't that a coincidence that she would have the same name as your mother," Colleen said. We all agreed silently. Lloyd seemed to take an immediate liking to Camille. He stretched his hand to reach for her and she finally gave in and moved closer to him.

"My mother's name is Camille Icilyn Thompson," Lloyd said to her.

"I know," Camille said.

"How did you know that my mother's name is Camille?"

"My mommy told me," Camille answered.

"How does your mommy know my mother's name? Who is your mommy?" Lloyd questioned not sure if this was a joke.

"My mommy said that she named me after my gran' mommy."

"Your grandmother? What's your mom's name?" Lloyd asked.

"My mommy's name is Hyacinth." Camille turned to point to a woman in her early twenties making her way across the floor in our direction. Hyacinth's approach was regal and timed as she sauntered over. She was breathtaking. She was fair skinned with sandy-brown hair she wore piled on top of her head except for a few curls that managed to escape, tumbling down the sides. The dress she wore clung to her like a glove, and the sequins on the garment shimmied with each stride. We were all in a trance watching her every step, and we didn't say another word until she arrived.

Hyacinth's smile was dazzling. She attempted to grab hold of Camille's hand and then she greeted us. Her presence was almost statuesque. I could sense that Colleen was feeling a little intimidated and she was marking her territory by taking her place in front of Lloyd. When Hyacinth arrived, Lloyd had a shocked look on his face like he had seen a ghost.

"Hello, Lloyd," Hyacinth cooed.

"Hi, Hyacinth." Lloyd introduced us all to her and stressed that Colleen was his woman when he made their introductions. "How are you?" he asked with some reserve, not really looking for an answer.

"I'm doing well. Life has been treating me very well, and I can't complain. How are you?" Hyacinth asked.

"Doing well myself. I see you have a daughter. She's cute," Lloyd said.

"Yes. Camille is going on four next month."

"She tells me that you named her after her grandmother. You remember that my mother's name is Camille Icilyn, too, right?"

"Of course I remember. I named her after her grandmother, Lloyd. Your mother is Camille's grandmother, and *you* are Camille's father."

Chapter Eight

The music grew faint in the distance, and the lights from the deck appeared like a beautiful swarm of lightning bugs dancing in the dark.

"He's a liar... he's a liar," Colleen kept repeating as the tears streamed down her face. Nothing I did or said calmed her. She stormed out of the reception after Hyacinth announced that Lloyd was Camille's father. Naturally I ran out after her, and poor Lloyd didn't know what to do. I told him to remain with Hyacinth to hear her out. She had a story to tell him, and he needed to see if what she was saying was true. He couldn't abandon his own flesh and blood, and it wasn't his fault that this was happening to him now. Lloyd was as much in the dark as Colleen was. The only difference was this was his problem and responsibility.

The night air was brisk as it quickly brushed across my cheek. I got an immediate chill and knew that the cool night air had no effect on Colleen. A blazing inferno was sitting in place of her heart right now.

Colleen was allowing herself to heal from the hurt and pain that her mother spewed at her earlier. Just when she thought it was safe to come out and play, she got pounced on again. She was choking and gasping for air, but she didn't know whom to turn to or whom to trust. She was feeling betrayed because the one thing she trusted to go right in her life was a mirage. This day was quickly turning into her worse nightmare. I sympathized with her, but she needed to understand that Lloyd did not deceive her. He didn't have control over the circumstances presented to him tonight. He loved her very much. Even I could see that during the short display of affection he showered her with during the reception.

Colleen headed toward my house, and I could barely keep up with her. Her short legs seemed like they were moving at the speed of light as I galloped alongside her in my heels. We were silent the rest of the trip to my house. I allowed Colleen time to clear her head.

When we finally made it up to my house, it was pitch black, and I had to maneuver my way around the porch. Years of practice enabled me to locate the light switch. When the light came on, the moths and mosquitoes came into full view. As a child I was afraid to sit outside by myself at night. It seemed like those insects only appeared when it was dark. One night my father sat me on his lap and told me not to be afraid because those bugs were just as afraid of me as I was of them. Then he made a muscle and made me do the same. When we did that together it made me feel big and strong. Hyacinth was Colleen's insect, and though she wasn't bigger in size, she was going to have to be a whole lot stronger. I wish I could afford Colleen that same kind of strength.

Colleen sat on the swing bench, her crying now down to a whimper. She was trying to regain her composure because she was all cried out. I took a seat beside her and gently rocked the swing so that it glided back and forth. The swing used to be soothing to me, and I only hoped that it would remedy Colleen the same way. Her breathing was now more controlled, which indicated she was calming down some. I put my arm around her shoulders, and she let her head rest on me. I asked her if she was feeling better, and she nodded. I wanted to try to lift her spirits, but I could see the pendulum of pain hanging over her head. It was more important that I be there for her since at this point I was probably the only person she trusted.

I didn't want to violate that trust by forcing her to speak prematurely. I knew how it felt to trust someone and how it felt to be betrayed. Besides Donovan, Colleen was the only other person that I really trusted. So as much as I wanted to speed up the healing process I decided to wait it out and not pry.

The night air was so relaxing that before I realized it I began dozing off. I woke up to Colleen's voice. She was asking me what she did to deserve this. I didn't know what the real answer was, because for some strange reason, bad things seemed to happen to good people. They just happen, and we have to deal with the results and hope for the best. The only thing that I could attest to was that she was a good person, and she didn't do anything wrong.

"Anne-Marie, what did I do for my life to turn out this way? My mother can't stand me and doesn't respect me, and the man that I'm falling in love with is no good because he's a liar too!"

"Your mother doesn't hate you. She's just a difficult person and doesn't know how to express herself or her feelings. She's probably never received or experienced love before, so it's hard for her to say or do the right thing. I'm not excusing the way that she behaves, because it's appalling. In spite of that, you have to stay strong. I know it's hard, but you can't turn your back on your mother because she's irreplaceable. She's the only mother that you've got, be it good or bad."

"She doesn't act like I'm the only daughter that she has. All I've ever wanted was for her to love me, talk to me, laugh and cry with me. A simple hug every now and then. I don't think that I'm asking for much. I understand if she can't display affection, but at least treat me like I count. Treat me like a person, a human being. You know in all my life the only show of affection that I've ever received has been from my father, Patrick, and now Lloyd." After Colleen said that, it occurred to me that my exposure to love and affection also came from the men in my life. All I could do was nod, because I knew exactly what she was saying and where she was coming from.

"Our parents weren't exposed to love and affection. It's no fault of your mother's really. Look at my mother. Her idea of conditioning and expressing love is by gossiping with Nadine. She likes to spread rumors. Look how close they are, and I bet you that she's still never told Nadine that she loves her. My mother loves Nadine unconditionally, and I'm sure that she loves me, too, but even with Nadine, the closest she has ever come to affection is a pat on the back. The men are different though. My father isn't afraid to express his affection to the family. Whenever he kisses my mother to express his affection, she acts silly and pushes him away. I realize it's not something she's ready to accept without a fight. She may never be ready because she doesn't want to allow herself that much happiness or pleasure. She won't give herself the chance to let go. Deep down my mother probably feels like she doesn't need to be loved that way. Your mother, though dismal and set in her ways, can still change. There's still hope for her, because she has Mr. Miller in her life now."

I didn't know how much of that I actually believed, but I had to sell it to Colleen. Plus to me it was implausible for a person to exist and not have at least an ounce of goodness in them. If such a person existed they would have to be the devil in the flesh.

"I really want to reconcile things between me and my mother. As cruel as she has been, deep down I still want her to love me, but I don't know how much longer I can put up with her shit. She tried to make a spectacle of me at the wedding," Colleen said.

"Ms. Margaret made a spectacle of herself," I said, laughing. It also brought a tight smile to Colleen's face. She was slowly lightening up and opening up to me. There was hope after all. "Did you see the way Mr. Miller dragged her out of the reception." I'd give anything to see that again."

"It was funny," Colleen said, trying to recover from her fit of laughter. "What I don't understand is why she carried on that way about Lloyd. She was so mean to him. I'm glad she left before that woman Hyacinth came along. Then she would have had more ammunition against him. I could hear her now saying, "How could you pick a man who has woman *and pikny*, and then bring him to the family wedding."

Colleen said that with so much emotion and fervency that it sent chills down my spine. Her imitation of Ms. Margaret was uncanny. It sounded exactly like her and was something Ms. Margaret would say.

"Do you think that Lloyd loves you?"

"I don't know anymore."

"Why don't you know anymore? What has changed between the two of you in the last couple of hours to make you feel differently? Has he done something to you?"

"He's a liar, and I can't trust him anymore." She couldn't even look at me after she said that. Colleen was secretly trying to convince me, and her efforts were pathetic. She couldn't even look at me. By now she had to realize that she was convicting the wrong person.

"Listen to yourself. Lloyd hasn't done a thing to you, except try to love you. He didn't lie to you about anything, Colleen."

"I can't believe that you would take his side. You are supposed to be my friend, Anne-Marie, not Lloyd's. I was having a hard enough time trying to prepare for this evening, and it turned out to be a disaster anyway. Nothing went right." She was rocking back and forth on the edge of the swing and biting on the bottom of her lip. She looked like she was on the verge of tears again.

"Colleen, please listen carefully. You know that I wouldn't say or do anything to hurt you. You're my best friend, and you know that I speak the truth when I say that you are being unfair to

Lloyd. What happened tonight was not his fault. He was just as surprised when Hyacinth came over to the table. I don't think that it's a coincidence that she just happened to waltz on in like that. I was sitting next to her in the church, and between you and me I think she set this shit up. She is a conniving, scandalous woman. Hyacinth is the one that you better keep a close eye on. You are trying to blame all of your problems on Lloyd, and that's not fair." I also felt that Colleen had other problems to worry about, but I would save that for another day. I had a bad feeling that Hyacinth was going to try and manipulate Lloyd by using Camille as bait to lure him back. There was no need to go in depth though. It wouldn't be long before the truth began to surface. "You're better than that, and you know that you have found yourself a good man. Didn't you see how confused he was when you were leaving? He didn't know whether to stay or run after you. If you weren't so self-involved, you'd have noticed. I told him that this wasn't about you, and he needed to handle his affairs with Hyacinth. I know how disastrous and painful this evening was for you, but you really should have stayed and supported him. Instead you left him with that malicious woman."

Colleen didn't interrupt me during my entire dissertation. She wasn't rocking back and forth anymore either. Instead she tilted her head back as if she were hit by a new revelation while gazing at the stars with her hands clasped on her lap. We sat there silently, the only sound was our breathing along with the singsong of the insects. I said enough for the evening, and it was up to Colleen to come to the realization that she overreacted.

In less than twenty-four hours, I would have my own set of issues to deal with. I would be telling my parents about my pregnancy and the possibility of me moving away to attend school overseas. As it stood now, I didn't have Donovan in my corner as far as school was concerned, and this saddened me. I was glad that Patrick offered to come to dinner to support me. At least I knew that he would be on my side.

My mind began to wander, and I realized how unprepared and uneasy I was feeling. I felt myself becoming extremely emotional. I leaned back on the swing to admire how marvelous the sky looked tonight. It resembled blue velvet decorated with tiny crushed diamonds. I was trying my best to control the tears that were forcing themselves down the sides of my face anyway.

Colleen sighed loud and hard and then proceeded to sit up straight. I followed suit in case she was ready to talk again. Instead she surprised me with a warm embrace. It was exactly what I really needed at that moment. It was an embrace that didn't need an explanation. Tonight was brutal for her. I couldn't imagine myself in her shoes. Colleen handled it all like a champ. She managed to hold on to her sanity.

"It's still pretty early," Colleen said.

"It is, so what do you want to do?"

"Let's go back to the reception. I've got a man to go look after down there, and I ain't letting Hyacinth get in my way."

"I hear you. Let's go."

"Let me go inside and freshen myself up. My makeup must be a mess right now with all that crying that I was doing."

"I should freshen up too. I want to change my dress."

"Anne-Marie, you can't put on that dress that Nadine had on."

"You're so funny."

"By the way you didn't say anything about my new hairstyle," Colleen said, as she patted her coiffure.

"It's really nice, girl. A lot of people are doing that now. It's popular because of Michael Jackson."

"Thanks. Are you really going to go change your dress now? The night will be over before you know it, so why dirty up another frock?" Colleen questioned.

"You're only saying that because you don't have anything else to change into."

"You know me too well." Colleen began smoothing out her dress and stood in front of me.

"That's the problem, but I love you anyway."

"Are you ready, crazy woman," Colleen said playfully with a big smile on her face.

As we were walking back down the hill I spotted the lights on at Mr. Miller's shop. I pointed it out to Colleen, but she was oblivious. I could tell she was still sorting out the night's events in her mind.

"What kind of business do you think Mr. Miller is taking care of this time of night?" I asked in an attempt to get her attention.

"Probably the same business I took care of the other night," Colleen said. She almost caused me to trip over a rock that was in our path. It was a rock that I always knew was there. I could climb up and down this hill blindfolded, but her last remark almost made me lose my footing.

"Repeat that, because I don't think I heard you clearly," I said.

"I'm just kidding, but we almost did it."

"Oh, really!" I replied, and we both linked our arms together laughing at the thought of Mr. Miller and Ms. Margaret being together.

It had been a long night, and we both needed a little light-hearted humor, if for no other reason than to just feel good.

Chapter Nine

B enjamin Miller's temples pulsated as he stood behind the counter with his hands firmly planted against the sides. He lightly tapped his left foot against the wooden floor plank while the right one steadily held its ground. Benjamin was highly disappointed in Margaret's display at the reception. Her performance was not only outrageous and appalling, but also inappropriate and loathsome. He couldn't fathom that the woman he was slowly developing an affinity for was capable of such behavior.

Benjamin was confused. It had been quite some time since a woman had managed to stir up such emotions and feelings in him. This wasn't the first relationship that he had been in since his wife passed, but this was the first one that he actually considered pursuing. He not only found Margaret to be a beautiful woman, but smart and compassionate. Tonight he discovered an entirely different person—the person that his friends had warned him about—and now he wondered if their relationship was based on deception. A farce. The entire scene was ugly and now he understood why Margaret didn't have many friends. Repeatedly, Benjamin had been warned about Margaret and should have seen this coming.

Benjamin wondered how he could have possibly missed all warning signs. First, his best friend remarked "Don't botha get yu tail caught inna de trap," but Benjamin didn't take the comment seriously. Desmond, his best friend, was infamous for giving false warnings, so he ignored his advice. Then at the doctor's office he noticed that Anne-Marie treated Margaret with such disdain. Another sign was when he mentioned Margaret's name to Donovan the other night. The look of disgust said more than he wanted to believe. Benjamin just figured most young people couldn't bear to be around adults anyway. So, he thought it was a natural reaction. He should have known better and taken the time to question why his son would respond in such a negative way, especially since he raised Donovan to be respectful to his elders.

Benjamin's relationship with Margaret was strictly platonic, and that was by choice. He was really starting to care for Margaret, and he was more than sure the feeling was mutual. The other night the relationship almost escalated to the next level, but he backed down. Not because he didn't want her, but because he wanted to court her the right way. After all, he was a good-looking man and could get sex from almost any available woman in Cambridge, but he wasn't about that. Women practically threw themselves at him on a daily basis. At first it was flattering to him, but then it got sickening. He dated a woman named Beryl. They used to get together every now and then, but then she started pressuring him about marriage. The original plan was that they would make appearances together and satisfy each other's needs, but he didn't love her enough to marry her. Beryl wasn't stimulating enough to consider marriage. She was nice and very attractive, but if the conversation didn't involve buying new clothes, getting her hair done, or sex she wasn't interested. Beryl lacked depth, and after being married to Sue he found that he needed a woman that had both depth and character. Beryl was only interested in getting married because her friends were telling her that she should do it. It wasn't even her idea to begin with, so that only let him know that she didn't think for herself, which was an instant turnoff.

When Margaret approached him a couple of months ago because of an ailment, he befriended her. Margaret was experiencing some mild symptoms that she felt were cancer-related, and she wanted some direction as well as support. Since she knew a little about his deceased wife, Sue, Margaret felt comfortable talking and sharing her fears and concerns with him. Benjamin started accompanying her to doctor's appointments and eventually started spending more and more time with her to insure that she didn't have to do this alone. When he was with Margaret he couldn't deny how much younger she made him feel. He felt rejuvenated and alive again. The stories that they shared about their childhood, marriages, and relationships made him even more curious about her. He only found himself wanting to know more about her. Margaret was different from the other women that he dealt with, and her motives were pure: She wasn't out looking for a man but they found each other. They talked about everything from A to Z, and spoke nonstop about their children and how much they treasured them. That's why he couldn't understand how her course of action tonight fit into that grand picture.

There were so many questions and concerns boggling his mind, and he needed answers. Why would she humiliate her own daughter in public? How could she pretend to be such a God-fearing woman and behave the way that she had? Now he had to re-evaluate exactly what it was that he originally saw in her, and what, if anything he wanted out of their relationship. Did he really want to know more about her after tonight? Did he really see such a deceitful and evil woman at his side as a lifelong partner? Maybe he was jumping the gun, but he would find out soon enough. Most importantly he needed to ask if he could ever see his son accepting her. This woman was practically scorned by the community, and after tonight's display he could understand why. She was actually about to strike her daughter in public.

In all fairness he decided that he should let her explain. There really wasn't much that she could say that would help her redeem herself, but Benjamin always prided himself on being a fair person and keeping an open mind.

Over the last couple of weeks he couldn't stop thinking about her because she made him smile and act like a little kid when she was around him. She even made him think about marriage again for the first time in years. But tonight she made him have second thoughts about even going forward with a relationship. After all, no one ever managed get under his skin or repulse him the way Margaret did tonight.

Margaret returned from the bathroom after cleaning herself up. She claimed that the ordeal upset her and that he had embarrassed and hurt her feelings. On the way to the shop he apologized for manhandling her at the reception. Benjamin was not an abusive person. However, he couldn't apologize for calling her "a snake of a woman." He realized that it was irrational to speak while upset, but given the circumstances, it was understandable. She was lucky that he was not harsher with her.

Margaret stood there with the kerchief in her hand, and her eyes were still a little glazed from the tears. Benjamin wasn't moved and in no mood for the fake tears. He knew she was crying wolf, and he was much more interested in finding out exactly what in the hell got into her at the reception.

Benjamin didn't even bother to look at her, because the sight of her only served to further infuriate him. She rested her hand over his to get a response. When he didn't make a motion to withdraw his hand she felt it safe to speak.

"Miller," Margaret voiced softly, trying to get his attention. It was almost a whisper, so he pretended not to hear her. Then she repeated his name again a little louder.

"What?" he replied snippantly.

"I want you to know that I am sorry."

"Sorry. You're sorry for what? What exactly are you sorry for?"

"My behavior. I mean what you witnessed tonight was not me."

"Then who was it, Margaret, because it certainly looked like you and as a matter of fact...it was you that I pulled away."

"Miller, please let me explain," Margaret pleaded.

"Nobody's stopping you, but I'm not the one you should be explaining or apologizing to. You should be saying this to your daughter. She is the victim here." Benjamin stressed the word victim to her. "And I'll be truthful with you, I'm troubled and embarrassed by the way you acted toward her this evening."

Margaret didn't say a word. For once in her life she was speechless and looked a bit baffled.

"Miller, I don't understand why you're upset with me. My dealings earlier were with my daughter and should be of little concern to you."

"Little concern? Margaret, are you serious, because if you are, you can leave my shop right now. I thought there was more going on between us than that, but if you feel that way, please don't even bother with your story or apologies. You don't even know what you're apologizing for."

"I didn't intend it that way. What I mean is, I don't know why you're upset with the way that I choose to discipline my daughter."

"Your daughter is grown and doesn't live with you anymore. What kind of disciplining does she need?"

"Since she's moved out she has become very fresh and out of order. You don't know my daughter the way I do."

"If that is the way you discipline her, who's to say that when we have a disagreement or grievance you won't attack me the same way. I'm more than sure that whatever problem you had with Colleen could have been resolved in a much more pleasant manner and behind closed doors. I also want to let you know that people are talking about us. They are starting to associate me with you, and I'm not sure if I'm comfortable with that anymore. The other day my son asked me about you, and I told him the truth—that we are friends. I didn't mention that there was a possibility of us becoming more, and right now there may not be a need to do so. If you treat your daughter like that, how would you treat my son?"

"I would never treat Donovan like that!"

"What makes my son different from Colleen? She is your flesh and blood," Benjamin said.

"Your son is not rude. You raised him to be respectful to his elders, and every time I've ever come into contact with him he has been nothing but nice. Exactly like his father."

"And you didn't raise Colleen to be respectful to her elders? Now you've confused me. Colleen is one of the most pleasant young women that I've ever come across. Tell me the real problem that you have with you daughter."

"Since she's moved out she's an entirely different person. She's staying with her aunt Lorna who is an unhampered woman and lives a very wild lifestyle. And it seems that my daughter is choosing to follow in her footsteps, chasing after men now. I don't even know who she is anymore. The person I saw tonight was a lost soul."

"There's got to be more to it, Margaret. The scene that I witnessed at the reception this evening is not something that manifested overnight. Now what did she do tonight to make you react in such a manner?"

"She had the nerve to try and introduce me to some Rasta man that she's seeing named Lloyd. You know those Rastas don't stand for anything good. All they do is chase woman and smoke ganja all day."

"Margaret, give me a break," Benjamin said, clearly annoyed. "I've known Lloyd for years, and he is a good and decent man, but that was a very narrow-minded remark. I'd expect more coming from you. Yes, it's true that Rastas smoke ganja, but that doesn't make them bad people. Furthermore, ganja is no worse than cigarettes. And what man do you know out there that's not chasing after some skirt."

"Well, Colleen doesn't need to be dealing with any man, good or not. She needs to go back to school like Anne-Marie is doing and make something of herself. Man will only breed her and then leave her alone to raise pikny. Next thing you know she will be coming back to me for support."

"Margaret, how old is Colleen?" Benjamin questioned.

"She's nineteen."

"Colleen's nineteen. She's not living with you anymore. She's obviously capable of supporting herself and should be entitled to date whomever she pleases. Now you're still young enough to breed. Do you think that's what I would do to you?" Benjamin stood there and stared at Margaret in awe. She just wasn't getting it. She was getting denser by the moment, and he was losing his patience with each passing second.

"No, but you're a good man," she replied as if that was definitely the answer she knew he was looking for. Margaret didn't realize that she was only digging herself into a deeper hole.

"But you're judging Lloyd, and you don't even know the man. Your daughter is trying to get you involved in her life. She was introducing you to someone that obviously means a lot to her, and you pushed her away. Let me ask you a question: Did you ever take the time to know your daughter while you were living together? Little things like her favorite color or food? What she wanted out of life?"

"Of course I know those things." She said with very little assurance.

"Then tell me," he said, and he stood there waiting for her to reply. Benjamin knew that she didn't have a clue.

"Miller, I know you can't be serious?" She said, hesitating. Benjamin simply nodded his head, and his face confirmed that he was very serious. "Colleen's favorite color is red, and she loves oxtails and gravy."

"I don't know if you're telling the truth or not, but I think you need to take the time to get to know your daughter a lot better. Colleen has more definition to her than a favorite color, food, or even being your daughter. Stop pushing her away. Judging from tonight's episode she did a brave thing coming to you with her new friend. Especially since she probably knew ahead of time that you would behave badly. For the sake of the relationship with your daughter, please go back and apologize to her."

"Margaret, you seem to be repeating everything that you've ever told me about your mother. She treated you very badly when she called you names and said she regretted having you and you were a mistake. Your mother was also wrong to kick you out when you got pregnant, forcing you to marry young. I'm sorry that you had to stay home and raise your daughter instead of following your dreams of becoming a nurse. But tell me what makes your behavior any different from your mother's?"

"But I never told Colleen that she was a mistake. I never told her that."

"Shhhh! Let me finish. I never said that you did say those things, but you hated your mother for mistreating you. Yet here you are today repeating the same mistakes with Colleen. Fortunately, Colleen is grown and has finished school. If she wants to be with a man, then that is her right. You also have to let it be her decision to go back to school. You can't force her to do something that she's not interested in. Margaret, you've already raised her, and your job is finished. You can't live her life out for her too. You should be asking yourself why your daughter moved out of your house in the first place."

"She felt that she was too grown for her own good. That's why she moved out," Margaret hissed.

"You haven't heard a word that I've said all evening, have you? You amaze me."

"I heard you. I'm plainly telling you the reason why she moved out, I've seen her a couple of times since she's moved out and each time she's been disrespectful to me."

"She couldn't have walked up to you in broad daylight and just been rude. You probably provoked her."

"Provoked her how? When I saw her the other day she had on this bright red lipstick and a tight blouse. I should have known a man was in the picture then, but I told her how I thought she looked. She blasphemously called me names and quoted scriptures from the holy bible."

"You seem to be very insensitive when it comes to Colleen, and you have a serious problem communicating with her. I'm warning you now that you are going to end up losing her altogether. That is, if you haven't already after tonight. Treat her like a person with feelings, because she is the only flesh and blood that you have. You should also consider telling her about your condition. Don't you think that she would be concerned to know that her mother may have to undergo surgery soon? I've been meaning to talk to you about that too."

"I'll think about it, but I don't want to worry her unnecessarily until I hear the final results."

"This is the last time that I'm going to mention it, but are you going to apologize to Colleen? Now don't do it because I'm telling you to; do it because you love your daughter."

"I promise that I will. I guess I overreacted a bit, and if you say that Lloyd is a good man, I know you wouldn't lie to me, and I'll give him a chance. He probably thinks that I'm a monster now."

"Probably, and you should also to apologize to him too."

"Miller, I'm so sorry. I'm sorry. I'm sorry what have I done?" Margaret broke down in tears. For the first time that entire evening, when Benjamin looked at her he could actually see in her eyes that she was sorry for all that she had done. He knew that what he saw today was probably a fit of rage. Sometimes people had a hard time telling the ones they cared about the most that they loved them. They resorted to violence or verbal abuse because they didn't know how to say I love you. Despite what she did tonight he knew that Margaret loved her daughter. Unfortunately, since she never received positive reinforcement when she was growing up, she had become a product of her environment.

Margaret was simply being overprotective of Colleen. Frightened that she left the nest too soon, she was still trying to capture Colleen by criticizing and making her feel weak in an ill attempt to coax her back home. He didn't agree with her tactics, but he felt her pain. He wanted to let her know that he would gladly help her through her transitional stage of re-creating a relationship with her daughter. The most important thing that he had in his life was his son, and everybody knew that, including Margaret. He lived and breathed for his son, and if it weren't for Donovan's smiling face he didn't know how he would have survived after Sue died.

Benjamin looked over at Margaret and saw how weak and vulnerable she appeared. He couldn't resist the temptation to hug her, and he did just that. This was the defenseless woman that approached him a couple of months ago. This was the woman that he was falling in love with. This was the woman that he wanted to get to know better, loved talking to, and couldn't get out of his mind. When Margaret wasn't around, he daydreamed about her. That woman that he witnessed making a scene earlier at the reception was possessed, and he was going to make sure that she never, ever surfaced again.

Chapter Ten

C olleen felt a lot more confident and secure after talking with Anne-Marie. She knew she was in denial and that it wasn't Lloyd's fault that the evening was a major disaster. After all, he didn't make her mother act a fool, and it wasn't like he handed Hyacinth a personal invitation to show up at the wedding.

Throughout Colleen's entire life she felt like a misfit, but she always had Anne-Marie there to set her straight. And as usual, whenever she was feeling bad or in a rut, Anne-Marie could be found standing in her corner.

Now that Colleen had someone else in her life to love, care, and hold her through the good times and bad, she didn't have to rely on Anne-Marie quite as much. She also didn't want to ruin this new relationship, which was blossoming so beautifully between she and Lloyd.

Colleen walked out on Lloyd when he needed her most. Wasn't he there when she and her mother got into it earlier? That was also a very awkward situation, but he stayed and consoled her with soothing words afterward. She just couldn't bear witness to the entire scene. Who was this woman claiming to be the mother of her man's baby? Colleen was the one who was going to have a future with him. She was supposed to be the one that would bear his children, not this intruder.

From the moment Colleen laid eyes on Hyacinth stepping across the deck, she could feel trouble. Colleen always had a sixth sense about things like that. Hyacinth's arrival couldn't have been at a more inopportune time. Colleen was just starting to relax and unwind and letting her guard down a bit, but then she saw the world around her crumbling, falling to pieces, and she was trying to use her inner strength to keep it all intact. All she wanted to do was make some progress with her mother. But as much as she wanted to build a relationship with her, she refused to further allow her to manipulate her mind. Colleen was determined to make her mother take her seriously and treat her with respect. Until her mother came to the realization that she was an adult, there was nothing left to be said.

Hyacinth's presence made Colleen feel inferior. The mere thought that her man once dated this woman bothered her. Hyacinth was beautiful; there was really no other way to describe her. Although she wore her hair pinned up, it was obvious that it was long and flowing. She had gorgeous high cheekbones and a stunning bronze complexion to accentuate her already astonishing looks. Her smile was mischievous as well as deceiving, but it could manage to melt any man's heart.

Colleen could tell that Hyacinth was a woman of many tricks. When she started to explain to Lloyd that Camille was his daughter, Colleen felt a sharp pain in her chest, and the rest of her body went numb. A throbbing headache accompanied the numbness, and she could feel tears stinging her eyes. Colleen couldn't control the intensity she was feeling and knew that if she stayed, she would break down in front of them. In order to save herself from embarrassment, she had to make a quick exit. It wasn't the most mature way to handle it, but it was the only way for Colleen.

Colleen wanted more than anything else for this relationship to work. She had no intention of letting every, and anybody in her bed, like her aunt. Aunt Lorna's lifestyle was a tad too slack for Colleen's liking. She also didn't want to end up like her mother.

She didn't want to push the man she loved away. Colleen had never experienced a feeling like this before, but she knew it was love. If Colleen had any inkling of Anne-Marie's panache or savvy, she would have stood her ground and patronized Hyacinth with a cross-examination. She wanted to knock Hyacinth out for disturbing her happy home. However, Colleen didn't have that type of strength or courage. Besides, she really didn't need to add another item to her already long list of problems. Colleen was certain about one thing, and that was Hyacinth was not going to be the cause of any discord in her newfound relationship.

Colleen conveniently placed herself in the vacant seat between Lloyd and Hyacinth. Colleen saw that she managed to momentarily startle Hyacinth with her intrusion, but Colleen didn't care. She turned to Lloyd. "I apologize for being abrupt earlier with my departure, but I needed some fresh air."

Lloyd graciously accepted her apology by caressing her hand and giving her a soft kiss on the lips. This gesture served only to assure Colleen that Hyacinth was not a threat—more of an unwanted obstacle. Colleen turned her attention to Hyacinth who was controlling the conversation and gave her a once-over. Colleen quickly noticed that this woman wasn't quite as beautiful as she perceived earlier. Her beauty was pure deception. Hyacinth's arrival and presence was probably timely and insidious. She had something up her sleeve, and Colleen intended to find out what it was. Why else would she wait four years to finally catch up to Lloyd and tell him that she was the mother of his child? Why didn't she tell him while she was pregnant?

Lloyd was kind and had a good heart. He wasn't a beast and would never deny the fact that Camille was his child. Colleen didn't know him back then, but from what she knew of him now and judging by his character, he was probably always this way.

Colleen glanced over at Camille sitting at the table behaving like a little lady, not making a fuss. She was simply busying herself with the paper napkins on the table. She had big brown eyes with long curved lashes like Lloyd's. Her crooked, innocent smile held dimples that resembled the moon, and she had a small gap between her teeth. The more Colleen looked at this child, the more she knew there was no denying Camille was Lloyd's child. She was his miniature twin.

Colleen was still miffed as to why Hyacinth would choose now, today of all days to return. Colleen was through allowing others to take advantage of her kindness. She reminisced the last year and some of the happenings were unsettling, but she was slowly learning how to gain control of her life. Being with Lloyd made her feel complete. He was the only man that made her swoon, but she really never had the opportunity to date before. The few guys she did allow to sneak into her life were selfish and only sought sexual gratification. That was out of the question until she met Lloyd. Everything that came out of his mouth made her think of a cool day providing her with the right amount of sun and warmth. With Lloyd, Colleen could wipe the slate clean and not look back. She didn't care if Camille stepped into the picture. Camille was a child, and on those grounds it granted her immunity.

Colleen turned her attention back to Lloyd and Hyacinth's conversation. Colleen was itching to ask why, and she couldn't hold back anymore, and she didn't care whether she was tactful. She turned to face Hyacinth, took a deep breath, and dove right in.

"So, Hyacinth… What brings you here today?"

"My boyfriend is in the wedding party, and he invited me. And, since I haven't been home in a while, I thought it would be nice to visit, but I had no idea that I would bump into Lloyd tonight," Hyacinth responded.

"Really and where are you living now?"

"I live in Kingston." Hyacinth peered over to look at Lloyd, hoping that he would intervene. Lloyd could sense the tension between Colleen and Hyacinth and tried to avoid direct eye contact with either. Instead he looked over at his daughter and beckoned. When she came over, Lloyd smiled from ear to ear. With this minor distraction, Colleen felt it safe to resume her cross-examination of Hyacinth.

"So, how long have you been living in Kingston?" Colleen asked.

"Well, I moved right after I got pregnant with Camille. My mother lives there, and I needed help at the time, because I wasn't working."

"Why didn't you ask Lloyd to help you? I'm sure Lloyd would have helped you," Colleen said, looking over at Lloyd.

"Lloyd didn't know I was pregnant, and..."

Colleen abruptly interrupted. "Was there a reason for you not telling him? Why did you wait so long to let him know that he had a daughter?"

"Honestly, at the time Lloyd and I weren't on the best of terms. Then when his father died, he took it hard, and shortly after, he moved. I didn't know where he moved to, and when my mother offered to help me raise Camille, I just never bothered. Like I said it's only a coincidence that we bumped into Lloyd today."

"But you knew where Lloyd's mother lived. You could have asked Mrs. Thompson where he had moved to, or even told her that she had a granddaughter."

"Mrs. Thompson never liked me. She wouldn't warn me if a car was about to run me down on the road!"

"My mother never really cared for Hyacinth, so she's telling the truth." Lloyd quickly defended.

Colleen was annoyed and frustrated that Lloyd felt the need to rationalize things for Hyacinth. Colleen couldn't understand how he could be so gullible. She was sure that it wasn't a coincidence that Hyacinth showed up. Colleen didn't believe in coincidences and intended on getting some answers.

"I'm sorry to hear that you and Lloyd's mom don't get along. She's such a nice woman. Mrs. Thompson and I have gotten along since I was a child. When Lloyd introduced me as his lady"—Hyacinth's face turned beet red as Colleen said that—"she seemed really pleased." Colleen was enjoying rubbing salt into the wound. "How did you hear about the wedding if you're living in Kinston now?"

"Colleen, baby," Lloyd said, "please don't chastise the woman. We had a long talk before you came back, and she explained everything to me. I know you're looking out for me, but I'm all right."

"Lloyd, I don't mind answering her questions. Colleen has every right to know. Like you said, she's your lady, and a strange woman has come from your past saying she's the mother of your child. She deserves an explanation," Hyacinth replied.

Colleen knew this was a performance, but as long as she got her answers she would play along. So she nodded her head in order to let Hyacinth continue.

"I came with Devon. He is the groom's younger brother, and we are dating." She proceeded to point to the table where the wedding party was seated.

"You see the guy sitting on the left side of the groom? That's Devon." Devon looked over in our direction and motioned for Hyacinth to come back over, she waved, and mouthed something to him, and he nodded.

Lloyd jumped in so Colleen couldn't continue questioning Hyacinth.

"Hyacinth said that I could take Camille on the weekends sometimes."

"Isn't that nice of you, Hyacinth," Colleen said facetiously.

"Yes, I want Lloyd to have an active part in her life. Camille has been asking me for her father for months now, so you can imagine how delighted I was when I spotted Lloyd at the wedding today."

"Exactly what have you been telling her about her father?" Colleen asked. "It's been four years, and all of a sudden you spot Lloyd across the room and tell Camille that he is her father."

"Well, I have pictures of Lloyd from when we were together, and I always told her that her father was a good man, but he and Mommy broke up a long time ago."

"I'm sorry that you had to do things by yourself for so long, but things are gonna change. I will do whatever I can for my daughter," Lloyd said wistfully, while bouncing Camille on his knee. "Things are definitely going to change, because it's important to me that I become involved in her life."

"Lloyd, don't worry, from now on you'll be very involved. But I warn you she can be a handful. Isn't that right, precious?" Hyacinth cooed at Camille.

"Don't you worry, I'm up to the task, and my sweetheart, Colleen, will help me. Won't you, sweetie?"

"Of course I will. Anything for you." Colleen thought about what she was getting herself into. Then it occurred to her that she loved Lloyd. Camille was his flesh and blood, so she would help him in any way possible. After all, it wasn't Camille she had to watch out for... it was her mother.

Colleen was truly happy for Lloyd. After Hyacinth left, all he kept talking about was Camille this and Camille that. It was almost the happiest she had ever seen him with the exception of the other night. Colleen didn't quite know why she continuously withheld information from Anne-Marie. They were just as close as they had always been. Yet lately she didn't feel compelled to confide intimate details with her anymore. It almost felt like when she told Anne-Marie something she was either asking for her permission or seeking her approval. Eventually she would break down and tell Anne-Marie that she had made love with Lloyd. She would never confide that with anybody else anyway. She wondered if while Lloyd dated Hyacinth, whether he made love to her or if they had sex. Colleen decided that it was definitely the latter, because before tonight, she never heard him mention her name as one of the women that he dated. On more than one occasion, Colleen questioned him about his past. His answers always seemed open and honest. He even remained friends with a few of them, and Colleen was made aware of it. She was comfortable because she knew the women, and they knew her. They were all pretty women and attractive in different ways, but Colleen could definitely hold a candle to all of them. The one thing that she was grateful to her mother for was for her good looks. At thirty-five her mother looked like she could be her twin. The one thing that she also wished that she had was her mother's height. Ms. Margaret was average height at about five foot six, but Colleen was petite. She was always self-conscious about her height. That's why she began making her friends call her by her proper name instead of her nickname, Minnie. Colleen always despised the name Minnie. It only served to remind her of how short she really was.

Although Lloyd was six feet, he didn't have any complaints. He said that she was perfect just the way she was and proved it to her the other night. He kissed every perfect part of her body like a delicate flower. The thought of that night sent chills up and down Colleen's spine. They had made love every night since the first evening, and Colleen was looking forward to a repeat performance later. That was until she promised to stay with Anne-Marie. Looking back at the previous two nights she knew what she would rather be doing, and it didn't include Anne-Marie. However, a promise was a promise and a friend was a friend.

Chapter Eleven

Ever since Donovan and I decided that we would tell my parents together I've been waiting in anticipation for today to arrive. Now that it's finally here, I'm a nervous wreck. I've been rehearsing a speech in my head, but all the practice in the world could never really prepare me for the real thing.

Last night, after the wedding and all of the drama that accompanied it, I was comatose. I cleaned almost every room in the house with the exception of the bedrooms.

Colleen was in my bedroom sound asleep. She stayed up with me for the first couple of hours talking and helping me cut the onions, and peppers and grate coconut for the rice and peas. When she got tired I told her to go to sleep and not worry about me. I needed some time to myself anyway. I continued to cook, and the baby kept me company until the early morning. The baby must have sensed that I was tense, because at one point I had to double over from pain. I lay down on the couch for about half an hour, rubbing my belly and drinking tea until the pain subsided. By six-thirty this morning, dinner was done. By seven-thirty breakfast was ready, and I still had so much pent-up energy that I decided to feed the few chickens that we had left out back. Then I saw clothes that had been washed yesterday on the line, so I took them down, folded them, and quietly tiptoed around to put them in their proper place. At a quarter to nine, my mother and father were up. I could hear the early Sunday morning revival being preached by none other than

Reverend Jasper Hendricks on the radio. In another fifteen to twenty minutes, Mama emerged from her room in her favorite purple-and-gold satin robe. She was ready to make a big Sunday morning breakfast for the family. To her surprise it had already been done, so she went back into the to her room to rest.

There was a lot of commotion going on in Nadine's room, and I heard a conversation going on between her and if I wasn't mistaken, a guy. I knew she didn't have the nerve to have a man in her room. When I heard feet shuffling about, I made myself scarce and went out on the veranda. Two minutes later the screen door opened, and out stepped the guy that I had seen Nadine with the night before. You can only imagine how surprised they both were to see me. They both stopped in their tracks and didn't say a thing, but the word *guilty* might as well have been stamped on their foreheads. On the inside I was cracking up. I could barely keep it together. Finally I said "Good morning," since they both appeared to be dumbstruck. I wanted to have a little fun with them, but I didn't intend on getting her in trouble. I then took the liberty of introducing myself.

"My name is Anne-Marie, I'm Nadine's older sister. We weren't properly introduced last night. And you are?"

"Good morning. I'm Percy, Percy Hendricks," he said with such cockiness and confidence, it made me wonder if I was supposed to recognize the name or know who he was.

"Percy, it's nice to meet you. Will I be seeing you again?" I asked.

"I hope so," Percy responded while gazing at Nadine. She smiled, welcoming the notion.

"Good. Well, I've got a lot of things to do, so you take care and get home safe."

Nadine walked Percy down the hill, and I ran back into the house and went into my bedroom. Colleen was sitting up in the bed fidgeting with my transistor radio. She, too, was a loyal listener of

Reverend Jasper Hendricks, so I knew that she was trying to locate the station that he was preaching on. Then it dawned on me the way Percy said his name with such assurance. He must be Reverend Hendricks' son or some relation. Percy was also a member of the wedding party yesterday, and Maisey's new husband's last name was Hendricks. Then I remembered them mentioning that the family had a lot of money. I began to wonder if they were related. The more I thought about it, the more I started to believe that they were all kin. Then I started to think, why didn't the Honorable Reverend Jasper Hendricks preside over the ceremony. I came in to gossip with Colleen, but once she found the radio station, I wouldn't be able to tell her anything until the service was over. Colleen was faithful to her church, and if she wasn't able to attend, she listened to the service on the radio. I ended up telling her breakfast was ready. I grabbed my robe and towel and headed to the bathroom for a soothing and much-needed shower. I had been up more than twenty-four hours straight, and I felt like a walking zombie.

By the time I got out of the shower, everyone was already at the kitchen table eating breakfast. I said good morning and fixed myself a plate then squeezed in between Nadine and Colleen. When I sat down, everyone was talking about the wedding, complimenting Maisey's dress and the food. We all agreed that everything was perfect. Then out of nowhere Nadine said, "Colleen, why weren't you in the wedding?" And without waiting for a reply, Nadine continued probing. "*Nuh true seh yu ah Maisey niece?*"

I wondered where that came from and why she was picking on Colleen.

Colleen calmly replied, "Aunt Maisey did ask me to be a part of the wedding, but when I moved to Montego Bay I had to withdraw."

"Are you dating that guy with the dreads that I saw you with last night?" Nadine continued.

"Yes, I am," Colleen said bashfully. "His name is Lloyd."

"I know Lloyd. He's a good guy. I knew his father very well. It's unfortunate that he died. What a tragedy, and such a young guy too," Daddy added.

"It is a shame. Lloyd talks about him all the time. His father was his hero, you know."

"I saw you and your mother quarreling at the reception last night. Was it because you're seeing him?" Nadine asked.

"Nadine, why must you be so inquisitive?" Mama said, surprising both Colleen and myself.

"Your mother is right. Colleen's business is none of your concern, so mind your business," Daddy stepped in.

I decided to give Nadine a dose of her own medicine.

"Daddy," I said, "is the honorable Reverend Jasper Hendricks any relation to the Hendricks that Maisey got married to last night?"

"I believe so, you know. Why do you ask?"

"I actually had the pleasure of meeting a Mr. Percy Hendricks, and he bares a striking resemblance to the reverend, and I was wondering if that was his father." I looked directly at Nadine when I made that last remark, but she tried to act like she didn't hear me by getting ready to leave the table. But before she could leave the table Mama chimed in.

"Isn't that the young man that I saw you with last night?" Mama asked.

Nadine shook her head and then busied herself with her breakfast.

"I also noticed a resemblance," Daddy said. "It also looked like he took a very strong liking to you, Nadine.

"If you only knew." I mumbled under my breath, but loud enough for Nadine to hear me.

"What was that, Star?" Daddy asked.

"It's not important, Daddy. It's nothing for you to worry about."

When we got back in my room, Colleen asked me what Nadine's problem was. I told her that Nadine was using her to get at me, but for her not to worry because I had a wicked little secret.

"What kind of secret?" Colleen asked.

"Remember I said that I had the pleasure of meeting Percy Hendricks."

"Yeah. We both saw him with your sister last night, but we weren't introduced to him."

"Who said anything about meeting him last night? Girl, I met him this morning."

"How did you meet him this morning? I didn't even know that you left the house this morning."

"Girl, I didn't leave the house. I met him on his way out of Nadine's room."

Colleen had an astonished look on her face.

"That's right. He was in this house, just this morning. Him when *de tek time creep out a de house!*"

Colleen and I started laughing uncontrollably until tears filled our eyes. It felt good to have something over little Miss Nadine's head.

"I came in here to tell you earlier, but you were about to listen to your morning worship service."

"I was wondering why you started asking your father all those questions when you could have asked me. *Gyal, yu crazy, yu knuh.*"

"Not crazy, just smart."

"I wondered why Nadine got quiet all of a sudden, but then I figured that your mother and father were responsible for that when they told her to mind her business."

"Like I said, I'm not crazy, just smart!"

The morning flew by, and I was starting to get extremely restless. I was a little exhausted, so Colleen suggested that I take a nap to relax and to take my mind off the scheduled events.

When I woke up I heard my mother and Colleen talking out on the veranda. Colleen saw me in the screen door and said, "You must have been really tired. I thought you were taking a short nap."

"I was. Why, what time is it now?"

"It's three-thirty. You've been asleep for more than three hours."

"Oh, my goodness! Why didn't anybody wake me? I have to get ready and warm up the food."

"Don't worry, your mother and I took care of everything."

"Where's Daddy?" I asked.

"He went down to the bar, but he promised to be back before dinner. He didn't open up. He said he had some paperwork that he had to complete," Mama answered.

"And Nadine?"

"That young man, Percy, came by for her, and they went for a short walk. He's a nice and charming fellow. I did find out that the reverend is his father, and he is the youngest of five," Mama informed.

Colleen looked over to me, and I knew she was thinking the same thing I was. We knew exactly what was taking place on that short walk.

Colleen and I went back into my room to rest up for whatever was to come this evening. It felt like it was only yesterday that I was trying to come up with the right words to tell Donovan that I was having his baby. Now I was trying to prepare myself for this evening.

Almost an hour had passed and neither Colleen nor I had spoken a word to each other. We were both consumed with our own thoughts. It never even crossed my mind to console her. She had been through so much over the past twenty-four hours alone. She really did have a rough life, and I didn't know how much more punishment she would be able to bear. However, a person can only conceal her true feelings for a short time before those feelings explode. It seemed like God wouldn't cut her a break.

Colleen needed my support today as much as I needed hers, but what could I possibly say or do to help ease the pain? My instincts told me that it didn't matter what I said as long as I was there. I was about to turn to ask Colleen what was on her mind, and she beat me to the punch.

"Girl, you been quiet for a while. Is everything alright?" Colleen asked.

I was stunned, because, after all, her issues weren't small ones. To sum it up; She had a mother that was more of an oppressor than a parent. A man with a secret past in need of reconciliation, who she is absolutely, positively in love with even if she won't admit it to herself. Lloyd was toting a load to put it mildly. If things worked out between Lloyd and Colleen, she would always have to deal with that conniving Hyacinth, which could make Colleen's life with Lloyd a living hell.

Then there was this beautiful little girl Camille caught in the middle of this whole charade. If Colleen decided to continue their relationship, she would need to ask herself if she was ready to become a stepmother.

Age wasn't the issue, because I am pregnant, and I'm looking forward to becoming a mother. My concern was the relationship that Colleen had with her mother. It was so negative.

Colleen is temperamental, fickle, and can become malicious like her mother, if provoked. I've seen Colleen take contenders on the road and while we were in school. She was timid and shy, but she wasn't a pushover. Colleen never sought out trouble, but trouble had a way of finding her.

In the midst of all that was going on in her life, she still had time to be concerned about my well-being. She never ceased to amaze me, and her act of unselfishness was only one of her beautiful qualities.

I steered the conversation from me and back to her. We discussed her present situation. Colleen confided that she had been thinking seriously about her relationship with Lloyd, and she was willing to put up a fight for her man. She felt that Lloyd was her soul mate, and she wasn't going to let little Miss Hyacinth walk in and destroy what they had.

Now this was Colleen's first real relationship with a man and quite personally I wouldn't go out on a limb for someone I hardly knew. Then I figured, there was more going on in this relationship than she was letting me in on.

After a few minutes of silence Colleen got up and began pacing the floor. Then she stood in front of me and said, "Anne-Marie, I don't know what to do. You know that I've never been seriously involved with a man before, mainly because of all the nonsense that my mother used to fill up my head with. I keep hearing her say, "Man will only breed you and leave you" or "All men treat women like doormats." Deep down I don't feel that Lloyd is using me, or would do either of those things to me. But I don't think he realizes the true nature of his situation. I'm glad that his daughter is going to be a part of his life, and I think it was cruel that he didn't get a chance to be involved sooner. But I agree with you when you said you felt Hyacinth was up to no good. I know it's too soon to really tell, but I can see it in her demeanor. Lloyd, on the other hand is blinded by his daughter. What am I going to do? I'm no match for Hyacinth and whatever game it is that she's playing."

I sat back to ponder the situation. If I had my way, I'd approach Hyacinth myself and find out exactly what she was up to, but she probably wouldn't reveal anymore to me than she would Colleen.

"This is only my advice, but I think you should simply give

Lloyd some time to adjust to the new situation. You don't want to put pressure on him, because he may feel like you're trying to come between him and his daughter. Let him be, and continue to be there for him if that's what you want to do. That's your decision, right?" I said, looking over at her at the far end of the bed.

"Yes, I've decided that's what I want."

"Okay then watch Hyacinth, and if you feel that she is up to something then tell Lloyd, but choose your words carefully. Remember she is the mother of his child."

Colleen nodded. We left it at that and got ready for dinner.

Five-thirty had arrived, and everyone was present with the exception of Nadine. She still hadn't returned, and I wasn't about to hold up dinner any longer to suit her. My father, Donovan, and Patrick were sitting on the veranda talking about cricket. Cricket was Patrick's other favorite pastime, and if he wasn't playing, he was betting on it.

My mother was in the kitchen helping me put the food into the serving bowls. She was quiet for the most part only making small talk. Earlier she asked what this big dinner was for, and I told her she would find out soon enough. Since I refused to give her any hints she stopped talking to me, and that was fine by me.

Colleen finished setting the table and putting the food down, so I called everyone inside. Donovan took a seat beside me. My parents both sat on opposite ends at the head of the table, and Patrick and Colleen sat across from Donovan and me.

My father was rubbing his hands together and licking his lips as he looked at the huge spread on the table. Then he grabbed my hand and Patrick's and said, "Let's bless this food before it gets cold."

While Daddy blessed the food, we heard voices outside the screen door. Nadine had returned with her friend. We could all hear her trying to invite Percy inside for dinner; I didn't want her ruining my plans. I could hear Percy declining to my relief. He said that he had to get back home to his family, but he would take her up on her offer the next time. Then there was silence.

"You coming in or what? You're already late for dinner!" Daddy exclaimed.

Nadine came in and sat at the end of the table closest to our mother.

We were midway into our meal when Mama broke the silence by clearing her throat, signaling Daddy to say something. She was still acting silly because I wouldn't tell her what the dinner was about earlier.

Daddy's mouth was still full, but he looked up at me and tried to chew his food faster. Then he rested the knife and fork on his plate.

"So, Star, what did you call all of us here for this evening aside from cooking up this good meal? You running a close second to your mother, girl, with this good cooking."

I smiled and put down my fork. I felt Donovan's legs fidgeting under the table. He used the napkin to wipe the sides of his mouth. Colleen sat attentively as I began to talk while Patrick and Nadine continued eating.

"Well, I have a couple of things that I wanted to share with you all this evening."

Donovan intervened and said, "A couple of things we want to share with you all this evening."

I put my hand on top of his for support as I continued, "Earlier this week I went back to school to get my grades, and the dean of my department, Dr. Ikembe, gave me some really good news. I was preselected for a program to go abroad to complete my medical degree."

I could barely contain myself, because saying it to someone

other than Donovan and Colleen felt so good.

"My, my... I knew you could do it. Going abroad is your dream come true," my father said, smiling from ear to ear. "My Star keeps rising." Then he bellowed a hearty laugh.

"Mmh humph. That sounds great, my dear," my mother said. "So tell us more about going overseas."

"Dr. Ikembe didn't have all the information about the schools available, only a few pamphlets. Six different medical schools accepted me, and from what I understand they are all very prestigious universities. The ones that I've heard of before are Oxford in London, England; Columbia University; and Johns Hopkins. The other three are Harvard University, Howard University, and Meharry. Dr. Ikembe used to be the dean of Howard's medical college and said that it was a predominantly black school."

Patrick asked me which school I was interested in. I told him that I didn't know yet because I still hadn't read the materials.

"My Star, going abroad to become a big time doctor," my father interjected.

"When do you expect the materials to arrive?" my mother asked.

"Well Dr. Ikembe is going to get in touch with me to give me the offer letters along with the incentive packages and the applications for my temporary student visa. The department wants me to visit all of the campuses to assist me in making my decision.

"We're not even sure that Anne-Marie's going abroad yet. Right, sweetie?" Donovan said, giving me a probing look.

"Why wouldn't she go? This is a great opportunity for her," my father said. "You know how many people would die to go abroad, much less go to school—and for free. Donovan, listen man, I love you like you were my own son, but if the relationship was meant to continue, and I'm sure it will, Anne-Marie will be back. It's only a couple of years."

"Maybe there's more to it," Patrick chimed in.

"Actually, there is more to it," I quickly responded.

I looked around at everyone at the table. My parents, and Nadine had an expression on their faces like... what more could there be?

"Well I'm going to come right out with it since there is no way to sugarcoat it. I'm pregnant! Donovan and I are having a baby."

Daddy made a face that I had never seen before, and he dropped his head into his hands. He was speechless. Nadine started smirking. My mother didn't miss a beat as she looked across at my father, "My, my, my... looks like your rising *Star* has fallen!"

Chapter Twelve

An awkward silence fell upon the table. Donovan was holding my hand above the table, and his palms were sweating. The truth was finally out, and I didn't know where to go from here.

I glanced at my father, and for the first time felt I had let him down. He still had his head buried in his hands, and he continuously shook it back and forth. Nadine looked more satisfied than I had ever seen her. It was almost like her prayers had been answered. Then she started to laugh uncontrollably.

"What's so funny?" my father asked her, finally looking up.

"I bet all of you thought that I was going to be the first one pregnant. Who would have thought that I'd live to see this day?" She looked over to our mother as she spoke, and my mother nodded agreement.

"*Just hush. Hush yu mout pikny gyal*," my father replied.

Patrick who had been calmly eating put down his fork to talk.

"No one died, you know. This should be a joyous celebration."

"A celebration of what?" Mama retorted. "Celebrate her pissing her life away. Anne-Marie had everything going for her and now she's ruining her life, please. *She mash up her life, and now she ca'an bada go away ah school. Well me done raise my pikny dem and me nah raise nuh more!*"

"Mama, let me ask you a question," Patrick said, and she turned around to look at him. "Do you really think that Anne-Marie is ruining her life and is a failure because she's pregnant?"

I loved my brother more than ever now. I knew there was a reason that I wanted him present.

"No, because she can always have an abortion. They are much safer now than they were in my day."

My mother was unbelievable, and I was speechless. Colleen looked as shocked as I felt. Donovan gave my hand a little squeeze and turned to speak to my mother.

"Anne-Marie's not having an abortion! She's going to have our baby," he said, and paused for a moment. "This pregnancy is not going to hinder her from her dreams or aspirations of becoming a doctor. She still has the option of going to school right here. Contrary to what you all may feel right now at this table, this pregnancy is a blessing and will make her a stronger person. I'm sure you all know I love Anne-Marie very much, and I intend on doing right by her." Then he turned toward my father. "Mr. Saunders, I know this evening has been difficult for you, but I would like to ask you a question."

He glanced at Donovan and said, "*Gwaan nuh!* Nothing you're going to say now can surprise me."

Then Donovan hesitated and looked around the table. "Mr. Saunders, I would like to ask for your daughter's hand in marriage."

My father's expression changed quickly along with everyone else's at the table. I think we were all stunned, and no one, including me, was expecting a proposal. Donovan pulled a blue velvet box out of his pocket and opened it to display an antique gold diamond ring with pearls. He pushed back his seat and got down on one knee.

"Miss Anne-Marie Saunders, will you marry me?"

If my parents thought the pregnancy was a surprise, this was really a complete shock to me.

I knew what my answer was because in my heart Donovan was always the one. I always felt that we were put on this earth for each other. Still, my heart was racing fast, and I was filled with so many emotions that I couldn't think straight. All eyes were on me, waiting for my answer.

I wanted to respond as I felt my eyes well up with tears, but my tongue felt heavy in my mouth. I lost all of my motor skills. In my mind I was screaming "yes" but my mouth wouldn't cooperate. Couldn't anyone else hear me? *Yes, yes, yes,* I kept repeating. I was fighting hard to move my tongue. Now I was shaking my head to let Donovan know my answer. Finally I felt the first tear free itself from my eyes, and my heart beat joyously.

"Yes," I said finally. "Yes, I will marry you, Donovan! I will marry you."

Then he got up off his knee to grab and hold me for dear life. We both looked over at my father, and he smiled giving us his consent.

Chapter Thirteen

My mother and Nadine were in the kitchen doing the dishes. Naturally they were talking about me, but I could care less, right now I was in heaven.

Colleen was in my room packing to go back home, and the men were in the backyard shooting the breeze.

I stepped out to the veranda to feel the cool night air. It felt so refreshing as it brushed my skin, leaving me with goose bumps. I admired the beautiful stretch of lush green foliage. In the distance I could see the sunset shining off the zinc rooftops of the homes, which would otherwise be buried with the night.

As I sat contemplating my fate, I heard a rustling sound behind me. I turned in the direction of the noise to find my father leaning against the mango tree staring at me.

"Hi, Daddy," I mumbled.

"Hello, Star."

There was an awkward moment of silence. It was almost as if we both wanted to say something, but we were holding back.

"I hope that I'm not disturbing you, but I couldn't help but notice your absence. Tell me what's going on in that big brain of yours."

"To be honest with you, Daddy, several things."

"Star, I'm all ears. Just talk to me."

"My future in general. Things like school, the baby and now my upcoming wedding. It's a lot to deal with in a matter of a week." As my father got closer to me I could see traces of tears in his eyes.

"You know, Star, while I was standing there looking at you, it's hard to believe how fast you've grown. It seems like it was only yesterday that you were my little baby girl. Now you've blossomed into a beautiful young woman. You were always my pride and joy, and you always will be."

I sat there staring and listening to the man whom I called Daddy and loved very much. He was always an amazing and nurturing father, and I wondered what he really thought about me being pregnant. When I announced the pregnancy, a look of horror covered his face. I knew that he expected so much of me, and I felt like I was letting him down.

"It feels as if it was only yesterday that I looked at you for the first time. I remember waiting outside the house back when we used to live on Water Lane. The midwife and your aunt Beverly were inside helping your mother deliver you. Patrick was about four or five, and he was so excited, and Uncle Sammy sat and watched me pace the yard. I prayed while I paced asking the good Lord to bless us with a healthy baby. Dusk began to fall, and you were being stubborn and gave your mother a difficult time," he said, laughing to himself as if he knew something that I didn't.

"Then I heard a loud wailing, and I almost busted the doors down trying to get into the house. There you were in your mother's arms. You were the most beautiful baby I had ever laid eyes on. From that day on I decided to call you Star, because of the brightness that shone in your eyes. I also knew that whatever path you chose to walk down later in life that you would always shine like a star. Now you're going to make me a grandfather. I still can't believe it. I'm not quite over the shock, but I want you to know that I think that Donovan is a good man. I've watched the two of you together over the years, and I couldn't ask for a better son-in-law or husband for my daughter."

"Thank you, Daddy. Be truthful. How do you feel about becoming a grandfather?"

"Honestly you were the last person that I expected to make me a grandfather, like Nadine said. I expected Patrick to come home and tell me *seh him get some gyal pregnant, yu know,* but what's done is done. I'll be a proud grandfather, but your mother on the other hand may not feel the same way immediately. I still have to ask how you two could have been so damn careless? Didn't you think about school? What's going to happen?"

"I'm still going to become a doctor. As a matter of fact, Dr. Ikembe is supposed to come by and drop off the information in the next couple of weeks. He assured me that I have plenty of time to make my decision since I don't graduate for another year. Even if I don't go away, I can still finish up at the university here, but I would prefer to go to one of the colleges that Dr. Ikembe told me about."

"That sounds good, but have you really sat down to think about your new responsibility of becoming a mother? I mean it's not easy."

"Well, kind of."

"What do you mean kind of? You know that having a baby will slow you down. Besides that, how can you expect to go abroad? Do you intend on carrying the baby with you?

"Nothing is definite yet, but I would like to go abroad if I can. I don't think that I would be allowed to carry an infant with me, but if Donovan is willing to help me out I'll be home as often as possible."

"Have you discussed that with Donovan yet? How does he feel about you having a baby and going away to school?"

"We talked a little, and he wasn't too keen on the idea of me going away, so I let it go. But Daddy he has to know how important this is to me."

"I'm sure he knows, and before the baby, I'm sure he didn't mind. Now that a baby is in the picture, it's different. I think that you should probably stay here and raise the baby together."

"Both you and Donovan act as though I'm going to just leave the baby. If I could take the baby with me I would, but Daddy I don't think that's an option. I would like to take advantage of this opportunity. It's a dream come true."

"Well, no matter what happens, Anne-Marie, you will always be my star. I will always be there for you, because I have faith and believe in you. But most importantly, Star, I love you!"

"Thank you, Daddy. Hearing you say that means the world to me."

Chapter Fourteen

I t's amazing to know that people can live on this island their entire lives and never leave the parish in which they live. I have always been fortunate to travel most of Jamaica with my parents, but this was to be my first visit to Negril.

Donovan decided to surprise me for my birthday by taking me on a little romantic getaway. This year my birthday fell on a Friday, so late Thursday night Donovan came by with a traveling bag and a big smile. I had the feeling something was up since he was being secretive all week. But I had no idea that we would be going on a little rendezvous. I was just about to go to bed when he arrived. He came in and led me to my closet and told me to pack a bag, he had a surprise for me and was taking me away for the weekend. I was so excited. I threw on the clothes that I had on earlier and put a couple of my favorite outfits in a bag along with my bathing suit. A few moments later, and I was ready to go. I needed to get away, because my mother and Nadine were getting on my nerves. I was sick and tired of being in the house with them every day and listening to them gossip about everyone and everything.

Apparently Donovan had been planning this weekend for quite some time, because he borrowed his father's car for the trip. Donovan rarely ever drove his father's car. For most of the trip I kept trying to inquire about our destination, but Donovan refused to tell me and insisted that I go to sleep. I was already tired, and it didn't take much to convince me since before long I was fast asleep.

By the time we got to our destination I was so exhausted I didn't know what was going on. All I remembered was Donovan talking to a guy in front of what seemed like a hotel, and everything in between was a complete blur. The next morning I woke up sprawled across a king-size bed, and the first thing I saw were double French doors.

As the day began to dawn, a beguiling mist gave way to the first rays of sunshine. The sky, which was capable of many moods, displayed a brilliant blue. The air was cool, and clear and smelled like seawater while the gentle breeze stroked my cheek. The sea with its crayon tincture and rhythmic waves entranced me as I stood on the balcony of the hotel room.

Donovan was wet as he entered the room swathed in a towel with a breakfast tray in his hand.

"Good morning, beautiful, and Happy Birthday," Donovan said.

"Thank you," I replied.

"Now I can call you my old lady. How does it feel to turn twenty?"

"Nothing's changed," I answered. "I feel the same way I did yesterday."

"How was your sleep?" he asked and gave me a long, wet kiss.

"Earlier this morning I had cramps. Aside from that it was pretty good. I haven't had a relaxing sleep like that in a long time. Having you by my side last night was so good. Do you realize that last night was the first time that we actually spent the night together?"

"Don't worry, baby, soon it will be like that all the time, and I can't wait." He put the tray on the breakfast table and kissed my forehead. "You had cramps again? Are you okay? We should tell Dr. Keene on your next visit."

"I'm fine. It's nothing to worry about. We just have an overactive baby in here," I said, rubbing my stomach. "So what time did you get up this morning?" I asked, taking a seat at the table.

"I got up at about a quarter to seven for some breakfast and a swim. It's beautiful out."

"Now are you going to tell me where we are?" I asked putting a forkful of scrambled eggs in my mouth.

"We're at a hotel."

"Donovan, sometimes you're too funny for your own good. I know that we are at a hotel, silly, but what hotel and where?"

"When you finish eating and get dressed, you'll see. I'll take you on a little tour," Donovan replied excitedly.

"I can't believe you won't tell me where you've taken me."

To avoid any further conversation he got up and headed to the bathroom to take a shower and said, "You'll find out soon enough."

I nearly choked trying to eat my food as quickly as possible. The baby must have been getting a mouthful, too, because it kicked me really hard to tell me to slow it down. The baby's movements were getting more and more frequent lately. My stomach was getting a little pudgier, and I was starting to put on weight. The other day the doctor told me that I was starting to retain water, and I had a slight case of hypertension. It was nothing for me to worry about, but he wanted to monitor the situation. I had some slight bleeding the other day, too, but I didn't mention it to Dr. Keene. I knew of many women that had their periods during their pregnancy, so I felt there wasn't really a need to alarm him. I was eating almost everything listed in the nutrition guide that he gave to me, so I wasn't worried.

Donovan was still in the shower when I was through eating so I got up and stripped myself to join him. It was hot and steamy in the shower, and he wasn't aware that I had stepped in with him because he was washing his hair under the showerhead. I snuggled up behind him and started massaging his chest with my soapy hands. Looking at his body glisten in the water was such a turn-on. He used the cloth to soap my body very slowly, and it felt so good. Then when he was done with my back he turned me around and began to wash the front of my body. Then he rinsed me off and bent down and began kissing me from head to toe. When he got up to my breasts he lingered to caress and suck them. He lifted me up by my waist and held me by my backside. I let myself be taken as he held me under the water. It was amazing. I felt my body beginning to release. Donovan must have felt the same way, too, because before I knew it we were both climaxing.

We got dressed and headed out to tour the hotel together. I did manage to find out that we were at Sunset Bay Hotel in Negril. It was a new all-inclusive resort. When we got to the front desk, Winston, one of Donovan's friends, was standing there to greet us. I looked over to Donovan to see if he was surprised, but from the look on his face he already knew that Winston was working there. I'm sure our large suite was compliments of Winston. It must have been the honeymoon suite, because I've never seen anything like it before.

"Happy birthday, girl! How are you doing today?" Winston asked.

"Thank you, Winston. I'm doing fine. I woke up in a gorgeous room this morning, and Donovan brought me breakfast, so I'm feeling very pampered right now." I smiled and looked at Donovan when I made the remark.

"I'm glad to hear that. We do all that we can to make your stay here at Sunset Bay Hotel a pleasurable one."

"So how long have you been working here at this hotel. I thought you were still working at the hotel in Montego Bay?"

"Let me see…" He paused and gazed up toward the ceiling as if the answer were somewhere up there. The hotel opened up about a month ago now, and both Joshua and I started the second week. So about three weeks now."

"Oh, Joshua is here too! So what is it that you and Joshua do at this hotel?" I asked.

"I'm the manager of reservations and guest hospitality, and Joshua is the senior staff manager," Winston answered.

Donovan chimed in and thanked Winston for the room and got a couple of brochures with the hotel amenities and bus tour schedule for additional activities. I stepped to the side to let them bond and share a few words with each other. Before long Donovan whisked me away for our day of adventure.

By this time it was already noon. As we walked along the beautiful white-sand beach, we passed a few humble cottages and saw fishermen paddling their small canoes to cast their nets. There were tourists everywhere, consuming the beach while eating, drinking, smoking ganja, laughing, playing volleyball, sailing, and surfing. Some even got their hair braided. Others simply laid out sunbathing, many in the nude. Donovan and I tried not to look as we continued to walk toward our destination. I couldn't help but think how happy these people looked visiting our island. In their eyes, I'm sure they think Jamaica is the land of ecstasy. To me it was merely a fool's paradise.

It was a good thing that I wore a white cotton dress, because the sun was scorching hot. We stopped where a man was using his machete to cut fresh coconuts and sugar cane. Donovan bought coconut for himself and sugar cane for me. Shortly after, we finally arrived at a little shack with an awning that read Sunset Bay Boat Ride.

We went on a mid-afternoon cruise that started out very romantic. Donovan embraced me as we stood at the railing on the deck marveling at the cool depths, coral reefs, and marine life under the tranquil sea. But as we got farther out to sea there was a flurry of rolling waves, and I started getting sick. I've never thrown up so much before in my life. The commander of the boat felt so sorry for me that he was inclined to turn the boat around, but I convinced him to continue the trip.

By the time I got back to the room, the only things that I could do were collapse on the bed and go right to sleep. I felt so drained, and I could tell that I was ruining Donovan's plans, but if anything was ruined, it was my birthday.

When I woke up, there was a bouquet of flowers on the pillow beside me with an envelope. Donovan was sitting on the balcony smoking a joint and was unaware that I was up. I hurriedly opened the envelope to see what was inside. Enclosed was a card accompanied with a document from Mr. Miller. I read the card, which expressed sweet sentiments and opened up the piece of paper. It was a deed that read, *This document indicates that ownership of said property belongs to Mr. and Mrs. Donovan Miller.*

Mr. Miller had given us property to build a home. I couldn't believe that he would be so generous to give us land, and for my birthday. As soon as we returned home I would have to thank him. Shortly after I finished reading the deed Donovan strolled into the room.

"Hey, beautiful. You finish resting?" he asked.

"I'm still feeling a little drained, but I'm much better than I was earlier."

"I see that you opened your card. What did you think?"

"I was surprised. That was very kind of your father," I replied.

"He thought it would be a nice gift for us. It's kind of a birthday and wedding gift together. We're going to start building in September."

"Who is we?" I asked in mock surprise. I knew Donovan to be capable of many things, but building a house was an entirely different story.

"Me, my father, your father, and your Uncle Sammy."

"Let's see… today is July twenty-eighth, so you have exactly one month, and three days left. I guess you all have been planning this for some time now, huh."

"Where did you think we were going to live, not under your parent's roof? We are more than welcome to stay at my house, but my father figured since we'll be raising a family that it would be best if we had our own home."

"I'm not arguing with that. By the way, I've been meaning to tell you that I got the materials from the colleges."

"Oh," he said distractedly.

"The package arrived earlier this week. Dr. Ikembe also wrote me a short note stating that he would be passing through Mo' Bay and would stop by Cambridge next week to review the information and help me with my choices."

"Well when he comes, you're going to tell him that you've decided not to go, right?" Donovan asked.

"I never told you that I wasn't going to go. I haven't made a decision yet."

"Well, let me help you, Anne-Marie. *No wife of mine is going abroad*," he bellowed.

"Since, I'm not your wife yet, I don't know who you're talking to. And don't you ever raise your voice to me like that again. That damn weed must have gotten to your head."

"I'm sorry that I yelled, and I'm not going to argue with you tonight. But as far as I'm concerned as long as you're carrying my baby, you are not going anywhere, and I mean that. End of discussion."

"End of discussion, my behind. It's my decision to make, and I haven't made it yet. You make it seem like I don't want to be here to raise the baby. Let me ask you this: how many people are fortunate enough to have such an opportunity? *Wha'pin yu wan me fi just dash it wey. No, mon, I ca'an do dat.*"

"Why can't you understand that we need you here. You've never lost a parent. Both your mother and father had a hand in raising you. I lost my mother, and I don't want our baby to feel that her mother doesn't care."

"Donovan, your mother didn't abandon you. She was sick and she died, and I'm not abandoning our baby, so please get that out of your head. I want you to understand that I would be coming home, but I want to see what else is out there."

"Exactly, Anne-Marie, my mother didn't have a choice, but you do. Why can't you see that? I don't want to do this alone. I love you, and I would sacrifice everything for you and our baby. Why can't you do the same for us?"

"Why won't you give me the chance to explore? The university here cannot offer me what some of these other colleges abroad can. All I want is a chance to do research elsewhere. I want to help our community. The university here doesn't have half the equipment that the ones abroad have. Please, Donovan, give me the freedom to make my own decision."

Donovan sat there thinking for a moment and didn't say a word. He cut his eyes at me and walked into the bathroom. I heard him turn on the faucet. Five minutes later he came out looking refreshed.

"Anne-Marie, you're right. I'll give you a chance to make your own choice. I only hope you make the right one. Are you ready to go to dinner?"

I was happy that he seemed to be coming around, even though I wasn't totally convinced. It still seemed like a sincere effort on his part. I got off the bed to hug him and thanked him profusely for being so understanding, then ran into the bathroom to get ready.

The hotel's dining room was beautifully decorated. The room was laden with ferns and hibiscus. The wicker tables and chairs had red chrysanthemums, which in the language of flowers meant I love you. We sat at a table that had a resplendent view that combined nearly all the joys of nature. There was a bewitching view of the coastline, which was absolutely breathtaking, and if you chose to look westward you could see the sensual beauty of the majestic and gently sloping hills.

The food was served buffet style, and by the time Donovan and I got to the line, it was long. The wait had to be at least half an hour. Donovan went to get the food, and I stayed at the table while the waiter took our drink orders. I got a rum punch for Donovan and Ting, a grapefruit soda, for myself. By the time the waiter came back with the drinks Donovan was right behind him with our food. I looked over at the line, and the person that he was supposed to be behind was still far in the rear. Donovan was grinning like he had done something he shouldn't have.

"How did you manage to get our food so quick?" I queried.

"I saw someone that we met from the boat ride today and made quick conversation with him. He asked me if you were feeling better, and I told him yes, but that you hadn't eaten since then. He remembered that you're pregnant, and he told me to go ahead of him," Donovan said, grinning.

"You think you're slick, don't you?"

"Hey I got us our food quick, didn't I? What did you get me to drink? Then he smelled it and took a sip to taste for himself. "Rum punch. *Dis taste weak, mon.*"

"You know they water it down," I replied. "This king fish and yellow yam looks good. Did they have any soup up there?"

"I didn't see any, but if you want I could go back and check for you."

"No, don't bother. So how long are we staying?"

"Monday morning. Why, are you in a rush or something? You're not enjoying yourself?"

"I was just curious." I didn't want to cause another fuss, but I was really concerned about getting back in time to see Dr. Ikembe. "So I see your father and Ms. Margaret are a real item now," I said, changing the subject.

"Whatever," Donovan replied.

"You're admitting it now. That's a surprise."

"My father and I had a talk, and I can't stop him from seeing whom he wants to see. He's a grown man, but he's probably only after the punanny."

"Donovan, do you really think that Ms. Margaret, the same woman who is always trying to preach the word is giving him some? Let me answer that for you. No!"

"Think whatever you want, but I know that it was Ms. Margaret that I saw strolling around in my father's robe the other morning."

"Oh, shit!" I said.

"My fatha been gettin' dat fi a while now. My fatha nuh easy."

"So did he get her pregnant or what? Why were they at the doctor's office together the other day?"

"He didn't knock her up. My father said something about a tumor or something. I really didn't concern myself too much."

"A tumor, my goodness. Donovan, that's serious, and that's Colleen's mom. We should be concerned."

"Listen I don't mean to be insensitive, but I don't like that woman. She's bad news, and I don't wish harm to her, but I don't want to be in her business either."

"I wonder if Colleen knows about her mother's condition."

"From what I gathered from my father she doesn't know. She's afraid to tell her."

Were my ears deceiving me? Ms. Margaret was sick, and Colleen had no idea. I wondered how long she'd been keeping it from Colleen.

"When we get back, I have to go visit Colleen," I said, snapping back to reality.

"Personally, I think you should let Ms. Margaret tell Colleen herself."

"How would you feel if someone knew something as critical as this about your father and kept it from you. It's not right, and I'm sure Colleen wouldn't turn her back on her mother."

"Can we stop talking about Ms. Margaret and everyone else and celebrate your birthday?"

"Of course we can." I reluctantly agreed to leave the subject alone, but only for the time being. How could we call ourselves

Colleen's friends if we weren't concerned about the welfare of her mother?

By the time the waiters and waitresses came over to sing happy birthday, the mood was dead. My only wish when I blew out the candles was for the day to be over.

Chapter Fifteen

S aturday went by without incident and was actually quite pleasant, but I still couldn't get Ms. Margaret off my mind. When Sunday morning arrived, I asked Donovan if we could leave the hotel later that afternoon. Donovan's original plan was to stay until Monday morning, but Ms. Margaret stayed on my mind for the remainder of the trip, and I was no longer in the mood to celebrate. How could I celebrate? You only get one mother, no matter how bad or mean that person was. Donovan of all people should have been able to relate to that. Especially since that seemed to be the hot topic we quarreled over lately.

As soon as I got myself settled the first order of business was to pay Colleen a visit in Mo' Bay. I loved her more than my own blood sister, and it really hurt me to know that her mother was sick. Someone had to make her aware of her mother's condition. Unfortunately I couldn't go to see her this week, because according to Dr. Ikembe's telegram he was due to stop by one day soon, and I didn't want to take the chance of leaving and missing him.

We were back in Cambridge by six in the evening. We weren't expected to be back until Monday, so when we arrived home the first thing that came out of Mama's mouth was whether Donovan and I got into an argument. Even if we did, I wouldn't share that information with her, so to appease her inquiring mind I told her about the boat ride and how sick I got. That seemed to be good enough for her, because she didn't question any further. I didn't tell her about Ms.

Margaret. The last thing I needed was for her to spread that around, although I knew that my mother would find out soon enough anyway. I wondered how she acquired her information and why people confided in her knowing her track record for gossip.

When I entered my room the first thing I saw was a huge gift-wrapped box sitting on my bed with a card. Beside the box were three different kinds of material of about two yards each wrapped with a bow. A card was between the material and ribbon signed Love, Mom and Nadine. I was more than sure Nadine didn't have anything to do with the card. All the same I appreciated the material. It would come in handy since I needed to make a couple of maternity dresses for the upcoming months. I ripped the gift-wrapping paper off the big box, and to my surprise it was the leather book bag that I asked my father for when I was making his suit. I hadn't given him a description of the bag, but he knew exactly which one it was.

The poem inside the card was beautiful and inspirational as it described our relationship.

> *My Star you are a glow of light*
> *A child born in the midst of night*
> *You've come to me from the heavens above*
> *To fill my heart with joy and love*
>
> *My Star, a growing ball of fire*
> *A dream come true, my life's desire*
> *To have a child who is full of life*
> *Grow to a woman and one day, a wife*
> *My Star, you are Daddy's little girl*
> *No matter what they say*
> *My love for you grows stronger with each passing day*
> *I'll be here for you, so come what may*
> *My beloved Star, have a glistening birthday*

I could feel tears welling up in my eyes. It was all I could do to blink them away. While I was unpacking my bag, my father walked into the room. I wasn't aware that he was home, but it was dinnertime, and he never missed a meal.

"Good evening, Star. Happy belated birthday! Your mother tells me that you got a little sick and decided to come home early."

"Thank you," I said. "Thank you for the bag too. How did you know that was the one that I wanted?"

"Don't you think I know my daughter after all these years? You have my good taste. Now tell me the real reason why you came home so early?"

"Mama told you. I was feeling a little under the weather, and the boat ride didn't make matters any better, so I asked Donovan to bring me back home."

It didn't look like he believed a word I said, and I hated to lie to him, but I couldn't risk telling him about Ms. Margaret either. He might use it as pillow talk with my mother later. It made better sense to me to keep it to myself. Especially since I didn't have the facts straight. Besides that, there were other issues that were bothering me. Donovan was still acting funny about me going away to school. The baby was making me moody, tired, and bloated, and I wasn't able to focus on my studies like I should have been. Dr. Ikembe kept his promise and sent me the materials for the nuclear medicine course that I have to take next semester, and I'd been unable to concentrate to say the least. Sleep seemed to be an issue as well. I could barely get enough of it lately.

My intention was to get up bright and early this morning when the rooster crowed. Unfortunately, by the time I showered and got dressed it was a quarter to twelve. I headed straight to the kitchen to feed my hungry baby and myself. My mother and Aunt Beverly were in the kitchen drinking Guinness Stout. Mama rarely drank alcoholic beverages, but if you placed a cold Guinness in front of her she couldn't resist it. I wondered what brought my aunt Beverly by this early in the day. When I entered the kitchen I immediately knew that they were talking about me from the expression on my aunt's face.

"Good morning, Mama. Good morning, Aunt Beverly."

"Good morning," My mother replied. "How you feeling today?"

"Good," I replied while I walked over to greet Aunt Beverly with a big hug. She returned my hug, but then she disdainfully pushed me off her as if she were upset. I had an idea why she was acting that way, but I figured that if I played innocent and pretended to act like my feelings were hurt she would let me off the hook easy.

"What's wrong, Aunt Beverly? What did I do?" I asked playfully.

"Nuh even bother wid yu good mawnin, yu hear. How comes yu nuh even tell yu big auntie dat yu pregnant?" Aunt Beverly scolded.

It was just as I thought. She was upset because I hadn't told her about my pregnancy. I'm surprised that she was only now hearing it. I thought that since my mother had firsthand knowledge about my pregnancy that more people would have known about it by now. As it turned out she seemed to be keeping it quiet and under wraps. She wasn't being quiet to protect me. She was only protecting herself from public embarrassment. My mother didn't want her family business on the front page of the daily *Gleaner*.

Aunt Beverly and I sat and chatted for well over an hour. There was no escaping her, and I didn't want to be rude and tell her that I had errands to run, so I sat.

In that hour I learned that Dottie and Clifton were rekindling the flames, because Dottie also had a little one on the way, and Clifton quit working at the bar altogether. He took a job helping Uncle Sammy out with his carpentry business, so it looked like there was hope for him after all. He finally realized that in order for there to be progress, sacrifices had to be made.

Eventually my mother went to prepare dinner, leaving and Aunt Beverly and me to sit on the veranda.

"So, I've been seeing Nadine and the Reverend Hendricks' son together a lot lately," Aunt Beverly said once we were alone.

"He comes by almost every day to pick her up. Then they come back really late."

"Well, she ain't the only one that I've seen him with, you know. I've seen him with that girl, Arlene, that works part-time at Mr. Miller's shop and my next-door neighbor's daughter, Pat."

"I'm sure Nadine doesn't know about that. I overheard her talking to my mother the other day, and she really likes him."

"You must warn her, you hear. Things may not be good between the two of you, but that's your sister. Tell her to be careful and that she mustn't put all of her eggs in one basket.

"You would think that since his father is a big time minister that he would lead a righteous life too."

"Anne-Marie, let me tell you something, just because Reverend Hendricks is a man of the cloth doesn't mean that his son is cut from the same material."

"Amen," I replied. "I'll try to talk to her, but you know that she won't believe me. Nadine is already in too deep, and Percy has already been beneath her cloth on more than one occasion."

"That sister of yours is something else *massa,*" Aunt Beverly said. "Didn't they meet at the wedding a few weeks back?" We laughed for what seemed like forever. I honestly didn't mind doing the right thing, but the chances of Nadine believing me were slim. She would think that I was lying to her, and based on our ongoing sibling rivalry, I really couldn't blame her. I told Aunt Beverly that it would probably be best if she pulled Nadine aside and spoke to her.

I wanted to get my aunt's perspective about me going away to school. Aunt Beverly was honest, objective, wise, and, most importantly, unbiased. I'd always dreamed of going away to school though I wholeheartedly understood Donovan's feelings.

"It sounds to me like you and Donovan are being selfish," Aunt Beverly said. "He doesn't want you to leave because of his mother passing when he was little, and that's a valid reason. I know you can understand his pain and where he's coming from. Imagine if you didn't have your mother, and your father raised you. And you can take that look off your face, because I am very serious. No matter what differences you all have, that is your mother," she said as she pointed toward the house. "She is irreplaceable, and you don't always have to see things eye to eye, but she did a wonderful job raising you and has your best interest at heart. Your father didn't do it alone. Faye, cooked, cleaned, washed your hair, and combed it, made sure that you and your clothes were clean when you went to school, and your father worked to make sure that food was on the table, you understand. There was no part-time mother or father involved there. They did it together. It wouldn't be fair for him to be a full-time daddy and you a part time mother. Yes, women have done it for years upon years, but that doesn't make it right. I'm not saying that it can't be done, but it's not fair to Donovan, and most importantly it's not fair to that baby you're carrying.

Everything that Aunt Beverly said was true, and I had known it to be true for a while now, but I wanted so badly to go abroad to take advantage of this opportunity. My aunt must have been reading my mind, because her next words emphasized my exact sentiments.

"I'm not saying that you should give up your dreams, but you asked me for my opinion, and I gave it to you. You have to reassure Donovan that you're not walking out and that your family will provide him with the support that he will need during your absence. Of course before you do that you need to check with your mother and father to see if that is okay. You know that you can count on me if you need to, because I'm looking forward to becoming a grand-auntie, even at my young age." Aunt Beverly had a big smile on her face as she spoke. "Now the way that you and Donovan have been handling this whole situation is wrong. You can't tell Donovan that you're going abroad no matter what he says, and he can't tell you that you can't go. Both of you need to sit down and talk. Try listening to each other and coming to a compromise. If you don't, trust me that baby's future is in danger."

Aunt Beverly's words resounded in my head for that entire week, and I decided to reevaluate my situation. The university was one of the best in the country, but it didn't have an oncology program, and the hospital facilities lacked the necessary equipment. My studies would be somewhat limited, but I would still have a healthy practice if I stayed home.

The following Saturday night my parents, Nadine, and I went to see Roots & Culture at Reggae Sunsplash. The band was hired to open for Ziggy Marley and the Melody Makers, Burning Spear, Musical Youth, and Yellow Man. Patrick came by earlier in the week and asked us to come to offer moral support. The only person that was a little hesitant about going was my mother, and that was because she didn't like crowds. She made an exception this time because she didn't want to miss Patrick's first professional performance. Plus it wasn't conceivable for her to pass up an opportunity to tell all of her friends that her son performed at Sunsplash, had a recording contract, and would soon be famous. She could redeem herself now, one daughter was a failure, the other a slut, but her son was going to be rich and famous. Patrick wrote and sang most of the songs for the group and when he got up on stage to perform, the crowd went crazy. My brother had the women mesmerized and the men envious. He was a hit. I couldn't believe that that was my brother on stage gyrating and strumming away on the guitar. When I use to go see him perform at the local clubs in Kingston the crowd was a little more reserved, but this one was much wilder. It also helped that my brother was very good-looking. When Danny, the other singer, got up front to perform his solo the women screamed, but he didn't have the same effect as Patrick. The women were screaming out Patrick's stage name and trying to climb up onstage, but that wasn't the case with Danny. At one point security had to stand up front to ward the women off during Patrick's performance. I could see that Patrick was living it up and loving every second of that spotlight. My brother surely had a gift to sing and play a guitar. We all used to wonder where he got his musical talent from, and of course both our parents try to take credit. Should the truth ever be told neither one of them could hit a high note no matter how hard they try.

By the end of the night we were all exhausted, but we wanted to wait around and congratulate Patrick and the rest of the band. It was a little after midnight when Patrick came out front to greet us, and he didn't look too happy. We found out that the record producers only wanted Patrick to sing, excluding Danny's solo off the album altogether. It was already established that Patrick was to be the lead singer, but now the producers wanted Patrick to redo Danny's song too. They felt that Patrick had the look and the voice that could carry the band all the way. Patrick said that he expressed his disapproval right away, but the band felt that he was somehow responsible for the sudden change.

When the Artist & Repertoire manager said that he wanted Patrick to sing and everyone else to concentrate on their instruments, he took the guy to the side to reject the idea instead of doing it in front of the group. To make matters worse after Patrick spoke to the manager the guy walked over to the rest of the group and declared that he could care less who played what, but if Patrick wasn't the sole singer they could forget the entire deal. Now the group thought that Patrick intentionally undermined them in an attempt to start a solo career. What bothered Patrick the most was that he and Danny had been friends for years, and he thought Danny knew him better than that. He was surprised that Danny was allowing the other members to sway his judgment. Now the band members were talking about possibly moving on and letting Danny be the lead singer.

Patrick was miserable for the entire night when he should have been celebrating. He wanted the band to work things out with the producers, so that they would keep Danny's song on the album. Unfortunately, he was going to have to wait until the following week when the producers returned from London, but this would give him a chance to talk to the other members and smooth things over. Surprisingly, our mother had said soothing words and even volunteered to talk to Danny for Patrick since she knew him and his family. Patrick declined the offer. He wanted to handle everything himself. My father was upset and wanted to personally speak to the A&R manager who started all this trouble in the first place, but Patrick assured us all that he would have everything under control. At different times Nadine and I tried to console him but he told me the only thing he needed right now was a woman to put his mind at ease. Patrick and I chatted for a little while longer, but I could see that the night had tired my parents out. So when an attractive woman approached Patrick in the middle of our conversation we left him to handle his business.

Chapter Sixteen

The weeks were starting to run into one another. I sat home waiting for Dr. Ikembe, and to my disappointment he never showed. My mother didn't have an encouraging word to say about the pregnancy since our big Sunday dinner. One morning I overheard her in the kitchen with Nadine.

"I've never known your sister to be so simple. That teacher probably doesn't want anything to do with her now. Why can't she see that she's making a big mistake? If she got rid of the baby she would still have bright future ahead of her. Donovan can always wait for her to graduate if he wants to marry her," my mother said to Nadine.

I've come to accept that she's against my having the baby, but she had no regard for my feelings. The fact of the matter was it was my decision, and she was going to have to deal with it whether she liked it or not. Day after day I tried my best to ignore her, but her comments were becoming abusive.

I was even starting to believe that Dr. Ikembe had just given up on me and was probably assisting a candidate worthy of going abroad to complete her medical degree.

The negative and sarcastic remarks were slowly starting to wear me down, and I didn't have a shoulder to lean on. I wrote my friend Keisha from school about the possibility of me coming to the States to attend medical school, but I hadn't heard from her. Then there was still no sign of Colleen. It was about time that I made an effort to go to Mo' Bay to pay her a visit at her aunt Lorna's house. It wasn't fair of me to expect her to visit me all the time. Besides a short break from Cambridge was exactly what the doctor ordered.

One sunny afternoon I decided to take the bus to Mo' Bay to see Colleen. I arrived at Lorna's apartment on Barnett Street a little after three. I remembered that she lived above a restaurant named Rosie's that made the best and hottest jerk chicken and escovich fish I ever tasted. During the school year on the weekends, my friends and I would come all the way from Kingston to eat at Rosie's.

It was late afternoon but the weather was still blistering hot. I decided to go inside Rosie's and sit under a fan to wait for either Colleen or Lorna to get home. I remembered that Lorna was a seamstress and worked walking distance from her apartment, but there were several dress factories in the area, and there was no telling which one she was employed by. I sat at a single table facing the big glass window, which would enable me to see them when they arrived. I ordered a banana-cola soda from the waiter and sipped on it until I spotted Lorna strolling up the opposite side of the street. Lorna was pretty and petite like Colleen, but she wore way too much makeup. Even from the distance I could see the heavy amount of powder and rouge applied to her face. It looked caked on and was at least two shades lighter than her natural complexion. The waiter was about to replace my empty bottle, but I stopped him and paid my tab. I wanted to go outside and meet Lorna before she went into her apartment. It took her a while to walk up the street since her dress was skintight. I was almost positive that the seam of the dress would bust if she attempted to move any quicker.

Lorna didn't recognize me immediately and stepped right past me. It wasn't until I called out to her that she turned around and took another look in my direction.

"Anne-Marie? Is that you, darling?"

"Yes it's me, Lorna. How are you doing?"

"I'm doing well, but I'm tired. I've been sitting at that machine since eight this morning, and I couldn't sew another stitch. What brings you by here today?"

"I'm here to visit my best friend. I haven't seen her in a while."

"Well, come on upstairs. Were you waiting out here long?"

"I've been here for a while, but I waited inside of Rosie's."

"Please excuse the mess in my apartment. I haven't had time to clean lately. That damn job has been tiring me out. By the time I get home in the evening all I want to do is sleep." She opened the apartment door, turned on the light switch, and dropped her pocketbook to the floor. "Whew, I had a rough day, I tell you. The fan at the shop isn't working, and I had to sew bridesmaids dresses today. Can you imagine, and the wedding is this weekend. We got the order in late on Friday, and I don't know why Mr. Walker even bothered to take it on such short notice."

"Why would they wait so long to get the bridesmaids dresses made? Especially if the wedding is this weekend, right?"

"This coming Saturday, my dear. It's my understanding that they weren't happy with the job that the other people were doing. But to tell you the truth I think that the girls in this wedding party are a little difficult to deal with. All they do is complain, complain, complain, but Mr. Walker made sure to get all the money upfront, and it's too late for them to go anywhere else now. Excuse me for a moment while I change out of these clothes."

Then she went into her bedroom and brought the fan out to the dining room. While she was in her room freshening up I saw a large photo album on the bottom shelf of her coffee table. It was an old one, and it contained pictures of Lorna, Colleen's father, and Maisey. The album started out with black-and-white pictures from their childhood; the older they got, the more photos that appeared in color. Then I came across pictures of Ms. Margaret and Colleen's father at their wedding. Ms. Margaret looked young, pretty, and *innocent*, but when she got married Colleen was already born.

Lorna was wearing a frilly bridesmaid dress with a huge sun hat to match. She appeared to be the only bridesmaid in all the pictures that were taken.

I was still flipping through the album when Lorna came sauntering out of her room wearing a light pink robe with matching slippers. She'd taken off most of her makeup and looked so much prettier without it. All that makeup only made her look older.

"I see that you've found my photo album."

"Yes. I hope that you don't mind me looking through it."

"Of course not, girl. If I didn't want people to look at it I wouldn't leave it on the coffee table."

"Can I ask you a question?" I asked, not waiting for a response. "Why are you the only bridesmaid pictured in Ms. Margaret's wedding?"

"Because I was the only bridesmaid in the wedding."

"Really?" I said, surprised.

"Yes, *gyal*, and my brother had to beg me to be in the wedding. Margaret didn't have very many friends back then."

"Then not very much has changed."

"Anne-Marie, don't get me wrong when I say this. Margaret i not the best person in the world, but she's not so bad either. She' always been alone, afraid, and misunderstood."

"What do you mean by afraid and misunderstood, because th Ms. Margaret that I know is as brazen as ever. Anyway, I though that you didn't want her to marry Mr. Rashford in the first place?

"You're right. I didn't want her marrying my brother, but no for the reasons you may think. Margaret and I fought a lot when w were in grade school because she was *fasty*. She had a piece o mouth on her back then, but that wasn't the reason that I didn want her with my brother."

"That was my impression, but if that wasn't the reason, then what was?"

"It was her family that I really disliked, and I didn't want him mixed up with them. There was a time when Margaret and I actually became friends. In that brief time I witnessed things between her mother and father that I knew she would repeat in her own relationship. And it wasn't all her fault, but she didn't know any better. Margaret's father was very abusive, and her mother was very timid. Margaret's mother never fought back when her husband would hit her. As soon as her husband left she would go in Margaret's room and beat the living shit out of her. Then she'd call her all sorts of names. Once right in front of me she told Margaret, *'All di try mi try fi kill yu, and yu wouldn't dead. I try fi dash yu away and yu wouldn't dead.'* She blamed Margaret for all of the problems that happened in their house. I felt so uncomfortable being there that afternoon. Then to make things worse, her mother turned to me and said *'Mek your wrenk friend leave and don't bring no more people over dis house. Friends don't mean you no good, only harm.'*

Lorna's descriptive narrative of Ms. Margaret's parents was sad and horrifying. Now I could understand the reason Ms. Margaret conducted herself the way she did. I wondered if Lorna ever told this story to Colleen. Lorna was right, Ms. Margaret was misunderstood, and I wanted to apologize for being mean to her in the past. My heart really went out for Ms. Margaret. She was carrying around years of deadweight and needed a friend that would show her compassion.

"Lorna, I never knew that. Does Colleen know what Ms. Margaret's been through?"

"We've talked a lot while she was staying here, but we never got hot and heavy over it. Colleen is not the inquisitive type, and she doesn't ask a lot of questions, so if she doesn't ask, I don't tell."

"I can understand that, and it would be better if it came from

Ms. Margaret anyway. Was Ms. Margaret's father any better than her mother?"

"Margaret's father looked very sneaky. He had a string of women, and his wife knew it, but she was too afraid to confront him. I think he use to take advantage of Margaret. Margaret never told me this, but my instincts told me something wasn't right. Especially since she was afraid to be left in the house alone with him. These are the things that made me tell my brother not to get involved with her, but he did love him some Margaret. *He loved her so much he turned fool!"*

"Ms. Margaret had it rough. They say you should never judge a book by its cover, and that's the truth."

"It's true, but that's what makes us human," Lorna replied, shaking her head.

"I'm sure Colleen told you about what happened at Maisey's wedding."

"She told me Margaret created a scene, but it doesn't surprise me. Not one bit. I'm only hoping that Colleen won't follow in her mother's footsteps. We all have our faults, but to live your life like Margaret is unhealthy. Look at Margaret. She doesn't have any real friends. All of her church sisters are hypocrites, and her daughter can't stand her. If she continues the way that she does, she'll always be alone."

"Colleen isn't anything like her mother. At least I've never witnessed her acting like that. She can be stubborn when she wants to be, but she's fun, caring, loving, and friendly. I think she tries very hard not to emulate her mother's habits."

"That's good. I don't see the characteristics of Margaret in her, but I still worry. Colleen has a good heart, but she seems to be easily influenced. It looks as if Margaret sheltered her from the wrong things, but that's another story."

Lorna got up off the couch and smoothed out her robe. Then

she reached across me to put the photo album back under the coffee table.

In the short time that I'd been at her house, Lorna answered questions that ran across my mind one time or another. They weren't the answers that I wanted to hear, but they explained a lot of things.

"I didn't see you at Maisey's wedding the other day, and in your photo album you only have pictures of her when you all were younger. Why is that?"

"Maisey and I had a falling out years ago. She invited me to the wedding, but I didn't want to be bothered. We haven't spoken to each other for more than ten years. I don't even remember why we stopped speaking, seems so long ago."

"Maybe you two should try to put your differences aside if you can't even remember what it was about."

"Girl, one of these days... one of these days, but not today."

I had been at Lorna's well over an hour and started to wonder what time Lorna expected Colleen to come home.

"Lorna, what time does Colleen usually get in?" I asked.

"Chile, I thought I told you. Colleen doesn't stay here anymore. The last time I saw her was last week when she stopped by my job to say hello."

My mouth dropped. I couldn't believe what I was hearing. Colleen wasn't staying at Lorna's anymore. Maybe she moved to Kingston with her father. She did mention that she wasn't comfortable staying at Lorna's because of her little escapades. But traveling from Kingston to Montego Bay every day had to be a hectic commute. Kingston was a two-hour drive from Montego Bay. I couldn't believe Colleen didn't even stop by to tell me that she was moving to her father's. She probably put in for a transfer to at the airport in Kingston. That girl was on the move, and I couldn't seem to keep up with her anymore.

"How long has she been working at the airport in Kingston?" I continued.

Lorna lit up a cigarette and puffed on it for a second. Then she looked at me like she didn't have a clue about what I was talking about. She tapped the ashes of the cigarette into the ashtray on the table, took a seat on the arm of the sofa, and crossed her legs.

"As far as I know she's still working at the airport right here in Mo' Bay," Lorna responded.

"Isn't she staying with her father?"

"*Gyal*, she live right here in Mo' Bay," Lorna said, with a smirk.

"Oh, I didn't know that she got her own place."

"You really don't know. *Pikny, Colleen tek up wid Lloyd. She and Lloyd deh shack up. She nuh tell yu?*" Lorna looked at me and chuckled while blowing a stream of smoke into the air.

Evidently my ears must have been deceiving me, because I couldn't believe a word that Lorna was saying. What was the world coming to? Colleen was living with Lloyd. She'd only been seeing him for a couple of months. She wasn't using the good sense that God gave her. Colleen had to be crazy to be living with a man that she hardly knew. That must have been what Lorna was talking about when she said that Colleen was easily influenced.

"How long has she been living with Lloyd?" I asked, returning to reality.

"I don't know maybe a couple of weeks or so. It was shortly after Maisey's wedding. As a matter of fact, it was the weekend after that." Lorna took her last puff of the cigarette, held her head up toward the ceiling and leisurely blew the smoke in the air. Then she smashed the remainder of the cigarette into an ashtray.

"Do you know where Lloyd lives?"

"No, but it's not too far from here though. I think it's walking distance." Lorna looked at the clock on the wall behind us to check the time. "Listen, it's only a quarter after six, and some evenings

A Fool's Paradise

Colleen don't get off until late. If you run now and get the bus down the road you might catch her."

I really wasn't in the mood to go back out into the blazing sun to catch the bus. If I went all the way to the airport, and she wasn't there then I'd have to wait for the bus again to get home.

"I wish I had the strength to go down there now, but I'm tired."

"Tired? Tired of what? You are a young girl, and you complaining that you're tired. I can't believe this young generation now. You all are just lazy."

"I don't know if Colleen has told you or not, but I'm pregnant. So I tend to get tired quickly, and I've been out all afternoon."

"Anne-Marie, you're pregnant? Well this is news to me. Colleen has not told me a thing. Well, are you ready to become a mother?"

"I'm learning to be ready," I replied.

"And who's the father?"

"Do you know Mr. Miller?"

"Not the same Mr. Miller who owns the shop there in Cambridge? That man is old enough to be your father," Lorna retorted.

"No, Mr. Miller is not the father. His son, Donovan, is the father."

"Girl, you nearly frightened me to death. Mr. Miller is a good-looking and strapping man, girl. I know Mr. Miller very well. I've been after him ever since his wife passed, but he's not ready for this," Lorna said.

I didn't dare reveal to her that Ms. Margaret was already getting the wood. Lorna probably wouldn't believe me anyway.

"Have you ever seen his son?"

"Not since he was little. I don't go to Cambridge often. It's not a place that I really like to visit."

"Well, Donovan resembles his father, but he has his mother's eyes."

"Good for you, girl. You are a woman after my own heart. Just make sure that he's good to you, because you will later learn that looks don't mean a damn thing."

"He's good to me. That's one thing that I can't complain about."

"Good. That's what I like to hear." Lorna got up from couch like she was ready to show me to the door. I got the hint and picked up my pocketbook to leave.

"Lorna, if you see Colleen again, please tell her that I stopped by, and it's urgent that I see her."

"Is everything okay," she asked.

"It's about Ms. Margaret."

"*Wha'pin?* Something wrong with her?"

"I don't want to worry her, but she needs to see her mother. I don't have much information to spare, but she's not doing so well."

"Okay then. I'll be sure to pass along the message when I see her."

"Lorna, thanks for taking the time to talk with me. I know how tired you are from work and everything."

"Anne-Marie, anytime you want to stop by to chat you can. I like you. You are a sweet young lady."

"Thanks, Lorna."

Lorna opened the door and a tall, handsome man who looked to be in his late thirties, was about to knock. Lorna startled him when she swung the door open. The gentleman politely greeted me and briefly stared at me since I was standing in the doorway. Then he quickly turned his attention Lorna. I stepped to the side to let him by. I attempted to say a final good-bye to Lorna, but she was clearly preoccupied with other thoughts for the night.

Chapter Seventeen

Donovan was taking inventory and stocking the shelves when Ms. Margaret came into the shop. He was growing weary of seeing her so much lately. She was either at the house or at the shop with his father. He felt like she was invading his space spending so much time in his home.

At home when he went to the bathroom he would find her pantyhose hanging above the shower rod. She even insisted on washing his clothes and cleaning the house. Donovan didn't want her doing him any favors, so he kept his dirty clothes in the hamper in his room to take to his aunt's house. Donovan loathed putting on airs by giving her a cordial grin from time to time and being polite. He didn't like Ms. Margaret, and his father knew as much. However, Mr. Miller still tried to convince him to feel otherwise. Donovan was also sure Ms. Margaret was well aware of his feelings simply by the way she tried so hard to impress him. Donovan never even acknowledged her kindness with a thank you. Instead he sought after his aunt or he would eat food that he bought.

Anne-Marie told him that this was Ms. Margaret's way of reaching out and that he should try to make the effort for his father. He was still trying to understand what his father saw in Ms. Margaret in the first place. Donovan was convinced that she was working *Obeah* on him. Only witchcraft could explain his father's sudden obsession. Donovan promised his father that he wouldn't be rude or disrespectful, but he damn sure didn't have to like Ms. Margaret.

Donovan was so involved in his thoughts that he didn't even take notice that Ms. Margaret had changed her shoes and put on Mr. Miller's apron, until she reappeared in front of him.

"Donovan, if you want to leave the shop now you can. Your father sent me down here to relieve you for the day."

Donovan wasn't quite sure if he was hearing right. He thought he heard Ms. Margaret say that she would be working in place of Arlene, but he had to have been mistaken. He acted like he didn't hear her and asked that she repeat her sentence.

"Your father had to take your aunt to town, and Arlene is off today, so he asked if I could work in the shop and relieve you until he returned."

There was no doubt in Donovan's mind now that *Obeah* was involved. He already knew that it had to be the answer. Now his father had Ms. Margaret working in the shop. Next she would be running it, but he wasn't going to let that happen. Donovan decided this was minor in contrast to the other things that he had on his mind. He decided to dismiss it and said good-bye to Ms. Margaret. He went to the back to hang up his apron and leave the shop.

It was still early in the afternoon, but he was feeling restless and didn't know what to do for the remainder of the day. Donovan knew if he went down to the schoolyard he would probably find Bigga, Hop, and the rest of his boys that didn't work playing cricket. He really wasn't in the mood to play any games now though. He really wanted to sit down and have a serious talk with Anne-Marie. He was losing his inner strength and could no longer deal with the fact that she still wanted to go away to school. The last time they discussed it was on her birthday.

They were getting into a very heavy argument. But since it was her birthday and he didn't want to ruin the evening, he lied when he agreed to let her make her own decision. Now Anne-Marie was avoiding the subject altogether, but they still needed to resolve the problem and put closure to the issue. Donovan started walking up the hill and got halfway to her house when he remembered that Anne-Marie had gone to Montego Bay to visit Colleen. It probably made sense for him to go and say hi to her mother, but he wasn't really in the mood. He turned around and headed back down the hill. On his way down he saw a man coming up the hill. He knew that he recognized the man from somewhere, but couldn't quite put his finger on it. The man was dressed strangely to Donovan. He had on a long navy-blue short-sleeved gown embroidered with fancy white and red stitching and a hat to match. Beneath the gown he wore pants. The stranger also wore horn-rimmed glasses and carried a briefcase that made him look very studious. When Donovan and the stranger were about to cross paths the man stopped to ask him if Anne-Marie Saunders lived in the house up the hill. He had an accent, and it didn't resemble that of the natives on the island. It was heavy and almost sounded British.

"Yes, sir. She lives right up there." Donovan pointed to a clearing that offered a view of the corner of the house. That's when Donovan remembered who the man was. He was the professor that Anne-Marie had been waiting to see. The last time Donovan dropped Anne-Marie off at the university they saw Dr. Ikembe. As they were driving by Anne-Marie told him that he was the dean of her department.

"Thank you, sir. Are you her brother? She told me that she has an older brother."

"No, I'm Donovan, her fiancé."

"Oh, I don't believe that I told you my name. I'm Dr. Ikembe. I'm one of Anne-Marie's professors and dean of the premedical department at the university. I wasn't aware that she was getting married, but I should have figured that out given her present circumstance. Congratulations!"

"Thank you very much. I recently proposed, and we've decided to have a small wedding before the Christmas holidays," Donovan anxiously replied.

"Is that right. I'm ecstatic for the both of you. I'm sure the two of you make a great couple. Congratulations again! I'd better be on my way to see Anne-Marie."

"Oh, Dr…." Donovan paused, trying his best to remember the pronunciation of the professor's name, "Emkambe"

"Almost," Dr. Ikembe replied. "But it's pronounced *Im-kim-bay*."

"Sorry about that, but Anne-Marie is not home right now. She's out of town visiting a friend."

"Really? I sent her a telegram a while back regarding my visit. I wonder if she received it?"

"She got it, but according to her you were scheduled to arrive the first week of August. She thought that maybe you forgot or that you got tied up and weren't coming. Anne-Marie was here all last week waiting for you."

"My goodness. I'm almost positive that I put the second week, because my summer schedule got pushed back. I must have sent the letter before I found out about my schedule change. This is not good. I really needed to talk to her. I guess I can go up and see her parents. I'd like to meet them and maybe they can give her the rest of this information to review. Can you believe that two additional medical schools have shown interest in Anne-Marie—New York University and Emory University? We are all so pleased with this outcome."

"I can believe it, and we are proud of her too," Donovan responded, trying to sound happy for Anne-Marie. "I'm sorry to disappoint you again, but I was just up at her house, and her parents aren't there either." Donovan was starting to see a solution to his problem, and he was going to take full advantage of it. He thought it over for a moment, and if he played his cards right he could walk away from this table a winner.

"This is a surprising turn," Dr. Ikembe said, and began scratching his beard.

"Dr. Ikembe, my father and I have a shop right down the hill called Miller's. Why don't you come down with me and let me get you something cold to drink. I know that you've probably been on the road all afternoon. You're coming from Kingston, aren't you?"

"Yes, and I'm exhausted. Sure, I'll gladly come down for a drink. Maybe I can relay this information to you," Dr. Ikembe said.

Ms. Margaret was taking care of a customer when they walked in. Donovan led Dr. Ikembe directly to the back of the shop and pulled up a chair for him to sit down at the table.

"What can I get you to drink? We have cola, Irish moss, ginger beer, sorrel, carrot juice…"

Dr. Ikembe cut him off.

"Carrot juice, please. That would be great." He removed a handkerchief from his pants pocket and lightly dabbed the sweat from his brow. Donovan went to the fridge to get the juice that he made earlier that morning. He poured it into a glass with ice and placed it before Dr. Ikembe. Dr. Ikembe drank the entire glass without taking a breath. When he was done Donovan refilled the glass for him, and Dr. Ikembe looked around. Then without hesitation, he proceeded to polish off the second glass

"I see that you liked the carrot juice."

"Thanks, it was very refreshing. The heat made my mouth parched. I wouldn't say no to you pouring me another glass," he added with a smile. "Whereabouts did you say that Anne-Marie went?" Dr. Ikembe inquired.

"She went to Montego Bay to visit one of her good friends."

"It's a shame that I missed her. I will be leaving the island for two weeks, and I wanted the chance to speak with her before I left. I won't be back before the semester starts. Do you know if she's had the chance to look over the things that I sent her?"

"As a matter of fact we both sat down and looked them over, and she would love the opportunity to go to the school that you taught at in the states."

Donovan didn't recall the names of any of the schools that Anne-Marie got information on, and he really didn't care. He did remember that at dinner she told her parents the dean of her department use to teach at one of the colleges she got accepted to.

"Howard University. Yes, she would love it there, but was she considering any of the other universities?"

"Honestly, she didn't. We thought it would be best if she stayed here since she's having the baby. We are in the process of building a new home, and she doesn't want to break up the family," Donovan said, trying to be convincing.

"So are you saying that she's no longer interested in the prospects of going away, because I would hate for her to pass this up without some serious thought."

"That was her final decision. She has decided to put family first. Family is our first priority. I'm sure you can understand that."

"Please forgive me. By no means was I expecting her to uproot and leave her family, but some of the universities may have been willing to accommodate her needs. As a matter of fact I was working something out at Howard University. There was a possible off-campus housing situation that would allow Anne-Marie to have the baby with her. She has so much potential. Anne-Marie was accepted to these prestigious universities based on her thesis about oncology along with her exceptional grades. Don't get me wrong, because she can get a lot of what she needs here at our university. However, she would accomplish a whole lot more abroad with hands-on training and unlimited facilities."

Donovan heard everything that Dr. Ikembe said, but it still didn't change the fact that Anne-Marie wasn't going abroad. No one could understand his pain. He was robbed of a mother, and he refused to let his daughter or son go through the same mental anguish he did. At the same time he was not a fool, and he would play along with Dr. Ikembe, telling him what he wanted to hear.

"Really. If Anne-Marie changed her mind and decided to go for this, how long would she be gone?"

"I'd say approximately five to six years at the very most, but she would be home during the holidays and breaks. In the states they have Christmas vacation and that lasts for about a month. Then there's spring break. I believe that's about two weeks long and then the summer vacation. The summer vacation is the longest and lasts for almost three full months. I'm sure she would have you visit her as well to fill in the gaps."

"That sounds like a strong possibility. I'll definitely see what I can do, but I'm telling you the truth, Anne-Marie was very firm about not pursuing this any further. Prior to the baby she would have jumped at the chance, but now she refuses to see otherwise."

"Donovan, it sounds like you have a very dedicated wife-to-be, and that's a wonderful thing. I commend both of you for staying together to raise your family. You are a good and responsible young man. Not many young people, or old for that matter, can to take the steps that you two are. They fail to see the importance of a two-parent home. Are your parents still together, Donovan?"

"No," Donovan replied solemnly. "My mother died from cancer when I was little. That's partially why Anne-Marie has taken such an interest in cancer research."

"Oh! Is that right? I'm sorry to hear about you losing your mother," Dr. Ikembe said sympathetically.

"It's okay."

"I can definitely understand her passion for the subject now. Anne-Marie is like a sponge. She's always ready to soak up some more information and turn it into something useful. With her brain, the sky's the limit! No matter what road she decides to travel, she will definitely be an asset to her community."

"I know that she will."

"Donovan, I appreciate your hospitality." He took a moment and finished his juice. "Ah, very refreshing. I'd better be on my way. I wish that I could have at least met with Anne-Marie's parents. I may try my luck again to see if they've returned home yet."

"No!" Donovan said, panicked. "I can guarantee you that they won't be home this soon. Anne-Marie's father owns the bar and restaurant down the way, and he and his wife went to town to take care of some business. They won't be back before nightfall." Donovan felt his heart race faster than he could ever recall in his entire life. Didn't this man ever give up or shut up? He told him earlier that they weren't home.

"I'll take your word for it then. If you could please give Anne-Marie these items for me and tell her that I'm sorry, and it's my fault that we missed each other. I must have miscalculated the times."

Dr. Ikembe got up to gather his belongings and held out his hand to shake Donovan's.

"Donovan, I'd like to wish you and Anne-Marie good luck on a successful marriage. You have a beautiful, bright, and dedicated wife-to-be. You are a very lucky man. Be good to her."

"I promise that I will be good to her, and as a favor to you I'll talk to her about the schools again," Donovan promised.

"I would appreciate that. This type of thing happens once in a lifetime."

"I understand, and I'll do what I can, but like I said before, her decision seemed final. Anne-Marie didn't even want to discuss options."

"All I ask is that you give it another try. Perhaps we can postpone the scholarships for a year if necessary, but I need to know as soon as possible. The universities can rescind the scholarship offer if we don't respond, and I want to avoid that should she change her mind. These institutions have an obligation to make sure each scholarship is accounted for and put to use. I'll need an answer sooner than later. I know the importance of a mother being present for the first year. Anne-Marie will need time to wean the baby. Tell her that I stopped by, and I'll be out of town for the next two weeks, but she can leave a message with the office. I'll see her when the semester begins, and please be sure to give her those materials."

"Of course I will give them to her. She'll be very disappointed that she missed you. Especially since she was here all last week hoping to see you."

"By the way, how is she coming along with the pregnancy? Good?"

"Not bad. She had a doctor's visit not long ago, and everything was fine. She had a mild case of hypertension, but we are taking precautions."

"Well tell her to be careful and relax. Take care now," Dr. Ikembe said.

"Okay."

Dr. Ikembe started to head to the front of the store, and Donovan followed closely behind him and when they got to the door he opened it.

"Good-bye"

"Good-bye, Dr. Ikembe, and it was nice to meet you."

"The same here." Dr. Ikembe headed in the direction of his car and Donovan watched as he got in. For a moment he was afraid that Anne-Marie might return and see Dr. Ikembe or that he would spot her coming off the bus, but neither happened. Donovan was home free, but he had several close calls. He had to play the concerned fiancé and patronize Dr. Ikembe for more than an hour. Of course he had no intention of telling Anne-Marie anything, and he would make sure that he trashed the package of information that he promised to forward. He would worry about her finding out about Dr. Ikembe's visit later. Donovan hoped that by then he would have already convinced her to see otherwise. If she felt that Dr. Ikembe gave up on her, maybe she would also give up on the thought and become complacent with the idea of staying home with her family.

All the worrying that he had done earlier was for nothing. It seemed that he finally had his closure and got exactly what he wanted. If Dr. Ikembe didn't get an answer, he would have to reply not interested to the schools, and they would take the scholarship money back. Then Anne-Marie would have no way of going anywhere. It seemed like a win-win situation. Donovan's prayers had been answered after all.

Chapter Eighteen

My summer vacation was almost over, and I was about to enter my last year as an undergraduate. I spent my last two weeks studying nuclear medicine and looking for Colleen, which was becoming a very difficult task.

During my last visit to Dr. Keene I was told to take it easy and relax a little more. Dr. Keene said that there was a slight chance of me developing toxemia in the latter part of my pregnancy. He was concerned because there was a slow rise in my blood pressure, and he noticed an increase on the visit before that one as well.

The arguments between my mother and me were becoming much more frequent and weren't helping my blood pressure any.

The first argument happened over a simple question. I wanted to know if Dr. Ikembe came by during my absence that week or if he sent me another telegram. A yes or no would have sufficed. Instead she had to tell me that I shouldn't worry about any damn professor or scholarship, because my place should be here with my soon-to-be family. We went at it for about ten minutes, until I decided that she wasn't worth expending that much energy. The second argument let me know how little she really cared about me, and my temper could no longer be restrained. I had just returned from visiting Dr. Keene, and my mother was in the kitchen preparing dinner. I asked her to set some food aside for me, unseasoned. Dr. Keene informed me that due to my condition it was necessary for me to eliminate salt from my diet completely. At the time I didn't think that I was asking for much, especially since this would help to keep the baby and myself out of harm's way. She went as far to say, "God gave you two hands and not fins, so cook for yourself." At that point I just lost it, and we went at it long and hard. I said some things that I know I shouldn't have, but there was one comment in particular that struck a cord with her, and there was no turning back from that point on. I told her "If that were your precious Nadine making such a simple request you would be kowtowing to her right now." That didn't sit well with her, because she knew that it was the truth.

My father came home and stopped us from arguing. I was shaking intensely, and I had a headache that wouldn't stop. He tried to come in the room to talk to me, but lately he had been noticeably distant, so I shrugged him off. He must have left to get Donovan, because half an hour later Donovan was by my side. At Donovan's suggestion I packed a few things, and I started spending more time at his house. It's been a little more than a week and I had been at Donovan's ever since. I only visited home during the day to pick up a few things. Occasionally when I stopped by I would see Nadine, and her behavior was rather peculiar. She was actually being quite pleasant throughout the entire ordeal by staying out of my way. I could only wish for the same treatment from my mother. Donovan has been extremely attentive and supportive ever since I've decided to stay at his house. I can't remember him ever being more affectionate and loving, but I'm not going to question his motives. He's been doing a great job of keeping me off my feet. He cooks my meals without salt the way the doctor ordered and makes sure everything that I could possibly need is within arm's reach.

I was lying on the couch in the living room with my feet propped up on the pillow while Donovan tried to repair his father's transistor radio. I had been reading for so long the words were starting to run together and looked blurry. I was unable to retain most of the material I had read in the last half hour anyway since I couldn't get Colleen out of my mind. I couldn't believe that she was living with Lloyd, and she still hadn't come by to tell me, or see how I was doing. When I saw her at the wedding I could sense something was different about her, and I figured she and Lloyd were probably sleeping together. Then I dismissed it, because I knew that Colleen would tell me something as important as losing her virginity. Now I'm starting to see that I was wrong, and I'm feeling a little hurt. I thought we were best friends and didn't hide significant things from each other.

"Donovan, I don't know where else to look for Colleen. She's not living with Lorna anymore. I have no idea where Lloyd lives, and Ms. Margaret's surgery is scheduled for next week."

"Did you try the airport? Didn't you tell me a while back that she worked there?" Donovan replied.

"I went to the airport twice already. The first time they said that she called in sick, and the second time she had the day off. Lorna said that she hasn't seen her since my last visit, but she would give her the message that I was looking for her if she stopped by. This is driving me mad!"

"Remember what the doctor said. You need to relax and put your mind at ease. I don't want you upsetting my little baby."

Donovan stopped tinkering with the radio and came over to my side of the room to rub my stomach. The last two weeks have really been hectic for me, and he's been gentle, sweet, and thoughtful. I also know that we've been getting along so well, because he probably thinks that I've dismissed the idea of going away to school. It didn't make sense to argue about it since Dr. Ikembe never even bothered to show up. Dr. Ikembe's telegram claimed he would arrive the first week of August to review the information and help me with my decision. His plans must have changed, because it was already the third week, and there was still no sign of him. Maybe the pregnancy had something to do with it, and he decided to focus on another candidate. That was probably it, and if that were the case, I was very disappointed in him. He didn't have to lead me on and go to such lengths of sending me a telegram. I almost made my way to the university to try to see him, but the chances of catching him in the office during holiday would surely be a wasted trip. I always thought very highly of Dr. Ikembe and for him to treat me with such disregard was unforgivable.

"Donovan, did I tell you that Ms. Margaret came to me the other day to ask for Lorna's address?"

"No, you didn't. What did you tell her?" Donovan asked, looking at me curiously.

"Well, as you can imagine I was shocked that she even would ask me, but I told her that I didn't know the address. I don't want her to find out that Colleen doesn't live there anymore. That's why I'm trying to find Colleen first."

"So, *wha'pin*?"

"She told me that she really needed to reach her, and it was urgent. I told her

that Colleen works at the airport, and she should go there."

"My father drove her to Mo' Bay the other day, but I didn't ask if they saw Colleen. I haven't heard them talk about it since, so maybe they saw her," Donovan replied.

"I wonder if she did find her? *When she come home dis evening I gwaan ask her*," I said.

Benjamin Miller was adding up the receipts and money for the day while Margaret folded material to return to the shelf. She had been quiet for most of the afternoon, which was unusual for her. Benjamin didn't say much to disturb her. He knew she had a lot on her mind and didn't want to add to the problems. Margaret finished folding and stacking the material and turned around to look at the clock on the wall to check the time. It was five minutes to nine. It was time to close up the shop for the night. Margaret started walking toward the door to put the lock on when Clifton and Dottie entered the store laughing and acting giddy. Margaret stepped to the side to let them in.

"Hi, Ms. Margaret and Mr. Miller," they blurted out clumsily as if they both had one too many to drink.

Margaret stepped back to take a good look at them and replied by waving her hand at them. Then she started fanning her hands in her face, because she could smell the liquor on them. She thought to herself, *when will they learn?*

They didn't pay her too much attention and headed toward Benjamin.

"Mr. Miller, *whap'in, mon?*" Don't tell me you locking up the store. Dottie and me just started to celebrate, and it's still early in the evening, *mon.*"

"Good evening, and to answer your question, Clifton, I close my shop at nine every Sunday evening. The shop hours are posted on the front door. Now if it's alcohol you seek, you know I don't sell any here."

"Who said anything about alcohol? We came by to share our good news." Clifton retorted. Dottie stood there blushing like a schoolgirl.

Benjamin put the receipts and the money away a tin box and turned his attention back to Clifton and Dottie.

"What good news do the two of you have to share?" Benjamin asked.

Clifton pulled Dottie by the waist to bring her closer to him, and she looked at him and smiled.

"Mr. Miller, me and Dottie are getting married. This smart and beautiful woman has agreed to be my wife."

Margaret stood in the background and grunted "idiot woman" under her breath. Benjamin had a feeling that she said what he was thinking, but he kept his thoughts to himself. He spoke loudly to divert their attention back to him since they turned to look at Margaret when she grunted.

"Well, I guess I should congratulate you both on this happy occasion. Congratulations!"

"Thank you, Mr. Miller. We really appreciate it," Clifton responded.

"It smells like you two have been celebrating all day," Margaret said.

"Actually, I had one drink, and Clifton has been very good. He only had one beer, and a glass of rum and Coke. It was mostly Coke though, I made sure of that," Dottie said.

"That's good, Clifton, so you been cutting back?" Benjamin said.

"That's right. It makes my lady happy, and I plan to make Dottie a very happy woman. I can't live without her. My life is very, very miserable without her." He grabbed Dottie by the waist and began to affectionately nuzzle her neck.

"So what can I do for you this evening before I close up for the night?"

"My lady wants to look at some material for a wedding dress, and I know that you usually carry the best fabric in the area."

"I really don't think I have anything appropriate for a wedding dress in right now, but I can order something nice for you. We already put the fabric away since we were about to close," Benjamin said.

"I don't want to wear white even though it is my first wedding. I'm looking for something off-white," Dottie replied.

"I'll see what we can do for you in the next couple of days. What's the date you're looking at?"

"The date?" Dottie replied and looked at Clifton. "We didn't set a date yet. How silly of us."

They both laughed like it was the funniest thing in the world.

"Like I said, I will let you know what I find in the next couple of days. We really are in a rush and would like to lock up now," Benjamin said.

"By the way, Ms. Margaret, do you still sew? I was hoping that maybe you could be my seamstress," Dottie said walking over to Margaret who was still standing guard at the door.

"I haven't sewn a wedding dress or bridesmaid dress in years. I only sew the children's school uniforms. Other than that I really don't do that sort of thing anymore," Margaret replied, distastefully.

"If you would please think about it. I don't need anything fancy because we're having a small wedding. The wedding party will consist of my sister, and Trevor will be the best man."

"I'll think about it, but I'm not promising you anything," Margaret said, to pacify Dottie in the hopes that they would leave.

"I appreciate it. It would mean a lot to me."

"I'll think about it, Dottie. I may have some other obligations that prevent me from taking on other projects. So we will see."

"Good night and congratulations again. I'm happy for both of you," Benjamin said as he walked them to the door.

"Thanks," Clifton replied. "See you around, Ms. Margaret, and take care of yourself. Listen, Mr. Miller, so when you and Ms. Margaret going to tie the knot?"

"We have a long time for that. We're taking it slow, you know. You can't rush a good thing," Benjamin replied.

"I hear you. Why buy the cow when you can get the milk for free, hmm?"

"What is that suppose to mean?" Dottie snapped.

"Not you, baby. I love you. Come let me show you how much love I have for you."

Benjamin watched as they left hand in hand giggling like school kids, and couldn't help but think about what they were about to do. The mere thought of sex got him aroused, especially being with

Margaret. He hadn't made love to a woman since he began seeing her. She spent the night all the time now, and he liked having someone there, but he needed more. She kept pressing her warm, shapely, and firm body on him night after night, and his needs weren't being met. Benjamin didn't know how much longer he would be able to handle the pressure. Before he and Margaret became an item he took care of business regularly. Now he was in dire need of giving and receiving passionate pleasure or he would soon end up with blue balls. Benjamin wasn't the type to take matters into his own hands either. He and Margaret attempted to gratify each other, but the fibroids on her ovaries made it very painful for her. The fibroids were causing a lot of complications lately, including mood swings. However, he decided to stick with Margaret through the ordeal in the hopes that things would get better. He knew that it had to be hard for such a young woman to have a hysterectomy.

"Margaret, you ready to go?"

"Give me one minute. Let me grab a cold soda from the fridge in the back."

Benjamin started turning off the lights and took the keys out of his pocket to get ready to lock up the doors.

"That's fine. Can you lock the back door while you're in there, please?"

Margaret grabbed her pocketbook, and soda and put the locks and chains on the door. She met Benjamin at the front door, and they walked out together.

The sound of their feet hitting the dirt pavement was the only noise to be heard. Benjamin stopped walking and stood in place. Margaret was so preoccupied by her thoughts that she was unaware that he was no longer by her side. She took a couple more steps before she noticed and turned around to see him standing a few paces back.

"Miller, what's wrong? Why did you stop walking?" Margaret asked.

"You tell me what's wrong? You haven't said a word all day, and I'd like to know what's on your mind."

"Nothing's on my mind. I'm okay."

"Something is on your mind, and I want to know what it is. Are you still concerned about the surgery? Are you worried about having more children? Talk to me, Margaret."

"Children? No. Did you want more children?" Margaret asked, alarmed.

"Not really. I'm looking forward to being a grandfather right now, but this is not about me. Tell me, is it because you still haven't been able to contact Colleen?"

"No, but that is bothering me too."

"Then we can make another trip out to the airport if you want. I know that you want to clear some things up with her, and the sooner the better."

"I agree, but that's not what's bugging me right now."

"Then what is it? Help me out, because I'm running out of ideas."

"It's nothing really. Forget it," Margaret said, and began to walk off.

"Forget what?" Benjamin said, flailing his hands in the air to express his impatience. "Margaret, I'm not going to ask you again, so please tell me."

"It's about Donovan."

"What about Donovan?" Benjamin asked

"I don't want to cause any problems between you and your son."

"You won't cause any problems. Now tell me," Benjamin said.

"It's not that easy. You and Donovan have a wonderful relationship. He loves you very much, and I know he's your pride and joy. The thing is Donovan is still not very accepting of the fact that you and I are together... and, Miller, don't lie to me."

Benjamin had his mouth open prepared to come to his son's defense. Instead he decided to hear Margaret out, because he would be lying if he said otherwise. Besides this was the most she had said all day.

Margaret continued, "He can't stand me, and that's understandable. I know that I haven't been the nicest person, and I have to live with that, but being with you these past couple of months has really enlightened me. I see the value of a strong relationship and bond between a parent and a child, and I don't want to damage what you and Donovan have."

"With all that said, are you going to tell me what's bothering you and let me decide for myself on how to work things out with me and my son," Benjamin probed.

"Fine, since you insist, here's the story: Two weeks ago Monday, a man stopped by the shop asking me for directions. It turns out that the man was Anne-Marie's teacher from her college."

"Why would that cause problems between me and Donovan?"

"Your son brought him down to the shop. They sat in the back, and they talked a while."

"What's so strange about that?" Benjamin asked, starting to get really impatient.

"I don't want you to think that I was eavesdropping, but I overheard a couple of things, and…" Margaret paused to arrange her thoughts.

"I'm not going to pry it out of you, just finish the story."

"Well the teacher said that he came to help Anne-Marie with some paperwork. Anyway she wasn't home, so Donovan brought the man back down to the shop. He told the teacher that Anne-Marie decided to stay here instead of going abroad because of the baby."

"Is that it? Maybe the girl made up her mind to stay here with Donovan and the baby. Nothing was ever written in stone that she was definitely going away. That's nothing to worry yourself over. Is that everything?" Benjamin asked.

"I bumped into Trevor on the road the other day, and you know how he loves to talk about his *Star*. He told me that Anne-Marie still didn't make up her mind about school, but the professor that was supposed to help her out never even came by."

"Is that so? Was this before or after the professor came by?"

"After, and I didn't tell him about the professor coming to town. I really didn't start to put two and two together until Trevor walked away. I feel so bad. Anne-Marie is a very nice girl. I always thought that she had a good head on her shoulders. Now that she's been staying at your house, we talk from time to time, and I really like her."

"None of this is your fault, but I will have a talk with my son," Benjamin assured her.

"I don't want him to know that I was listening. Please don't involve me. He can't stand me as it is. I don't need to be the cause of any more confusion."

"Don't worry about a thing. I think that after all these years I know how to handle my son. I really can't believe that he would do something like that deliberately."

"I was surprised myself, but I figured that I better mind my business. Then I started feeling bad, because Anne-Marie's been very kind and pleasant to me. Sometimes we talk, and I know she is very disappointed about the whole school business. I would hate for her to miss out on a dream."

"Margaret, don't you worry about a thing. You made the right decision by telling me, and I will certainly deal with Donovan in my own way."

Benjamin stood with his hands in his pockets and shook his head in disbelief. He raised his son to behave better than that. Donovan couldn't possibly have a legitimate reason for betraying Anne-Marie's trust. Poor Anne-Marie, he thought to himself. That poor girl didn't know the wool had been pulled over her eyes.

Chapter Nineteen

A couple of days passed before Mr. Miller was able to get Donovan alone to talk about what Ms. Margaret had shared with him earlier that week. Donovan never left Anne-Marie's side. They seemed inseparable. If it weren't for Keisha, Anne-Marie's friend from college, stopping by to pay her a visit Mr. Miller would never have had an opportunity to get Donovan alone. When Keisha arrived, Donovan politely left to give Anne-Marie and Keisha privacy to chat. At first they sat inside, but Mr. Miller encouraged them to go outside to enjoy the nice weather. Keisha was more than happy to oblige, because the house was not air-conditioned like her home in the United States. She complained that the fan was only blowing the hot air around. Anne-Marie was used to the heat, but didn't mind getting out of the house for a while and happily followed.

Mr. Miller headed to Donovan's room and knocked on the door. Donovan invited him in, and he took a seat on the chair beside the bed. Donovan was sitting on the edge of his bed folding the clean clothes that his aunt washed for him the day before. Mr. Miller wanted his undivided attention so he waited patiently for Donovan to finish.

Mr. Miller took a brief look around the room. He could see subtle changes that suggested a woman now shared the room with his son. Small things like the doilies and the figurines meticulously placed on each side of the dresser. Framed pictures of flowers in vases and a picture of the countryside replaced the posters of Bob Marley, Sugar Minot, and Yellow Man that once graced the walls. Although Mr. Miller was still a little perturbed with Donovan, he was still proud of his son's wise decision to make Anne-Marie his wife.

Anne-Marie Saunders, a smart, outgoing, strong, and caring young woman was about to make him a grandfather. The thought of it provoked an urge to smile that was too powerful for him to resist. These last couple of months gave his life new meaning. It wasn't that long ago when Donovan prematurely made him a grandfather before. Mr. Miller sighed a breath of relief to himself, because that was over. This pregnancy with Anne-Marie was also a little premature, but it was also a blessing. Anne-Marie had a good head on her shoulders, and this would only be a minor setback for her. He also sympathized with his son's devotion to Anne-Marie, but he disliked Donovan's possessive behavior. He taught Donovan the right way to pursue a relationship, and that involved trust. Donovan's recent actions were far from trustworthy. He was betraying the most sacred element essential to a successful relationship. Mr. Miller felt the need to do an early intervention to save Donovan from a potential disaster. He couldn't stand to bear witness to such wrongdoing, and this blatant act of dishonesty went against everything that he believed. Donovan couldn't possibly think that he could enter a marriage based on lies. Once you started to lie, it was a never-ending circle. One lie begat another lie to cover up the original one, and the pattern continued. Son or not, he was going to find out the truth from Donovan. If Ms. Margaret was right, and Mr. Miller was almost certain that she was, he planned to set Donovan straight. He realized that he had to be careful in the way that he approached the subject. He didn't want to start off accusing Donovan. Mr. Miller didn't want any offense/defense tactics even though it would be inevitable.

Donovan was rolling up the last pair of socks, and he got off the bed, took a few steps backwards, aimed and shot the balled-up pair of socks into the drawer like it was a basketball hoop. When he made the shot he held his hands in the air and looked at his father with a big smile.

"I still got it, Pops," Donovan exclaimed as if he achieved a major accomplishment.

"So I see. You're quite the superstar. I always knew that you had it in you," Mr. Miller said, humoring him.

They didn't say much after that, and Donovan was short on things to say or do. Donovan knew that something was bothering his father, but he thought that it had something to do with Ms. Margaret. Donovan linked his father preoccupation to the fact that Ms. Margaret was due to undergo surgery soon. He was actually a little curious about what the operation was for. Anne-Marie finally managed to peak his interest by bringing it up almost daily, but he wasn't going to ask his father unless he brought it up. Donovan realized that whatever it was could be rather sensitive, so he didn't want to push it. Especially since his relationship with his father seemed to be strained over the past couple of weeks. It was almost like walking on eggshells, and Donovan knew that it was partially his fault.

Mr. Miller had genuine feelings for Ms. Margaret, and all he asked of Donovan was for him to be respectful and pleasant toward her. At the time it seemed like his father was asking for a lot, so he gave him hell over it. Donovan knew that he was being harsh on his father and should have been elated that he was able to find happiness after all these years. After all, his father was extremely supportive when he told him that Anne-Marie was pregnant and he wanted to marry her. Mr. Miller never turned his back on him in his hour of need and here he was being selfish. He even gave them a deed for land as an early wedding/birthday gift.

Donovan realized that he wasn't the one that had to be with

Ms. Margaret. In all honestly she had never done anything to him personally. Sure she spoke to the youth in a condescending tone, but most adults did. She wasn't the only person guilty of that. It really had more to do with the way she treated Colleen.

Mr. Miller was right, he was being too judgmental, and people could change. It was very wrong for him to think that Ms. Margaret was incapable of reform. Donovan wanted things to get back to normal between him and his father, and he was committed to making that happen. He decided to break the ice.

"How is Ms. Margaret feeling?" Donovan asked.

"She's doing okay, considering you know. Her surgery is scheduled for next week. I'm surprised you asked."

"Honestly, I hope that everything goes well for her."

"It will, I'm not too worried about it. While we're on the subject of health, how is Anne-Marie doing with my grandbaby? No more complications, I hope."

"She's doing much better. I've been making sure that she stays off her feet and cooking for her every day. I want to make sure that nothing goes wrong."

"That's good, and I'm glad to see you're taking such good care of her. That's what a man's supposed to do—take care of his woman, and if that means cleaning her bedpan, then so be it. Don't let these chores make you feel like less of a man either, because it takes a real man to stand by his woman."

"Pops, you don't have to tell me that. I enjoy taking care of Anne-Marie. She's taken care of me ever since we were small. I was always her favorite patient."

"I'm sure you were," Mr. Miller said, trying to imply a different kind of patient, and Donovan caught on right away. Then they shared a hearty laugh together.

"By the way, how is she getting along with her mom? Did they make up yet?"

"Well she goes over there every other evening to pick up books or clothes and mail. I think she's hoping that her mother will apologize. Pops, you know Mrs. Saunders is not the type of person to apologize even when she's wrong. Mr. Saunders on the other hand has stopped by almost every evening begging for Anne-Marie to come home. He tries to apologize for his wife, but Anne-Marie wants to hear it directly from her mother. I tell you one thing though, Mr. Saunders loves his Star. He comes over here showering Anne-Marie with gifts and sits here talking with her for hours, but the one thing he can't control is Mrs. Saunders' mouth."

"Faye is human, and I think that she wants to give in, but she's too stubborn to come out and admit that she's wrong," Mr. Miller added.

"You always manage to see the good in people, but Pops I think you're wrong this time."

"You think your old man is wrong? Why?"

"When Anne-Marie stops by the house her mother barely says two words to her. She doesn't breathe in her direction, much less ask how she's doing, and Anne-Marie is a little hurt. Things have never been this bad between them, and it doesn't seem like Mrs. Saunders is concerned."

"Trust me, son, Faye is very concerned. She came by the store the other day pretending to shop. I say pretending because she walked around the aisles for about ten minutes, but I didn't really pay her any mind. Finally she came up to the register and asked me if I had mackerel. Now Faye knows damn well that I don't sell mackerel, saltfish, or any other kind of fish. The fish use to smell up the entire shop, so I stopped carrying it. Anyway that's when I knew she didn't want anything from the store, but she did want some sort of information. Finally she asked me if Anne-Marie was holding up okay and how we were managing at the house."

"You're kidding?" Donovan said, surprised.

"No, not at all. Then I told her what I knew, and she seemed pleased. Then she thanked me for taking Anne-Marie in, and said to tell her that she could come home whenever she wanted to. If she's waiting on me to tell Anne-Marie, she'll be waiting for a while. I'm not a messenger," Mr. Miller said sarcastically. "Faye needs to stop playing the fool and talk to her daughter."

"I can't believe that she said Anne-Marie could come home whenever she wants. Anne-Marie goes there all the time, and she never says a word to her. It's really hard to believe, and if you told Anne-Marie, she would probably think that you were making it up."

"All I'm saying is, don't think for one moment that Faye's not concerned. She is, and her conscience is riding her bad. It wouldn't surprise me if she gave in soon."

"It sounds like it, but you really have to see how she acts when we go over to the house." Donovan said.

"She has a problem expressing herself and her feelings. Margaret has the same problem, but she's learning, and I'm going to continue to help her as long as she needs me to."

"I'm glad that you're there for her. You're a good person, Pops!" Donovan thought that Ms. Margaret could use all the help that she could get, but he was willing to be sympathetic if it appeased his father.

"I'm glad to see you're coming around son. Always remember it's not our place to judge, and not everyone is a lost soul."

"Like you always say, where there is hope there is promise. Right, Pops?"

"True, always remember that. Donovan, seriously how is Anne-Marie really doing, and be honest. Has she been back to see Dr. Keene lately?" Mr. Miller figured he would casually ease his way into the conversation and let it take its course.

"She's doing a lot better since she's been staying over here. I see to it that she has everything she needs and gets plenty of rest. Of course like I said before she's still vexed over the thing with her mother, and I do what I can to take her mind off it. She was really depressed this week over not seeing Colleen, so I am really happy that her friend Keisha is here."

"I haven't heard her mention anything about going away to school again either. She still hasn't heard anything from her teacher?"

"He sent her a letter saying that he was coming the first week of August, and Anne-Marie waited and waited, but he never came. I guess she's not interested anymore. She hasn't brought it up, and I'm not going to encourage her either. Honestly, if it were up to me, Anne-Marie would stay right here with me and the baby like I told you before."

"Like I told you before when you first came to me for advice, you can't keep her locked up. You have to let Anne-Marie follow her heart, and if her heart tells her to stay here, that's great. If her heart tells her something else you have to deal with that too. Anne-Marie has to make her own decision, and she needs you to be there for her."

"Pops, that's what I'm doing day in and day out. I'm here cooking, cleaning, and being the man that you taught me to be. I support whatever she wants to do."

"And you're letting her make her own decision about going away to school?"

"Pops, of course I am. Why do you ask?"

"All I'm asking you is did Anne-Marie hear anything from her teacher?"

"I told you that she didn't hear anything from him. Do you think that I'm lying about something?"

"Are you? Because I've heard differently."

Donovan could feel his heart racing, and he took a deep breath. He couldn't believe that the bitch snitched on him. She actually told his father that Anne-Marie's teacher was there. She was even more conniving than he thought, but it didn't matter because who was his father really going to believe? His son or some woman that recently stepped into his life? Even if it were the latter he would simply deny it all.

"I can't believe you're accusing me of lying. Why would I lie?"

"That's exactly what I want you to tell me, because I would never raise my son to be a liar, much less hurt someone he loves. I told my son not long ago that it's okay to love, but not to smother or suffocate that person to death. You have to leave room for a person to breathe, grow, and bloom. People are not possessions and cannot be treated as objects or animals where you can control their every move."

"I know that, Pops, and I'm not trying to control Anne-Marie's every move, and I'm not being possessive either."

"Really? Then why haven't you told her that her teacher dropped by? Why does she think that he's forgotten about her, and why are you still standing here telling me lies?"

Donovan raised himself off the bed, and Mr. Miller stood. Donovan didn't know exactly what he had in mind when he decided to stand, but he regretted it right away. His pride wouldn't let him back down, and he remained standing.

"I don't know who told you what, but I'm not lying about anything. The person who told you that is a liar and trying to cause trouble." Donovan felt his voice rise with each word. He was standing only inches away from his father, and he never realized how much bigger his father was than him.

Mr. Miller had one arm across his chest while the other hand gently massaged his chin as he listened to his son. He was growing tired and refused to subject himself to these flagrant lies.

"Donovan," Mr. Miller said in a serene tone, "I suggest you have a seat and lower your voice."

Donovan was at his peak, but knew better than to challenge his father and immediately sat back down.

"Now I know that a man came to town the other day looking for Anne-Marie, and if I'm not mistaken, he was from the university. And for your information, my source has nothing to gain by lying about Anne-Marie's teacher coming to town. You on the other hand have a lot to lose. You have good intentions, but your motives are wrong. I'm starting to lose my patience, so I'd appreciate it if you would stop the lies at once. Now you have two choices: You can either find a way to tell Anne-Marie the truth or you can let me tell it for you. Don't doubt me, because this has gone on long enough now. Do you understand?"

Mr. Miller didn't wait for a response, he simply exited the room and shut the door behind him. He left Donovan fuming with his thoughts.

Donovan felt no remorse for his actions, because he wouldn't allow himself to see the error of his ways. He wasn't about to rest the blame on himself either, because he did what was necessary to protect his family. He was angry that Ms. Margaret decided to open her big mouth. He hated her to begin with, and if this ordeal had a negative outcome she would definitely be the one to blame. If Ms. Margaret thought that he was being difficult and uncooperative before, she could go to hell. She had only begun to feel his wrath.

"Keisha, I'm so happy that you came by to see me. How did you know where to find me, and what brought you back to Jamaica so early? We still have two weeks before the semester begins," I said.

"Girl, one question at a time. I'm staying with family in Montego Bay until school starts, and I remembered where you lived. Did you forget that I came home with you twice before, and your sister told me where to find you. I was really hoping to run into your cute-ass brother, but I guess my luck ran short. Anyway, when I got your letter, I was ready to come back right then. I wasn't doing much at home anyway. I didn't get a job this summer, because my father wanted me to catch up on my studies. He made me take a couple of summer courses at NYU, and I met some fine men while I was there, but what kind of relationship can I possibly keep when I'm more than two thousand miles away for most of the year? Some summer vacation! Anyway enough about me, tell me about the scholarships that you got and stuff. Girl, I'm so excited that you're coming to the States!"

Keisha was even more excited than I was when Dr. Ikembe first told me the news. She was what we called a real *Yankee gyal*. She was full of energy and talked a mile a minute, but that's what I liked about her. She was average height, attractive, but not immensely pretty, but her body and long hair more than made up for her anything that she lacked in the looks department. Keisha didn't have any problems finding men. She was overly animated and never let a bad situation get to her. Keisha was always able to see the bright side to things. I really needed her positive energy right now.

"Well that's not the only news that I've got for you. I'm not too sure that I'll be coming to the States anymore."

"Anne-Marie, what in the world are you talking about? In your letter, you said that Dr. Ikembe submitted your application for the foreign-exchange program and that you got accepted to like six schools."

"He did, and he sent me a telegram that said he was coming to Cambridge. Dr. Ikembe was supposed to come visit me two weeks ago, but he never showed, and I think I know why."

"First of all, girl, that does not sound like Dr. Ikembe. He is a man of his word. If he says that he was gonna come by, and he didn't, then something mega major must have happened. Second, what makes you think that he would up and change his mind out of the blue? Why would he go through the trouble of getting you accepted into all these schools and then forget about it?"

"I wanted to tell you in the letter, but I'm pregnant, and when Dr. Ikembe told me about the scholarships and the program I mentioned it to him."

Keisha's mouth fell open. We stopped walking, and she grabbed my forearms with both hands and shook me numerous times in jubilation.

"Anne-Marie," She exclaimed. "Oh, my goodness. Get the hell out of here, girl. Little miss thang is pregnant. Holy shit, I can't believe this. What did Dr. Ikembe say when you told him that you were pregnant?" Keisha asked, doing a jig.

"He was a bit surprised to say the least, but he said that he would try to postpone the admittance date and work something out for me. But why should he go through all this trouble for me? I think he didn't want to hurt my feelings and only said what he thought that I wanted to hear."

"Anne-Marie, bullshit! You are going to be either valedictorian or salutatorian at graduation. He better go all out for your ass! What I don't understand is why you told him? Are you planning on keeping the baby?"

"I don't know about any valedictorian or salutatorian. My GPA isn't a perfect 4.0, and you have couple of people with perfect GPA's. And to answer your question, of course I'm keeping the baby."

"I would, too, if my man was as fine as yours. Girl, he looked good in that T-shirt and those khakis. Dark chocolate with those pretty eyes and that crooked smile. I see why you don't bring him up to school often. *Mmh-mmh-mmh*!" Keisha uttered, fanning herself to show how hot Donovan made her.

"Keisha, you are crazy, but you better stop looking at my man so closely."

"Anne-Marie, it's okay to look as long as you don't touch, and you are too good a friend for me to even go there."

"Seriously, I had to tell Dr. Ikembe, and even if I didn't, he would have found out eventually anyway."

"That's true, but I don't think that he would say something he didn't mean. He doesn't have to play games with you. I'm telling you that there has to be a reason he didn't show when he was supposed to. Maybe you read the letter incorrectly. Did he tell you the actual date?'

"He said the first week in August. The first week of August has come and gone already."

"School starts in a couple of weeks, so don't get discouraged. I think the first thing that you need to do is head straight to his office and get this stuff cleared up and find out the real deal. Before I forget to tell you, I got accepted to Howard's medical school, too, and I know it's probably too early for you to decide, but I was hoping that maybe we could go to the same medical school. Wouldn't that be awesome? I got accepted into Meharry, too, but that's in the boonies way in Tennessee. Ain't nothing happening in Nashville, Tennessee, girl. Washington, D.C. is where it's happening. You can only imagine how happy I was when you wrote Howard as one of your prospect schools. I didn't apply to Columbia because I didn't want to be in New York. I need to keep the distance going between my father and me. He is so fucking controlling, and it's only because I'm a girl. My younger brother, Craig, is only eighteen, and he doesn't have to go through half the shit that I go through, and I'm twenty-one."

"It would be fun to have someone that I already know at school, but there's another problem. I'm having the baby, so I can't be expected to up and leave my child behind," I reminded her.

"Why don't you bring the baby with you? Most men don't want to be tied down watching babies anyway," Keisha said.

"Donovan is not most men. We've been arguing all summer about me leaving to go to school and the baby. He wants full responsibility, and he doesn't want me to leave. He is very family-oriented, and I love him for that. The more I think about it, the more I think that he's right. I would be pissed if he left me to raise a baby alone. It's not fair."

"Anne-Marie, are you trying to talk yourself out of the whole thing? I think that you're the crazy one. It's not like you're leaving your past life behind. You can come home during the holidays and breaks and when you're not doing that, they can come visit you. It's a small sacrifice. In the long run you'll gain your degree and an experience that you can't get here. Girl, you need to pursue this. When I was little my mother went to graduate school for her MBA. She attended Harvard University in Cambridge, Massachusetts, which is a little distance from Brooklyn, New York. It's about a three to four hour drive, depending on who's doing the driving. Anyway, she would come home on the weekends and during the holidays. My point is she was still a full-time mother, and my father explained to me why my mother was always absent during the week. Why can't Donovan do the same for you?" Keisha said poignantly.

"The thing is, he grew up without his mother. She died when he was small, and I think he's afraid that our baby will grow up not knowing me. I don't know how it is not to have a mother. My mother's always been there to witness my first steps, my first words, my first cut, and everything else. Those are moments that she was there to experience firsthand and even when your mother left you, it sounds like you were old enough to understand everything going on around you. I would be leaving a newborn, and every time I came home I would be a stranger to the baby, and I don't want that to happen."

"I kind of see what you mean, but I still think that you should see what Dr. Ikembe has to say and then think it over. Don't give up so soon. It's only the first inning."

"What?" I asked confused.

"Baseball, you know the game?"

"Oh, yeah, but I don't follow it."

Keisha simply shook her head. She thought that everyone knew baseball and the terminology. Jamaica was the home of cricket and soccer.

"I simply mean to say that this is only the beginning, girl. Listen, I have to take Tissue Mechanics and Endocrinology this semester with that witch of a teacher, Dr. Thorton. What did she end up giving you last semester?"

"You are not going to believe it!"

"Was it that bad? Oh, shit, and those are the last two classes that I have to take for our major. I kept putting them off and waiting until the last minute. I swear she better not mess up my GPA. I can't afford another C on my transcript. I already have two, and that's more than enough."

"I don't think that you have to worry about Dr. Thorton. She left to pursue her studies at Columbia University."

"*Yes, yes,*" Keisha screamed. She held her hands above her head and blew a kiss to the sky. "There is a God."

"I don't know who is taking her place though, but guess what?"

"What?" Keisha answered still elated that Dr. Thorton was no longer there.

"She gave me an *A*." I screamed.

"Get the hell out of here. You're lying. Oh, my goodness! Anne-Marie, didn't she give your ass a hard time last semester, or were you just pulling my leg?"

"Keisha, you know I don't complain to hear my voice. She gave me nothing but headaches the entire school year. Then she explained why she did what she did before she left. She even bought me a stethoscope engraved with my initials."

"Damn, girl! What did you and Dr. Thorton have going on?"

"Don't play with me, girl. I was surprised too. I was ready to settle for my second *B*.

"Your second, shit I wish I had your transcript."

"I got a *B* in Physiology during my sophomore year when my father got sick, and it was just too much for me to handle at the time. I almost got another in advanced statistics. What was that class called again? I think it was inverse problems, but that was because the teacher Dr. Hunter, was lousy, and I barely understood anything he said. I had to get by on my own. Did you ever have him?"

"Girl, I was warned beforehand, and I took Dr. Fowler and skated in that class. Dr. Hunter talks like he has a mouthful of spit and he looks like a pit bull," Keisha said, bellowing out a hearty laugh and hitting me on the shoulder.

I smiled not to hurt Keisha's feelings. I liked Keisha and truly enjoyed her company, but she had a wry sense of humor that I didn't always think was funny. I usually brushed it off as a cultural difference since I noticed the same wry humor and mannerisms with the other American girls that we associated with at school.

The afternoon turned to evening while Keisha and I talked about everything including the night that she spent with Patrick. Since Patrick asked about her at Maisey's wedding and the other day at Sunsplash, I figured it would be nice for them to hook up again. Especially since they both seemed to be after the same thing. Keisha must have really turned my brother out for him to keep asking for her. It wasn't as if he couldn't get laid on a regular basis. It felt good to finally be able to tell someone besides Donovan all the drama that I had endured during my summer vacation. Keisha was shocked that my mother would talk so harshly to me. We walked and talked for about two hours until heard Keisha's stomach begin to grumble.

"Girl, I'm hungry. Where can we go around here to get something to eat?" Keisha asked.

"We can go to my father's bar. We have a little restaurant around the back that my mother tends to."

"I remember that your mother can throw down, girl. Sounds like a plan to me. Let's go."

"I'm not that hungry. Donovan cooked for me right before you came, and I had a decent-size lunch," I said.

"It doesn't matter. I'm hungry enough to eat for the three of us, okay!"

Chapter Twenty

C olleen realized that she hadn't seen Anne-Marie in a while because of her preoccupation with Camille. She decided to take a couple of days off from work to spend time with Anne-Marie in Cambridge. Colleen packed her traveling bag and told Lloyd that she would be going to Cambridge after work the following day and would be back later in the week. Camille had been spending a lot of time with them lately, but Colleen was doing most of the work. She knew that Lloyd meant well, but he was putting all the responsibility of Camille on her. It was due time that he bonded with his daughter. Colleen knew the only way that would happen was if she left for a couple of days.

When she visited her aunt Lorna's house, Colleen found out that Anne-Marie had come by to see her and mentioned something about her mother. Then her boss told her that her mother stopped by the airport looking for as well. Colleen didn't know what her mother was up to, but she wasn't in the mood for another battle. She tried to reach out to her mother on numerous occasions, and none of her attempts were successful. Over the past couple of months Colleen underwent a personal transformation, and she was now at peace with herself. Her new perspective on life, love, religion, and relationships evolved from the connection that she and Lloyd shared. Colleen was finally able to come to terms with the fact that not everyone shared the same beliefs that she did. All her life she had lived in darkness and now that she could see the light, Colleen was no longer afraid, uptight, or callous, nor did she feel the need to be accepted by everyone she knew. People would have to learn to accept her at face value. For years she tried to live the life that her mother wanted for her and even tried to emulate Anne-Marie's strength. Then Lloyd helped her realize that she wasn't put on Earth to satisfy Ms. Margaret, and she shouldn't pretend to be something that she was not. She had to find her true self and strength from within.

Anne-Marie was right when she commented on Colleen's newfound attitude. It was all an act. Even the times she stood up to her mother were a façade, because after each incident she worried herself sick for days at a time. It wasn't what Anne-Marie said that made her upset the day that she walked out on her and went to pack the rest of her belongings. The words that she chose were painful, because every ounce of Anne-Marie's statement rung true. And she loved Anne-Marie for being so brutally honest even when she wasn't prepared for it. True friends didn't always tell you what you wanted to hear. They told you the truth, no matter what the circumstances.

Colleen had to go to work, and Lloyd promised to pick her up and take her to Cambridge afterward. He had taken the week off, because once again Hyacinth was missing in action and had left Camille in their care. Hyacinth never picked Camille up when she was supposed to. Then when she did arrive she always had an excuse. Colleen didn't mind having Camille around because she was a lovable little girl. Colleen even suggested to Lloyd that they take her full time and enroll her into school.

Hyacinth didn't seem to value education much, because Camille never attended preschool, and it was apparent that Hyacinth didn't teach her anything. When Colleen started taking care of Camille, the little girl had no idea what the ABC's were and couldn't even count to ten. Camille was eager to learn, and Colleen enjoyed teaching her, but she wasn't able to provide Camille with attention that she really needed. Lloyd's reason for not asking Hyacinth to take Camille full time was that he was afraid she might take Camille away for good. It seemed more than obvious to Colleen that Hyacinth would be more than happy to have Camille off her hands.

Colleen thought that Hyacinth only saw Camille as a burden. It was obvious to Colleen that Hyacinth had a higher regard for her freedom than for Camille. Hyacinth loved to party, and mingle and needed lots of attention to feel good about herself. With Camille away she could do those things. Colleen on the other hand enjoyed being a part of a family and didn't have the urge to party or mingle because she had everything she needed at home. Colleen had already decided that whenever the opportunity arose she would ask Hyacinth herself about Camille coming to stay with them.

A lot of things had happened to Colleen since she last saw Anne-Marie. She got a promotion at the airport and was now training the new ticket agents. She and Lloyd went into business together at the record shop. Now she helped him run the store. She finally convinced him to fire his lazy friend who was putting most of the profit in his pockets. She and Lloyd were also talking about building a new home together, because the house that they lived in now was rented. Lloyd was even ready to start a family, but Colleen wanted to hold off on that since they already had the responsibility of Camille. Things were looking good for Colleen all the way around. She thanked the Lord every day for bringing Lloyd into her life. He was the one who told her to put her differences with her mother aside and find out what she wanted.

Colleen knew that Lloyd would be outside waiting to take her to Cambridge after work. Just as she predicted he was waiting out front, and Camille was sitting in the back of the van. As they drove on the bumpy road to Cambridge, Colleen was preoccupied with looking out the window at the scenery. Men crossed the road with their goats and donkeys in tow. Horses grazed in the tall green grass

Children in their blue-and-white uniforms, on their way home from school, ran on the side of the road racing the cars and buses as they rode by. Adults sat on the verandas of their bright colorful houses, as they ate roast corn with friends while Rastas with their long swinging dreads were armed with handheld radios as they rode by on their bicycles.

When they arrived in Cambridge, Colleen got out of the car with her overnight bag. Camille cried and carried on because she thought that Colleen was leaving her for good. Colleen reassured her that she was only visiting her friend and would be back before the end of the week. Colleen's heart was filled with warmth when Camille began to cry. Camille never acted that way after Hyacinth left her at their house.

Colleen had Lloyd drop her off at Anne-Marie's house, because she figured that Anne-Marie would have some idea about what Ms. Margaret wanted. When she got up the hill, the only person home was Nadine. She informed Colleen that Anne-Marie no longer stayed there. Colleen was curious to find out what happened, but didn't want to ask Nadine. She only asked where Anne-Marie was staying. Then she headed to her mother's house to get it over with, but when she arrived no one was home. It didn't look like anyone had been there for a while either. The tables were dusty, which was unusual for her mother. The refrigerator was almost empty, and so was her mother's closet. Now Colleen was concerned, because it was unlike her mother not to be at home. Was she in the hospital or did she move? Colleen hauled ass to get to Donovan's house to see Anne-Marie. She needed to know what the hell was going on and why it appeared that her mother hadn't been home in days.

Donovan's house was a little ways from Colleen's mother's house, so by the time she got there she was out of breath. She didn't want to appear panicked so she waited to catch her breath before she knocked on the door. When she finally did knock, to her surprise her mother answered the door. It was a relief to see her, but what the hell was she doing there, answering the door nonetheless?

Ms. Margaret's face lit up when she saw Colleen. She immediately invited her in, shutting the door behind her. There was so much Ms. Margaret wanted to say and apologize for. A flood of emotions swept over her, and she had an overwhelming desire to hug Colleen, and she went with it. Ms. Margaret was starting to lose hope that she would ever see her daughter again. Colleen was surprised by this bizarre display of affection and stood almost lifeless while her mother embraced her. She didn't know what to attribute this sudden change of heart to, but wouldn't waste time trying to find out.

"Good evening," Colleen said. "I heard that you've been looking for me."

"Yes, I have, and Anne-Marie has been, too, but you've been hard to find."

"Is Anne-Marie here?"

"No, she and Donovan went out earlier and haven't come back home yet, and Mr. Miller is working at the shop. We're the only ones here," Ms. Margaret confirmed.

Colleen looked her mother over, and Ms. Margaret looked like the picture of health. Nothing appeared to be wrong. She was a little thinner, but that was all she noticed. Her hair was well maintained as usual. There was one difference that Colleen noticed immediately though. For the first time in years her mother had on earrings and a matching necklace with pendant that Colleen had never seen before. Ms. Margaret discarded her jewelry several years ago when she joined the church. Her belief was that men worshipped possessions more than they did the Lord.

They entered the living room, and Colleen put down her bag and sat on the chair beside the couch. Ms. Margaret sat on the end of the couch that was closest to the chair. Then she asked Colleen if she wanted anything to eat or drink, but Colleen declined. Colleen simply wanted to get the conversation off the ground.

"I went to Anne-Marie's and heard that she's not staying at her mother's house anymore."

"That's right, she's staying here with us. She and Faye had a big falling out, and Anne-Marie hasn't been back since."

"Us?" Colleen said, instantly picking up on her mother's choice of words.

"Yes. Mr. Miller invited me to stay here, because it was lonely at the house. I'm sure you've heard by now that Mr. Miller and I are seeing each other."

Colleen was surprised that her mother openly admitted and volunteered information. Ms. Margaret was a very private person and never spared details with her like this before, and if she were willing to share, Colleen would continue to pry.

"I figured that out from the wedding, but how long have you two been dating?"

"Before I go into that, I do want to say how sorry I am for my behavior at the wedding. It was wrong of me to carry on like that. Even if I didn't approve of your friend, I could have spoken to you in private. I hope that you can find it in your heart to forgive me."

"It took a while for me to get over it, but Lloyd, my friend from the wedding, helped me get through it. But what is really going on with you? Why were you looking for me in the first place? I come over here, and for the first time since I was a child, you hugged me. Then you tell me about you and Mr. Miller. Are you okay?"

"Colleen, things could be better, but all things considered, I'm fine. I just want things to be good between us. I would like for us to have a relationship," Ms. Margaret said, sounding remorseful.

"Why now? Why after all these years?"

"I realized that I was making the same mistakes that my mother made with me. And I would like the chance to start over with you, if you let me."

"Why should I?" Colleen asked. "I have tried to reach out to you time and time again to the point of humiliation sometimes. I don't know if..."

"Colleen, please, I'm asking you to forgive me. Let me tell you something: It kills me to know that you hate me the way you do. I can see it in your eyes, and it hurts. It always has, but for some reason I thought that you would tolerate my behavior no matter what—like I did with my mother. But you got tired, and you left me. I felt helpless when I realized that you were doing well on your own and didn't need me anymore. But I don't want to lose you altogether. I'm begging you to forgive me."

Colleen's heart went out to her mother, but she didn't know if she was ready to let her in her life again. The wounds were gone, but the scars were still there. If Lloyd were here he would tell her to give her mother a chance, and deep down that's exactly what she wanted to do. However, something was preventing her from accepting her mother's offer.

"I need to know the real reason behind this change. Are you doing this because Mr. Miller told you to make amends with me?" Colleen asked.

"I won't lie to you, Mr. Miller did talk to me. He wanted me to apologize for the night at the wedding, but I want to ask you something. Have you ever wondered why you never met your grandparents?"

"Not really. I figured that they were dead."

"You're close. My real father died when I was little, and my mother remarried when I was about nine. Anyway the man that she married was mean and treated her very badly. He was never like a father to me. He did things to me that no man had a right to do to a child, and my mother knew. She hated me so much that she told me that it was my fault, and that she regretted the day that I was ever born. I even believed that it was my fault, and those words have stayed with me until this day. My mother didn't even treat me like I was her child. When I got old enough to take care of myself I did. I stayed out of the house as much as I could, because I hated being home. I went to school and worked part-time for a nice woman who was a seamstress. She taught me how to sew, and she was my only friend. Then I met your father. He was the kindest man that I had ever met. It wasn't long that I got pregnant with you, and my parents kicked me out of their house. Your father took me in and asked me to marry him. I don't know what I would have done without him. The one thing that I never regretted was having you. There's a lot that I wish that I could change, but having you is not one of them," Ms. Margaret finished.

Colleen took a couple of moments to let her mother's words sink in. Her mother was molested by her stepfather? That was awful, Colleen thought, but why didn't her mother tell her these things before?

"I'm so sorry that you went through all of that. I wish you had told me this before, because it explains a lot of things. Why would your mother tell you that it was your fault that your stepfather took advantage of you?" Colleen was enraged and even though she didn't know her grandmother or grandfather, she felt a very strong dislike for them.

"I really don't know the answer to that, but everything that went wrong between them she found a way to blame me. As far as she was concerned, I was the reason that he beat her, cheated on her, and tried to leave her. When I left home, I shut my eyes, and they were dead to me. I don't want you to do the same thing to me. If you have children, I want them to know me. To love me."

"My God. I'm not trying to be mean, but carrying that around for years would make anyone miserable. Do you know if they are still alive?" Colleen asked.

"My stepfather was gunned down by the police during an election a couple of years ago. To my knowledge my mother is still living somewhere in St. Ann's, but I don't know where exactly."

"They say the wicked always live long," Colleen replied.

"To this day she doesn't know if I'm alive or dead, and she never even tried to come by to see her grandchild. After all these years not even once has she tried to find me, but to tell you the truth, it doesn't surprise me."

"I'm so sorry that you went through all that. Mom, I'm really sorry."

"It's not your fault, and I don't want you to be sorry. I want you to know that I'm trying to change, but I still need time. I'm asking you to have patience with me."

"I'll give you time. I've waited this long, and I'm glad that we are finally talking. This is all that I've ever wanted from you. This was long overdue. Is that why you were looking for me, because I was surprised when my boss told me that my mother came to the airport asking for me. I asked the man over and over if he was sure that it was my mother and when he described you I knew that it was you."

"That was part of the reason."

"What's the other part?"

"Now I don't want you to worry, but I'm going in for surgery this week. And I was truly hoping that I would see you before I went in to the hospital."

"What's wrong? Are you going to be okay?" Colleen said with alarm in her voice.

"I'm going to be just fine. I'm having a hysterectomy."

"Why?"

"A couple months ago I went to the doctor complaining abou

a pain that I was feeling in my pelvic area. Dr. Keene ran some tests, and I have fibroids. I've had them for years, but they were smaller and didn't cause me any pain, but now it's unbearable."

"Doesn't a hysterectomy involve removing the uterus?"

"It does, but don't worry about it. I'm not planning on having any more kids. You're all that I can handle, and I'm sure one of these days you'll be having kids," Ms. Margaret said, trying to bring humor to the situation.

"Aren't you scared? I would be. I hate hospitals and operations. Goodness!" The thought of it made Colleen uneasy.

"Of course I'm afraid, but it's not that bad. It's either I do this or I risk the chance of things getting worse."

"Are you sure that you need to get a hysterectomy? Can't they just remove the fibroids?"

"They could, but the fibroids could always come back. I'd rather remove everything. I'm getting old and tired. I don't want to be visiting the doctor's office every couple of months to see if the fibroids have come back. They are the most painful things you could ever imagine. If I am going to be cut open then I'd prefer that everything be done the first time around," Ms. Margaret replied.

"Now I'm worried about you. What day is the surgery? I want to make sure that I'm here, and if I necessary I will take the additional time off," Colleen fussed.

"It's in two days."

"Good, I'm here for three days. This way I can come to the hospital the day of, and I'll take an extra day to see after you."

"I'm glad that you'll be here. Mr. Miller has been so kind to me. He's also planning on being there. I keep telling him not to worry and that everything will be fine. God doesn't give anyone more than he or she can bear."

"It's only natural for him to worry if he cares for you," Colleen said and moved over to the couch to sit beside her mother.

"He does very much," Ms. Margaret replied bashfully.

"I still can't believe that you and Mr. Miller are a couple. No one would have guessed this in a million years."

"I could!" Ms. Margaret said, laughing to herself. "I've been liking that man for years, but I never knew how to approach him."

"My mother was after a man. Well it was about time."

"What did you think? I was a mule or something. I love men, too, but not every man that comes around should get fruit from the tree. Now since we are on the subject of men. Are you still seeing the young man that you brought to your aunt Maisey's wedding?"

"Lloyd and I are doing very well," she said trying not to give away anymore information than necessary. Although Colleen felt a lot more relaxed talking to her mother, she didn't know how she would react if she told her about Camille and the fact that she was living with Lloyd now.

"That's good to hear. After the surgery and everything, I would like for you to bring him by again. I know that he must think that I don't have any upbringing but I want to apologize to him."

"I'm sure that would make him feel better. Lloyd's very family-oriented, and he didn't like the fact that you and I weren't getting along. He and his mother are very close and so is the rest of his family."

"That's nice. It sounds like the relationship between Donovan and his father. They discuss ev-er-y-th-i-n-g," Ms. Margaret said and smiled.

Colleen and Anne-Marie sat outside of the hospital waiting for Ms. Margaret to come out of surgery. Because of her fear of hospitals Colleen chose to wait outside. The doctors told them that the surgery would be about an hour long, and Ms Margaret would be in recovery for at least three hours. For the first time ever, Colleen told her mother that she loved her, as they wheeled her off into surgery. Colleen never exchanged those words with anyone else except recently with Lloyd. Those words were new to her vocabulary. Even though Anne-Marie was her best friend, they never said I love you to each other. They just knew it and that was enough. Ms. Margaret echoed the same sentiments before she was wheeled off on a gurney. She held Colleen's hand in a tight grip and released it only when she was pulled away. Colleen bit her bottom lip, trying her best not to cry. It took this long for her to finally have a functional relationship with her mother, and she didn't want to lose her. All she could do was pray that her mother would get through the operation without any complications.

Anne-Marie was glad that Colleen and Ms. Margaret were overcoming their differences to begin a new relationship. She wanted to take Colleen's mind off her mother, and since they hadn't really spoken, Anne-Marie figured that she would tease Colleen about Lloyd.

"I hear that you have a new address?" Anne-Marie said in jest.

"You are such a joker. Yes, I have a new address. Is that okay with you?" Colleen said unable to keep a straight face.

"We're grown, and you don't need my permission. You been shacking up for some time now, and you didn't even tell me."

"I'll tell you this, it is the best move that I've ever made in my life," Colleen replied, head held high.

"Really. I'm surprised to hear you say that. I never saw you as the kind of person to live with a man and not be married."

"Trust me, that will happen in due time. But I had to get out of Lorna's, because she had one too many visitors for me. In the middle of the night her men would knock on the door, and you know that I slept in the living room on the couch. I hardly got any sleep. Then after I caught her in bed with a man, I knew that it was time for me to leave. She seemed fine afterward, but I was uncomfortable."

"You caught Lorna in bed with a man?" I said in disbelief. "If that were me, I would have been so embarrassed. I probably couldn't face you for... I don't know how long."

"The same here, but she wasn't bothered one bit. She just told me to shut the door and when she was done all she said was 'if my bedroom door is not ajar or you knock and I don't respond, I beg you please do not enter'. Can you imagine?" Colleen said mockingly.

"I can see why you wanted to move. When I went over there looking for you a couple of weeks ago, just as I was about to leave a man was at the door. I was barely able to say good-bye before she shut the door *inna mi face*!"

"I'm telling you the truth, men came by day and night. You would think that she was running a friggin' brothel."

They shared a good laugh.

"I wonder if the men ever bumped into one another or if they know about each other," Anne-Marie asked.

"She had too many men for my taste. Aunt Lorna is a nice person, but I tell you this, my mother was right when she said that Lorna was skettel."

"It sounds like it to me. Colleen, I'm really glad that things are working out with you and Lloyd. How are things going with his daughter?"

"I left this week so Lloyd could spend more time with her. Camille practically lives with us, and we love it. She's full of energy, and I don't think that her mother really wants her, but that's another story. Then Lloyd works so much that I end up spending most of the time with her, and she needs to get to know her father."

"That's true," Anne-Marie agreed. "I see that you picked up a little weight."

"Yeah, it's because I've been cooking a lot more lately. We can't eat out every day since Camille is there so often."

"You know that's not what I mean."

"What do you mean?" Colleen asked.

"I mean you're screwing now, and you picked up weight because the sex is good. I can see that you weren't going to tell me about that either. You've been very secretive lately," Anne-Marie said, trying to sound offended.

"Not really secretive, but you don't have to talk about everything. Some things are private."

"Since when? We use to talk about everything under the sun and now we keep secrets from each other?"

"Anne-Marie, look, we did it, okay I'm having sex now, and I know what your next question is, so let me answer it. We did it a few days before my aunt Maisey's wedding," Colleen said, anxious to get off the subject.

"You make it seem like I was going to ask you details. I don't want to know how you carry on in the bedroom. I only thought that this was something that you would share with me."

"I haven't seen you in a while, so when was I supposed to tell you?"

"At the wedding. I told you about my pregnancy."

"There were so many things going on at the wedding that I forgot. You know what I went through that night."

"You're right. So, you know that my mother and I had a falling out?"

"I figured as much. I stopped by your house first when I got to town, and Nadine told me that you weren't staying there anymore."

"As usual, my mother was being difficult, and I couldn't take it anymore. Dr. Keene told me to take it easy, and she was making me miserable."

"Well, you have to do what the doctor says. I want my little niece or nephew to be healthy. By the way, did you ever hear from your teacher about the schools?"

"He never showed up, so I'm not even thinking about it anymore," Anne-Marie replied despondently.

"Anne-Marie, I'm sorry to hear that. I know how much it meant to you and that you really wanted to go away to one of those schools."

"It's probably for the best. Donovan and I were arguing about it every second anyway. He didn't want me to leave him and the baby. Going away to school was causing more problems than it was worth."

"You can always finish school here, right?"

"That's exactly what I'm going to have to do whether I want to or not," Anne-Marie replied.

Before Colleen knew it the hours had passed, and they went up to the recovery area where Ms. Margaret was supposed to be. When they got to the room Ms. Margaret was nowhere to be found. Colleen started to panic and ran to the nurses' station to find out where her mother was. Apparently the nurses had changed shifts, because there was a different one at the desk, and she wasn't very helpful. She appeared to be in her early twenties, not overly attractive or bright, but you could tell that she took pride in her appearance. Her uniform was starched to a crisp. The nurse said that she didn't see any record of admission for a Ms. Margaret Rashford. Colleen started thinking the worse. Colleen knew something like this would happen, and she was starting to lose all patience with the stupid woman behind the desk. Anne-Marie knew Colleen couldn't stand to be in the hospital.

There seemed to be a shortage of doctors and nurses, because the waiting area was full of sickly looking people. Colleen briefly stared at them and felt a twinge of disgust. Anne-Marie had to calm her down and talk to the nurse to get the information. Anne-Marie explained what Ms. Margaret came in for and told the nurse that she was supposed to be in the recovery now, but Ms. Margaret couldn't be located. The nurse told Anne-Marie to wait a moment and went down the hall. Five minutes later the she returned with a chart in her hand, which must have been Ms. Margaret's. The nurse asked if the person we were looking for had a hysterectomy, even though she was told several times along with Ms. Margaret's name when we first approached her. Then she pointed them to a room on the right side at the far end of the hall. Colleen mumbled something under her breath and swiftly walked down to the room.

Mr. Miller was sitting in a chair beside the bed pouring Ms. Margaret a glass of water. Ms. Margaret smiled when she saw Colleen and Anne-Marie enter the room. It was also evident from the look on her face that she was in a lot of pain. Mr. Miller got up to give Colleen his chair so she could sit beside her mother. Ms. Margaret sipped the water that Mr. Miller poured for her. With each swallow she closed her eyes and twisted her nose in pain. When she was tired of drinking she handed Colleen the glass to place on the side table.

Before she went in for surgery Ms. Margaret was the picture of health. Now Colleen thought she looked like the people that she saw sitting in the waiting room a few moments ago. Her mother's eyes were sunken into her head, her lips were chapped and her hair was all over the place.

Mr. Miller and Anne-Marie left the room to give Colleen and her mother a little privacy.

Ms. Margaret attempted to speak, but the words were strained. Colleen merely put her hands to Ms. Margaret's mouth and told her mother not to speak. She didn't want to hold the tears back anymore. She hated to see her mother like this, but realized that it could have been worse. She could have no mother at all. Colleen found a bible in the drawer of the side table. Then while holding her mother's hand she read the Twenty-third Psalm. It was Ms. Margaret's favorite, and Colleen read it for her until she fell asleep.

CHapter Twenty-One

It was nice to have a female companion to talk to, and I was already missing Colleen's company. She ended up staying two extra days, because she wanted to make sure there were no complications before her mother was released from the hospital. When Ms. Margaret got out of the hospital Mr. Miller went back to work at the shop. During his absence Donovan had been taking care of the store. Mr. Miller no longer employed his part-time help since Ms. Margaret started working for him.

When we all got back into our groove I noticed some tension between Donovan and Mr. Miller. It was so thick you could cut it with a knife. When I asked Donovan what was going on, he told me that he and his father had an argument caused by Ms. Margaret. He said that he didn't want to go into detail because it would only get upset him again, so I left it alone.

The following week I was in the kitchen preparing some food for Ms. Margaret. She was doing a lot better, but was unable to stand for long periods. Donovan had brought me lunch earlier, so when he saw me in the kitchen he asked if I was hungry again. I told him the food wasn't for me that it was for Ms. Margaret. He got real upset and left the kitchen. Shortly after I heard him talking to Ms. Margaret in a way that I never heard him talk to any adult before. I overheard him when he said, "Anne-Marie is not your maid, so if you want something to eat then get it yourself."

When I went into the room to give Ms. Margaret the food I

apologized for Donovan's behavior. She said that it was okay and for me not to worry myself over it, but his behavior was inexcusable. Later that evening Ms. Margaret and I were in her room talking when I heard Donovan calling me. I told him that I would be there in a minute, but he became impatient and came to get me. Donovan grabbed my hand and pulled me out of the room. He told me that he didn't want me around that nosy, lying wretch. What made it worse was that we weren't even out of the room yet when he said it. I knew that Ms. Margaret had her ways, but she didn't deserve this, especially in her condition. Ms. Margaret didn't put up a fight. Again she let him slide. Donovan's attitude toward her during her recovery was downright malicious. I didn't know what she had done to upset him so, but he hated her more than ever now.

That night when Mr. Miller got home I was tempted to ask him what was going on. I didn't want him thinking that I was trying to get involved or stepping out of line so I didn't let my curiosity get the best of me. Still I couldn't help but feel bad for Ms. Margaret. If she told Mr. Miller about Donovan's behavior it would only cause another argument between them, and things would only get worse. Ms. Margaret was between a rock and a hard place.

Donovan's behavior didn't improve as the week went on. He was starting to show me a side of him that I didn't care for. He started acting foolish whenever I was alone with Ms. Margaret, questioning me about our conversations. I continued to ignore him because I was getting tired of his pettiness.

One particular afternoon the tension in the house seemed almost unbearable. The attitudes were flaring, so I decided to take a walk to my aunt Beverly's. When I left Donovan's house, it was muggy and humid. Before I got back, there was a sun shower. Donovan was home and took everyone's garments off the clothes-line with the exception of Ms. Margaret's, which he left out on the line to get wet. That was one of the first mean things that I noticed he did.

On another occasion he deliberately hid her pain medication, and although he didn't admit to it I knew that he was responsible. The final thing that he did was locking her out of the house. Early one morning Ms. Margaret said that she was feeling a little better and went to morning prayer. When she came home that afternoon the door was locked. Since it wasn't normal practice to lock the door, no one ever bothered to carry keys. Ms. Margaret didn't want to make a big fuss, so she went to her house. When Mr. Miller came home that evening he asked me if I had seen her. Of course I told him I hadn't since early that morning. He didn't trouble to ask Donovan, because he already knew what his answer would be. It was getting late, so Mr. Miller went out to look for her knowing that she still wasn't in the best of health. First he went to the church, which was closed and then to one of her church sister's house where Ms. Margaret visited from time to time. Ms. Margaret wasn't at either place. Finally he went to her house. Mr. Miller found her at home sitting in the dark crying. Ms. Margaret broke down and told Mr. Miller everything that had happened. Apparently there were other things going on that I wasn't aware of. Things only got worse after that.

Mr. Miller gave Donovan a stern talking to that evening and even I felt ashamed for him. Donovan walked out in the middle of the argument, and the last thing out of his mouth was "They should have chopped off her mouth while she was on the operating table."

This change was sudden and made me very uneasy. At this point, I was more than appalled at Donovan's behavior but I didn't want to say the wrong thing and tick him off either. Donovan came home at about three in the morning. I tried to talk to him, but all he did was babble the same thing over and over. "If you knew what that witch did, you'd be upset too."

Still he refused to tell me exactly what Ms. Margaret had done to him.

Donovan and I weren't in the habit of keeping secrets from each other, so it really bothered me to see him this upset and not know the reason. The more he refused, the more curious I became. I knew that whatever it was had to be the root of all of these problems going on in this house.

The following week Mr. Miller came and said he wanted to have a talk with me.

"How are things between you and Donovan?" he asked.

"There seems to be a lot of things bothering him lately," I replied. "Something is tormenting him, but I know he's not really comfortable with Ms. Margaret being here. I think he feels like she's trying to take his mother's place."

Mr. Miller shook his head defiantly to disagree. "It's much more than that," he exclaimed. "Has he mentioned anything to you at all about the disagreement that we had?" Mr. Miller asked.

"No, but I know that it had something to do with Ms. Margaret, but he won't talk to me," I said with worry in my voice.

Mr. Miller told me Donovan had some issues that he needed to resolve right away. Then he went on to say that if Donovan didn't handle things soon he would be forced to take matters into his own hands. He expressed concern for the baby and me, because he noticed that Donovan and I also argued a lot lately. Mr. Miller wanted to know if it had something to do with me wanting to go away to school, but I reassured him that school was no longer a problem, especially since Dr. Ikembe never bothered to contact me. When I told him this he seemed very upset and immediately asked me about Donovan's whereabouts.

"He's down at the schoolyard playing soccer," I answered.

"This has been going on long enough," Mr. Miller said as he stood. "There's something that we both need to tell you, but I have to go to the schoolyard to get him first."

"Is everything okay?" I asked, concerned.

"Not right now, but they will be soon," Mr. Miller said as he left the room and headed toward the door. "I'll be right back."

"O.K." I said, not giving it a second thought. Before he walked out of the door he turned back like he wanted to say something, but didn't. Then I heard the screen door slam. Not a minute passed before he came back in the house and apologized for slamming the door and said that my mother came to the store asking for me. He strongly urged me to go see her as soon as possible. I was taken by surprise, and shortly after he left I didn't waste anytime going to the house to see my mother.

My mother and Nadine were sitting on the veranda talking and eating tamarind. They both greeted me, and I was a little startled by their enthusiasm. My mother even offered me some tamarind. I knew this was her subtle way of trying to apologize. I sat down on the white patio chair that was opposite the swing and joined them. We sat there quietly eating the tamarind, but I figured there was some other reason for my mother asking me to come to the house.

"Mr. Miller told me that you came to the store yesterday asking for me. Was there something in particular that you wanted?" I asked.

She was still eating the tamarind and didn't answer me immediately. She was trying to avoid the question, so I patiently sat and waited for her to finish.

"Can't a mother come by and ask for her daughter?" my mother asked coyly.

"Of course you can, but that's not like you."

"Well you haven't stopped by in a while, and I wanted to make sure that you were all right."

"I'm doing fine. Thanks for your concern." She was acting very unusual and even Nadine sat there just enjoying her tamarind. I thought for sure that they were up to something, but the entire time nothing out of the ordinary happened.

Then we all started talking, and my mother mentioned that she had a dream the other night about her teeth falling out. Whenever someone dreamed about teeth falling out, it usually signified death. My mother, Nadine, and I sat there thinking aloud about who we knew that might be sick. We couldn't come up with one single person. My mother said that she and my father had already discussed the dream, and he didn't know of anyone on his side of the family who was sick, so she was going to call her sister in England to find out if their father was ill.

All the tamarind was starting to make me thirsty so I got up to get myself something to drink. While I was in the house my mother said that a letter came for me, and it was on the dresser in my room. I poured my drink and went into my bedroom to get the letter. As much as I hated to admit it, I enjoyed being able to sit and chat with my mother and sister. It had been a long time since we all got together and talked. I listened to my mother tell me the latest gossip, and of course she asked me about Ms. Margaret and Mr. Miller. I didn't give her details, but I said that they seemed to be serious about each other. My mother and Nadine were questioning me about everything, and it seemed odd that I would have most of the information, but I confirmed a lot of things for them.

All the laughter and good vibes that I was feeling really started lifting my spirits. I loved being in the house with Donovan, but things weren't the way that I pictured them to be. It started out pretty good. Unfortunately it seemed that the novelty of it all was starting to wear off. I never, ever had second thoughts about anything, and I was sure once Donovan and his father made up things would start to fall back into place. Even though Mr. Miller didn't feel that Ms. Margaret had anything to do with all the unpleasantness I thought she did.

All of a sudden the sun began to set its sights on the house, and it became brutally hot. I used the letter in my hand to fan myself, and Nadine asked me when I was going to read it. If she hadn't mentioned the letter I would have forgotten that it was even in my possession. I thought that it was a scrap of paper that I picked up. I proceeded to open the letter since they seemed anxious to know whom it was from. Immediately I recognized the handwriting to be that of Dr. Ikembe. I wanted to know exactly what his excuse was for canceling his visit to see me.

Dear Anne-Marie:

I hope that you had a great summer, and look forward to seeing you in a couple of weeks. Unfortunately, I got the weeks confused, and I missed you on my recent visit. However, I did have the pleasure of meeting your fiancé, and you've made a wonderful choice.

Donovan took the liberty of telling me that you've decided to decline the opportunity to attend school overseas. Although I was a little disappointed, your decision is definitely understandable and the dedication that you have to your family is very admirable. I'm sure the future has something grand in store for you.

Best Regards,
Dr. Ikembe

Chapter Twenty-Two

C olleen thought for sure that she had spotted Hyacinth a-cross the floor at the airport. Camille had been in the care of Lloyd and Colleen for more than two weeks, because Hya-cinth had disappeared.

Lloyd was beginning to worry and thought that something must have happened to Hyacinth. He even went looking for her at the address she had given him. When he went to inquire, the neighbors told him that Hyacinth never lived there. They confirmed that Hyacinth's mother, Mrs. Livingston, used to live there with her little granddaughter, Camille, and Hyacinth used to visit from time to time, but she never, ever lived there. They also informed Lloyd that Ms. Livingston had died six months earlier.

Apparently, Mrs. Livingston got sick earlier in the year and that was when Hyacinth decided to try to find Lloyd. Her mother had passed long before Lloyd came into the picture, and Hyacinth lucked up when he showed up at Maisey's wedding as Hyacinth hoped he would. Hyacinth desperately needed someone else to tend to Camille, so that she could once again abandon her responsibili-ties as a mother. The fact that Hyacinth lied didn't upset Lloyd one bit. He was only concerned about the welfare of his daughter, and now that he seemed to have full custody, along with Colleen's sup-port he was happy. Lloyd treasured Camille, and Colleen adored her. However, Colleen was upset and didn't like the way Hyacinth misrepresented herself.

As usual Hyacinth dropped Camille off for what was supposed to be a weekend visit. However, Colleen found Hyacinth's behavior to be a little peculiar. Colleen also noticed that Hyacinth packed three bags for Camille instead of the single bag she usually sent with her. It was also the first time that Hyacinth stepped foot in the house. Normally she dropped Camille off at the gate even though both Colleen and Lloyd invited her inside on several occasions. On this day she asked if she could come in and stay until Lloyd came from work, because she needed to speak with him about something. This only made Colleen more suspicious, but she figured Lloyd would get to the bottom of things when he got home.

Colleen obliged and was even kind enough to offer her something to drink. She accepted, and Colleen watched as she slowly sipped from the glass, but it was clear that she was uncomfortable being there. Colleen didn't really feel like sitting with Hyacinth, so she pretended to be busy with chores that she had already done the day before. Dinner was already prepared, and Camille was taking a nap. There wasn't much else for Colleen to do.

Finally, Colleen decided there was no harm in being cordial. After all, Hyacinth hadn't done anything directly to her, and it was clear that she was no longer interested in Lloyd. Colleen had always wanted to know why Mrs. Thompson, Lloyd's mother, didn't like Hyacinth. She hoped that she and Mrs. Thompson would get close enough and that one day she would voluntarily reveal her reasons, but she never budged.

Colleen went into the kitchen and washed the mangoes that she picked off the tree earlier that day. She got the knife from the dish drain and proceeded to peel off the skin. Colleen sliced the mangos and put them into a small serving bowl, and went to sit at the table with Hyacinth.

"Colleen, do you think Lloyd will be arriving soon?" Hyacinth asked.

"Fridays are usually Lloyd's busiest day of the week. More tourists fly in and leave on Monday, but lately since you've been dropping Camille off he tries to leave a little earlier."

"What time is it now?" Hyacinth asked.

"It's a quarter to seven," Colleen said, looking at the clock on the wall behind Hyacinth. "He'll probably be here by seven, seven-thirty. Would you like some mango?" Colleen asked, pushing the bowl before Hyacinth. Hyacinth nodded, and took a piece from the bowl. "They're nice and ripe now too."

"They're sweet. Where did you get these mangoes from?" Hyacinth said, trying to wipe the juice from the fruit from her mouth.

"I picked them off the tree in the backyard this morning," Colleen replied.

"They really are good."

"I'll give you a couple to take with you before you leave if you want."

"Sure, I'll take one."

"Good," Colleen responded. "Hyacinth, is everything okay with Camille, because you seem a little worried."

"Camille is fine. She's a little angel. I couldn't ask for a better daughter!"

"She's a little woman. Sometimes I forget that she's a child until she doesn't get her way and starts throwing a tantrum," Colleen said, smiling. "But you really did a great job raising her. Lloyd is very happy that she is a part of his life now."

"You know, I'm glad to hear that. I thought he would resent me for the rest of his life. I know I should have tried to find him sooner, but time simply flew by. The days turned into months, and the months, before you knew it turned into years. But as the saying goes, it's never too late. Camille needs to have her father in her life, and Lloyd is a good man."

"He really is. I'm glad that I found him. He's very together and doesn't play games. I like the fact that he knows what he wants in life."

"He's always been that way. His only fault is that he can be a little too passive. He takes things too lightly for my liking."

"What do you mean?" Colleen asked.

"The whole thing when we were together. I mean we broke up because like I told you his mother never liked me, and I've never done anything to her."

"Right," Colleen said encouragingly. Hyacinth was finally going to tell Colleen everything that she wanted to know.

"My mother and Mrs. Thompson never really got along. So when Lloyd and I got together Mrs. Thompson disliked me immediately. First, she was only polite to me when Lloyd was present. Then one day she told me she didn't like my family or me. When I told Lloyd, he didn't believe me. Over time it only got worse, and she would tell me off. Lloyd worships his mother and never believed me or took my side. She could do no wrong and told me that the things I accused his mother of were false. I knew that it was a lost cause, and there was no competing against his mother. Then his father died, and Lloyd took it really hard. His mother wouldn't tell him when I stopped by, and I got tired of trying. Two months later I found out that I was pregnant. I went to his mother's house again when I was about four or five months pregnant. I wasn't really big, she may not have known I was pregnant, but she chased me away and said Lloyd didn't live there anymore."

Colleen listened to Hyacinth's story and could understand where she was coming from when she said that Lloyd was passive. Colleen saw it as stubborn. She, too, had told Lloyd that her mother could be unbearable before the wedding, and he took it lightly, not believing her. But he had to experience Ms. Margaret's wrath firsthand. After the wedding that night he apologized profusely for not listening to her. He figured he could charm his way in with Ms. Margaret. What he didn't know was no one could charm her mother unless she wanted to be charmed.

Colleen wasn't convinced that Mrs. Thompson disliked Hyacinth solely over some quarrel or disagreement that had nothing to do with her. There had to be another explanation, because Mrs. Thompson wasn't like the woman Hyacinth described. Hyacinth was deliberately leaving out something, and there were always two sides to every story. Colleen knew that Lloyd worshipped his mother. That much was true, but if she told him that his mother mistreated her, Colleen was sure he would question her.

"If Mrs. Thompson disliked you so much why would you name your daughter after her?" I would think hearing the name every day would bother you every time you said or heard it."

"Regardless of how she felt about me, I knew that Lloyd would sell his soul to the devil for his mother. He loves the ground she walks on. So when I had a girl, my first thought was for her to be loved like that one day. She deserved to be named after someone who was loved and worshiped that way," Hyacinth replied.

Colleen wasn't buying it. She thought the real reason was probably because she wanted to make sure that Lloyd knew Camille was his child from the beginning. But she didn't have to go through all that trouble because Camille resembled her father. The only features she shared with her mother were the thin lips, perfectly arched eyebrows, and widow's peak. Lloyd couldn't deny that Camille was his child. Colleen wasn't about to make a big deal over it though. She would know the truth before long.

Colleen heard Lloyd's van pull up and immediately got up to go to the door and greet him. He looked exhausted from a long day of hard work, but Colleen was there to take care of him. He was so sexy to her. She loved the way his locks framed his face. She couldn't be happier since she moved in, and she had no intentions of going anywhere. When he got to the door he hugged her and gave her a kiss on the lips and though he was tired he still managed to grope her. Colleen cleared her throat and quickly informed him that they had company. Lloyd looked over her shoulder and saw Hyacinth sitting at the table trying to act like she didn't witness the scene by picking at the remaining mango in the bowl.

"Wha'pin, Hyacinth. How are you today?" Lloyd asked, turning to Colleen and whispering, "What's she doing here?" Colleen shrugged her shoulders and told him that she had been waiting for almost two hours.

"I'm okay."

"Is everything all right with Camille? Is she sick?" Lloyd asked, concerned. He left to go check on her.

"No, Camille is fine. She's taking a nap," Hyacinth answered.

"She'll be up all night wanting to play with her father," Colleen said.

"Would you like to stay for dinner?" Colleen asked from the kitchen. "I made oxtails, mixed vegetables, and rice and peas. I also made some bread pudding."

"Colleen, that sounds good and smells even better, but I'm really not hungry. I have a lot on my mind," Hyacinth responded.

"O.K., but if you change you're mind your more than welcome."

"Change your mind about what?" Lloyd asked, sneaking up behind Colleen.

"That was quick," she said, reaching up for a kiss. "I was telling Hyacinth that she could stay for dinner, but she said she wasn't really hungry. She has a lot on her mind, so stop being fresh and go find out what it is that she wants. I'm going to go wake up Camille and get her ready for dinner." After turning the fire down under the food, she playfully showed him the way out of the kitchen. As she was passing by him he grabbed her by the waist to embrace her.

"Fresh," she said as she laughed and walked away.

"What can I say? I can't get enough of you." He took a seat at the table with Hyacinth. He could tell something was troubling her because she was not her usual lively self. She appeared distracted.

"Colleen said that you were waiting for me. Is there something wrong? Is everything really okay with Camille?" Lloyd asked.

"Trust me, Camille is fine. And now that she has you, she couldn't be better. She loves her daddy, you know."

"I love her too. She means the world to me. She's even taking a liking to Colleen. Look, I'm sorry that I couldn't be there before, but I'm glad that I can be a part of her life now."

"I appreciate that, Lloyd. It means a lot to me. I have a big favor to ask you, and you can say no if you choose to. I'll understand."

"Okay. What's the favor?"

"My mother has gotten worse, and it doesn't look like she's getting any better."

"I'm sorry to hear," Lloyd said.

"She's really sick, and I want to go stay with her, but I don't have anyone to watch Camille. I don't want to have Camille around her while she's sick."

"I understand. Say no more. I'll watch her."

"It should only be for a week or two at the most. I don't want to inconvenience you or anything. I took the liberty of packing enough clothes for her," Hyacinth pointed out.

"It's fine. I make my own hours anyway. I'll just take this Monday off, and Colleen has Tuesday and Friday off, and I'm sure she won't mind watching Camille. If it should be longer than a week, I'll get my mother to baby-sit. She loves Camille."

"I really appreciate it. You know if I had someplace else to leave her, I would. It's only because it's my mother, and I need to spend some time with her."

"You don't need to explain. She's my daughter, too, and I don't mind," Lloyd declared. "You go take care of your mother. She needs you right now, and don't worry about Camille. She will be fine."

"Thank you so much, Lloyd." She got up and gave him a hug. He was sincerely concerned. The thought of losing his mother frightened him.

When they were through embracing, Hyacinth looked like she was about to cry. Lloyd pulled the chair out for her to sit back down. Colleen walked out with a sleepy-eyed Camille. Rubbing her eyes from sleep she looked up and saw her mother crying.

"Why are you crying Mommy?" she asked.

"Hyacinth, are you okay?" Colleen asked, looking at Lloyd with alarm.

"I'm okay. I was just telling Lloyd that my mother is sick." Hyacinth said.

"I'm so sorry to hear that. Is she going to be okay?" Colleen asked.

"We don't know. The doctors say it doesn't look good. She has sugar and high blood pressure. I asked Lloyd if it would be possible for me to leave Camille here for a week or two, while I take care of my mother."

"Of course you can," Colleen said.

"Granny's gone. Granny's not coming back," Camille said.

"No, baby. No, Granny's not gone. Granny's really sick, sweetie, so don't say that. Mommy doesn't want to hear you say that again. Okay?"

"Granny Livie's gone," Camille said again and started to cry.

Colleen tried to calm her down.

"She thinks that her grandmother is gone because I won't take her over there anymore. I don't want Camille seeing her like that."

"I understand, "Lloyd said. "Don't worry about it. She'll calm down."

"I'm going to get out of here. I have a long ride ahead of me and a lot of business to take care of," Hyacinth said.

"You go ahead and take care of your mother. If you need anything, please stop by and let us know. I hope everything turns out well with your mom."

"Thanks, Lloyd. You are helping me out more than you know," Hyacinth replied.

That was the last time Lloyd or Colleen saw or heard from Hyacinth. And now Colleen was standing just a couple of feet from her at the airport. Hyacinth was standing in line getting ready to check her luggage, but she wasn't standing in Colleen's line. After finishing with a customer, Colleen walked over to where Hyacinth stood and asked the ticket agent to switch lines with her for ten minutes. The girl looked over to Colleen's line and saw fewer people and agreed. Hyacinth never even looked up until she was right up on Colleen at the counter. She was busy reading a magazine and wearing sunglasses inside the airport. She handed Colleen her ticket and put the luggage on the scale. Colleen smiled politely and said, "Ms. Hyacinth Livingston, may I see your passport, please?"

Hyacinth recognized the voice and looked at Colleen like she had just seen a ghost. She lost all color in her face. "Are you okay, Hyacinth? How is your mother?"

"Excuse me?" Hyacinth asked.

"How's your mother? You know Lloyd and I were concerned about you."

"Oh, my mother died last week," Hyacinth said dismissively.

"Did she really!"

"Yes. As a matter of fact I'm flying her body to London to be buried today."

"Is that right?" Colleen asked, unconvinced.

"I'm sorry that I didn't contact you and Lloyd, but everything happened so quickly."

"Cut the bullshit, Hyacinth. Stop your damn lying. I'm tired of all the lies, so let's end it now."

"I don't know what you're talking about, and I don't know who you think you are talking to."

"Your mother has been dead for more than six months now. You sold off her property two months ago, and she's buried right in Cambridge. What did you do, dig up her body to bury it in London?"

"What I do is none of your damn business. I am a grown woman!"

"What you do is my business. You left your daughter in my care."

"You're going to make me miss my flight. Listen, I'll call your supervisor and file a complaint against you!"

"I'll call the police and tell them that you abandoned your daughter, so go right ahead and try to call my manager!"

Colleen was trying to keep her voice down to a whisper, but she was getting stares from her coworkers as well as the passengers. She wasn't going to jeopardize her job over this woman, but Colleen wanted Hyacinth to be aware that she wasn't stupid, and she was in on her little game.

"Let me tell you something. Lloyd has escaped the responsibility of being a father for four years now. So he can afford to spend some quality time with his daughter," Hyacinth retorted.

Colleen was livid. She couldn't believe the nerve of this woman.

"How dare you! You have the audacity to stand here and call Lloyd an absent father? We know that you have been absent in the upbringing of your daughter Camille. Your mother raised Camille. You only took her for the past few months, and who knows, you've probably been pawning her off on other people the same way you've been leaving her with us. It's okay though, because Lloyd and I love that little girl. Quite frankly, she's better off without you in her life. Camille doesn't need you to keep playing disappearing acts because you only confuse her more. She deserves better...much better than you. So, Ms. Livingston, I'll grant you passage without question to London, but you make sure you never come back and disturb our happy home!"

Chapter Twenty-Three

My head was spinning. I couldn't understand why Donovan would do this to me. How could he act like everything was okay? Dr. Ikembe came by, and Donovan had no intention of ever telling me. He was just waiting for it to be too late for me to do anything about attending school overseas. My last couple of weeks of living in bliss had all been one big lie.

My heart was racing so fast that I had to sit down for a minute and think things out. I could feel myself getting a little lightheaded, and I went into the kitchen for a glass of water. My mother and Nadine were both still sitting there chatting, but when my mother saw how flushed I looked she asked what was wrong. I couldn't even tell her, I simply handed her the letter to read for herself.

"When was this?" she asked, handing the letter back to me after she read it.

"It had to have been a day when I wasn't home. He probably tried to come up here, and no one was home."

"So, what are saying? Donovan didn't tell you anything about your teacher coming by?"

"No, he didn't say one blessed word to me and…I gotta go. I have to go see him now."

"Anne-Marie, sit down for a minute. You can't go over there upset like this."

"Mama, I have to go!"

She continued pleading, but I ignored her cries and ran down the hill like there was no tomorrow. She stood at the top of the hill and yelled after me "Take your time going down the hill. If you run you may hurt yourself." For a quick minute I almost forgot that I was pregnant, and I slowed my pace.

I still couldn't believe what I read just moments ago, even though the letter, now crumpled, was in my hand. How could Donovan be so deceitful and pretend everything was fine? Donovan was everything to me, and I thought that I meant the world to him too. Deep in my heart I still didn't want to believe that Donovan would do something so deceitful. My heart raced faster with each long stride I took. I was physically fit, but I don't think that my legs ever moved this swiftly before. I concentrated on lifting each one as high as possible. It was still early afternoon, and as I whizzed by people on the street looked at me as though I was crazy.

The sun was hotter than ever causing my dress to cling to my back and my brow to drip with sweat. I was so upset that I wasn't sure if it was tears or sweat stinging my eyes. A lump began to form in my throat, and my breathing became rapid and more intense. I could see Donovan's house in the distance, and it wouldn't be much longer now. I was starting to feel dizzy and lightheaded. I finally made it, and I climbed the rickety steps two at a time. I had no idea what I was going to say to Donovan, but no explanation could possibly exonerate him.

The screen door was closed, but the main door to the house was open. I flung the screen door open, and it clanged loudly against the house. My chest heaved up and down, and I couldn't catch my breath, but with all my might I yelled out Donovan's name. Seconds later I saw his shadow approaching along with his father's, and before long they both stood in front of me. The look on Mr. Miller's face told me that he knew that I had gotten wind of something, and he tried to reach out to me.

Everything started coming together for me. Now I knew why

Donovan was so upset with his father and why Mr. Miller wanted to speak with me immediately with Donovan present. It all started making sense. At that moment the mere sight of Donovan made my head spin, and I felt like all the air had been sucked out of me. I could feel my legs beginning to buckle and right then everything went black.

Jamaica, West Indies

1985

Epilogue

Tomorrow by noon my plane would be touching ground at LaGuardia Airport in New York. Everything is happening so quickly. It's hard to believe that only a year ago I was pregnant and yesterday was my graduation.Yet, here I am today packing my bags and getting ready to leave for my trip to America, and I didn't know when I would return to Jamaica.

My father was so proud of me at my graduation, and I was glad to see that familiar smile again. It made me feel good to know that things were getting back to normal between us. Things were strained for a while because of the pregnancy, but ever since the miscarriage he has been nothing but apologetic for his negligence toward me. I really wish things would have turned out differently, but everything happens for a reason, and I believe that God has something good in store for my future.

I was still devastated over the loss, of my baby, and it took a lot to get me through my last year of school. I managed to maintain a decent grade point average, but I wasn't the valedictorian or salutatorian like Keisha had predicted. However, I did manage to graduate magna cum laude and in the top ten of my class.

For months I wanted to give up on everything, and I would cry myself to sleep. There was a vacant spot in my heart, and at times it seemed irreparable. There were days that I felt like I had no place to turn, but I thanked God daily for school. It helped me take everything off my mind during the day, and Bob Marley's tunes helped me through the evenings. School, Keisha, and Bob Marley pulled me through those rough moments that would have otherwise seemed endless.

Keisha and I were inseparable for a while, and that was why I finally made my decision to attend Howard University with her. Keisha lived in Brooklyn, New York. She said that she couldn't attend Columbia, because it was only a thirty-minute train ride from home, and she and her father needed the distance between them. I knew that I didn't want to attend Oxford University, because London was gloomy year-round. I declined the offer to attend Harvard because Keisha said Cambridge got really cold in the winter, and I had no idea what cold weather felt like, but if she was complaining, who was I to argue? She didn't apply to Meharry because she said it was too *country* and she didn't get accepted to Johns Hopkins, so that left Howard University.

I liked having Keisha as a friend. She was different from Colleen, but no one could ever replace what Colleen and I shared. Keisha was aggressive, energetic, and the life of the party wherever we went, and I looked forward to her company once I got to Howard. Dr. Ikembe was thrilled with my choice and said that I would not regret my decision about attending Howard University. He was very helpful during my transition this year, and he couldn't believe all that Donovan had put me through. And without hesitation he managed to arrange everything for me at the last minute. I will forever be grateful for his help and the faith that he has in me.

Surprisingly my mother and Aunt Beverly were in tears when I accepted my diploma. Mama and I never did resolve things between us. The day that she, Nadine, and I sat on the veranda chit-chatting, eating tamarind, and sharing a couple of laughs was the closest she ever came to an apology—if you want to call it that. But she wasn't as ugly to me as she was before, and for Mama I realize that was her way of trying to make amends. Even though Dr. Keene

referred to my tragedy as a threatened miscarriage, to a certain degree I still blamed Mama. She was unrelenting when I needed her
most, and though I'm willing to orgive, I'll never forget the stress
and strife she caused me to endure. Well, I guess my ignoring the
bleeding and cramping didn't help matters.

Colleen came to visit when she could, but she had other responsibilities now. She didn't miss my graduation though. Colleen
came with Lloyd, and I was glad to see things were still going strong
between them. Who knows, maybe one day in the near future she'll
write inviting me to her wedding. I could definitely see wedding
bells in their future. Colleen makes a great stepmother, and Camille
loves her unconditionally. Hyacinth hasn't been seen or heard from
since Colleen confronted her at the airport. This made things a lot
easier for Colleen and Lloyd to move on with their lives and give
Camille the attention that she needed. I never would have thought
that Colleen would be a mother before me. It was strange to see her
holding Camille's little hand. It was even stranger hearing Camille
refer to my best friend as Mommy. They were a nice-looking family, and Colleen decided to grow dreads, but she didn't bear any
resemblance to Rita Marley.

Mr. Miller and Mrs. Margaret Miller also attended my graduation. They finally tied the knot, and Mrs. Margaret was almost a
changed woman. When she found out that Colleen and Lloyd were
living together she wasn't very pleased, but Colleen was quick to
point out to her that she wasn't a saint either. Once Mrs. Margaret
met Lloyd she became very fond of him and on occasion even took
care of Camille.

Nadine and I were on better terms lately. Percy Hendricks, who
was still her boyfriend, lived in Kingston not far from the university that I attended. She stopped by twice during my last semester to
ask for my advice. She came once to talk about Percy and the other
time to ask about her career options. I was very happy to be of

assistance, and it felt good to finally have a relationship with my sister. I never really did like the way things were between us, and I'm thinking that she didn't either, but our mother had a lot to do with that. I think Nadine was growing up and starting to develop her own personality. She emulated our mother's habits before, and I think that Percy helped her to see that. Percy wasn't the most honest person as far as their relationship was concerned, but he seemed to be a very good friend. I told Nadine that if she felt that Percy was being unfaithful to her that she should confront him. I don't know if she ever did, but they're still together.

Clifton also made it to my graduation, but Dottie had to stay home and watch their newborn baby girl. I heard that Clifton really cleaned up his act. He was now a doting husband and a loving father. He found his niche when he began working with my uncle Sammy, and the carpentry business was booming for them.

Donovan didn't come to my graduation, and I was kind of relieved. I wasn't quite ready to face him yet. Seeing him would only rehash the pain and loss I was trying so hard to forget. After I recovered from the miscarriage I left for school. Donovan made several attempts to contact me, but Keisha and my roommate did a good job of keeping him away from me. Soon his visits became less and less frequent, and eventually he gave up. There was nothing that he could possibly say or do that would ever make me forgive him. Donovan was the one person that I loved and trusted more than anyone in the world, and he let me down. He betrayed everything that we ever had and caused me the most sorrow.

At the graduation Mr. Miller handed me a letter from Donovan, and I was tempted to tear it to shreds when he walked away, but decided to save it for later.

Throughout the entire school year Dr. Thorton and I had been exchanging letters. When Kathryn found out that I lost the baby she was very consoling. She ended up visiting Jamaica for the Christ mas holiday, and I spent the whole break with her in Kingston. It was the first Christmas that I spent without my family, but my heart was still too fragile from my loss, and I didn't think being at home would help the healing process. At any rate, my father and Patrick came by to see me on Christmas Eve. They understood my reasons for not wanting to spend my vacation at home, but I still saw the disappointment in Daddy's eyes when he hugged me before he left.

Shortly after, Patrick and his band went to Europe on tour, and the band was getting rave reviews. They ended up replacing two of the members, but Danny, Patrick's friend wasn't one of them. Their next tour was going to be in the States, so we made plans to get together when he hit New York. I made arrangements to spend half of the summer in Manhattan with Kathryn, and the other half with Keisha in Brooklyn. I wanted to be as far away from Cambridge as possible, so that I could move on with the next chapter of my life.

I sat down on the edge of my bed and looked around to see if there was anything else I was forgetting to pack. My blue dress that Nadine wore to Maisey's wedding was hanging on the back of the bedroom door. I planned to give it to Nadine as a peace offering, and quite honestly it fit her much better than it did me anyway. Then I looked over at my dresser, and the letter that Mr. Miller gave me was leaning against my jewelry box. I took a deep breath, because I figured that I might as well get it over with and see what Donovan had to say. Carefully, I opened the envelope. My hands began to tremble as I stared at the sheet of paper neatly written in Donovan's handwriting.

Dear Anne-Marie,

I want you to know that I will always love you, and I will never forgive myself for hurting you. Anne-Marie, you are the best thing that has ever happened to me, and my life will never be the same without you. At the time I thought that I was doing the right thing. I was afraid that I was going to lose you and the baby. I made a mistake and as a result I've lost everything that ever had any true meaning to me. Looking back, I know that I should have handled things differently and taken heed from my father. Instead I had to learn my lesson the hard way. If I could take back all the hurt and pain that I've caused you, I'd gladly do it. I would give my life for yours and there isn't a day that goes by that I don't regret the mistakes that I've made.

These words don't come easy to me and will never make up for all that I have done, but I hope that one day you will find it in your heart to forgive me. I will truly miss you, and I will forever keep you in my heart.

Love always,
Donovan

Colleen arranged for Lloyd to take me to the airport, and at 6:00A.M. he was knocking on the door. My family woke up at around five, so when he arrived he didn't disturb anybody. My mother got up to make me my favorite breakfast, and we all sat around the table talking for almost an hour.

Daddy helped Lloyd take the bags down to the van. Mama, Nadine, and I said our last good-byes. For years I had always pictured this day, and I was always happy to be leaving and thinking *good riddance* as I walked away. But I was actually a little sad when we all hugged. Like I said before, my mother wasn't very emotional, so her hug was a bit dry. When we embraced, she didn't pull her body all the way into mine. She merely patted me on the back and then stepped away. Nadine's hug was truly sincere. I whispered "take care of yourself" in her ear, and it felt like she didn't want to let go, but we heard Lloyd blowing the horn. I grabbed my purse and headed for the door. Mama and Nadine stood out on the veranda and watched as I walked down the hill. I know that they were waving at me, but I never looked back for fear that I would turn into a pillar of salt like Lot's wife in the Bible.

Daddy was standing beside the van talking to Lloyd, and I knew that it was going to be hard to say good-bye. I had the best father in the world, and he is the one person that I wish that I could take with me. I was going to miss him tremendously. When we hugged I didn't want to let go. I felt the stream of tears rushing down my face. I knew that this was going to happen. That's why I asked my father not to accompany me to the airport. It would only make leaving harder.

As we drove off I saw him wiping the tears from his face, because he knew that the chances of me returning were slim. Lloyd was sweet and tried to strike up a conversation so that I would stop crying, but it didn't work. I bawled the entire way to the airport.

When we finally arrived it was a couple of minutes to eight, but my flight wasn't scheduled to leave until nine-thirty. The check in line was ridiculously long, but Lloyd walked me right up to the front of Colleen's line. She was in the middle of taking care of another customer, but as soon as the customer left she processed my paperwork. Then she took her break and walked me to the gate. We sat there and talked about everything imaginable. We laughed together until we cried. I was really going to miss Colleen. She stayed until my flight was about to board and watched as I walked outside and down the steps toward the plane.

I looked at my ticket to check my seat and I turned back to wave good-bye. Only Colleen wasn't standing in the window anymore. To my surprise Donovan was standing in her place with his hands pressed up against the glass watching me. When he saw me turn around he waved at me and for a moment I hesitated, but I waved back. Then he mouthed, "I love you." My mouth wanted to return the sentiments, but my heart wouldn't let me. Instead I did what I had always seen them do in the American movies: I simply blew him a kiss good-bye.

Glossary

Afoe - before

Ai door – outside, at the door

Back a bush – yard person, having a country background
        or upbringing

Bada – bother

Buguyaga – a tramp

Ca'an – can't

Cotch – to stay somewhere temporarily

Dash – to discard, throw away

Dem - them

Dis - this

Dread – a person with dread locks

Fas – to meddle with, fresh. The act of being rude.

Fayva – to resemble, to appear as

Feisty – cheeky, impudent, rude

Fenneh – mess, defecate

Ganja - marijuana

Gwaan – to go ahead, going to

Gyal – girl

Haf – to have

Hoh - how

Inna - inside

Knotty – matted together or unruly hair

Knuh – to know

Ku ya – look here

Labrish – talk, gossip

Lawd – Lord

Mash – to mess up or ruin

Massa – Mr., Mrs. or Miss

Mek - make

Mi – me or my

Nuh – don't, no

Nuh true – isn't that right

Obeah – the practice of communicating with spirits. To
    cast a spell.

Pikny – child

Pon - on

Punanny - vagina

Ratha - rather

Shet – shut

Skettel – a loose woman

Spliff – a joint, reefer, blunt

Tek - take

Wah - what

Warra-warra – politely omitted profanity

Wrenk – to smell, stink

Wha'pin – what's happening or how are you?

Wid - with

Yu - you